Overkill

Lou Wilham

PRAISE FOR OVERKILL

"I finished reading in three sittings and was almost late for work one day because I couldn't tear myself away. It gave all the feels of watching Buffy for the first time, but now with characters like me!"

   - **V.S. Holmes**, Author of *Blood of Titans*

"Overkill has everything from vampire hunting to mystery, romance, twists and turns, and pristine descriptions. There are even some pop culture references sure to give the reader a chuckle or a smile."

   - **Cynthia Brubaker**, Author of *Gomada Academy*

"Buffy who? Eric and Tony are the vampire hunters you want to be reading about! Wilham has a way with words that completely immerses you in a fictional world. The characters are so relatable, diverse, and *real*, that it makes it so easy to fall into the storyline."

   - **Whitney L. Spradling**, Author of *These Dangerous Fates*

This book is for all the tired "chosen ones" out there who answered the call, followed their passion, and are just trying to save the world one kid, one person, one piece of art at a time

CHAPTER 1

"WELCOME TO IRONPORT, Maryland. We've got a bit of a vampire problem." With a click of a button on the keyboard, the PowerPoint slide shifted to a picture of a dark-haired man mid-lunge, stake held aloft. "And that's me, Eric—"

The tiny classroom erupted in a series of annoyed groans, along with one very vehement "Not this again."

"Shhh," Bert hissed, kicking Nik's ankle from across the aisle, a movement Eric's Venator sight could track even in the dark of the classroom. "Let him finish."

"He does this speech *every* semester," Kate grumbled, her head falling forward with a hard *thunk* against her desk.

"And it gets better *literally* every time." Bert's eyes were round with excitement, his jaw slack, and his hand already furiously taking notes.

Well. At least someone is paying attention. Eric would count that as a win, however small.

"Are we done?" Eric asked, lifting a hand to brush a bit of floppy dark brown hair back from his eyes.

To be fair, the kids were right. Eric—Professor Marcelino—*did* do this speech at the start of every semester, meaning most of them had heard it at least a couple of times, if not more. Bert had heard it at least ten, but he seemed to relish it every time, and Eric couldn't be more grateful for the one kid in his

Venator—*vampire hunters*, to the layperson—class who seemed to think hunting vampires was actually cool. It wasn't. Hunting vampires fucking sucked—pun not intended. But it was nice to get a bit of hero worship after so many years of being treated like a glorified exterminator.

"The sooner you let me finish, the sooner I hand out your syllabi and you can all fuck off back to the dorms."

"Can he say *that*?" Chase whispered. He looked positively terrified of Eric and everything this class entailed, which probably had to do with the fact that he was one of the new kids—the other two would join them in a couple of days. It would have been funny if, you know, he wasn't Eric's best friend Hunter's kid brother, and Eric didn't hate himself a little more every day for how his class was growing. Three new students this semester; that was never a good sign. He hadn't had a new student since Nik joined a couple years back, and before that it had been just Bert and Kate for what felt like decades.

Everyone knew that the amount of Venator genes—a gene that only popped up in Huntsmen, a species of supernatural with slightly elevated abilities, but mostly still human—in a population was directly proportionate to the amount of vampire activity in an area. And with three new kids testing positive in a span of months? Something big was coming. At least none of them had active genes. Yet.

"Dude, he's Eric Marcelino, Ironport's longest living Venator. He can say whatever the fuck he wants," Bert informed Chase primly.

Chase nodded as if that were a completely valid argument —or maybe he just didn't want to have an argument with Bert, that was completely possible—and returned his attention to the PowerPoint.

"Please continue." Bert flapped a hand vaguely like a white knight or a politician yielding the floor, and Eric was gratified to find that the others were silent at least for the moment, giving him leave to return to his presentation.

"Like I was saying"—Eric cleared his throat, standing up a little taller, trying to play into the hero Bert seemed to think he was—"that's me, Eric Marcelino, resident Venator, getting my ass handed to me as I struggled for the third night that week to get patrol done so I could get to bed at a reasonable hour." The picture was actually from a few years prior, when Eric had been younger and only slightly less good at the whole slaying-vampires thing. Not much had changed since then. Aside from a few gray hairs—which he pulled out immediately, and did *not* have an existential crisis over, thanks—and an investment in a *really* good mattress, but Eric still liked to pretend he'd learned something since turning thirty a couple years back. It made the whole crushing-weight-of-disappointment-from-his-parents thing less . . . crushing.

"It wouldn't happen," he narrated, playing a video Hunter shot for him to show off to the kids that same year. God, he'd been such an arrogant asshole then, hadn't he? Flipping his stake around and wiggling his hips like he was about to pitch a no-hitter. What a prick. "It never has. Not since I turned thirteen and the whole *chosen one* thing kicked in."

Not really chosen *one*, so much as chosen *few*. Active Venator genes usually cropped up only one to a huge portion of the human population—like whole countries. There were two Venator the US for the last few years or so, but that was before kids in Ironport started testing positive like a chicken pox outbreak.

"But it's always worth a try," Bert called, finishing Eric's speech for him, and damn it if Eric didn't feel his eyes burn a little at the warmth in his tone. Humbert Miller was a good kid. More family to Eric than his own blood had ever been. And something about his unwavering loyalty and faith in

Eric always made the shit-show he called a life seem vaguely worth it.

Vaguely.

"But it's always worth a try," Eric repeated, fighting back the smile that threatened to spread over his face and crinkle his eyes. He really did not deserve that kid. Another click on the keyboard brought up a slide with the most recent vampire stats, courtesy of Hunter, and Eric cleared his throat to dislodge the fondness that settled there. "But now that I've adjusted your perceptions of what it's like to be a Venator, let's talk about some statistics, shall we?"

More groaning followed, but Eric watched as each of his students picked up a pen or opened their laptop and started writing.

—————

"All right," Eric said, clapping his hands together to regain everyone's attention after a half hour of running through data that—if he were being honest—*he* didn't really understand.

Nik had fallen asleep in the back row. His head tilted back so far, his ball cap was falling loose, and at the noise of Eric's clap he awoke with a loud snort that had the other kids giggling like they weren't all approaching legal drinking age.

"That's it, shitheads. Get outta here." Eric made a shooing motion with his hands, his eyes flicking to the time on his phone. It was getting late, too close to dark already with the way the winter sun sank so fast from the sky. "Class dismissed or whatever."

He didn't have to tell them a third time. The room filled with the sounds of shuffled notebooks and zipped backpacks, and one muttered "Shitheads?" from Chase. Poor kid, he'd get used to it eventually. Or Eric hoped so, anyway. If not, Eric would probably have to suffer through another lecture about professionalism from Moondale U's dean, Vanessa

Cochburn—which was kind of hilarious given how the kids liked to pronounce her name. Not something he really wanted. She was a nice enough woman, a powerful witch, but every time he was called to her office it felt like being called in to see the principal all over again. Stirred up too many flashbacks for comfort—to schoolyard fights in high school and that disappointed look from his father.

"And remember," he said, forcing his mind away from the memory of how Daniel Marcelino would suck on his teeth right before he geared up to say something scathing to his son, "on Monday we have two new students, and I expect you all to be—"

"Respectful and welcoming," the kids parroted his earlier words as they filed out.

All except Bert. Who flicked on the lights from where he stood next to the door, bouncing on his toes like he might take flight at any moment. Fuck, how could one kid be so full of energy? A tightly wound spring just waiting for the moment to let loose. Was Eric ever like that? He didn't think he had been. And if he was, his Venator gene had surely killed that part of him. Making him tired and achy 90 percent of the time, and too-caffeinated the other 10.

"Are you going on patrol tonight?" Bert bounced more, his shoes squeaking against the polished floors. Eric huffed, resisting the urge to hang his head, and finished stuffing his laptop into his bag, crushing the power cord in the bottom.

"Of course I'm going on patrol tonight." The strap on his messenger bag cut into his skin where it was too close to the collar of his sweatshirt, but Eric didn't bother adjusting it. "I go on patrol every night. It's in the job description."

"Can I—"

"No."

Bert's face fell for a moment, then he perked up, redoubling his efforts. "Oh come on, Eric. I'm twenty, that's gotta be—"

"After your performance in last semester's final?" Eric slanted Bert a look, his dark brows raised high enough they almost disappeared into his hair. Bert had the decency to blush at the mention of that *particular* debacle. Eric could still hear the startled yelp when the animatronic vampire leaped at Bert, knocking him to the ground. It had been funny until the damn thing short-circuited and caught fucking *fire*, almost burning Bert to a crisp with it. And then it wasn't anymore. "Not on your life, kid."

"But I've been practicing," Bert pleaded, picking up his pace so he could keep up with Eric's longer stride to his car. It was fucking freezing out, but not cold enough to snow, a watery slush soaking in through his shoes. He hated that. Hated cold weather without a hint of a flurry. If it was going to be cold, it needed to fucking *snow*. Otherwise, it should be warm. Not that snow kept the vamps at bay, but at least it was pretty for a little while, and it caught his fall when one of them threw him off a roof—a not infrequent occurrence. "All break. I swear."

"Good." The front door to his beat-up old beamer stuck a little in the cold, making Eric wish—not for the first time—that he hadn't needed to buy a new laptop last year and could have bought a remote start instead. Well, there was always this year, he supposed. Provided nothing else broke. Which it would, if he'd learned anything at all about adulthood.

Bert perked up. If he'd had a tail, it would be wagging, and Eric hated himself more for having to rip that out from under the kid. But it was for Bert's own good. Bert was too young, too green, to be out there fighting vamps. And Eric didn't have the resources to protect some kid along with covering his own ass.

Funny how no one had bothered to protect *him* when he'd been too young and too green to go slaying. Not funny haha. They'd just handed him a stake, patted him on the butt, and sent him on his way. Good luck, Ricky, hope you don't get sucked dry! We're rooting for you!

"Then you'll ace the midterm." He yanked the door shut before Bert could say anything else, leaving him standing there in the cold, his cheeks going pink and his upturned nose curled in frustration. But he didn't try to pull the door open, and Eric counted that as a win as his car kicked on with a dull *thunk*, and he pulled out of the parking space.

The wards spat him out when he left the mountains of Moondale U campus. They always did, as if he were a popcorn kernel in their teeth that they'd finally wriggled free. A nuisance. An annoyance. Not meant to be there. Which made sense, because they weren't made for him. Not really. They were made for the kids and the nonmagical folk that lived there. Erected to protect a plot of land that was outside Moondale and thus didn't benefit from the town's magic. He wondered, regularly, why the Moondale Board of Magic didn't extend the town's borders to include it, but that might put them too close to Ironport. And he supposed no one wanted that. Which was . . . fair.

Or maybe it had to do with ley lines, like Ava always said. Eric didn't know enough about magic to bother with such knowledge. It was just one more thing to crowd the brain space he needed for fight styles and battle tactics, and besides, he couldn't use magic anyway.

Venator, for all they were magical creatures in their own right—adjacent to werewolves in some ways, and witches in others—didn't possess the affinity to harness magic the way most others did. Some sort of cosmic joke, in his opinion. Create a species of hyper-sensitive warriors to combat the leech problem, but don't give them magic. *Noooo*, that would be too much of an advantage. That would make too much sense.

The stoplight blinked, flashing an eerie red glow on the single road that led from Ironport to Moondale, and curved around Moondale U. One way in. One way out. Easier to defend. He glanced back in his rearview once to see the mountains that Moondale U sat nestled between, then pulled through the light without even really looking to make sure nothing was coming.

Beyond the trees, lights twinkled to life, blotting out the stars with their own miniature galaxies. Buildings grew out of a flat space of land, more swamp than prairie probably, the skyline so different from Moondale, it made Eric ache a little. Moondale had maintained its small-town charm, not allowing for big businesses and too much modernization, but Ironport was a whole different beast. All industrialization and chains. Densely packed in some areas like a city—particularly in sections where the bars, restaurants, and clubs were—and spread out in others. It was a strange place. Not a city. Not a town. Not anything really. But it was where Eric Marcelino had been born and bred.

Eric pressed down harder on the gas petal as he pulled into Ironport.

There were a few places vamps liked to congregate in particular: abandoned buildings and busy hospitals were high up on the list, but most of the time they went where the people were—like the Little Mermaid. Following their instincts to the easiest hunting grounds. Which meant only one thing for Eric: another night at the clubs.

Fuck. He was too old for this shit. Maybe this is why Venator didn't usually live past twenty-five.

It took him approximately ten minutes to find a parking spot along the strip of bars Ironport liked to pretend was some kind of party district, change out of his stuffy *professor* clothes into something more likely to get him in through the front door, and take a pre-emptive dose of ibuprofen. Pulling the collar up on his shirt, he hoped to whatever gods were listening that the line wasn't too long. The sooner he got in, the sooner he could feel the place out.

The question was . . . where to start?

His hands stuffed into his pockets, Eric hummed to himself, eyes flicking over the crowd of twenty-somethings stumbling from one bar to the next, completely unaware or uncaring of the danger they put themselves in.

It was an innate thing, something in the blood or the genes or whatever—Hunter had tried to explain it once, but there had been a lot of science-y words Eric didn't know so he'd kind of stopped listening—that let a Venator hunt vampires. A special sense no one else had. And as Eric stood, waiting, the hair on his arms raised in a way that wasn't strictly from the chill late-January air.

The hum of awareness he was never quite able to explain, even to his class, guided his eyes to a bar down the row. "Gotcha, you sonuvabitch."

There was a small line outside, but as Eric's gaze flicked over the people, it was easy to see that none of them were the source of the threat. Inside, then. Well, at least that meant he could warm up a little before having to fight.

Jogging across the street, he headed for the entrance, putting on his best smile for the guy at the door. A shift in the man's face told Eric that the Venator charm had worked again, and he tried to ignore the way his gut churned with it. That particular ability was too close to how the vamps lured their prey, and he hated it. Hated how easy it had made life at one point in time for him. Hated how it made him feel like a predator.

Almost as soon as he brushed past the bouncer, the smell hit him square in the face—another gift from his active Venator gene and heightened senses. Metallic and rank. Death. Decay. Blood. It hovered over top the scent of alcohol and sweat, so thick he was surprised no one else could smell it. Maybe if there was a were-creature present, they would have, but as far as he could tell, these were all humans. Normies.

Eric closed his eyes, gave himself a moment to focus on the tingle on his skin and the thickness of death in the air. Based on the hum against his skin's intensity, there was one vamp, maybe two. Nothing he couldn't handle. Easy. But the scent? There were at least four separate layers to it that he could pick apart like notes in a perfume. A mama vamp, then. Out on the hunt for their brood.

Fuck, but those were the worst, weren't they? Because they were just doing what came naturally to them. Just following their instincts and trying to keep their children alive. Kind of like him and his class.

A long slow breath left him, and he opened his eyes to peer through the murky darkness of the club, letting the crowd carry him toward the bar. It didn't take long to find the vampire in the room of humans. Their stillness gave them away, something no living creature could mimic even if they tried, because breathing was a thing. They were leaning over a short ginger with a smile stretched dopey-soft across her full lips, the vamp's long blond hair curtaining their face so Eric couldn't make out any identifying features.

Two options, that's all he had.

Option one: go drag the bitch out into the alley and stake them there.

Option two: hang back, wait a bit, and hope they hauled their prey back to the nest.

He knew which the Huntsmen code dictated: the lives of the few were a fine sacrifice for the needs of the many. But the thought of letting the pretty little ginger die just because she wanted some action didn't sit right with him. Wavering, instincts warring against duty, Eric shoved his hands deeper into his pockets.

Before he could say fuck it and go with his gut, the choice was made for him. The pair slunk toward an exit near the bathrooms. And he cut through the crowd to follow them.

The nest it was.

CHAPTER 2

WITH MIAMI—AND everything it represented—in the rearview, Tony McMahon's shoulders unhitched from where they'd been up around his ears for what felt like decades. He slumped back into the driver's seat, fingers drumming against the wheel to the music. The world lay ahead of him and Lu. Well, maybe not the world, maybe just Ironport, Maryland. But still. It was a fresh town. A fresh school for Lu. Fresh leeches for Tony to hunt.

A fresh start, hopefully, for both of them.

"Still can't believe you wouldn't let me drive," Lu muttered, grumpy. She'd curled her legs up into the seat with her after kicking off her shoes, because fuck if Tony was going to let anyone, not even his baby sister, put their shoes on his leather interior.

"We'll be there in less than an hour, there's no point." That wasn't really why he hadn't let her drive, and they both knew it. Because if that were why then he'd have let her take a leg at some point during the fifteen, almost sixteen, hours it took for them to get from Miami to Maryland. "'sides"—he sniffed, rubbing at his running nose. Fuck, it was cold this far north. He missed the heat of Miami already—"no one's getting to play with Harry Styles's gear shift 'cept me."

Lu made a gagging noise, curling over her knees as if she were going to throw up on Tony's impeccably clean floor mats, but he could see her lips curving into a smile. "You're so fucking gross."

Wiggling his eyebrows for effect, Tony had to press his tongue between his teeth to choke back the laugh crawling up his throat. It was good to be like this with Lu again. To see her happy. To know she was safe, at least in the most basic sense. He couldn't protect her from everything, he knew that, but he'd be damned if he let anyone touch her the way—

No. He shook himself, forcing that *man*, the one who had the audacity to call himself their *father*, from his mind. He wasn't doing that. Ironport was a fresh start. A way to put distance between themselves and the life they'd lived in that house before that man died. Declan Brenner's shadow had hung over them for seven long years while Tony worked through the process of adopting his sister, paying off Declan's debts, and saving enough money to get them the fuck out of there. But they were free now, and he wasn't going to let the bastard ruin it.

"We should get into town just before dark," Tony said, needing the conversation, however monotonous, to keep his brain on track.

A hum came from the passenger seat, and Lu threw herself back against the headrest again, turning her head to look at him through the tangle of red hair she refused to so much as fucking braid. "You gonna go out on patrol?"

"Don't see any reason not to." He sucked on his teeth, pressing his tongue into one pointed canine. The need to fight, to hunt, to slay, sat like an itch under his skin. More than once during the trip up, he swore he was breaking out in hives from the sheer inaction of sitting in a car for hours. Lu checked his back for him, told him to stop being a fucking baby, and for the love of the Goddess to stop itching or he really would have a rash. But there had been no hives. No outward sign of the jittery, unsettled nerves lingering too close to his marrow.

In retrospect, the fact that he'd only stopped wearing a binder a few months ago, after his top surgery, probably didn't help. Thank the Goddess for Venator healing, or he probably wouldn't have felt like making the trip at all for at least another few weeks. But it left him with an uneasy feeling of not being held together. The skin where his binder usually sat now too exposed to the elements. He sniffed again. "Gotta get the lay of the land, and all that."

"Right." Lu snorted, her fingers tapping an unsteady beat against her knees. "The lay of the land."

"I don't know what you're talking about." But it sounded forced, even to him, a hint of aggravation at being called out by his sister adding bite to the words that wouldn't otherwise be there if he were, in fact, totally innocent. He gripped the wheel a little tighter, fingers flexing.

Lu, however, was taking none of his shit, as usual. "Cause this has nothing at all to do with my new teacher."

"New teacher?"

Green eyes, so much like his, so much like their mom's, narrowed under thick red brows as Lu stared him down, unblinking.

"Fine," Tony said, running his tongue along the inside of his cheek where a scar lingered, if only to prolong the inevitable. "Maybe I wanna feel this—this King Ricky guy, out."

"King Ricky?" Lu scoffed, turning back to look out the window again. "The fuck does that mean?"

"Come on Lu, I know you know what I'm talking about." The leather creaked under him where he shifted in his seat. It was embarrassing to be so fucking transparent to his sister. It sent heat crawling up his neck and trickling out across his cheeks. Maybe she wouldn't say it. Maybe she wouldn't point out how Tony had taken one look at Eric Marcelino's picture and decided he wanted nothing more than to see how good he was in a fight. To know what that neatly coiffed head of hair looked like after it'd been mussed up. He'd look good bloody, Tony had little doubt.

Before Lu could turn back to him and fix him with that look like she could see down into his very fucking soul, knew all his dirty little secrets—fucking sisters, man—he pressed, "He's the oldest living Venator in at least a century."

He was, also, cursed if his file in the Huntsmen database was to be believed. Some prophecy about being the last of the Marcelino Venator family line, or some shit. Honestly, Tony kind of skimmed that bit; it wasn't as interesting as checking out Marcelino's slay average. Which was only a couple points higher than his own, to Tony's delight, in spite of their age difference.

"Yeah," she said, short, clipped, disbelieving. "Sure. That's why."

But she didn't call him on his shit for once, and Tony was able to relax back into the drive.

"What's with the crab billboards?" Lu asked, a laugh on her lips.

"Fuck if I know," Tony muttered, squinting at one that appeared to be from PETA that said something like "I'm ME, not meat. See the individual, go vegan." followed by another from a seafood restaurant of some kind that said "Savor the sacrifice. See the individual put Old Bay on it."

"Marylanders are fucking wild." Lu pulled her phone out of her lap to take a couple of pictures.

Tony grunted his agreement.

They pulled up outside of the townhouse Tony rented for them as the last rays of the sun set the sky on fire, streetlights kicking on. 201 Crescent Lane, on the corner of Crescent and Wolf, was one in a row of five little brick houses, all huddling close together.

It was a nice part of town—*quaint*, his mom would have called it. He could only hope it would be safe for Lu. The rate on vamp attacks in this place was higher than Miami, and that was saying something. It was part of the reason he'd chosen Ironport as their next destination. Well, that, and Moondale U's Venator class, led by one very handsome Eric Marcelino. It was the only program like it in the country, and Tony would do literally anything to protect Lu. Even move up the coast away from the sun and the sand that was practically engrained into his skin to a backwater town like Ironport. She was fucking seventeen and she'd been through enough. She deserved a someplace steady and safe to finish out her schooling, even if he knew damn well she could take care of herself most of the time.

"Don't get on his bad side," Lu said, leaning over to peer into the car from where she stood at the curb. Her eyes narrowed in something like a threat, and Tony had to fight down the manic chuckle that burbled up his throat. "I don't want him failing me just because my brother is a dickhead."

"Me? A dickhead?" Gasping, Tony held his chest in faux offense. "I don't know what you're talking about, Louie, I'm a *delight.*"

Instead of answering, she just stared unblinking back at him, clearly unimpressed with his act. Tony didn't look away, wouldn't, because Lu was like a bear that way. If he looked away first, it would be seen as a sign of weakness. She'd be insufferable after that, and he'd never get her to do what he told her to ever again, which would fucking suck as her guardian. So they stayed staring, Tony's eyes slowly drying out enough to burn.

Lu blinked first.

With a soft "Whatever," she slammed the door and headed up the sidewalk to their house. The car idled on the curb, Tony waiting until the door was shut and locked, the wards in place behind Lu before he pulled away.

The thing about having an active Venator gene, Tony had learned, was that it kind of turned a person into a bloodhound of the hunting-dead-things variety. In Miami, he'd been known to follow a scent for upward of a mile, tracking a vamp for hours at a time. Criss-crossing busy streets and slipping down alleyways until he was able to corner the bloodsucker and dust 'em.

So, in a place as small as Ironport—more town than city when compared to Miami—it was almost easy to follow his nose to the nearest nest.

And lo and behold, it was in a cemetery. *Real original.*

"Gotta love a classic," Tony muttered to himself, pulling the hair tie from his wrist so he could twist his strawberry blond curls up into a bun. They probably wouldn't stay there, but it was always good to start a fight without hair in his face. With Lu not there to judge him, Tony flipped down the visor so he could give himself a quick once over before getting out of the car. Eyeliner on point, shirt slightly rumpled, stubble a little ragged . . . it'd do in a pinch. He looked like he'd slept in his fucking car, honestly, but if his guess was right, Marcelino wouldn't be much better off.

Reaching into the backseat, he grabbed the beat-up old duffle that made up his hunting kit. Stakes clicking against each other, silver jangling in the bottom of the bag, Tony set it on his lap. He tucked a paperback copy of *The Happy Prince and other tales* by Oscar Wilde with a broken spine into his breast pocket and jammed a couple of stakes into the pockets at his sides. Then it was just a matter of slipping two silver hair pins into the bun at the crown of his head, and he was ready for a fight.

From start to finish, the whole process took maybe five minutes, but with winter still having her claws in the land, it was full dark by the time Tony all but rolled from his Mustang. The slam of his driver's side door echoed too loud in the silence of the cemetery. Which would have made Tony's hair stand on end, if he wasn't so used to the way vamps could suck the life right out of an area, leaving nothing behind, not even color, really.

With a quick pat at his pockets to make sure he had every-thing, he pushed the screeching gate to the cemetery open farther. Someone had already taken it off its hinges to get past the chain holding it closed. Probably Marcelino. Vamps usually just broke things that were in their way.

No insects chirped. No animals rustled. Not even the breeze through the trees dared make a sound in this cold, dead place. Leaving Tony able to hear, perfectly, the soft grunts of a fight somewhere off to his right. He had a handful of seconds, a single *thu-thunk* of his heartbeat, before Eric Marcelino came into view and tore the breath from his lungs.

The other Venator was beautiful.

There was no elegance in his movements—he was all brutal efficiency. Looking for the quickest, cleanest way to shoot past the vampire's guard and stake it through, then jerking back out of the way when he missed. Not a single wasted step.

Tony couldn't take his eyes off him.

His lack of attention to his surroundings made him sloppy, careless. Goddess, his father would have smacked him into next week if he saw the way Tony stood there star-ing, mouth hanging open like some starstruck teen.

Awareness crawled across his skin, the gentle hum of some undead thing getting a little too close, raising the hairs on his arms, the back of his neck, and Tony had just enough time to turn and meet the vamp's washed-out eyes before the creature slammed him into the ground. It knocked the wind from his lungs, sending the stakes in his pockets skittering across the frostbitten dirt. Stars danced in front of his eyes, a hazy sort of feeling taking over his mind. Was he going to pass out? Was *this* going to be the end of Tony McMahon? Oh, what an impression that'd make on Marcelino. Forget showing him what a "dickhead" Tony was, he was going to be sucked dry in the middle of some hick-town graveyard and prove himself entirely useless.

Fuck.

Rookie move, kid.

The leech lunged for his throat, fangs already extended. Tony reached into the front pocket of his jacket to rip out the worn little paperback. Putting all the belief, love, and faith he had into the bent pages of the story his mother read to him over and over again as a child had the creature shying away, hissing with contempt. Saliva still dripped from its fangs, but there was enough space for Tony to move.

He scrambled blindly for the stakes he'd lost, not willing to take his gaze away from the imminent threat for a moment. Which was still hissing and snapping its jaws, trying to find a way past the little bubble of protection the book provided Tony. It wouldn't. There was too much history tucked between the pages. Too much of his mother clinging to the spine. But leeches always tried.

"Almost there." Tony gritted his teeth against the jerk of his arm as the vampire tried to press past the paperback. His fingers scraped at the blunt end of the stake. If he could just wiggle his hips and shift his back a little, he'd—

Another body slammed into the vampire, a grunted exclamation leaving the person when they hit the ground. Grass crunched under the pair as they rolled across a couple of graves before a dull *thud* rang out through the silence.

"Fuck me," one of the figures hissed, and with them not rolling around anymore, Tony could make out the fluffy dark hair of Marcelino where the vampire had him pinned against a headstone, teeth snapping toward his neck. "Throw me the stake, newbie, and get the fuck outta here."

"What?" Tony blinked, because why not make even more of a jackass of himself in front of someone he wanted to fuck. Sure. Let's do that.

"The stake!" Marcelino yelped as the vampire slammed his head against the grave marker again, leaving behind a smear of blood that glistened in the moonlight. "The stake!"

Understanding finally settled in, and Tony scrambled to grab the stake and throw it toward Marcelino. With the precision of someone who wasn't practically being strangled by an overpowered undead creature, Marcelino snatched the stake out of the air. It slid through the leech's shoulder blade with a crunching sound but very little resistance on Marcelino's part as he buried it into the creature's heart.

A single heartbeat later, the creature burst into dust, leaving behind the soft clatter of fangs on stone where only the leech's canines bounced off a grave marker. Marcelino covered his nose and mouth with the sleeve of his soiled jacket, so he didn't inhale. Then he scooped up the fangs to tuck into a little baggy.

"For fuck's sake, you're as bad as my kids!" Marcelino sniped as he rose to his feet, brushing dust from his clothes. "What the fuck are you doing out here anyway, man? Normies usually stay to the populated areas."

"I'm not a fucking *normie*." Tony's hackles rose at the tone, his blood still pumping too fast and too hot in his veins. The vamps might be dusted, but he was itching for a fight and pretty boy Eric Marcelino was going to give it to him.

"Sure fucking look like one to me." Marcelino spat on the ground, a split in his lip dribbling crimson down toward his chin. Tony had been right, the man *did* look good bloody. Fuck. "Go home, kid. Let the *adult* handle things."

And that. Well, that was enough to have the itch under Tony's skin catch fire with rage and burn through every bit of sense he had left. So, he did the only reasonable thing he could think of in that situation. He reared back and punched Marcelino right in the face with all the strength he had.

Marcelino stumbled back a half-step then turned to fix Tony with a bloody smile, sending his heart skittering in his chest. A second passed, just enough time for Tony to realize that perhaps he hadn't reacted correctly to the taunt.

Then Marcelino was on him, slamming him against the

ground, his knee connecting with Tony's stomach hard enough to knock the air from his lungs. Tony's fist slammed into Marcelino's shoulder, his temple, anything he could reach, trying to get the other man off him where his weight pressed Tony into the ground. But for as lithe and lean as Marcelino looked, he was surprisingly heavy, all muscle and finely honed precision.

If Tony had any sense at all, he might have recognized what deep shit he was in right then and there, but Tony McMahon had always been a sucker for a pretty face. Marcelino pressed down hard with his knee, making Tony wheeze for air, but he hadn't hit Tony yet. Instead, he seemed to be trying to get his hands around Tony's wrists, to stop the wild volley of punches splitting his lip open further, blackening his eye, bloodying his nose. Thank the Goddess the vampires were gone, or they'd both be fucked.

Marcelino's hands were cold around Tony's wrists, tight as steel and twice as unyielding as he pinned him to the ground. His chest heaved with panted breaths, and there was this *look* in his eyes. The pupils blown so wide, they almost ate up all that honey-brown hazel Tony had seen in his database picture. There were more moles littering his pale skin than had been visible in the picture. Constellations of dark spots on his neck, his cheek, that Tony wanted to trace with his fingers, his tongue. Maybe someday soon, he would.

With a wiggle of his hips, Tony finally got enough leverage to flip them, sending Marcelino sprawling onto his back. He didn't let go of Tony's wrists. But that was okay, because Tony had the upper hand now. He just had to—

Pain erupted across his forehead, a startled yelp ripped from his lungs as Marcelino head-butted him so hard, Tony saw stars.

"Jesus, *fuck*." Tony's hands jerked away from Marcelino's vice-like grip to rub at the ache quickly spreading through the rest of his skull. "Did you just fucking—"

Marcelino took advantage of Tony's inattention and lack of balance to shove him to the ground, pinning him thoroughly with knees and hands. His pretty face hovered over Tony's, blood dripping from his nose to splatter against Tony's cheek, but it was hard to care about that when those big doe eyes were so wide, so round, Tony was pretty sure they might swallow him whole.

"What was that about not being a normie?" Marcelino asked, his voice a rasp with how out of breath he was. He was smiling though, fierce and feral, and Tony had to fight against every instinct he had to not grab Marcelino and kiss him until their heads spun from lack of air. He was thoroughly fucked.

"Oh, fuck off, pretty boy. I gave you a run for your money." But for all the offense in the words, Tony found himself laughing, relaxing back into the wet grass, moisture seeping in through his tight jeans.

Marcelino hummed, leaning back on his heels to give Tony enough room to breathe and sit up, if he wanted to. He didn't want to. He wanted to see how long Marcelino would let him lie between his thighs in the grass, even as his ass went numb from the cold. "No one told me an active Venator was moving into town." His dark brows creased in the middle. Then, because he'd been raised right, unlike some people, he said, "I'm Eric."

"Tony," he grunted, taking the outstretched hand Marcelino extended to help him to his feet. "We just got in a couple hours ago."

"We?"

"Me and my little sister. She tested positive a few months back, but her gene isn't active yet." And Tony thanked the Goddess for that every single day. She was only fucking *seventeen*. Too young. Too scrawny. Too unprepared for the big bad world of vampire hunting.

"Louisa or Finnley?" Marcelino started toward the gate

without a backward glance, clearly expecting Tony to fall in line beside him.

A smile twitched at Tony's lips, something warm settling in his belly as he matched Marcelino's long strides with his own. Marcelino knew his kids off the top of his head, even the ones he hadn't met yet. That was . . . *cute*. "Louisa."

"Well." Keys jingling in Marcelino's pocket, his eyes cut to where Tony left his Mustang. His tongue poked out to brush over the congealed blood on his split lip with a tiny wince. "I look forward to meeting her on Monday."

"Do you want a ride back to your car?" Because Tony wasn't ready for this, whatever *this* was, to end. Not yet. It'd been so long since he'd spent time with someone who wasn't a teenage girl. Someone who *got* the whole vampire hunting thing. Maybe if he could hang out a little bit longer . . .

"Nah. I'm going to run a quick sweep." Marcelino shrugged, tapped his nose, and said, "Works better walking" like Tony wasn't already fully aware of the limitations hunting in a car posed. Then, before Tony could ask if he needed a hand, Marcelino grinned, his head tilted just so, dark hair falling across those bottomless honey-brown hazel eyes. "See you 'round, Tony."

He was gone before Tony could unstick his tongue from the roof of his mouth.

CHAPTER 3

A WINCE RIPPED itself from Tony's throat, his body jerking away from Lu's gently prodding fingers. "Watch it there, Nurse Ratched. I'd like to be able to walk in the morning."

"Stop being such a baby," Lu said, giving his ribs another experimental poke. Feeling out the damage, checking to make sure it wasn't too severe, just like he'd taught her. Honestly, she'd probably make a better Venator than him someday soon. The girl absorbed everything like an over-eager sponge. "Right, well, they're just bruised."

"Could have told you that." Tony grunted, taking another hit off the sloppily rolled blunt between his fingers. More to help with the sleeping than the pain. Lu hated the smell of pot. But so long as he didn't get paranoid, she couldn't really say anything. He was paying the bills, which included any cleaning charges they might accrue for the smell. And besides, no one wanted a sleep-deprived Tony on their hands, least of all Lu.

"Probably, but it's good practice," she reminded him, reciting the same words he'd said to her what seemed like forever and a day ago. When she'd first helped him patch himself up after a particularly nasty round with *that man*. Tony had talked back, under his breath, and what might have been a quick slap from their father morphed into an all-out beating. He still had the scars from it. "Let me see your knuckles."

"They're fine." Bruised and bloodied, but nothing was broken, and Tony always counted that as a win.

"Why didn't he go for your face?" Lu pulled back to close the first aid kit, which she'd already had sprawled across the counter when he walked in the door. Likely because she heard his car pull up. "If it was me, I'd have gone for your face."

Tony taught her that. Taught her to go for the eyes first thing, because people would protect their eyes before they'd protect their torso. Covering their face was always a person's first instinct, and it left the rest of the body open to attack. Tony would know from personal experience. "Sure you would have, Louie."

With a huff and an eye roll, she stood to return the first aid kit to the cabinet by the fridge where it would live for the foreseeable future. "He must suck at fighting if he didn't know that."

"He doesn't suck at fighting." But Tony didn't really know why Marcelino *hadn't* gone in for the kill. It wasn't like Tony was holding back. But there was a gentleness about Marcelino that Tony hadn't expected. Something so contradictory to who and what they were, it left Tony wrong-footed, his stomach swooping as if he'd missed a stair in the dark. Tony licked over his teeth before taking another deep drag off the blunt. It was getting down toward the end, the cherry inching closer and closer to his fingers, but he hated to waste it. Maybe he'd put the last of it in the bowl he kept in his nightstand. "I think he wasn't trying to hurt me."

"Musta realized what a wuss you are." When Tony's narrowed eyes flicked back to her, Lu was inching her way toward the doorway that led upstairs, her socked feet skidding a little.

"I'll show you a wuss!" He leaped from the stool at the

counter, knocking it over to clatter against the ceramic floor in his haste to get to his sister. Yelping, Lu took the stairs two at a time. A breathless giggle echoed behind her, filling the mostly empty house with light and life like Tony had never known when he was her age.

The warmth settling into his chest like heartburn would take some getting used to, but Tony thought he just might be looking forward to it.

———

"Get in a fight with a lawnmower?" was the first thing out of Hunter's mouth when Eric dragged himself into the lab the next morning, still nursing an aura from last night's migraine. Or maybe it was today's? Who was to say.

"What the fuck does that even mean?" Eric winced when he miscalculated how high the last stair was and stepped down too hard on an ankle that was probably sprained. Why couldn't the steps in this old-ass building be even like everywhere else? Why didn't the dean have them replaced? Why did Hunter insist this was the best place for his lab? Eric had answers to none of these questions and likely never would, so he chose to be grumpy about it instead.

"Means you look rough, hon."

"Yeah? No shit." Was the bite in his tone necessary? Not in the strictest sense. But Eric was tired and sore, and he was pretty sure he still had vamp dust in his hair even though he'd washed it like five fucking times that morning. That shit was like glitter. Eric had to swallow down a manic giggle at the thought of glittery vampires. He shook himself. Goddess, he really was tired, wasn't he? Scrubbing at his face, Eric slumped onto the wobbly wooden stool across from Hunter at one of the big lab tables. "Didn't Britt tell you?"

"She gave me your list of injuries." Hunter shrugged, sitting up a little more so he could tie his long curly black hair back out of his ebony face. A glint of knowing seemed to appear in his brown eyes, but it was hard to be sure with his glasses reflecting the light from above. "She didn't tell me the story."

"There's no story." If that sounded petulant, it's because it was. Eric loved Hunter. He loved Britt. But the idea of them cozying up together and talking about their days enough that Britt had given Hunter a rundown on Eric's treatment made something snarling and snappy curl up in his chest. Jealousy, Ava would say. But Ava could go fuck herself.

Eric pulled a plastic baggy from his messenger bag and slid it across the smooth black surface to where Hunter was fiddling with a microscope. "Just had a run in with a new Venator last night, and the jackass decided to start swinging."

"Before or after the vamps were gone?" Hunter's long brown fingers fiddled with the bag, clearly excited at the prospect of some new samples to archive, but his eyes didn't leave Eric, pinning him in place. Fuck, Eric hated that. Hated how his best friends could see everything on his face. Why couldn't he have one of those faces that hid things? Like Kate. Well . . . then he would look like a perpetually disgruntled French Bulldog, but it'd be worth it!

"Does it matter?" It did. They both knew it did. And Eric didn't really think for a single second that Hunter was going to let him get away with not talking about this. Eric was an optimist, but he wasn't stupid. That was a lie. Eric was stupid —if his grades from high school said anything. But still, he knew people. He knew *Hunter* specifically. There was no getting out of this.

Hunter didn't dignify that with an answer, just raised his right black-brown eyebrow, the one that had the piercing through it, and waited for Eric to cave. Because he would cave. He *always* caved.

"After," Eric said after about ten ticks of the loud clock

hanging above the door. Which might have been a new record for him, but probably wasn't.

"Oooooh ho ho." Hunter laughed, leaning dangerously back on his stool, the legs tilting off the floor with a groan like they might give out at any second. It was a struggle to not reach over and grab his wrist, tell him to take it easy on the furniture the way Eric would tell one of his kids. "Somebody's got a crush."

"Fuck off. I do not." Curling his arms over his chest, Eric huffed. He was not pouting. Except. He definitely was pouting.

"I meant the newbie." The plastic bag opened with that soft clicking sound of the seal being broken, and Hunter fished the fangs out of the bottom. "Telling that you thought I was talking about you, though."

Heat licked up Eric's neck, making him suddenly too hot, stifling in the worn yellow sweatshirt he'd pulled on before heading to the lab. "Shut up."

"The lady doth protest too much, methinks."

"Whatever the fuck *that* means."

Hunter hummed, his long elegant fingers making quick work of putting the teeth on a slide so he could look at them under the microscope. They were silent for a few scant minutes as Hunter focused on mineral buildup, or calcium deposits, or tartar, or whatever the fuck he used to identify the age and region of the vamps Eric had dusted. He'd told Eric once. Sat him down in front of the microscope and shown him the differences between two separate vampire's fangs, hoping to impart some wisdom. But none of it made any sense to Eric. Too much science-y shit, and it had been kind of hard to focus with Hunter's warm breath rustling the short hairs at the back of his neck. Besides, that's what the university paid Hunter for.

"Huh," Hunter said, his brows raised high enough that

Eric could see them over the little eyehole thingies, "that's weird."

"What's weird?" Eric kind of hated it whenever someone said something like that. It was always bad news. Always one more problem for *him*, the only active Venator in all of Iron-port, to deal with. Fuck, he was tired already.

"The mineral buildup on these teeth." Hunter's tongue brushed over the inside of his cheek, poking out a little as he flicked a switch on the table beside him. The image he was looking at projected onto the white wall off to the side.

"You're going to have to tell me what I'm looking at." Eric pinched the bridge of his nose, a headache already forming. He should have stayed in bed. Definitely.

Letting out a soft sigh, Hunter turned to look at him with a pitying gaze and instead of sucking in a breath for an over-enthusiastic explanation, he said, "These were local vamps."

"Wait. What?" Eric's head whipped around so hard, his neck screamed from the action. He squinted at the projection again. He couldn't see what Hunter was seeing, but if Hunter said they were local then . . . "They can't be local vamps. We only get transients. Idiots drawn to the magic of Moondale who can't get past the wards."

"Historically, yes, that's been true."

"But?" Goddess, Eric hated when there was a but. Even more than he hated when someone said, "Huh, that's weird." This was definitely going to turn into an Eric problem.

"But these teeth aren't transient. Haven't been, ever, as far as I can tell. I'll have to run some other tests to be sure, but it looks like these were locals. The minerals on these teeth perfectly match some local human teeth I've examined."

Eric decided he didn't want to know why, or how, Hunter was examining human teeth.

"Fuck me." Eric's head slammed against the table, not even cushioned by his arms, reigniting the pain he'd felt the night before when he head-butted McMahon. "That's not good."

"No. It is not." There was some shuffling of papers, and Eric could only assume Hunter was writing down his findings to report them to the Council of Creatures.

"Can you hold off telling them about this?" Not that he knew what good it would do. If anything, waiting would just piss them off when they *did* find out. But Eric needed to get himself straight first, needed to figure out what the fuck he was going to say, what solution he was going to propose. Because he sure as fuck was not going to let them suggest putting his kids into the field. They weren't ready. They would *never* be ready, as far as Eric was concerned. And he'd die a thousand times over before he let some out-of-touch rich bitch put them in danger like that.

"I can give you a week, tops." Hunter sounded apologetic, and when Eric dared to peek at him from where he was smashed against the tabletop, he looked it too. Brows creased together, nose wrinkled just so. Goddess, Eric really had gotten lucky, hadn't he? Shame he hadn't been smart enough to get his head out of his ass and become friends with Hunter and Ava earlier. Maybe then he'd have . . . But no way was King Ricky, the vampire slayer, going to be caught dead hanging out with two band geeks.

"I'll take it." Eric pushed up from the table to run his fingers through his already hopelessly mussed hair. It wasn't a lot of time, but it was more than he'd have if Hunter turned the report in right away. Maybe it would be enough for Eric to come up with something semi-intelligent. A plan. He'd have to poke Ava for ideas.

"Okay but what if—I just think—" Hunter stopped himself, humming, his fingers drumming against the tabletop. He shook his head, seemingly dismissing whatever he'd been about to say.

"You just think what?"

"I just think maybe you should accept—"

"I am not getting the kids involved in this. None of them even have active genes yet, Hunter. They're not capable of handling a newly sired vamp, much less a local infestation. No." His nails bent back where he'd gripped the table a little too tightly, scratching into the smooth surface. Yanking his hands away, he tucked them into his lap. "I'll come up with something else."

"I wasn't talking about the kids." A frown wrinkled Hunter's face, and Eric scowled back at him. "I was talking about this newbie. Let them lend you a hand. Teaming up with someone wouldn't be so bad, would it?"

"No. No way in fucking hell. Not a chance. Nope. Not happening. No, thank you. No, sir." Eric was already up off his stool and grabbing his bag by the time he got the last declaration out of his mouth, clean white sneakers squeaking against the white and black tiles on his way to the door.

"And why not?"

"Because McMahon's an arrogant little jackass, that's why not." Eric braced his hands on his hips, spinning around to fix Hunter with a wrinkled nose. "He ran in half-cocked and almost got himself fucking killed."

"What's his Cross?" Hunter had narrowed his own gaze, brown eyes flicking over Eric's face, searching for something. Eric didn't like it. It made him feel like one of Hunter's experiments. Like he was under a microscope. What would Hunter see if he examined Eric closely enough? The fear? The loneliness? The longing?

Shifting his weight from one foot to the other, Eric sniffed. "He didn't use a cross."

Where others might have backed down, might have looked away from the irritated stare of the most accomplished Venator of their time, Hunter didn't. He stared back. Probably because Hunter had held Eric's hair while he was puking his brains out more than once in his twenties, and it was tough to be afraid of someone after that. But that didn't make it any less fucking annoying.

Eric sniffed again and answered through his teeth, jaw clenched. "Looked like a paperback."

Expression shifting, opening up, Hunter opened his mouth to say something—

"Don't. Don't even start." Eric pointed at him, brow creased. "You know damn well I don't believe in that bullshit you and Britt spout about how a person's Cross says a lot about them. So I don't want to hear a single word about the history of the paperback, and stories, and how they affect a person." And then he was on a roll, his words tumbling out of him in irritation before he could even really think about the analysis it had taken for him to say them. Because he *had* given it some thought. He *had* looked into the history of Crosses, and who the last person to use something like a book —not a religious text, just a book—to ward off vampires was. Fuck having no filter when he was tired. "Or who the last Venator to use a paperback was. Nothing about what a unique Cross it is, and how much faith, and love, and strength had to go into using something with absolutely no religious significance as a shield. None of it. It's just a tool. Just something he chose to protect himself. It doesn't *mean* anything."

He was panting with exertion and how wound up he'd gotten. And Hunter was looking at him with wide brown eyes and a smile quirking one side of his mouth, stupidly handsome.

Fuck it.

Fuck it all straight to hell.

He was getting out of there. He was going to go back to the house and take a nap, hopefully get a couple hours in before the kids got back from the library for lunch. Yup. That's what he'd do. He'd nap. He'd chill. He would not think about Tony McMahon and his bright green eyes, which had been so intense, so strangely vibrant in the middle of the night, near a vamp's nest no less. He wasn't. Because that way led to disaster.

And besides, Eric had enough to deal with. Local vamps. Magic councils. Papers to grade. Class prep. Patrol. There wasn't *room* for Tony McMahon.

"Yeah," Hunter said softly, just as Eric reached the door to his lab, "cause that pretty necklace from your grandma says absolutely *nothing* about you, man."

Eric didn't turn, and he didn't slam the door behind him, although it was a near thing. Instead, his hand flew to the medallion pressed warm against the skin under his sweatshirt. He had almost rubbed it smooth over years of running his thumb along the image of Diana, but he refused to give it up. Even when his mother offered to get him a new one, a gold one of all things. A stupid suggestion anyway—a Venator couldn't just *replace* their Cross. Not that his mother knew that, seeing as how she'd never even tested positive.

"It doesn't mean anything," he repeated to himself, and headed for his car.

It *couldn't* mean anything.

CHAPTER 4

THE PUNCHING BAG swung hard on its chain, squeaking loud enough that Tony could hear it above the sound of a guitar solo in his ears.

"Should you be doing that with a concussion?" Lu called over the music blaring through his headphones. She sat over to the side of the little workout room he'd managed to cobble together in their basement with the help of his Venator strength. Her tiny form was curled up against the wall, a textbook perched against her knees, forgotten for the moment. There were still boxes to unpack upstairs. Shit like pots and pans that he'd have to deal with when he was done his workout because he wouldn't have time once the week started. But he needed to get in some exercise before then or he'd wind up with a mean case of cabin fever.

"I don't have a concussion." His voice sounded oddly garbled by the earbuds, but he refused to take them off, even as he reached to turn the music down using the buttons along the cord. Because Lu didn't respect the sanctity of the earbuds, and Tony wasn't about to have her shouting loudly enough to irritate the people living to either side of them. If he could go the entire time they were in this armpit of a town without having to meet the neighbors, he'd consider himself blessed.

One red brow lifted high enough on Lu's face that it almost disappeared into her hairline. "That goose egg on your forehead says otherwise." She clicked her tongue, clearly unimpressed. "What the fuck happened anyway?"

"Goose egg." Snorting, Tony swiped sweat from his temple before swinging another hit at the punching bag. His knuckles were still bruised from where he'd pummeled pretty boy Eric Marcelino, and the ache that followed every hit was a reminder. Not a bad one. *Definitely* not a bad one. "What are you? Eighty?"

"I notice you didn't answer the question." Her pale finger marked her page, the book flopping closed on her lap. It was a text for Marcelino's Venator class. Some kind of Huntsmen history book. Tony hadn't given it much thought, but he supposed it was a sign that she was excited for the class. Getting her to do homework in high school had been like pulling fucking teeth.

"I notice you didn't answer the question," he repeated, forcing his voice to go too high and too nasally in a poor imitation of Lu. Freckles blurred as she scrunched her nose at him in her displeasure, but she didn't comment further, just glared at him, willing to wait him out. Because he was predictable as fuck, and his little sister knew how to play him. He might hate her for it if he didn't love her so damn much. Licking his teeth, Tony smirked at her. "He head-butted me."

A blink then "Ew! Gross." Lu gagged, her face scrunching up in distaste. "You're totally gonna try to fuck my teacher, aren't you?"

"Probably." Tony shrugged, his smirk stretching wider, tongue poking out lewdly in a way that had Lu making even more aggressive gagging noises.

"Don't do that. Please! I'm begging you." Her hands pressed together in front of her lips, green eyes gone pleading and too wide in her pale face, but the corner of her mouth twitched. Something light and teasing. Like this was all some elaborate game for her. Maybe it was. Tony didn't pretend to understand teenage girls. "Please, Tony, don't."

"And why not?" She had to know she couldn't convince him, even with this little act. He was going to do what he wanted—he always did. "I mean . . . have you *seen* him?"

"Because he's my teacher! Come on, Tony. What if it's bad? Then he'll—"

"Hey!" Tony cut her off, pointing his finger directly at her in warning. "It *won't* be bad."

"Ugh. Gross." She pushed up from where she'd been curled against the wall and shot him another glare, but it was only halfhearted. "You're impossible."

"Impossibly sexy!"

"Disgusting!" Lu stormed up the stairs, her steps so heavy it sounded like her feet might go through the floorboards. "You're so gross! Do whatever you want! I don't care!" she shouted from the top of the steps before slamming the door behind her.

In all honesty, if Lu had seriously asked him not to, if her eyes hadn't held a glint of mischief through the entire conversation, if she'd done anything other than storm off like a drama queen . . . Tony would have put the whole thing to bed right then and there. He wasn't actually willing to sabotage her chances with her new professor just to get laid. He wasn't an asshole.

Well. He *was* an asshole. Just not that much of one. Point being, if the whole conversation hadn't felt like they were playing, he would have called it off before it even began. But it had, and now . . .

Now Tony had *permission.*

His tongue flicked out across his bottom lip in a quick swipe, the smirk turning into something slightly more feral and toothy.

Yeah. Marcelino wasn't going to know what hit him.

———

"All right, you little shits, listen up." Eric clapped his hands once loudly, bringing the shuffling class of early twenty-somethings and late teens to order.

The soft murmurs of conversation cut off, then Eric had four sets of eyes fixed on him, four matching expressions of mild annoyance. Because *hormones* or whatever. The two girls standing to his side shifted uncomfortably under the combined attention of his class.

He hissed, "Be nice."

And most of them—except Kate, who was perpetually pissy—had the good sense to wipe the expressions of irritation from their faces. Good. That was a good start. Now if only he could get them to stop having a base reaction of bitchiness to everything, but he supposed he couldn't win every battle.

Taking a deep breath and running his fingers through his hair, he straightened up further. "These are the two new girls. Finnley"—he motioned toward the tall brunette who could almost have been his sister, if he squinted, then toward the redhead—"and Louisa—"

"Lu," Louisa said, her chin tilting back just a little, lips pursed like she'd tasted something sour.

"Huh?" Because of fucking course Tony McMahon's kid sister was going to be a pain in Eric's ass. And of fucking course Tony wouldn't have corrected him on the spot when he got it wrong the other night. They couldn't let him get through these fucking introductions so he could get into the important shit. No. Of course not. *Fuck me.*

"My dickhead dad named me after his dickhead sister. I've always hated it." She licked her teeth, a tic Eric would be willing to bet she'd picked up from her brother. "Mama and Tony have always called me Lu."

"Okay then . . ." Eric scrubbed at his face, ignoring the soft snort of laughter that was no doubt directed at him, not the girls, from one of the kids seated at the desks. "Lu. Finnley and Lu."

"Finn," the other girl corrected, clearly not to be outdone, and when Eric looked over at her, one corner of her lips twitched upward as if she found this whole thing very funny. Because of *course* she did.

"Sure. Why not?" Goddess, he was fucking tired, and it was only Monday.

The weekend had been a complete wash, spent mostly trying to figure out how the fuck he was going to explain *local* vampires to the Council of Creatures. Two days later, he still had fuck all to show for it, and Hunter was going to have to turn in that report soon otherwise the Huntsmen would start asking questions. That'd be worse. So much worse.

He dragged a hand down his face, tugging on the delicate skin under his eyes that was no doubt dark from lack of sleep before announcing, "Lu and Finn everybody!"

Bert clapped awkwardly, as if he wasn't sure how he was supposed to react. Kate crossed her arms over her chest, her expression still pinched with annoyance. Nik looked absolutely thrilled by the whole interaction, smile curling up the side of his face. He'd probably been the one laughing. And poor Chase . . . well, Chase looked like he wanted to die from secondhand embarrassment. At least *someone* felt for Eric's pitiable state.

"Go take your seats." Flicking a wrist toward the vacant row of desks, Eric waited until the girls had settled in, pulling notebooks from their bags. "Before we get started"—he licked his dry lips, anxiety crawling at his skin because he hated asking this—"do either of you have any questions for me?"

Lu's hand shot up right away, her green eyes bright in the

yellow lights from above. She waited, shifting in her seat, until Eric nodded toward her. "Is it true that you've been active since you were thirteen?"

Bert hissed through his teeth but didn't say anything, because if anyone loved the *legend* who was Eric Marcelino, it was Bert. Legend. Right. Eric was just some stupid kid who'd gotten lucky. *Very* lucky.

But instead of saying all that, he merely shrugged. "Yeah. My gene activated at thirteen when my grandmother died."

There was more to it than that. So *much* more to it than that. But if Eric could avoid talking about it, he—

"Is it true you lived alone after that?" Kate asked. She leaned forward in her chair, her eyes glittering.

"I—"

"Man," Nik said, brows raised high on his tawny brown face, "I wish my gene activated and my parents dipped when I was in high school."

And here's the thing, the kid didn't know what the fuck he was talking about, Eric knew that. Nik *didn't* want that. Because he didn't know what being a Venator was really like. He didn't know how it was to be thirteen and alone with the monsters, the ones who were supposed to support and protect him off traveling the world when he came home bloody for the third time that week. Nik didn't know. Neither did any of the other kids. Eric did. All too well.

He shook his head, opening his mouth to say something else, get them back on topic, but Kate Regan—his ex-fiancée's younger sister, of all fucking people—cut him off.

"Kalla said you used to throw all these wild parties," Kate supplied unhelpfully, clearly not seeing that her teacher was on the verge of switching topics. Unobservant little shitheads. This was why they weren't ready to be Venator, why they never *would* be ready. Because they couldn't see past the noses on their faces to know what was going on around them. If he took them out on a hunt right now, they'd be sucked dry for sure. "Sounds pretty awesome to me."

"Dude," Bert hissed, his hands curled into fists on top of his desk. "You can't say shit like that to a Venator. Who *raised* y'all?"

Nik's and Kate's eyes went wide, brows knitted as their gazes jerked up to Eric, but they didn't say anything. Didn't press any further. And an awkwardness settled over the class, each student looking increasingly more uncomfortable the longer it stretched.

So Eric took pity on them. "It's fine, Bert."

It wasn't fine. It would *never* be fine. What Eric had gone through was the exact opposite of fine. Which was why they were all there, in that room—so Eric could make sure no one else ever had to go through what he had. He'd gone out of his way, called in favors, bribed away his trust fund, all so that he could make sure these assholes never had to know the terror of being a young Venator without someone to look after them.

"But, Eric—"

"I said it's fine, Bert." Eric waved him away and forced a smile onto his face. It was a struggle to stand up straight, to not curl over the wound in his chest, the reminder of all he had lost over the years left behind. But Eric was nothing if not obstinate. So he pulled himself upright and forced the smile wider. "It's fine. Any other questions?"

The kids all blinked back at him, looking thoroughly cowed. Lu's jaw worked, like there was something else she wanted to say, but she didn't let the words off her tongue and she didn't raise her hand.

Eric nodded and decided to move on.

"Great, then let's get started. Open your texts to page fifty-nine." Eric flipped through the notes on his desk. Originally, the lesson plan for the first Monday with a full class had been introductory games. He needed them to get to know each other, to become a team—including the new kids. Especially when he knew how easy it would be for those who'd been with him for years now—Kate, Nik, and Bert—to leave the others out. Vampire hunting was a numbers game, and the better they were able to work together, the more likely they were to survive. Not that he knew from experience or anything, but it felt right and Eric had always been a man who followed his gut instincts.

Either way, after his hunts over the weekend, two of which turned up nests with yet *more* local vamps, things had to change. He couldn't drag the kids out on hunts, but that didn't mean they couldn't help out. And they were much better at research than he was, so . . .

"Local versus transient vampire activity," Bert read out loud, tone skeptical. "We don't get local vamps in Ironport, Eric."

That was the sticking point. They *didn't* get local vamps in Ironport. Biting his lip, Eric sent up a quiet hope that the kids wouldn't shoot off at the mouth anywhere someone from the council could hear them, and turned on the projector, the lights dimming automatically.

"Historically," he said, showing them the pictures of the teeth Hunter had examined alongside a sampling of the data, "Ironport has been known for transient vamp activity. But over the weekend, I broke up three nests with vampires whose teeth showed markers of being Ironport locals."

"How old?" Kate asked, her fingers drumming against her textbook. There was something unsettled in the way she shifted from side to side. Something familiar in the crease of her brow, and Eric was reminded all at once of *Kalla* Regan, the local sheriff. Beautiful, confident, capable Kalla Regan. The woman who'd broken his heart and left him bleeding. He shook himself.

"Hunter is still running tests, but as far as we can tell, the oldest was at least sixty." Rubbing his itching palms on his jeans, Eric clicked over to the full run-up on the oldest vampire.

"And there was no indication that they'd maybe moved from somewhere and settled here?" Nik frowned, scrubbing at his nose nervously. He knew what it meant—all of Eric's kids knew what it meant. It meant they had a big fucking problem.

"None at all. Hunter is digging into census information to figure out who they were before they were turned, but based on teeth alone, he says these vamps were born here, raised here, turned here."

"So?" Lu piped up, her head turning this way and that to look at the other kids in the class. Eric couldn't see her eyes with how dim the lights were, but he was willing to bet the last of his trust fund that they were wide and wild, confused. She didn't understand. Of course she didn't. She wasn't local. How could she possibly understand? "Everybody's got local vamps. They're like cockroaches, they're everywhere."

"Not Ironport." Nik shook his head. His foot tapped beneath his desk, making the entire thing shake a little.

"What do you mean, not—"

"We've never had locally sired vamps before," Bert cut in, his eyes narrowed on the report on the projector, textbook forgotten. He, unlike Eric, could probably understand all the data Hunter provided them with. "We don't know why, but there has never been a report of a local from Ironport being turned. They're always transient. Dumbass wandering bloodsuckers who are drawn to the strong magical aura Moondale puts off because it's a town literally made by magic. They come this way, sniffing out all that power, hoping to get a taste, and then can't get in because of Moondale's wards."

"So they settle for the next best thing," Nik added with a shrug. "Ironport."

"Okay, but that doesn't explain why Ironport wouldn't have its own vampires. Are you telling me none of those transients have ever turned one of the people who lives here?" Lu was gripping the front of her desk now, her face pinched in upset, and Eric felt for her. Ironport was an anomaly, and it took some getting used to for anyone who hadn't grown up there. She'd adapt. Or . . . maybe she wouldn't have to if what Eric saw became a trend.

When Bert shook his head at her, Lu pressed, "Well, why the hell not?"

"We don't know," Kate said, her voice getting louder as she ramped up for a fight. "No one knows! We just know that as far as the records show, there has never been a local turned."

Silence settled after that, and Eric flicked his gaze back to Chase and Finn, who had watched the entire volley of conversation without saying a word. Chase looked anxious, terrified, but Eric was having a hard time getting a read on Finn. The girl's face gave nothing away as her head turned to follow who was speaking.

"Either way," Eric said, cutting through the quiet, "that's what the next assignment is. I want you all to head to the archive and do some digging. See if we can't find any record of a local being changed. I know it's common knowledge that there's never been one, but sometimes common knowledge lies."

Bert squinted at him.

"What is it, Bert?" He huffed, tapping the button on the podium again so the screen would roll back up into the ceiling.

"Is this just so *you* don't have to do research?"

It most certainly *was* so Eric didn't have to do the research himself. Because dyslexia was a fucking bitch, and these nerds could get through the archives at least ten times as fast as he'd ever be able to. But he wasn't going to tell them that. "Just for that, it's due Friday. A thousand words each."

There was a collective groan and a murmured "You just

had to open your mouth, didn't you, Bert?" from Kate that had Bert looking embarrassed.

"Now, like I was saying"—Eric rubbed his hands together, glancing down at his notes—"the difference between local and transient vampires comes down to two things: territory, and pack dynamics . . ."

CHAPTER 5

WITH CLASS DISMISSED, Eric was left following his herd of baby Venator out the door into the cold late-January air. Bert kept glancing at him from where he was smashed between Kate and Nik, their shoulders jostling each other, but Eric refused to meet his eyes. To face the hurt that still lingered in his chest like a gaping hole head on.

Besides, Bert's sympathy wouldn't solve anything. It was an old wound, one that had healed over wrong and still ached when it rained. There was no fixing something like that. There was only living with it.

"Can you drop me off at Hunter and Britt's before you head out?" Chase had snuck up beside Eric, his footsteps too quiet under the noise of five other kids. If not for Eric's expert training, he might have flinched . . . he *did* flinch. "Sorry."

"You're good, kid." Eric tried to offer him a smile as the group of them shuffled out into the parking lot. The kids would have to cross it to get back to their dorm, and Eric had little doubt at least one of them would try to climb into the back of the beamer and go hunting with him before he left. Probably Bert. But he wasn't counting Lu out; she seemed the type to cause him trouble. "I'm meeting Hunter at Spin a Yarn tonight. Gotta do a quick patrol first."

Chase slumped slightly, his shoulders curling inward in a way that left Eric aching to fix it. To make the kid smile. He was so small, with big sad eyes and too-sharp features—more bird than Venator—but still, Eric couldn't help but see a kicked puppy every time Chase did that.

"I can drop you off on my way off campus." Because Eric was now, and forever would be, soft and helpless in the face of one of his kids' disappointment. Even if that kid was relatively new to his class like Chase was.

"But no one else is going," he said louder for the kids crowding around the car. Bert already had his hand on the handle, ready to open the door the moment it was unlocked. Nik made a soft noise of protest in the back of his throat, his jaw falling open like he was about to argue. "No one else. Just Chase. You all need to go back to the dorm and start on your projects."

A collective groan went through the three kids who had been with Eric the longest. Clearly, he'd been spoiling them. But now that he had a total of six in his class, he couldn't afford to drive them all over the place. Plus, the beamer wouldn't fit six unless someone was riding without a seat belt, and fuck off if Eric was going to test his luck with the cops in Ironport. Not with his ex being the sheriff. And especially not with her younger sister riding shotgun.

"No arguing. You all need—"

The roar of an engine and the noise of tires that hadn't been properly treated to handle the icy pavement drowned out anything else Eric had been about to say as a cherry-red Mustang swerved into the parking lot. It screeched to a stop two spots over from Eric in the empty lot, just before Tony McMahon climbed out, hair tied back in a messy bun, leather jacket stretched across broad shoulders. He gave Eric one quick once over, his tongue flicking out over his lower lip, and grinned, sharp and feral. "I must be dreaming! Is that you, Marcelino?"

"Fucking hell," Eric muttered under his breath, and turned to fix the full force of his glare on Tony. He did not have time for this shit, not today. Not with the lights in the parking lot flickering on, and evening plans with Ava and Hunter already on the docket. They'd skewer him if he was late. "What do you want, McMahon?"

"Did it hurt when you fell from the vending machine?" Tony's sharp green eyes raked over Eric once more, the attention making a shiver roll down Eric's spine that he was definitely going to pretend was revulsion. Because what else *could* it be?

Lu groaned, banging her head against Finn's shoulder while the other girl merely looked on in confusion. The rest of the kids had fallen oddly quiet on the other side of Eric's car, and all he could hope was that it would stay that way, or that they'd fucked off to the dorms per his instructions. Doubtful though.

"What the fuck are you talking about, man?" Eric rubbed at his face, tired already from a long day and not looking forward to more of whatever tomfuckery Tony thought to drag him into.

"Cause you look like a snack," Tony all but purred.

A collective groan from all present parties—apart from Eric and Tony, of course—followed. And Eric thought he heard a muttered "This is so embarrassing for you, bro" from one of the boys, but he couldn't tell which one.

Tony's lips curved further up his face, his eyes crinkling a little with the smile, just enough to let Eric know that he found himself hilarious. Which was . . . which was *annoying.* All right? It was annoying. It was also annoying how boyishly charming Eric found those tiny crow's feet around Tony's too-bright eyes.

"Does that line actually work? Like on *real* people?" Eric crossed his arms over his chest, the sleeves of his peacoat pulling back a bit, making his wrists cold. "Or just on your reflection?"

Tony barked a laugh, his eyes crinkled further as his head

fell back to reveal an expanse of gold-tanned skin. He was beautiful, Eric could admit that in the privacy of his own head. The way that a tiger or a lioness would be beautiful. All sharp teeth and killing intent. And Eric knew enough about himself, enough about his history, to know that anything he wanted half as bad as he wanted Tony McMahon in that moment couldn't be good for him. So he kept his distance, pressing his back harder against the driver's side door of his beamer, letting the cold seep in through his coat and jeans.

There was a beat of silence, something fraught with tension pulled too taut, near snapping, and Eric willed the little shitheads to say something. To break it. To do what they did best and turn the conversation elsewhere. But they didn't. They remained quiet. Probably hanging on every word so they could make fun of him for it all later. Assholes.

Tongue poking through his teeth, Tony narrowed his eyes, inspecting Eric more closely, and Eric fought tooth and nail not to squirm under it. "You always dress like an eighty-year-old librarian, or is today just special?"

"If this is you flirting, no wonder you're single," Eric shot back, cheeks heating as he tugged his tweed coat further around his frame to hide the woolen sweater underneath. It was cold, all right? And he liked being cozy. He shouldn't have to dignify his fashion choices to someone wearing a white T-shirt that looked like it came out of a plastic package of ten in barely above freezing temperatures.

"Is that you asking if I'm single?" Tony's tanned face crinkled gleefully, his shoulders falling back a notch to puff his chest out. And okay, maybe it *was* Eric's way of asking if he was single. But Tony didn't need to know that.

"Enough already," Lu huffed, drawing both men's attention back to the small huddle of college kids now whispering frantically near the hood of Eric's car. Fuck. They were definitely going to make fun of him. He didn't need this. He didn't need this *at all*. He had so much else to do. So much else to worry about. Local vamps. And magic councils. And three freshly positive Venator genes. He didn't have time for Tony and his bullshit.

Tony clicked his tongue, his gaze flicking to his sister, who had moved to lean against the corner panel of his car. "Ready to head home, shitbird?"

"Yes, please." Lu sagged a little, her bag seeming to suddenly weigh a ton where she'd looped it over one shoulder.

"Yeah." Tony's smile went a little softer around the edges, less sharp and feral, and Eric wondered for a moment what it would feel like to have all that softness and warmth turned on him. Fuck. He didn't even *know* Tony. Had one good fight with him in a graveyard, and now he was thinking about soft smiles. Maybe Ava was right—maybe he *did* need to get laid. "All right."

Shifting forward onto his toes, Tony pulled the passenger door to his car open for his sister and turned to head back around to the driver's side. As Lu's door slammed shut, Eric snapped out of whatever fugue state he'd been in and said, "I meant to ask."

"Yeeees?" Tony tilted his head just so, a curl of stupidly pretty strawberry-blond hair falling loose from his bun and settling against his collarbones. A tease, even if it was an unintentional one, that had Eric really hoping the kids weren't paying attention as he shifted his weight against his car again.

"Why isn't Lu living in the dorms with the rest of my kids?" He tried not to think about how the words *my kids* felt at home on his tongue. Because the moment he took ownership of them like that, the moment he went from mentor to Mama Bear—which, let's face it, had happened a long-ass time ago—was the moment he knew he couldn't ever let them become active Venator. Couldn't let the Council of Creatures push them into service, not the way they'd pushed *him* into it. Fuck. He was in over his head on all fronts, wasn't he? "Campus is safer, and we've got plenty of room."

A soft hum left Tony as if he was thinking about his answer, considering his options. Then he raised both brows, his face lighting up again. "Why don't you come to dinner with me, pretty boy, and we'll talk about it?"

The kids behind Eric snickered softly, and heat crawled up his neck, making his scarf feel choking and stifling all of the sudden.

"I've got plans." Eric lifted his chin a little, a clear challenge for Tony to act like a dick and see what happened.

But Tony just shrugged and said, "Maybe next time then" before getting in his car and peeling out of the parking lot without another word. And that was . . . that was a hell of a lot different from the reaction Eric had been expecting.

"You need to get laid," Ava confirmed a few hours later when she, Hunter, and Eric were curled into three of the deeply cushioned chairs in the middle of Ava's yarn shop, Spin a Yarn. Somehow, they'd gotten on the topic of Tony McMahon —Eric knew *exactly* how, and it was all Hunter's fault— instead of focusing on the things they were supposed to focus on. Which was local vampires. And Council of Creatures meetings. And three new Venator genes in as many months. Because, apparently, Eric's inactive sex life and the sudden appearance of someone who *might* be a willing partner, was more important. Eric was too fucking sober for this. Way too fucking sober.

"That's what I said!" Hunter laughed, slumping further down in his chair. He'd abandoned his crochet project at some point and taken to unspooling the skein of yarn Ava was using, turning it into a ball. Eric wasn't sure if she'd asked for that or not, but she wasn't yelling at Hunter, so it must be okay.

"This has nothing to do with that. And Tony isn't like . . ." Eric glared down at his own messy attempt at a beanie. It wasn't turning out right. Maybe he'd miscounted the stitches? Or the rows? Fuck, he was going to have to frog it and start over, wasn't he? He hated that. "We're not doing that."

"Not doing what? Having a nice dinner with a nice-looking guy?" The chair creaked under Ava's weight as she leaned over to get a better look at Eric's mess of a beanie. "You need to start over, dingus, there's no way in hell your base chain was big enough. And what stitch even is that? Is that a treble?"

"Fuck off, Ava, let me make my hat in peace." Huffing, he pulled the hook from the loop and started to unravel the whole thing. She was right. It was probably the base chain or some shit. "Damn it, where's my pattern?"

"Think Hunter used it for his gum." Ava's hands reached for the yarn Eric was ripping apart as Ava helped him roll it around the skein so it wouldn't knot up.

"Hunter!"

"I didn't!" There was some mad scrambling, chair legs creaking dangerously as Hunter leaned over and wound up finding the wrinkled-to-the-point-of-almost-being-unreadable paper stuffed between the seat cushion, the arm, and his ass of all places. "Found it!"

"How did it even get over there?" Eric took it, trying to smooth it out across his thigh, but it seemed hopeless.

"You're avoiding the question." Ava tossed a skein of yarn from her basket at him, and Eric didn't even bother to move out of the way. She'd just toss another one if she missed.

"There wasn't a question. There was an untrue statement. I don't need to get laid. I'm fine." He wasn't fine. He knew he wasn't fine. Not that getting laid was going to suddenly *make* him fine. Because his relative fine-ness had nothing at all to do with his lack of sexual activities, and everything to do with the stress of something lingering in the air of Ironport. Like blood in the water, ready to draw the sharks, and he was just one helpless, hapless seal trying to fend them off long enough for all the other idiotic seals to get away . . .

That analogy had gone too far. He needed to stop putting on Discovery Channel when he went to sleep at night.

Ava and Hunter went still in the corner of his eye, and although Eric wasn't looking at them, too focused on restarting his awkward little beanie, he could see them glance at one another. A whole conversation passing between heartbeats. And he hated that. Hated how worried they were about him. Hated how his two best friends in the entire world thought they needed to protect him. Especially when he knew that they couldn't. No. It was *his* job to protect *them*—them and everyone else.

"All right," Ava said, her tone slow, measured, "tell me again about the local vamp problem."

Not that she could do anything about it; she was a coven-less witch. It wasn't her *place* to do anything, and magic didn't really work on vamps anyway. Not in the strictest sense. A witch could ward against them, could create protection amulets. But most spellwork wouldn't take on a vampire. No offensive magic of any kind would do *anything* to them, and very little defensive did either. Something about the way their blood wasn't pumping anymore, but they also weren't dead, making them an anomaly that not even a necromancer could control.

Still, Eric took a breath and dove in. Repeated everything he and Hunter had told her the moment they'd walked in, hoping Ava would see something they missed. That somewhere in that too-clever mind of hers, she'd find a solution that wasn't Eric taking six kids who were barely through puberty out to hunt vampires.

By the time he was done, they had all abandoned their

various projects into the basket at Ava's feet and fallen quiet, still. Which made it all the worse, because stillness meant thinking, and thinking meant that nothing had struck them through the entirety of Eric's explanation. For someone as quick-witted as Ava, as knowledgeable as Hunter, that was never a good sign.

"You need help, Eric," Ava said, her voice soft enough that he almost couldn't hear it over the sound of Taylor Swift belting out her rage at whatever real or imagined adversaries she faced. Eric had been in charge of picking the tracks for the night, and he had needed Taylor's optimism, but now the music seemed a little macabre.

"I know that." He slumped back into his chair, raking his hands through his hair. "Do you think I don't know that?"

"No." Sitting up, Ava reached for his wrists, her fingers tight around the bone, hands strong from years of soft crafts. "No, Eric. No. You need help."

"I'm not taking the kids—"

"Not the kids, you absolute tool." She squeezed his wrists tighter, making his fingers tingle from the pressure on his nerves. "And not that—that dipshit, Tony, either. You need *real* help. Trained help."

"Okay, and where would you like me to get that, Ava?" Clicking his tongue, he shook her hands off him, flexing his fingers to get the blood flowing back into them properly. "Should I just pull it out of my ass?"

"Ask the council for reinforcements." Hunter's tone was eerily soft, thoughtful. It sent Eric's heart skittering in his chest. Because if fun-loving, bright-eyed, laughing Hunter was being serious then . . . then this shit was *serious*. Not that he didn't already know that but, you know. "From some of the other Huntsmen communities. I know there aren't many Venator in the country, but there are a few in North America, a handful maybe. Two in Canada at least. One in Mexico, right? That's better than nothing. Isn't it?"

Eric stopped, waited, considered this. His lungs expanding, expanding, expanding, pushing against his ribs, lending him a sense of calm he didn't really feel. "Yeah," he said when he finally allowed himself a slow, shaky exhale. "Yeah, that could work."

CHAPTER 6

BY THE TIME Ava finished the skein of yarn she was working on and glared down at the next one—likely trying to decide how she wanted to join the two separate threads—Eric felt better about everything. They hadn't solved his problem, but they had formed a plan at least, and that was more than Eric had when he walked into Ava's shop hours ago. So, he would take what he could get and choose to look on the bright side of things.

The alternative was too depressing.

"I'm riding home with you." Hunter stuffed his hands into his pockets, leaning back on his heels where they stood next to the door. A cold rain had started up outside, making the street sparkle in a way that indicated ice. Because *that's* just what Eric needed on top of everything else.

"Britt drop you off?" The zipper on Eric's parka-like coat got caught on his scarf, and he cursed under his breath, lifting the fabric up to his mouth to hold it out of the way as he tried again. Maybe he shouldn't have bothered changing before he went out on patrol. But the tweed one was a little small these days, had less manueverability. Ava could fix it easily using her magic as a Stitch Witch, he just kept forgetting to bring it for her to look at.

"Yeah, something about me never being sober when I

leave one of our craft nights." Hunter rolled his shoulders in a shrug and shooed Eric's hands away to help him zip his coat. There was a glassy sheen to his eyes that told Eric Britt had been exactly right about that. He hadn't thought whatever edibles Hunter brought tucked in his brown paper bag for he and Ava to share had been that strong, but it was always better to be safe than sorry.

A huff left Eric as he tightened the scarf around his neck. It wasn't that he hated being the responsible one. It wasn't. But it seemed to be all the time. Like every day since he'd turned thirteen and his Venator gene had activated. And, sure, he knew part of it was his own fault. He tended to mother hen people, even friends his own age. It was in his nature. Hammered into him by his grandmother telling him it was a Venator's job to protect others all the damn time.

"Zip your jacket, it's fucking frigid out," he muttered, slinging the tote bag carrying his own yarn and crochet hooks over his shoulder.

"Yes, Mom." Hunter laughed softly, but there was no bite in the words, only fond teasing that left something warm in Eric's chest. It was good to have friends who really liked him, really cared about him. Good to have people in his life who worried about him and his problems. Even if he didn't want them to, it was good to know they did regardless. The warmth spread out to his fingertips, humming like family, but Eric didn't let himself lean into it too much.

Leaning over to get a better look at where Ava was tucked up into her chair still, Eric waved theatrically and said over-loud, "We'll see you on Friday, Ava."

"Yeah. See you." She sounded like she was only half paying attention, and then she popped up over the back of the chair, her loosely tied back deep-green hair falling into her eyes. Soft. Mussed. Her brow crinkled a little in concern, and Eric hated that he had brought his drama and his troubles here, into her safe space. She didn't deserve that. None of them did. He should keep it all to himself. "Good luck with your new *lover boy*, King Ricky."

A choked-off guffaw left Hunter, then he was bending over holding this stomach, his ebony brown face crinkled up in laughter. Ava's own shrill giggles followed shortly after, and in spite of being the butt of the joke, Eric basked in it. Let it chase away the fear that crawled constantly along his skin like ants. Let it lighten the air, make it sparkle, almost.

Once outside of Spin a Yarn, everything would have to go back to how it was. He'd go back to being Ironport's sole line of defense against vampires. And he was hesitant to leave. To push out into the street where it was cold, and dark, and the monsters waited.

He knew this sense of safety wasn't correct. Wasn't true. Wasn't *real*. But he also felt that so long as he didn't cross that threshold, so long as he stayed tucked among the shelves that towered to the ceiling—stuffed full of yarn—and the too-thickly padded armchairs Ava bought from a thrift shop and reupholstered herself, with only minimal help from him and Hunter, he was *safe*.

It was an alien feeling: safety. Left him staggering the first time he experienced it upon walking into Ava's shop. He was sure there was some science behind it, some magic. Something about the wards that Ava wove into the walls and the floors. Something about the soft lighting and the gentle hum of music from the speakers. Maybe even the smell of the yarn. But he liked to think it was because this space, this shop, was sacred. The one bright spot in the world that was untouchable for the darkness that lay beyond the door.

Childish.

"He is *not* my lover boy." Eric rolled his eyes, puffing his chest up to play into the annoyed tone that didn't dip any lower than surface level. How could he possibly be annoyed with these two? They were his family. They were his *people*.

"Mm-hmm. Sure." Flopping back down into her chair,

Ava effectively ended the conversation, and Eric was left to stuff his hands deep into his pockets, reaching for his keys.

"Come on, Hunter, I've got to make sure the gremlins are asleep."

"And make sure they didn't eat after midnight!" Ava called, a snort of laughter leaving her.

"You're hilarious," Eric sniped back, shouldering out into the cold. He didn't look back to see if Hunter was following, his gaze already cutting to the street to search for threats.

Beyond the soft yellow light of Spin a Yarn were several streetlights out—not an unusual occurrence in Ironport, but it put Eric's teeth on edge. Had they been out before he'd entered? He hadn't noticed them . . .

"All right, Mama Bear, let's go tuck your cubs into bed." Hunter's voice shook lightly with laughter still, and it was enough to settle the bubble of safety from Spin a Yarn onto Eric, even out in the cold and the dark of Ironport's streets. Enough to make him relax as Hunter looped their arms companionably, warmth blooming and burning through the thick padding of their coats, as they walked carefully down the slick sidewalk toward Eric's parked car.

It wasn't far. Not even half a block down the road. And it had seemed even closer when Eric parked it there hours ago after his patrol around Ironport turned up nothing. But now . . . *now* it seemed miles and miles away. With darkness and decrepit alleys standing between Eric and the safety of the beamer and its warded panels.

Fear crept along his senses, raising the hair at the back of his neck.

Hunter didn't seem to notice. He was humming quietly, whatever buzz he'd gotten from the edibles while they'd been crafting still lingering warm and smooth in his veins. Loose limbed and content at Eric's side where his too-warm arm was wrapped around Eric's own. It would have been good, fine, any other night. But Eric's mind buzzed with local vamps, and three new Venator genes, and too many coincidences to settle.

Thus, he was distracted, his attention elsewhere, when the hair on the back of his neck and along his arms raised. When *warning* settled against his skin. Easy enough to brush off in the change in temperature from Ava's warm store to the frigid winter night as he focused on keeping Hunter upright and getting them both to the car safely. Too busy to notice the way someone or some*thing*'s gaze lingered on them and pressed in closer.

They were passing an alley, Eric's tennis shoes skidding against a patch of ice, when the awareness finally hit him all at once. The smell—they must have been downwind till then—smacking him so hard in the face, he stumbled.

Death. Rot. Decay. Blood. Blood. *Blood.*

There was just enough time for Eric to shove Hunter away from him, toward the car, pressing the button to unlock the doors. "Get in!"

"What? What? What?" Hunter scrambled against the slick pavement, his Chucks providing no traction at all as he reached for the handle.

Thankfully, his first reaction was to follow Eric's orders. Anyone who'd ever been around Eric when the vampires came calling knew that the one thing a person never did in a situation like this was ignore an order from Eric Marcelino. Especially when it was in that Tone. So it was only instinct, it seemed, for Hunter to get into the backseat of the beamer—the nearest door—and slam it behind him before banging his hand so hard against the lock button, it gave a decisive *thump.*

Eric spun. Reaching into his tote bag, he pulled out one of the thin wooden crochet hooks he'd been using to make his beanie. It wasn't perfect, didn't even really have a point, but it would do in a pinch. And as he'd stupidly left all his stakes in the trunk, in a pinch he was.

Even with the lights from what few stores remained open

—just Spin a Yarn, a liquor store, and a twenty-four-hour pharmacy some doors down—it was hard to see. The darkness beyond the streetlamp his car was parked under shifted, writhing. That was all right. That was fine. He was trained for that sort of thing.

Eric planted his feet, his fingers curled around the crochet hook in his hand, and readied himself for a fight. Between one breath and the next, he heard the soft shush of clothing, movement in the dark. He locked on to something moving out of the corner of his eye off to his right, adjusted his stance, and was ready when the vampire lurched for him, fangs gleaming in the light, already dripping with saliva.

It should have been a one-and-done kind of thing. *Would* have been a one-and-done kind of thing. Only the moment Eric got his impromptu stake into position, Hunter shouted something muffled and unintelligible from the car, and movement caught Eric out of the corner of his eye, awareness of another threat sending a shiver down his spine. Eric had just enough time to spin, to see the three fucking *other* vampires materializing out of the darkness—human-like apart from their glowing red eyes, birdlike movements, and glinting fangs—before the one who'd already lunged toward him barreled into his chest. His body hit hard, denting the door of the car probably enough that Hunter wouldn't be able to open it, and cracking something in his ribs.

His vision darkened around the edges, threatening unconsciousness, but he somehow managed to kick the nearest vamp away before they had the chance to sink their teeth into his jugular. Pulling himself away from the car—mourning the money that was going to cost him to fix (there went the remote start)—he settled back into a fighting stance. The crochet hook was, thankfully, still clasped tightly in the palm of his hand, but the pack of vamps didn't give him enough time to work out a plan. They were on him. All four of them dogpiling him, snapping, snarling, and going for any bit of soft skin they could get to. Pressing down heavily against his injured ribs, their combined weight making it hard to breathe.

Eric lost track of his weapon at some point, too focused on trying to shove them off so his lungs could properly inflate. Darkness pressed in harder along the edges of his vision. Fresh blood, metallic and over-warm, ran thick in the air, coating his jeans, his coat, cooling against his skin. Limbs pulled in fifty different directions, each vamp taking an arm or a leg, threatening to rip him apart like one might a fucking gingerbread man.

Fuck.

This is how he went, wasn't it? This is how Eric Marcelino —King Ricky—died.

There were too many of them to keep track of. Too many mouths. Too many teeth. Too many clawed hands. And they'd caught him unprepared, too focused on getting Hunter to safety. This was why he'd been hunting alone for so many years. This was why he couldn't let the kids out into the field.

One of the vampires yanked so hard on his arm that his shoulder dislocated, pain shooting through him so quickly, he was nauseous with it. Another ripped into his fluffy coat with its teeth—the seams tearing loud enough he could hear it over the ringing of his ears—trying to get to his wrist. He couldn't see what the other two were doing. Which might have been for the better, because even as he squirmed and thrashed, even as Hunter screamed, his voice muffled by the car and by Eric's pain, Eric's vision darkened, bit by bit, and he knew . . .

Yup.

This was how Eric Marcelino died.

He had just enough time, just a moment, to let out a strangled, breathless, choked-off chuckle as he looked into the face of his best friend from high school. The kid who'd followed him around like he was Diana's gift to Earth for the first three years. Right up until Eric got his head out of his ass and stopped pretending he was cooler than he was.

Noah M.

Then the darkness of blood loss and lack of air pulled him under.

TONY WASN'T STALKING MARCELINO.

Lu could say whatever she wanted to say. But Tony wasn't *stalking* Marcelino. He wasn't. Scout's honor. It was just coincidence that on his after-work patrol he happened to wander past the street on which Marcelino's signature beat-up green beamer was parked.

Tony knew cars. It wasn't Marcelino's car in particular he'd memorized. That had nothing to do with it. It was just . . . it was just that he was a mechanic, a car guy. So yeah, he noticed cars. Knew what they said about the person who owned them. Marcelino's beat-up four-door BMW in a sensible color said that once upon a time he'd had money, or his parents had gifted him the car when he turned sixteen. It also said that he'd wanted to be able to drive people around. It also said—

Nevermind.

And so what if he'd gone out on patrol specifically looking for the other man? So what if when he saw the car, he perked right up and decided to turn down the street and see what Marcelino was up to?

He wasn't spying. He wasn't stalking. He wasn't being a weirdo.

Thank you very much, Lu.

And it was a good thing he did!

Because he saw the moment Marcelino went down.

It all happened so fast. The leeches melted out of the darkness like fucking shadows made real in a cartoon, only faster. Between one heartbeat and the next. Quick enough that if he weren't a Venator, if he weren't trained for this, he wouldn't have even noticed the movement. Then they were on Marcelino. Slamming him to the ground.

Tony's step had stuttered the moment he saw them, some stupid thing in his brain telling him to hang back a minute, to see Marcelino at work, for real this time. He'd missed most of the fight a few days ago, and now he wanted to see what Marcelino was made of.

Only . . .

Only the guy in the car shouted, and the extra leeches came out of nowhere, and Marcelino seemed distracted. And instead of showing off what a badass he was, he slipped on the ice and went down. The vampires piled on top of him.

"Hey!" The word ripped from Tony's throat, his boots skidding against the slick cement. He was too far. At least two blocks down. *Too far.* "Hey! Get off 'im!"

And the vamps . . . those vicious fucking bloodsuckers, they weren't going to let up so long as they had a meal like Marcelino in their grasp. They didn't even bother to pause in their feast. Which, to be fair, if Tony had Marcelino sprawled out below him like a damn buffet, he wouldn't let himself be distracted either. But that wasn't the point! That was entirely beside the point!

The point was that it left them open. Their attention drawn elsewhere. Their backs to Tony. They were easy fucking targets. So easy, in fact, it almost felt wrong to add them to his slay tally, but Tony was going to do it anyway.

The nearest vamp went down without much of a fight, Tony slamming a stake through the bone of its back, slicing like butter straight to its cold dead heart. It burst into a cloud of dust a moment later that had him coughing enough to make his eyes water, but he didn't slow down.

He couldn't.

Because he was throwing the next nearest leech away from Marcelino, refusing to note the blood that splattered across the pavement as Tony got his feet under him again and faced off against the vamp. The thing hissed at him, blood dripping from its fangs, its pale hands curled into claws, nails long enough to rip, to tear, then slammed its entire body weight into Tony's chest.

Which hurt like absolute hell, but he managed to angle the stake in his hand just right and dust the damn thing before it could take Tony to the ground the way one of them had Marcelino. But it also distracted him from the fact that a third leech had separated from the meal on the ground and come up behind him. It landed a blow to the back of his head with a fist that felt more lead pipe than bone and skin. He stumbled, vision going a little hazy around the edges. If he didn't have a concussion before, he sure as fuck had one now.

There was a grunt from beside him, and Tony looked over just long enough to see that Marcelino seemed to be coming to. He still struggled under the weight of the fourth leech, but the creature had, oddly enough, stopped feasting for the moment. Likely to wait and see how Tony's fight with its friend turned out. Strangely intelligent for a creature driven by thirst and instinct, in Tony's opinion. Especially since warm blood trickled down from where the other leech had bashed him on the head.

"You good, Marcelino?" Tony called, grabbing another stake from his pocket and fixing his attention on the threat in front of him now. He wasn't going to be taken off guard a second time.

Marcelino grunted again, but Tony would take that as a good sign. At least he wasn't unconscious anymore. He might be a little anemic for the next couple of days, if Tony knew anything about a vamp bite, and he did, but Venator were built to bounce back, and Marcelino was strong. So he'd be fine.

"Glad to hear it." A vicious smile curled up Tony's lips, more feral than a grin had any right to be really, and he lunged at the vamp in front of him.

He took a knee to his stomach for his troubles but managed to smack the leech hard across the jaw, drawing a small trickle of blood before it healed over, and knocking it sideways. The leech swung wildly, catching Tony's arm and knocking one of the stakes from his hand, but he managed to keep hold on the other. And as the vamp rounded for another manic swing, Tony jammed it into the creature's sternum.

It didn't hit home at first.

The vamp struggled to push the splintered wood away. But Tony twisted his wrist, vicious and brutal, creating a gaping hole in its chest that knitted back together almost as soon as it'd been torn open, and dragged the stake over to where its heart was. It wasn't easy. The vampire howled and squirmed the whole time, swinging wildly in an attempt to get away from its certain end. But Tony managed to push past bones gone brittle and flesh gone sallow, and sink the tip of his stake into the creature's heart.

If it weren't for that last vamp still hovering over Marcelino's prone form, the thick metallic scent of blood in the air, the other man still watching from the backseat of Marcelino's car, and the jingling of a bell from a shop nearby, Tony might have made a "just the tip" joke right before the creature was dusted. But as circumstances stood, it didn't seem entirely appropriate—not that the level of appropriateness for a crude joke had stopped him before, but anyway.

A scream rent the air, drawing everyone's attention for a moment to the woman with the green hair who'd just come out of a shop a little ways down the block. Then the stillness that had settled over them was broken, and Tony lunged for the last vamp, grabbing it by its shoulder to drag it in closer to him.

Just as he was lifting the stake still clutched in his bloody hand, Marcelino shouted, "No, Tony! Don't kill Noah!"

The surprise of it made Tony stumble, his movements stuttered, giving the fucking leech enough time to scramble out of his hold and disappear into the night.

"Who the *fuck* is Noah?" Tony growled.

But he didn't get an answer because a moment later the guy from the car and the woman with the green hair were both hovering over Marcelino like two overprotective parents. The woman's voice went a little raspy as she muttered, "Eric. Eric. Are you all right?"

"I'm fine, Ava." Marcelino brushed her off, but even as he said it his knees buckled under his weight, and his two friends grabbed him by the armpits to haul him into the passenger seat of his car.

"You aren't fine, man," the guy said, his voice deep but shaky as he bent at the waist to get a look at Marcelino in the overhead lights of his car. "Britt is gonna shit the bed over this."

"Huuunter," Marcelino groaned, tilting his head back against the headrest and squinting at everyone around him for a moment.

"Don't *Hunter* me." Hunter turned to Tony, still bent awkwardly over Marcelino's form as he dug around in his coat pocket for something. "You good to drive, Tony?"

Tony jerked at being addressed directly when he'd felt only a moment prior like he was intruding on something, a family moment where he didn't belong. "What?"

"I can drive, Hun!" Marcelino tried to swat Hunter away from where he was digging through his pockets for his keys, but his attention was quickly drawn away when Ava started talking into her phone. "Fuck me, Ava, don't call Britt!"

"I'll do what I want. Shut the fuck up, Eric," Ava snapped,

moving off to the side to continue her phone call at the same time Hunter found the keys and gave a victorious crow. He turned the full force of his sharp eyes on Tony.

"So, you okay to drive?" He held the keys out to Tony, not seeming to really need an answer.

"Aren't you?" But Tony was already taking the keys, not even bothering with the fact that it meant he'd have to have someone drive him home tonight.

"Not really." Hunter laughed, and that's when Tony saw his hands shaking just before he stuffed them into his pockets. "You can drive me and Eric back to the dorm, and then Britt will give you a ride back to your place once we've got big boy back here patched up."

"I told you I'm fine!" Marcelino huffed, but it was starting to sound faint, and when Tony looked past Hunter, he found Marcelino slumped against the seat, almost melting into the floor.

"Yeah, you're fine all right." Tony rolled his eyes, spinning the key ring around his finger.

Hunter offered Tony a wide smile and clapped him on the shoulder before moving off to check in with Ava.

"Who's Britt?" His weight pressed into the dented passenger side door where he could monitor Marcelino's breathing based on the rise and fall of his chest.

"Hunter's wifey." Marcelino waved his hand vaguely in the direction of where Hunter and Ava were murmuring into the phone in Ava's hand. If Tony tried, he'd be able to hear what Britt was saying on the other end of the line, but he didn't try. He was too focused on watching Marcelino. "The nurse at Moondale U."

"Ah." Tony nodded. "She any good?"

"Been patching me up since I was about twenty." He shrugged then winced when it seemed to jar something. "Fucking broken rib."

"They busted you up real good, didn't they, pretty boy?"

Marcelino grunted, his face pinching a little like he was going to say something else, but Hunter was beside them again. When Tony glanced over Hunter's shoulder, he noted that Ava had gone back inside. "Britt's gonna meet us at the dorm. Let's head out."

There was a note of protest from Marcelino but both Tony and Hunter ignored him as they piled into the now *more* beat-up beamer, and Tony peeled away from the curb.

———

1106 Moonshadow Way.

The dorm, as Hunter called it, was less a dorm and more an old house with peeling siding and a slight lean to it that looked like it was sliding down the mountain it had been built on. Every window in the front shone brightly in the gloom of the late evening, and Tony heard Marcelino mutter, "Fucking gremlins" from the passenger seat as he parked.

Hunter rolled out of the car before Tony even got his seat belt unbuckled, and moved quickly to help Marcelino from his seat, effectively stopping him from trying to do it himself and injuring himself further.

"I'm fine, Hunter," Marcelino grumbled for what might have been the hundredth time since Tony stumbled upon the scene about a half hour ago. But Hunter wasn't taking no for an answer and already had Marcelino slung over his shoulder, half-crouching to accommodate his shorter height, by the time Tony shut the driver's side door. Tony moved to his other side to help balance him out and take the weight off Marcelino's likely cracked ribs.

The door to the house swung open before they even reached the crooked front porch, a head full of curly hair silhouetted by the lights in the house as it poked through the crack.

"Oh shit, you lose a fight?" the kid asked, stepping back

away from the door and leaving it open for Hunter and Tony to all but drag Marcelino over the threshold.

"Fuck off, Bert," Marcelino growled as he pulled away from the two men helping him stay upright. He straightened his spine, likely to hide the weakness from his student. But Tony didn't miss the soft wince he released as he leaned heavily against the wall to kick off his shoes.

Tony's and Hunter's followed, joining the collection of sneakers and boots on the mat along the right-hand side of the short hall that led into the house. They varied in size and stages of wear, all stacked neatly in a row.

"Oh, for fuck's sake," Marcelino bitched. He'd rounded the corner from the short hall into the main house, and Tony followed behind, hands tucked into his pockets but gaze fixed on the way Marcelino favored his right side. "It is well past your bedtime!"

"We don't have a *bedtime*. We're *adults*," one of the kids sniped back.

And chaos descended as every other kid in the room—which was a fucking mess, soda cans and pizza boxes strewn among board game pieces around a cluttered coffee table—started arguing their point against bedtime. Hunter nudged Tony lightly in the arm, nodded toward the kitchen without a word, and Tony followed him.

There were bandages and disinfectant already laid out on the counter where one of the kids, presumably, had gathered whatever first aid things they thought Marcelino might need. Hunter went to the fridge to pull out a couple of ice packs along with a bottle of water that he tossed to Tony before opening his own with a crack.

The shouting from the other room intensified.

"Shouldn't they listen to him? He's their teacher." Tony frowned, leaning against the counter so he could peek through the doorway into the living room where Marcelino had taken to leaning against the couch, his face pinched. He wasn't saying anything, just letting the kids get it all out as they bitched and moaned about being too fucking old for a bedtime and how they weren't technically breaking curfew because they were inside the house. "And what's the deal with them anyway? They fight like . . ." He drifted off, unsure how to end that sentence. He wanted to say siblings, but it didn't—Well, he didn't want to presume anything.

"Like family?" Hunter asked. He braced himself on the other side of the island, his elbows planted firmly against the scuffed laminate countertop. "That's because they are."

Tony tilted his head, narrowing his eyes on the scene playing out before him as the kids grumbled and shouted but ultimately started cleaning up the living room as instructed while Marcelino just waited with his hands on his hips.

"Here's the thing," Hunter said, his voice going soft and warm, fond in a way Tony didn't think it had any right to, but somehow also getting louder like he was leaning in closer to Tony to share with him some great secret of the universe. "Eric practically raised those four. Every single one of 'em. Even my brother, who didn't test positive until about a month ago. Any kid from a Huntsmen family who looks like they might have the slightest inclination toward testing positive for the Venator gene gets taken under his wing."

"Oh yeah?" He could see it. Could see the way Marcelino had parented all of them, annoyed them, but there was a bond there, a trust. Like the one he had with Lu. These kids knew Marcelino would keep them safe. Knew he had their best interest in mind with everything he said.

"He's the reason we even have the Venator program at Moondale U." Hunter's voice grew firmer, pride lining every syllable, but there was also an edge of warning to the words. Like he was gearing himself up for a shovel talk. Which was kind of hilarious, because Marcelino hadn't even agreed to dinner yet. And it wasn't like he needed protecting, least of all by some low-grade witch like Hunter.

"No shit?"

"No shit."

Tony's world view realigned a bit, with Marcelino at the center of it. All he managed after that was a singular grunted "huh" right before the door opened and a woman—presumably Britt—poured in with a medical bag over her shoulder.

"All right, nerds, get out of my way so I can look after the mama bird," Britt said, shooing the kids toward the stairs with absolutely none of the trouble that Marcelino had.

"Stop calling me that," Marcelino grumbled, slumping down onto the couch now remarkably free of debris. One of the kids had even folded the crochet afghan neatly and laid it over the back of the couch.

"Never." Britt turned on him, her blond ponytail swaying, and flashed him a feral smile. "Now show me where it hurts."

"Oh nurse, all over," Marcelino grumbled playfully, wiggling his eyebrows at her in what was clearly meant to be a ridiculous way, and Tony snickered softly to himself.

"That your girl?" He turned back to Hunter, brow raised.

"Yeah. That's her." Hunter laughed, his eyes settling fond and warm on Britt. They both leaned more comfortably against the counter to watch Marcelino and Britt trade barbs as she looked him over and patched him up quickly. Fuck, was that woman efficient.

CHAPTER 8

"FUCK, your room is boring, pretty boy," Tony said as he all but hauled Eric into the small bedroom Eric had chosen for himself all those years ago when the Venator classes first started.

It wasn't much, hardly big enough for the twin bed and desk in the corner. It looked more like a traditional dorm than any of the other rooms in the house, but it was his sanctuary. The one place on all campus where the kids weren't allowed to storm in and bug the living shit out of him without knocking first. Which, arguably, should have meant that it was more personalized. At the very least, he should have had some art hung on the walls. But there had never been time for all that, and he only slept and graded papers in there anyway. He spent most of his time in the common areas, the living room, and the small study he'd set up for the kids, which sported big overstuffed furniture, tables for them to do their projects on, and shelves overflowing with more books than he'd ever manage to read in his life. So, yeah, his room was kind of . . . basic.

"There's rules about what kinds of decorations we can put up in our rooms here," Eric lied and hoped the wince from his broken ribs covered it. Britt had wrapped them tight, but even that couldn't change how they caught on each other, snagging skin, when he jostled them too much.

"What?" Bert asked, popping his head in where it looked like he'd been on his way back to his room after his nightly routine; he had toothpaste on his shirt. "No there aren't."

"Really, kid?" Eric cut Bert a glare as Tony helped him settle onto the edge of his bed. "Who are you helping right now? Who? Literally no one. Go to bed."

Bert huffed but didn't say anything else, just slunk down the hall toward his room, leaving Eric alone. In his room. With Tony McMahon. Which . . . why was he still there, anyway? Britt said she could take him home whenever he was ready. And it wasn't like Eric needed Tony to tuck him in. Hunter was perfectly capable of manhandling an injured Eric up the steps to his room and throwing him in bed. He'd done it so many times, it was probably muscle memory by now. But Tony was still there, making a slow circuit of Eric's room like it would tell him the secrets to life, the universe, and everything. Maybe it would. Eric had never tried looking for those answers here.

"So," Eric said, clearing his throat when the silence between them stretched on for too long. "I think we need to talk about what happened tonight."

"What about it?" Tony set down the half empty mug of day-old coffee he'd been sniffing.

With a long inhale, Eric geared himself up to say the one thing he'd been thinking since he came to lying on the ground outside Ava's shop. The one thing he didn't even want to so much as *think*, much less say out loud, because he knew what it meant. Knew how dangerous it was not just for Ironport, not just for his kids, but for the Huntsmen community as a whole.

"That attack was targeted."

There was a beat, a single tick of the clock, as Tony considered those words then turned to pin Eric in place like a fucking lab specimen with that penetrating green stare. "How do you figure that?"

"Because they were waiting for us." A shiver crawled across Eric's skin as the words left his mouth, lifting the hairs on his arms and making him want nothing more than to hide under the blankets. But he couldn't hide from this. He had never been able to hide from this. Because this was his destiny. Fate had well and truly fucked him. Picked the wrong guy too, if you asked him. He wasn't cut out for this. Wasn't built for it. He'd just learned to make the best of a fucked-up situation. "There was glass on the ground near my car that wasn't there when I parked. And it looked like someone had tried to jimmy it open."

"So? Might have just been an attempted burglary. Doesn't mean the vamps were waiting for you." But even as Tony said the words, Eric could see he didn't really believe them. Could see the way he was doing the mental math just how Eric had. Two plus two coming up seven.

"Not likely." Eric scoffed. "That car is older than some of my kids, and there's fuck all in it that's worth the trouble of jimmying the door. Besides, I have wards set up on it. Hunter checked them while Britt was patching me up. They were tripped, and not by something human."

"Why would vamps want to break into your car?" He had pulled the swivel chair from under Eric's desk and settled into it, giving Eric's theory his full attention. Which Eric was grateful for because he knew how this sounded. Vamps didn't do stuff like that. They weren't *organized*. Especially not transient vamps. But then . . . these weren't transient vamps, were they?

"Like I said, it was targeted. They knew I was going to be there; Hunter and I head to Ava's on the same day every week. They tried to break into my car to lie in wait. When they couldn't get past the wards, they broke the streetlights so they could surround me more easily."

"That's a lot of planning ahead for a gang of leeches."

"You got a better theory?" Eric leaned back against his

hands on the bed, ignoring the way it pulled at his ribs. "I'd like to hear it."

"I didn't say you were wrong. I just said it's a lot of planning ahead." Tony sniffed, his eyes darting around Eric's face as if he was trying to judge if Eric was serious. Or maybe he was nervous, wary of the implications of this theory. *Join the club.*

Eric nodded, and they settled into an uncomfortable silence as they both thought over everything that had happened that night. Well. *Eric* thought over everything that happened that night—who knew what the fuck Tony was thinking—and the planning that would have had to go into it. They would have to know his schedule. His haunts. His friends. Fuck. They knew his *friends.* They knew he frequented Ava's at least once a week, sometimes more. Eric's stomach churned. He'd have to warn her. She was gonna be pissed. *So* pissed.

"So what's the game plan here?" Tony asked, ripping Eric from the downward spiral. "Want to get a kit together and go hunt the bastards down before the trail gets cold? I'm sure lighting their nest on fire would solve all this shit."

A glimmer of violence settled into Tony's eyes, making them sparkle in the yellow light coming from Eric's bedside lamp. It sharpened his edges, proved once and for all how dangerous he was—and also, unsurprisingly, lit Eric's blood on fire, made it sing in his veins as Tony licked his teeth. Eric wondered what they'd feel like biting into his skin. Blunt and bruising.

"No," Eric made himself say, licking his lips and scratching at the bandages Britt had wrapped almost too tightly around his wrist, cutting off the circulation in her upset over his injuries.

"No?" Tony barked a laugh, incredulous. "What the fuck d'ya mean, no?"

"I mean, no. Not yet. Not right now." He picked at the edge of one of the bandages, sliding the pad of his thumb over the sticky residue left behind on his skin.

The bite marks would be mostly healed over by morning, scabbed and already preparing to scar. But he knew Britt wrapped them more to hide them until they faded. To hide his shame for him. Not that he *was* ashamed. He had nothing to be ashamed of. But a Venator getting bit by a vamp? All Huntsmen were taught as children to see that as a mark of weakness, failure, and Britt knew that—even if she was a normie. Eric, on the other hand . . . if any of the fuckers on the Council of Creatures or among the Huntsmen elders had anything to say about him getting bitten, he'd personally volunteer to take them out on a hunt sometime. So they could see exactly what he was up against. Let them try shaming him for a couple nibbles in the line of duty after that.

"Why the fuck not?" Tony snarled, bracing himself on his knees as if at any moment he'd get up and storm from the room, race down the steps, and flee into the night to slaughter the vamps who'd done this to Eric.

Eric had to remind himself Tony didn't feel protective of him. They didn't know each other from Dick. There was nothing between them. It was just in Tony's nature to crave the hunt. Eric had seen it on him that first day in the cemetery, smelled the bloodlust on his breath. Tony lived for the fight, for the slay. There wasn't anything else, except maybe his little sister. And that's all this was: his need for the hunt.

"Not until we've spoken to the Council of Creatures."

"The what now?"

"They're the ruling magical body in Ironport." Eric scrubbed at his face and felt the weight of his exhaustion dragging him down. Goddess, he was so tired. When was the last time he really slept? A week? More? Likely not since before Hunter told him about those local vamps. And then there was the twinge starting up at the top of his spine, the sign of an impending migraine. "I don't want to do anything until I've spoken to them. Ava said . . ." He pressed the bandage back down, but it was sticking up oddly now. It would likely get caught on his shirt when he went to put it on tomorrow. "She said we should ask them about if the Huntsmen can reach out for reinforcements. There's at least a few other Venator in North America that could maybe help us clear this up."

"What? Am I not *enough* for you, pretty boy?" Tony snapped.

"Stop it with that shit."

"What shit?" Tony leaned forward, all smooth lean lines and biting smile.

"*Pretty boy.* Cut it out." But even as Eric said it, heat crawled up the collar of his shirt, making him shift where he sat.

"Question stands." One strawberry-blond brow raised. "Am I not enough for you?"

Eric opened his mouth to respond, an explanation ready, then he caught the way Tony was biting his tongue, lips twitching into a smile. "You're teasing me."

"I like to think of it as flirting."

"This is serious."

"It usually is." Tony shrugged, lounging back in the chair again and spreading his knees wide to give Eric a mouthwatering display of the way his muscular thighs flexed under the denim. *Fuck.* How did one even *get* that ripped? It didn't seem fair. "That's the name of the game here, isn't it?"

"Huh?" Eric blinked, jerking his eyes from where they'd strayed to staring at Tony's chest. He shook himself, frowning, and forced himself to focus on the wall over Tony's shoulder instead of trying to look him in the eye. That seemed safer. At least for the duration of this conversation. "Oh. Right." Eric rubbed at the ache in his neck. "But yeah, so we'll talk to the Council of Creatures. There's a meeting this Friday at midnight."

"Friday? You think this can wait that long?"

"It's gonna have to."

"You're telling me you can't just like . . ." Tony flapped his wrist to indicate something, but Eric wasn't exactly sure what. He raised his brows in confusion and Tony huffed, rolling his eyes. "Call an emergency meeting."

"I don't have that kind of authority." If he sounded bitter about it, it was because he was.

The fact that Eric had no authority—at fucking all—in Ironport was as stupid as it sounded. But it was the way things were in the Huntsmen community; every one of them knew that. Venator were lesser, expendable foot soldiers in the war against the vampires, even though they were rare. Whereas the remainder of the Huntsmen population, those who didn't test positive with a Venator gene—people like Eric's little brother, for instance—were allowed to inherit, allowed to hold seats of power, allowed to make something of themselves. But a Venator?

A Venator's destiny was predetermined.

That's why the Marcelino parents had been so disappointed when Eric not only tested positive, but his gene activated a few years later. *That's* why they'd dumped him on his grandmother's doorstep and decided to try again. And now had their darling little boy. Their sweet, perfect, little Oliver. Who could do no wrong and was the apple of his parents' eye. Who would inherit fucking *everything* when they died.

So no, Eric couldn't call an emergency meeting for the Ironport Council of Creatures. And yes, he was bitter about it. That, and a whole rack of other things.

"No need to jump down my throat, sweetheart. I was just asking." Tony held up his hands in surrender, and Eric forced himself to relax, to let his shoulders fall away from his ears and unclench the fists he'd made in his bedding. It wasn't Tony's fault this situation was fifty different shades of fucked.

"Shouldn't you be heading home?"

"Probably. Probably. But I have one more question, princess." As Tony scrubbed at the tip of his nose, his eyes flicked down and away from Eric's face, seeming to find the carpet very interesting all of the sudden.

The words "I'm not your fucking princess" sat heavy on Eric's tongue, a knee-jerk reaction, but he bit them back. Because . . . well, because he found he didn't entirely mind it. Just like he didn't entirely mind Tony calling him *sweetheart* or *pretty boy*. What did that say about him? Nothing good, probably.

"What is it?" Eric asked instead, shelving the existential crisis that knowledge would bring for later. Preferably after the pain medication Britt forced down his throat kicked in, and he was feeling nice and fuzzy.

"When are you gonna let me take you out to dinner?" The words were accompanied by a playful wink and a yelp when the pillow Eric hurled at Tony hit him with deadly accuracy right in the face. "Is that a no?"

"Of course it's a fucking no." A grumble left Eric as he flopped back onto his bed, hoping this would be enough to dismiss Tony and his stupid questions. But the chair Tony was in didn't even so much as creak, his weight not shifting to rise and leave.

"And why not?"

Why not. Wasn't *that* the million-dollar question. There were at least half a dozen reasons why not, not the least of which was that they had other shit to worry about right now. But instead of saying that, Eric said, "Because I'm fucking cursed, that's why not. Check my file. You'll see."

With a grunt, Tony stood so Eric could see his face from where he lay on his back. Then he said, "I don't believe in curses" and headed for the door, the pillow tossed over his shoulder landing beside Eric on the bed.

"I'll see you at the Town Hall on Friday, at eleven," Eric called after him.

"I'm picking you up at seven. We're doing dinner first."

"The fuck we are!"

But Tony didn't respond, even if Eric was sure he'd heard just fine. Asshole.

Chapter 9

BECAUSE I'M FUCKING CURSED, Marcelino had said, and it niggled at Tony. Echoed through his head the whole ride home. He thought to ask Britt about it—surely, she'd have the details—but didn't.

By the time Britt pulled up to the curb outside the townhouse, all the lights were off inside with the exception of one soft yellow bulb in the kitchen. Likely the one over the stove left on by Lu so he wouldn't trip over all the boxes still stacked high in the open-plan first floor. Sweet of his sister to try to keep him from tripping and braining himself.

"Welp," he said looking over at Britt and offering her a wide smile. She was a petite blond woman with sharp brown eyes and a severe mouth. Who looked like she took no bull-shit. Exactly the kind of person one would expect to work as a nurse on a college campus. Tony liked her on sight. "This is me."

Britt nodded, flexing her hands around the steering wheel like she was gathering the courage to say something. Hopefully not a fucking shovel talk. Tony and Marcelino were nowhere near that stage in their relationship. Although not for lack of trying on Tony's part. He was going to have to redouble his efforts in the coming days. Maybe even *cook* for their date. Fuck, that meant he'd have to finish unpacking the kitchen, didn't it? It'd be worth it. Marcelino was worth it. Tony wasn't sure how he knew, he just did.

"Thanks for tonight," Britt said, when she'd finally gotten herself together. "For stepping in and protecting both of them. If you hadn't . . ."

She let the words drift off, but the implication was clear. If Tony hadn't acted, Marcelino would be dead, or worse, and Hunter might very well have followed right behind him. Not to mention Ava. Tony had saved more than one life that night, and it was nice to receive a little gratitude for once, though it made him shift uncomfortably in his seat, something warm crawling under his skin. He was used to being taken for granted. Used to his efforts either being brushed off as just what he was supposed to do, or in the case of *that man* being outright criticized for his mistakes.

"It was nothin'." Tony shrugged, not taking his eyes off the dark house. "Quick question though," he murmured, sucking on his teeth. "How does the pretty boy feel about Italian?"

Britt blinked at him for a moment, seeming to process what he'd just said to her, maybe trying to understand who "pretty boy" was, then she snorted. "His last name his Marcelino."

"Yeah. So?"

"I wouldn't make Italian," she deadpanned, meeting his eyes with a narrowed look, her lips twitching up at the corners as if she was mocking him. "Wouldn't want to embarrass yourself on the first date, would you?" Then she hit the unlock button on her door pointedly and nodded for him to get out of the car.

"Fair point." Tony laughed and rolled from the vehicle to saunter up the front walk without a backward glance.

He waited approximately as long as it took him to shower, change into a pair of low-slung sweatpants, and flop down into bed before he grabbed his tablet and pulled up Marcelino's file again.

Tony meant what he said before he left. He didn't believe in curses, or prophecies, or fate, or any of that shit. Never much had. In his mind, those things were just an excuse for bad behavior. *It wasn't my fault, the universe made me do it!* No. It made more sense to him that people controlled their own destinies. That the circumstances that befell him were either his fault, or someone else's directly.

But if Marcelino believed in it enough to let it keep him from dating, then Tony needed to know what it was. How else was he supposed to combat Marcelino's doubts?

His thumb tapped against the shell of the tablet while he waited for the Huntsmen app to boot. It was slower than fucking molasses and twice as clunky, a remnant of an age long past that someone had tried to make more functional by turning into a tablet app. Which, in turn, made it *less* functional. Probably because the Huntsmen didn't see any point in putting money into developing it correctly. Especially when the only people who really benefited from the files were Venator.

Tony wasn't stupid. He had spent much of his life outside of the Huntsmen community thanks to his father being a hateful, spiteful, transphobic piece of shit, but he wasn't stupid. He knew enough about how the Huntsmen worked and how they treated the Venator to know that Venator were seen as glorified exterminators. No better than a garbage-person, in their eyes. Necessary, but not someone you'd want to have over for a Super Bowl party lest they bring the stink of their profession along with them. Instead of the warriors—the protectors—that they were.

It had been that way for years, as far as Tony knew, each generation of Venator treated worse than the last. Which rankled, when he could be bothered to think about it, because he knew the history of their people. Knew where their species had started all those centuries ago. A mutation in the human bloodline spawning something new, and better, something to protect the human race against the bloodsuckers. And for a while, they were revered. Someone like Tony, like Marcelino, would have been given all the resources they needed to do their job, and then some. But now . . .

Now Tony chewed on the inside of his lip as he watched the app boot up and crash for the third time in a fucking row. Fucking hell. His fingers squeaked against the glass as he swiped out of the app, then pulled up everything currently running on the tablet and closed out of every other program.

When he opened the Huntsmen database back up, it finally loaded, and he slumped against his headboard with a relieved sigh. From there it was a few minutes' work to find Marcelino's file, scroll down, and read the prophecy, curse, whatever the fuck it was, more carefully.

There will come two Venator, and all Huntsmen will rue their existence for they will bring about the end of the Huntsmen. And one will be of the house Marcelino. The other the house Mac Math-ghamhna.

"Okay," Tony murmured to himself, licking his lips as he squinted down at the screen in the dark. Maybe he shouldn't have taken his contacts out. "But why do you think this means you, pretty boy?"

Marcelino's file was dense. Packed tight with thirty-three years of life, from birth to his current day slay average. But Tony didn't see anything that would point to Eric being "the end of the Huntsmen" much less something that would connect him to someone from the house of Mac Math-ghamhna—which to his knowledge had been extinct for at least a generation or better—until he got to the bottom of the last page.

Eric Marcelino is the first active Venator of the Marcelino line.

"Well, fuck me sideways," Tony breathed and thumped

his head back against the headboard, letting that information seep into his bones.

———

Still, by the time Friday rolled around, Tony decided he wasn't going to let a little thing like a prophecy stop him from getting what he wanted. First of all, because prophecies were stupid, and he didn't believe in them. Second of all, because now that he knew about it, he just needed to be on the lookout for this Mac Mathghamhna person. Easy.

He saw no reason at all why he and Marcelino couldn't see each other.

Except of course that when he knocked on the door to the dorm at precisely seven on Friday evening, the pinched face of a young Black woman peered at him from the crack just long enough for her to give him a once over, find him wanting, and let out a soft derisive snort. She proceeded to slam the door in his face. He thought it might have been one of Marcelino's students but it was so quick. . .

"Eric, your date's here!" Tony heard her shout, the sound muffled through the thick wood.

"His *what*?" someone squawked from inside, and the door opened again. This time to reveal a face with rounded cheeks, braces, and long curly hair tucked beneath a ball cap. Tony thought maybe Marcelino had called the kid Bert the other night, but he couldn't be sure anymore. "Oh." The kid twisted his face up into a wrinkled expression of contempt. "It's *you*."

Tony opened his mouth to ask who the fuck else it would be but was cut off by Bert calling, "Eric! It's Lu's brother!" over his shoulder in a voice so loud it made Tony's ears prickle.

"I'm coming!" Marcelino shouted back.

The polite thing to do would be to invite him in, or at least stop standing there looking at him like he was some door-to-door salesman who would push his way in regardless of invitation if the door was opened more than a mere crack. But it seemed like Bert had missed that memo, so he stayed where he was, guarding the entrance like a very short sentinel, and blocking Tony from getting past. "What's in the bag?"

"None of your business, Curly. Why don't you go back to Moe and Larry and let me in?" Tony's lips peeled back from his teeth, his gaze flicking to look at the room beyond Bert's hat, but he couldn't see anything through the gloom of the darkened entryway.

"What the fuck are you talking about?" Bert tilted his head, his brow wrinkling in the middle.

"The stooges? Moe, Larry, and Curly?" Tony frowned and looked at where Marcelino was making his way toward the door *finally*. "Honestly, Marcelino, what the fuck are you teaching these children?"

"Usually?" Marcelino asked as he nudged Bert out of the way with a murmured, "I've got this, buddy."

Bert continued to stare at Tony, backing down the hall and into the main room before he disappeared around the corner.

"How not to die." Marcelino shrugged. "What are you doing here, man? I told you I wasn't going out with you."

"And thus, I have brought everything we need for a night in." Tony smiled cheekily and held up the reusable grocery bags in his hands. They were heavy, weighed down with all the fixings for homemade tacos. Lu had been a little put out that he didn't make her any, but that was mitigated by him offering to drive her to campus. He'd dropped her off outside the library a few minutes ago for her to hang out with Finn and work on some homework together.

Marcelino frowned at him, his head tilted to one side so a piece of dark hair fell into his honey-brown hazel eyes brushing against the moles on his cheek, and Tony felt his mouth go dry. The desire to brush the strand aside and play connect the dots with the moles using his tongue rushed through him with such force that he had to tighten his hold on the bags to keep from doing just that.

"What about Lu?" Marcelino asked after a beat too long. Tony was pretty sure he felt his soul leave his fucking body and then return to make his heart beat double time at the mere thought that Marcelino was concerned about Tony's *sister*. Sure, Lu was one of his students, but the care Marcelino offered his kids outside of the classroom—at least, from what Tony had seen—went above and beyond what was expected of even a dorm parent.

Seriously. Who was this fucking guy? A Disney princess? Next, Marcelino would tell Tony that he did his impeccably coiffed hair with the help of mice and rabbits every morning.

"Lu was given enough cash to feed your whole pack of brats." Tony flicked his gaze to the space over Marcelino's shoulder pointedly. He couldn't see the kids, but he didn't doubt they were all still standing right fucking there, listening. Nosey little shits. "C'mon, Marcelino, give a guy a chance. I brought tacos. You gotta eat, don't ya?"

He jiggled the bag again, giving his best smile, the one that usually got him laid. Eyes hooded in that way that made Lu make gagging noises and anyone else swoon. So sue him, Tony knew what worked, and he wasn't afraid of pulling out all the stops to get Marcelino to let him in, just a bit.

"Fine," Marcelino said, sighing loudly as he stepped away from the door to let Tony inside. "But I don't put out on the first date."

"Well, good thing this is our second date." Tony pushed past him. The kids sat in the living room, and they all watched him from their respective places on the couch like he was about to lunge for them, going for the throat. He wasn't exactly sure what he'd done to earn their mistrust. Maybe it had something to do with the fact that he kept making eyes at their most beloved teacher . . .

"What?" Marcelino trailed behind as Tony made his way to the kitchen to unload his bags. "This isn't our second date."

"Sure it is." A six-pack clanked together when he sat the bag on the counter before unpacking everything, spreading the little tubs of guac, queso, beans, etc. across the island. "You remember the other night in the cemetery when I let you win our—"

"Let me win?" Marcelino snorted. He'd come to lean against the island, arms crossed over his chest, hip pressed into the edge of the laminate countertop. "You didn't *let* me win!"

Tony looked up from where he was still unloading everything, his tongue between his teeth and asked, "Didn't I?" with a wink that made Marcelino blush a lovely shade of red and sputter.

Tonight was going to be a good night.

Chapter 10

ERIC KNEW BETTER. Arguably. He did. He knew the kind of trouble that Tony McMahon would bring with just one look at him.

But . . .

Well . . .

Ava was kind of right; Eric did need to get laid. Badly. It had been one hell of a dry spell. Years, in fact. And Tony was —Tony was arguably *very* hot. Like . . . exactly what Eric needed. Ava would be all for it, or at least he thought so. Aesthetically, anyway, because Ava was 100 percent only into women.

So . . .

"No. No. Seriously, you just—" Eric snickered, leaning in closer to Tony. At some point while they were talking, Tony had draped himself over the back of Eric's chair, his thumb brushing thoughtlessly against Eric's shoulder. The warmth of his skin burned almost too hot through the thin long-sleeved shirt Eric had put on to lounge around the house pre–Council of Creatures meeting. "You just said, 'What're you gonna do, stab me?'"

"And then the little fucker *did*." Tony laughed, the sound deep and echoing through where Eric's side was pressed against Tony's into Eric's chest.

And oh. Oh, that felt nice. Too nice, probably. But the

alarms that normally shouted "caution," "danger," "contents may be hot" in the back of his mind were not nearly loud enough to deter him as Eric leaned in to run his nose along Tony's jaw.

Tony stilled, his hand fisting in Eric's shirt for a moment, his breath stuttering. Like a spooked animal, not sure how to react for a second almost too long. Long enough that Eric started to pull back, thinking maybe he'd read the signs all wrong, maybe Tony wasn't as into this as he was. But he didn't make it far before Tony lifted his free hand, his nails digging into the soft skin along Eric's jaw, and crashed their lips together. A soft moan left one of them, but they were pressed so close together now, chest to chest, Eric couldn't tell who as he practically climbed into Tony's lap.

With a muffled groan, Tony fended him off, getting enough space between them to stand, swipe one arm over the table to push their dishes to the side, and pull Eric onto his feet. Eric watched, half-dazed, as Tony bent down, grabbed him by his hips, and hefted him onto the kitchen table without a single grunt of exertion.

"The kids," Eric said, not even really a protest, because fuck the kids. They were all adults. If they didn't want to see their teacher making out with some guy in the kitchen, maybe they should be at the library studying like good little students, not hanging around the house spying on him while he was on a date.

"Fucked off ages ago, pretty boy," Tony mumbled from where he was making small swiping motions with his tongue across Eric's neck. Kitten licks. Following first one mole, then another, then connecting them with the tip of his tongue. Eric's skin exploded in goosebumps, his body slumping forward to lean heavily against Tony, who was now standing between his spread thighs, grinding down against where Eric had hardened in his baggy sweatpants.

"Where'd they go?"

"Who the fuck cares?"

"Good. Cool. Cool." Fuck, there were too many layers of clothing between them. Tony's hand skimmed the line of Eric's side, leaving a trail of heat in his wake that made his shirt, and the bandages around his ribs, feel stifling all of the sudden. He reached down to tug at the hem, chanting, "Off. Off. Off."

Tony chuckled, reaching for the bottom of the shirt and peeling it from Eric quickly enough that Eric would swear he heard some of the seams rip, then threw it across the room to land somewhere over by the massive couches sitting in front of the fireplace.

"So eager," Tony cooed, tone light and teasing, but he didn't waste any time following a new path of moles down over Eric's chest toward his nipple, leaving behind a slowly chilling trail of saliva that did nothing at all to cool Eric's heated skin.

A grumbled "Shut up" left Eric as he grabbed for the hem of Tony's shirt, pulling it up—he couldn't pry Tony away long enough to really remove it—to reveal a toned stomach and bronzed skin, the bottom edges of a scar under each pec that Eric's mouth watered to get his teeth on. But he couldn't. Not in the position he was in, with Tony's tongue swiping ever closer to his nipple, his other hand slipping down his soft belly to brush over the tie of Eric's sweatpants. He didn't want Tony to stop. Didn't think he could pry him off even if the kids did decide to make a reappearance. But it would be nice to be able to reciprocate. "Bottom."

"What's that, sweetheart?" Tony didn't even pull away, just pressed the words into Eric's skin, teeth nipping lightly at his nipple and dragging a shiver from him.

"Bottom. I'm a bottom. I want to be on the bottom." His hands flapped through the air, nervous energy making him jittery. Fuck, it really had been a long time, hadn't it? Too long. Much too long. He was so out of practice. And Tony probably thought he was an idiot. He definitely sounded like an idiot to himself. Tony was going to laugh in his fucking face and walk away and—

"I don't think we're gonna get that far, baby." Tony chuckled darkly, his hand moving to brush the backs of his fingers against Eric's cock, making him jolt and let out a soft hiss. "Besides, I didn't bring everything we'd need for that."

"I've got lube and stuff upstairs." But Tony was probably right—Eric likely wouldn't make it that long. Not with the way he was straining against his pants. Not with the way every nerve ending in his body was alight with sensation. If Tony really got his hand on Eric, it'd be all over. And wouldn't that be embarrassing? Shooting off in the first five minutes like a fucking virgin. Like he wasn't a thirty-year-old man. Fuck. Ava was going to laugh so fucking hard when he told her about this.

"A strap?" Tony asked, pulling back from where his teeth had still been worrying Eric's nipple, leaving it red and swollen, to meet his gaze. There was a nervousness there, Tony's bright green eyes, although hooded with lust, shifting around Eric's face as if he didn't know where to look, what to focus on. Like he was laying himself bare in a way, and fully expecting Eric to reject him. Which was fucking stupid, really.

But he was . . . confused? Unsure? What did Tony mean by —OH! Oh, okay. Tony was trans. Yeah. Eric could get behind that. He'd never been with a trans guy before, but he could definitely get behind that. He just—he just needed to think . . . Did he have anything upstairs that would . . . What did Tony need for . . . Fuck, he couldn't just ask, could he? He didn't want to look like a complete asshole. And he didn't want to make Tony any more self-conscious than he already was . . . Fuck. He was fucking this up already, wasn't he?

When Eric didn't respond quickly enough, still trying to process everything, do the mental math about what he had upstairs and what they'd need, Tony pulled back further, his chin jutting out in something that might have been arrogance. But Eric saw it for what it was: fear. Tony was steeling himself so it wouldn't hurt as badly when Eric ripped away from the embrace. "Problem?"

"No. I just . . . I was trying to think of what I have upstairs. I don't think I have—I mean, there's toys. Not anything like— I've never been with—And it's been so long—And—I'm not trying to—Fuck, I suck at—"

But he didn't get to finish because Tony pressed in even closer, grinding his hips down roughly enough against Eric's that they drew a hiss, and pressing their lips together so hard he tasted blood. His blunted teeth bit into Eric's lower lip, giving it a tug that reeled him in even closer. "Fuck, you're cute when you babble, sweetheart."

Eric whimpered, hands fisting in Tony's shirt, his hips lifting off the table to grind back into him in spite of how Tony's jeans scraped rough through his sweatpants. His skin was going to be red, maybe bruised, but it was going to be so fucking good. Worth it. Tony pulled away again, his teeth leaving behind a bruising bite on Eric's lower lip that made Eric whine, hands trying to haul him in closer, keep him from moving away.

"Shh. Shh," Tony murmured, soft and soothing as he sank down into the discarded chair. "I've got you, pretty boy."

The thought was there to ask what the fuck Tony was doing, why he was nipping a trail down through the thatch of hair on Eric's chest, toward his navel. His mind unable to process the actions after too long without, and then Tony nudged him to lift his hips just a little, and he was sitting bare ass on the dorm kitchen table. He figured out exactly what Tony was doing right before Tony's mouth descended on him.

"Not gonna—not gonna last," Eric chanted, his fingers fisting in Tony's curly strawberry-blond hair, trying to pull him off, but Tony wouldn't move, seemed to understand that Eric didn't *want* him to despite his protests.

Tony hummed, the sensation vibrating where Eric's length was pressed against his tongue, traveling all the way up to his chest as he fought the urge to keep his hips in place. His toes curled into the fluffy bunny slippers on his feet, one foot kicking out as Tony's tongue brushed the underside of his cock, sending the slipper across the kitchen. Another quick bob of Tony's mouth as he relaxed his throat, his hand tight enough on Eric's hip to leave behind bruises, and Eric was gone. Lost to the sensation of warmth pooling in his stomach, and a mouth around him that was too hot, too hot, too hot. Fuck. No. He wasn't going to last. There was no way in fucking hell. Then Tony did that thing again, with his tongue, and Eric lost what little control he had over himself.

"Tony. Fuck. No, I'm gonna—" He yanked on Tony's hair, trying to warn him, trying to pull him off. In response, Tony swallowed him down deeper, and the orgasm hit him like a fucking truck, leaving him boneless and panting as he flopped back against the table, no doubt getting fucking guacamole in his hair.

Tony worked him through it, mouthing at him until Eric hissed in over-sensitivity, all but shoving him away. Then he pulled back, a wide smile splitting his face as he brushed the spit from his chin with his wrist and offered Eric a wink. "Feelin' good, sugar?"

"Fuck you," Eric croaked.

"Next time," Tony said, patting his thigh lightly.

"What about . . . ?"

"Hmm. I'm all good, sweetheart." He rose from the chair and started cleaning up their dinner. "You should put your pants on though. Dunno when the brat pack will be back."

"Fuck." Eric squeaked, lifting his hips to at least cover himself should the kids come back. "What time is it?"

"Quarter to ten. When's the Council of Creatures meeting again?"

"Midnight. And I still need to find something to wear."

Eric sat up, running his fingers through his hair, and finding . . . Yup, that was guacamole. Damn it. "I'm going to need to shower too."

"You want company?" Tony leered at him from over his shoulder, pressing his tongue between his teeth in a smile that was almost too cute for the way he'd been able to bring Eric to a boiling point with very little prompting. Yeah, Ava was definitely going to get a kick out of this. Hunter too, if Eric told them both. But like, when was the last time he'd hidden anything from his two best friends? *Five-minute Ricky strikes again.* He was never going to live it down. "Pretty boy?"

Eric cleared his throat, heat crawling along his neck. "Nah, I'm good. Thanks." He scurried from the table, nearly knocking what was left of their food onto the floor in his hurry to put some distance between himself and that heated look before he did something *else* embarrassing.

"You can't smoke in here" was the first thing Eric said to Tony when he returned from his shower. He stood in the doorway to his ensuite bathroom—his was the only room in the dorm with a bathroom attached, and he thanked the Goddess for it every day (sharing with five young adults would be hell on earth)—his hands on his hips, nose curled up in disgust. The smell of skunk weed was seeping into every soft surface of his room, he knew it. He was going to have to Febreze the living daylights out of the place to get it smelling even close to normal again. Seriously, where did Tony even buy that shit?

"Fuck off. Who says?" Tony asked around a mouth full of smoke, his tongue poking out to lick at his bottom lip in a gesture that made Eric's dick twitch with interest. Which was fucking ridiculous. It'd only been forty-five minutes; he did not have that kind of recovery time anymore, and likely never had. *Down, boy.*

"We're on school property. It's the rules." It wasn't really. Because if it were then the dean's office would be inundated almost twenty-four-seven with students and teachers alike. It was a magic school, for fuck's sake. They all needed some way to take the edge off.

Tony made a show of looking around the room for a minute, his lips ticked up at the corners in a smile that was arguably adorable. "I don't see them posted anywhere."

"Yeah, well." Eric made his way over to the dresser to pull out underwear and some socks. "This is a dorm. It's common fucking sense."

"Mm-hmm, mm-hmm, I hear you." And although Eric couldn't see him, he imagined Tony nodding in a way that was distinctly mocking. When he glanced at Tony from the corner of his eye, he found him leaning against the head-board, the blunt between his teeth as he took another long inhale. He held it for a minute before releasing it along with the words, "Then tell me about that little baggy sitting on your desk."

"That's medicinal." Well. Kind of. Sometimes it was just to get high, to get that nice fuzzy distance from the world that made everything seem very funny, like looking at the world through a fishbowl. And other times it was because if he didn't look at the world through a fishbowl, he might lose his fucking mind entirely. If he didn't distance himself from the blood, and the gore, and the vampires, he'd never sleep again. Super fun byproduct of PTSD and being the only Venator in a hundred-mile radius for most of his life. When it wasn't those two reasons, it was to ward off a migraine, because some-times traditional meds just didn't do it. One too many blows to the head could do that to a person.

"Sure, it is." This time Eric did watch Tony nod, slowly, as if he was listening to some bit of sage advice that he was taking into consideration. Eric never thought a nod could be sarcastic before, and yet here they were. It would have been funny, endearing, if it weren't so fucking annoying and aimed at him specifically.

"What're you? A cop?" Eric pointedly ignored the raised eyebrows as he wriggled on his boxer briefs under his towel like Tony hadn't gotten up close and personal with his dick not even an hour ago. Maybe he should have told Tony to wait downstairs while he got ready. But it hadn't seemed that important, or like something that even needed to be said. Kalla wouldn't have followed him up to his room like this. Then again . . . Kalla wouldn't have been game for sex in such a public space either, so the rules were probably different with Tony. Maybe more nebulous.

"Consider me a concerned parent," Tony said in a tone of faux seriousness as he tried to keep himself from smiling. But his lips twitched involuntarily and there was laughter in his eyes. All Eric wanted to do was move to the bed and crawl into his lap. Shotgun the smoke from his lips and curl up there, happy and fuzzy. Let the world move on around them outside the fishbowl of his room. He couldn't do that. There wasn't time for it. But he wanted to. Even if just for a little while. Even if whatever this was with Tony wasn't permanent. Which it didn't seem like it was. He wanted to enjoy it while he had it.

"Pretty sure concerned parents don't fuck their child's teacher on the kitchen table of the dorms." Eric snorted, grabbing the blunt from Tony's fingers to take a short drag off it and hold it in for a beat too long until he was coughing up smoke, his lungs burning in that way that felt like swallowing fire more than being held underwater for too long. Which was a nice change of pace considering Eric spent most of his life drowning.

"Maybe not in Ironport, they don't. But in Miami . . ." Tony barked a laugh, his eyes squeezing shut for a second and his face contorting in something that looked like honest amusement. Joy. Contentment curled up warm and languid in Eric's stomach, and the alarms in the back of his head that screamed "danger" went off for the first time since Bert opened the door and revealed that boyish smile stretched wide across Tony's face.

He shook himself, heading for his closet to find something to wear, putting distance between them and leaving Tony to finish his blunt in peace.

Chapter 11

THE COUNCIL of Creatures was a bureaucratic nightmare, in Eric's honest and *correct* opinion. They were too busy trying to keep up with Moondale in all the ways that didn't really matter, and ignoring the one way in which Ironport would never hold a candle to the small town nestled to the east of them: safety. Sure, it had a mall and big box stores, but what it made up for in metropolis vibes, it lacked in innate magic.

To be fair, there was really nothing the Council of Creatures could do about the safety/magic problem. Ironport wasn't built on a nexus the way Moondale was. It didn't have nearly half as many ley lines weaving a patchwork quilt through its landmass as Moondale did. And the coven system in Ironport was . . . Well. There was a single coven, and most of the witches—like Ava and Hunter—had chosen not to join it.

"The head witch is a dick," Ava said the single time Eric asked why, and she never bothered to explain herself further.

Now, faced with said dick—a male witch by the name of Connor—Eric thought he understood a little better. Connor was one of the five "creatures" who made up Ironport's Council of Creatures. There was also a werewolf named Melinda; a human named Asher—one of the few humans *in* on the whole magical creatures thing; a Huntsman named

Janet—also the mayor, and wearing too much fucking perfume, all over ripe fruit and strong florals, if you asked Eric; and some type of fae named Brooke.

None of them particularly looked like they wanted to be there, and Eric wondered if it was because usually their monthly meeting was a formality. Yes, they all technically had to agree on any changes made in Ironport, but Eric was willing to bet the last of his trust fund that they all kind of let Janet do whatever she wanted. She was a Huntsman. She was the mayor. She held the most political and financial pull in the community.

If Eric hadn't tested positive as a Venator, and his gene hadn't activated, it might have been him sitting in Janet's seat —the Marcelinos were well known in Ironport, probably more so than the Chadwicks. But his gene had activated. And now he was on the other side of a laminated fold-up table pleading with the Council of Creatures to finally do *something* about the vamp problem in their city.

"*Local* vampires?" Connor asked, his tone disbelieving as he looked down at the report Hunter printed up for the council. It was all very official. Hunter even put all the papers in those plastic folder thingies, although Eric didn't think the presentation of the information was likely to change the outcome. The council was going to do whatever the fuck it pleased. It always did. Hence him using his own fucking money to fund the start of the Venator class at Moondale U.

"At least five nests that we've come across in the last week, sir." Eric resisted the urge to smooth his hands down his dress shirt again. It was wrinkled beyond recognition to the point that Lu and Finn had taken one look at him before he and Tony left, and started cackling. Which seemed grossly unfair. It's not like he had to dress up every day for work. Teaching college courses usually meant finding a pair of clean jeans and a sweater without holes. He was lucky there had been a dress shirt stuffed into the back of his closet at all.

Likely left over from a funeral or a job interview back before Moondale U. It was a little snug.

"And you want us to do . . . *what* about it?" Asher looked twitchy. Humans usually were when there was a discussion of vampires. Well, most living creatures were, really. Hard not to be when you were a food source—so this wasn't any different than normal, but it still chafed a little. Eric thought it was pretty fucking obvious what he expected them to do about this. It was all laid out in their packets in black and white. Clear as day.

Eric heard Tony's chair creak behind him and hoped he wasn't thinking of getting up and shooting his mouth off. That wouldn't make this any better. If anything, Janet would see it as someone challenging her authority, and since she was head mean girl in Ironport, no one wanted that. She'd shut down, and she'd take the rest of the group with her. So, Eric waved behind his back at Tony, hoping to stay his hand if only for the moment. Give him a chance to talk this through with them before resorting to intimidation tactics.

"We're requesting reinforcements from the other Huntsmen communities in North America." It was absolutely the stupidest shit Eric had ever heard that he couldn't simply file the request *himself*. As a Venator, and not just any Venator but the *oldest* Venator in North America, he shouldn't have to go through a bunch of red tape to reach out to others of his kind. Especially when his city was in danger. But that was where he was at—tied up in red tape. "That request cannot be filed by me; it must be filed by the Ironport magical community."

Janet hummed, drumming well-manicured nails on the table in front of her. She hadn't even bothered to open her packet, but Eric wasn't stupid enough to believe that meant she hadn't read it. They'd all received them days ago, giving plenty of time to review the information and make a decision without first hearing what Eric had to say. Which fucking sucked, if he was being honest. They should have had to face him while they debated the efficacy of his claim. But they didn't.

"And what about McMahon?" Brooke leaned back in their chair, arms wrapped in billowy sleeves crossing over their chest.

"What about him?" Eric frowned. He knew where this was going, because how could he miss the signs? How could he ignore the way everyone's eyes kept flicking back to Tony as if looking for some clue as to his capabilities? Or the extra folders sitting next to the ones he and Hunter made up. Likely Tony's file, now that he thought about it.

"Is he not enough backup for you?" Connor's tone had gone snide, his nose curling as if he had judged how good Eric and Tony were at their jobs and found them wanting. As if he saw them asking for help as weakness. Like Connor had any right to judge. Eric knew for a fact he'd never even seen a vampire in person, much less been tasked with staking one. Fucking politicians, man. "Surely having a second Venator in Ironport should be enough to stave off this infestation."

Eric's jaw clenched, teeth grinding against one another to bite back words he knew wouldn't help his cause at all. Words that would turn this entire council against him and make this and any further asks an automatic no.

"Let's take a recess," Janet said, her eyes narrowed on Eric where he stood as if every emotion that raced through him showed on his face. He wasn't sure if she was blessing him with the space to cool down, or if her plan was to talk about him where he couldn't hear. Either way, he didn't get the chance to stop them as the council rushed to stand, retreating to their offices for further debate.

———

The metal of the chair dug into Tony's thighs where he pressed them harder against the seat, forcing himself to remain seated even as Marcelino railed against the idiocy of the Ironport officials. Suddenly, Tony missed not being beholden to anyone but his abusive tyrant of a father. It was easier to go around Declan Brenner than it would be to go around this whole council of idiots. A smack he could take, but political double-talk made his head spin.

"You good, pretty boy?" Tony asked, pushing to his feet when the last of the council members had disappeared behind a door at the back of the hall. The main meeting space was a small room off the side of the Ironport court house's campus, barely big enough for twenty people to sit comfortably, with grungy tile, yellowed lightbulbs, and peeling metal chairs. All typical markers of a political organization running mostly unopposed. Which was fan-fucking-tastic.

"Yeah. All good," Marcelino said. He slumped into one of the chairs, his spine curving as he leaned against his knees so he could run his hands through his hair. All the blushing, smiling good humor from their date was long behind them now, leaving only a tired, worn man who looked like he was fighting an uphill battle. Tony wished he knew how to shoulder some of that weight for him.

"McMahon," Janet called from the door the entire council had disappeared behind, her perfectly crimson, perfectly manicured nails tapping on the doorframe, "a word."

Tony didn't particularly want to leave Marcelino, not right now, not like this, and something of that must have shown on his face as he shifted his weight from one foot to the other.

"It'll only be a minute." And she didn't really look like someone who was going to take no for an answer. Plus, she was the mayor. The *may-or*. He didn't particularly want to get on the bad side of the fucking mayor.

"Go on. I'm good," Marcelino said again, flapping his wrist without looking up from where he was carefully examining his sneakers against the cracked tiles beneath them. Not for the first time, Tony wished Ava, Hunter, Britt, and even the kids had come along. It seemed logical that Marcelino would take his support system into a battle like this. But he hadn't. He'd just brought Tony, and Tony was . . . Tony was out of his fucking depth.

"A'right." Boots squeaking against the floor, Tony headed for the door Janet had once again disappeared behind, and pushed inside. There was a short hall on the other side, lined in doors spaced slightly apart. Likely offices for the council members.

Janet waited for him outside of her own, which was shut behind her. Tony could make out the movement of people through the frosted glass that bore her name: Janet K. Chadwick. Murmured voices drifted from the crack beneath it just loud enough for him to hear, but not loud enough for him to make out any of the words over the buzz of the lights above.

"I need you to do me a favor," she whispered once he was close enough.

"And that favor is . . . ?" Raising his brows high, Tony stuffed his hands into his pockets and hunched his shoulders forward—a coping mechanism he'd learned he'd had in therapy a while back. A way to make himself a smaller target when he was nervous about what might come his way. Even if his therapist explained it to him, he'd never quite gotten out of the habit. And then there had been other things to worry about, and therapy became something to deal with "later." For him. Not for Lu.

Her ass was still *in* fucking therapy, because he wasn't having her turn out as absolutely fucked up as he was, even if their father's abuse had never really been directed at her. Tony acted as a shield, taking any and all of the heat he could.

"I want you to look after Eric for us." There was an expression on Janet's face that Tony couldn't connect directly to an emotion he recognized. Her too-blue eyes sharp and demanding as they homed in on him, pinning him to the spot. This was an order, not a suggestion. "He's our golden boy, you see," she said with a smile that didn't show any teeth, her hand reaching out to run one long fingernail down the length of his bare arm where he had rolled up his flannel sleeve. "And we're terribly fond of him."

"What's not to be fond of?" Tony huffed then frowned a little. He hadn't meant to say that out loud, even though it was *true*. He found himself increasingly fond of Eric Marcelino. And not just because he had a really pretty O-face. Still, there was something unnerving about Janet. Something that reminded him very much of his therapist. Whatever it was made him want to spill his guts to her regardless of how stupid that idea was.

"I'm so glad we agree." Her smile widened but still showed no teeth. Then she dismissed him with a light, "That's all."

"Uh. Sure?" Tony spun on his heel, making a beeline for the door again to escape the feeling of Janet's eyes on his skin and keep himself from saying something *else* completely fucking stupid.

Marcelino was where he left him, not even bothering to look up until Tony had returned to his side.

"You ready for round two?" Marcelino asked, his big brown eyes narrowed in determination, his spine straightening as he sat up. With his chin lifted, he rose from his chair, taking on the air of a man going to war, and Tony's heart lurched into his throat at the nobility that lined Marcelino's silhouette. Fuck. Could one man get any hotter? Seriously. Where the fuck did he get off looking that sexy in a fucking cardigan and wrinkled dress shirt? Who gave him the right? Tony itched to drape himself across Marcelino's lap like a lazy cat and stay there all day. Forget the Council of Creatures. Forget the vampires. Forget his slay average. Maybe he could get a witch to curse him—

"Ready as I'll ever be, sweetheart."

The smile Marcelino shot Tony at that was enough to send his pulse into overdrive, making it hard to hear much of what came after the council returned to their seats. He didn't tune back in until Marcelino leaned on the front of the laminate table where the council sat, his posture predatory, his ass on full display where his slacks were a little too tight. And damn if that didn't make Tony's blood rush south. What the fuck was with him tonight? Couldn't he keep it in his pants for a couple of hours? *Especially* after he'd already gotten off. Not around Eric Marcelino, apparently.

"So you aren't going to put my request through?" Marcelino asked through his teeth, voice huskier than it ought to be outside of the bedroom and Tony's wet dreams.

"Currently, I don't see any reason to leave other communities unprotected when we have two very capable Venator right there." Janet leaned forward on the table, putting herself in Marcelino's space more, like they were playing chicken and she intended to win. *Joke's on her, I think Marcelino's into that.* "Right, Tony?"

"Right," Tony responded as if on autopilot, then had to take a half-step back when Marcelino whipped around to shoot him with a betrayed look. Shit. He'd fucked up, hadn't he?

"There, you see?" Janet smiled that closed-mouth smile again, gesturing toward Tony. She reached forward to brush her hand against Marcelino's where it still rested on the table —a gesture of comfort maybe, although if it was, it didn't seem to work. Marcelino's posture remained rigid, stiff. "If things have grown worse by our next meeting, we will reconsider. But until then, I think this influx in activity is due to the Moondale centennial. It's in a few months, you know."

"What if it gets worse before then?" Marcelino's voice shook, from fear or irritation, Tony couldn't be sure without seeing his face.

"Then let me know, and we'll call an emergency meeting. I promise, Eric." Janet gave his hand a squeeze. "I've got your back."

Marcelino nodded once, tight and sharp, then pulled back. "If your decision is final?"

"I'm afraid that it is."

Another sharp nod, and Marcelino spun on his heel to head toward the door so quickly that Tony nearly tripped over a chair in his hurry to grab his coat and follow.

CHAPTER 12

THIS WAS A RETREAT, it wasn't a surrender, as Ava would say. Goddess, she was so fucking smart, far smarter than he was. Eric really needed to start listening to her more. About . . . everything. Maybe not about guys, though. Because, apparently, she was a *shit* judge of character when it came to guys.

Prime example, Tony McMahon. Fucking prick.

Eric wasn't giving up. He was falling back. Regrouping. A thought that should have made him feel less like a failure, but it didn't. It didn't take the sting and ache out of walking away from the Council of Creatures empty-handed. It also didn't protect Ironport. Didn't save the countless lives Eric knew would be at risk thanks to this decision. Anxiety buzzed under his skin, making every step toward his car a struggle against simply tearing off his jacket so he could claw at his arms.

"Don't worry, Marcelino." Tony clapped his wide hand onto Eric's shoulder, giving it a squeeze that might have seemed companionable if he hadn't shown his whole ass about five minutes ago in front of the council. "We've got this."

Rage simmered just below the surface of Eric's skin, burning away the anxiety with a flame so hot it threatened to make him bubble and boil.

"We've got—*we've* got this?" Eric scoffed, shrugging Tony's hand off as he spun to face him, his hands shaking at his sides. He clenched them into fists, hoping that would hide the shaking, but it seemed to make them tremble *more*.

Because here was the thing—the thing Eric had come to understand at a very young age: It was now, and would always *be*, up to him.

Ironport was his responsibility, always had been, always would be. Another Venator in town? An uptick in vamp activity? None of that mattered. At the end of the day, it was Eric's problem, no one else's. All of this would fall onto *his* shoulders. And the fact that Tony thought he could sweep in and agree with Janet fucking Chadwick like she was Diana's gift to Ironport, then make it sound like they were a *team* . . .

Fuck that. He was out of his fucking *gourd*, as Bert would say.

"You—" Eric lifted a hand to point at Tony as he took a step backward, keeping the carefully placed distance between them. It was safer that way. Safer to keep Tony at arm's length. To not let himself fall into the trap of thinking he could depend on someone again. He'd been there before, hadn't he? Learned that the only person he could truly depend on was himself. The only person Eric could count on to watch his back was *Eric*. "*You've* got nothing."

"Nothing?" Tony spat the word, a frown marring his handsome face. Goddess, he was so handsome. And Eric . . . Eric had thought they had something, maybe. Thought maybe there was something special there. Hours ago, when they shared tacos, and laughed, and Eric had cum so hard he couldn't breathe for a minute. When Eric let himself connect on a real level for the first time since he'd been in his twenties, since Kalla, since Hunter. But the nervously charming smile he'd seen on Tony's face when he finally made it to the door was long gone now. "My slay average is—"

"Your *slay average*?" Eric barked a laugh and stuffed his hands into his pockets. "Is that all you fucking *think* about?"

"What else is there?"

And that was the crux of this whole argument, wasn't it? The thing Tony didn't *get*. How could he? From all Eric had learned about him over the last week or so since Tony moved to Ironport, Tony had never really been part of a community. He'd lived in Miami before Ironport, and somewhere in Indiana before that, and Las Vegas before that, and LA before that. He didn't know what it was like to have a home that needed protecting. He didn't know what it was like to rail every fucking day against a tide that kept fucking *coming*.

Sure, all those places had high vamp rates, but they were nothing on Ironport. Nothing on the way vampires seemed to flock to the border of Moondale. It had always been that way, since before Eric was born. The heady smell of a magical community as densely packed as Moondale drawing any vampire who came within a state's distance to its border. Like a hound on the hunt. Eric could spend his entire life slaying vampires and not put a dent in the ones that passed through Ironport. He *had* spent his entire life doing *exactly* that.

"What else *is* there?" Eric spat, taking another step away from Tony.

He needed to get in his fucking car and go. Before he took a swing at Tony and they wound up fist fighting in the middle of the courthouse parking lot. Goddess, he could only imagine what his father would say if he heard Eric had gotten a bloody lip right out in front of the Council of Creatures hall.

"What else is there." He laughed, but there was no mirth in it. It rose hollow from his chest and left him aching. "What else is there. There's—there's *everything*!"

Tony's frown deepened, his lips pursing in a confused line. But Eric wasn't going to explain it to him. If he couldn't see what was right in front of his face, so be it.

"You know what?" Eric licked his lips. "It's been fun, but I'm out."

"You're out?" Tony asked, and it sounded a little like it was choked. Like maybe there was heartbreak in it. Which made zero fucking sense. "Out of what?" Tony followed him to the car, his steps thudding and angry, but Eric didn't turn back. Didn't spare him a second glance. There was still patrol to do. The cold winter air hummed with not-quite-life, and Eric had to make sure it didn't snuff out the *actual* life. There wasn't time to fuck around with—

"*This*. Whatever *this* is." Eric gestured between them, one hand flapping while the other struggled to get his keys out of his pocket, his hands still trembling but no longer from fury. He was coming down from it now, the lack of adrenaline leaving him jittery. Fuck. He needed to get out of there. He didn't have time for this, for Tony, for anything resembling a normal life. Not when there were local vamps in his city and no backup was coming. "This team up, or tag up, or whatever you think it is. I don't have time for it. And I'm just—I'm just *out*."

"So . . . what?" Arms crossed over his chest, shoulders hunching forward, Tony leaned his weight back on his heels, looking for all the world like he was ready for a fight. Which made a manic laugh burble up Eric's throat that he choked down. "We went on one date and you're just calling it quits?"

"Yeah. You know what? Yeah. I think I am." His keys fumbled out of his pocket and onto the cold ground, the sound echoing in the empty air around them. "We had a good run though, didn't we?"

Confusion wrinkled Tony's brow further, his bright green eyes dropping to watch Eric as he swooped down to grab his keys. "What are you talking about?"

"Who the fuck knows," Eric mumbled, only loud enough for himself to hear and whipped around to rip his car door open before Tony could try to hold him up further. His heart was in his throat, and he couldn't explain why, didn't understand why. *Had* there been some chance there? Some *something*? And it was all out the window now that Tony had shown his true colors? Or was there a vamp lurking nearby watching the whole exchange? He couldn't tell. All he knew was he needed to get away. As quickly as possible. The need was a physical ache in his muscles, screaming *Run. Run. As fast as you can. Get away. Escape.*

"Wait, Marcelino." Tony reached for the door, but Eric had already yanked it shut, and he could hear Tony shout, "We only had *one* fucking date!" at him as he backed out of the spot and drove away.

———

For all the blood and the carnage. For all the aches and pains and the concussions leading to chronic migraines. For all the sleepless nights and inability to walk into a room without first turning all the lights on. For all of that, and so much more, there was still one thing Eric loved about Ironport, about being a Venator, and that was the lack of silence, the lack of downtime. Ironport was always humming, always noisy. The vampire problem kept him on his toes, kept him moving. And those two things combined meant he usually didn't have a whole lot of time to think, to dwell.

Which was fucking fantastic for a person who suffered from the inability to *not* rehash a conversation over and over again. To *not* replay every awkward word choice fifty times in his head, trying to find hidden meaning behind every shift in a person's face. Ironport never left him time to overthink and over-examine every conversation he ever had. Never left room for that one really weird thing he said to his teacher in third grade.

Only . . .

Only Ironport was silent now. Holding its breath. Like the

argument between the two Venator was thunder rumbling in the distance, and the city waited for the inevitable lightning strike.

And in the ensuing quiet, Eric found himself replaying the conversation over and over in his head. Every run through making him feel more and more guilty. He'd been too hard on Tony. The emotional whiplash from how they were on their date and Tony agreeing with Janet was the cause of that, obviously. It tore at something deep and scarred in Eric's being. Something not even years of therapy would probably cure.

Because he was used to that, wasn't he? Used to being treated differently in public than he was in private. It's how his parents had always treated him. How Kalla had treated him. Used to people choosing someone else instead. Used to being left behind. It was how all his relationships ended. His parents. Kalla. Hunter. Eric Marcelino was never anyone's first choice for long.

"You deserve better than that," Ava would say, and maybe she was right. But it didn't feel like she was right in that moment as he crouched among the grave markers, his breath fogging in front of him, his muscles tightening up from being still and cold for too long, and the conversation playing over and over in his head. He felt like an asshole, his hand twitching for his phone to text a number he didn't have because he'd never even *asked* Tony for it. They'd gone out. They'd fucked. And he hadn't even bothered to ask for Tony's number. What the fuck was wrong with him lately?

"And where the fuck are all the *vampires*, anyway?" Eric hissed, a little too loudly, the sound echoing off the emptiness of the cemetery around him.

The clubs were closed by the time he drove past them, the bars too, so he wound up here, in the cemetery. Which maybe seemed a bit ridiculous, but on his last run through he'd noted traces of a nest recently abandoned, and vampires had a tendency to return to their nests, never leaving them empty long.

Unfortunately, for the first time in his entire career as a Venator, he was sitting in a graveyard and there were no bloodsuckers in sight. In fact, he hadn't felt any vampires since leaving the courthouse. The smell of death was still here, but it was stale, fading, like the vampires hadn't returned in a few days.

"Of course. The one fucking time I need to punch something, and they're all holed up somewhere else," he muttered to himself, standing and stretching out his legs. It felt silly to remain crouched behind a gravestone when no one was even there. Nothing but the crickets keeping him company as he trudged across the cemetery through the crunchy grass, thanking the Goddess that the only bloodsuckers he had to worry about in the winter were vampires, not ticks and mosquitos.

The mausoleum door creaked on rusty hinges as Eric pushed inside, his eyes adjusting quickly to the low lighting while his nose curled at the smell. Death lingered here. Death and blood, blood, blood. But it was stale, just like everywhere else. Remnants too long left behind. Even digging through the personal belongings left by the vampires turned up nothing.

"Guess they wouldn't leave a forwarding address lying around." Normally he might have laughed at his own joke, but it fell flat, landing lifelessly among the debris left over from at least five vampires living in close proximity. Blood-soaked clothing, empty blood bags, and ironically a Game Boy that wouldn't even turn on anymore, it was so drained.

"I should go home," he told himself, and while he knew it was good advice, knew it was exactly what his friends would tell him to do, he didn't. Because to go home was to admit failure. To go home was to look the kids in the eyes and tell them reinforcements weren't coming. That it was just him, and Tony fucking McMahon, against a problem Eric didn't quite know the scale of yet.

So he didn't go home.

He didn't go home, and he didn't go back to his car, and he kicked around the graveyard until the sun came up and his fingers were stiff from cold.

Chapter 13

THE OLD RUST bucket Tony had up on the lift was a pet project for some rich little shit who had more money than sense. Someone who could appreciate the aesthetic of a vintage car but knew absolutely fuck all about how to maintain one. But that was fine, because if it were up to Tony, he'd rather work on something pre-computer. Rather get his hands greasy up to the elbows as he tried to diagnose the problem himself without Siri telling him it was something completely mundane like worn down brake pads.

That was the thing about being a mechanic in the modern era: it'd lost most of its shine. Tony had gotten into cars because he liked the problem solving. He liked puzzling things out. That's probably why he was so attracted to Marcelino—the man was a Rubik's Cube. But modern cars? They didn't need someone to listen to the strange noises they made and know by instinct what those sounds meant. No. They just needed someone smart enough to follow directions. It was disappointing. But he could see the draw of it. Could see how it would make people's lives simpler to know the problem and fix it. How it would streamline the process, make it easier to get more cars in and out of the shop. He could respect that. It was a sound business model. That didn't mean he had to fucking like it though.

So when the Impala had come in at the beginning of the

week, and all the other mechanics took a collective step back, Tony raised his hand and volunteered. Because why wouldn't he? It was a chance to do some *real* mechanic work. The kind he'd actually gotten into cars to do.

Besides, it was a decent enough distraction from the shit-storm that was his personal life right now. If he had a Face-book—which he didn't because it was too damn easy for people he didn't like to find him there, honestly, who the fuck wanted to keep up to date with all those people they hadn't really liked in high school?—then his relationship status would be "complicated." Which was so fucking cliché, it made him want to hurl, but also so very *very* true.

"Is this where you've been hiding yourself?" a smooth, light voice said from outside the sanctuary of the engine block, and Tony groaned softly. Because he recognized that voice. That voice was the whole reason for the "complicated" status in the first place.

"Mrs. Mayor," Tony cooed, forcing on a charming smile that didn't penetrate past skin deep, "to what do I owe the pleasure?"

He pulled himself from the car, mindful of his head, and turned to face Janet Chadwick while he wiped his hands on the rag hanging from the back pocket of his coveralls. She looked just as neat, just as well-pressed, as she had the other night at the Council of Creatures meeting. Her blond hair was pinned back into a neat bun, not a strand out of place, and the crisp pale-blue pantsuit she wore looked like it didn't even know what a wrinkle was, much less how to get one.

"It's *Miss*," Janet corrected softly, taking a step closer, almost too close. Tony raised his brows, but she didn't acknowledge the way she leaned into his bubble. She winked and said, "Mrs. Mayor was my father."

Tony barked a laugh, but he could see Lu and Finn on the bench in the corner miming throwing up. He didn't know why the fuck they'd decided to come with him to the garage, but he had to admit he kind of liked the company. Their useless chatter about classes and Marcelino had been a welcome break from the silence in the garage this late in the evening after everyone else had gone home.

"Miss Mayor then." Tony smiled wider, but it still didn't reach his eyes, and he knew it. He knew what a real smile felt like, and this wasn't it. There was something off about Janet Chadwick. Something he couldn't quite pinpoint. "Question still stands. Or is this a social call?"

"No. No, I'm afraid not." Janet straightened up, lifting her chin, but the closed-mouth smile didn't leave her face. "I heard you haven't been patrolling with Eric these last few days."

"What about it?" He didn't bother to ask her how she knew, although the knowledge that she had spies out there watching him and Marcelino didn't sit right. Maybe she was worried about the threat they'd brought to her attention, or maybe it was something else. Either way, being spied on by the mayor was usually a bad thing. Maybe he shouldn't have gone to that meeting with Marcelino the other night after all, not if it was going to draw this much attention to him.

"I thought we agreed you were going to keep an eye on him, keep him safe. You can't exactly keep him safe if you aren't with him, can you?" Her blond brows raised high, but her forehead didn't wrinkle, which was really fucking creepy if you asked Tony.

"He doesn't exactly want me around him after the Council of Creatures meeting."

"And whose fault is that?"

"Yours, actually," Tony growled, his eyes narrowing on Janet, who looked like she'd just swallowed something rotten. Clearly, she hadn't thought she would get any pushback from him. Maybe she never had any before, but it was really stupid to come at him like this. Especially as she didn't know him. She must know fuck all about battle tactics, because Tony would never go after an unknown entity like this, not without backup. "After that stunt you pulled, any chance I had at a partnership went up in smoke."

"The stunt *I* pulled?" She leaned back on her heels, her arms crossed over her chest as she frowned. It was almost a pout. But if she thought that was going to work on him, she was sadly mistaken.

"Yes. The stunt you pulled. You put me on the spot back there, and made me choose between you and him. Not my fault my knee-jerk reaction was the wrong one. Maybe you should have thought of that before calling me out like that." Tony gnashed his teeth at her, eyes narrowing. He saw Lu and Finn sit up straighter out of the corner of his eye, readying for a fight, readying to step in if they had to. Good for them, maybe Marcelino was teaching them something useful after all. "And now you're here to what? Scold me?"

A breath whooshed out of Janet and her shoulders relaxed, her posture going congenial, pliant. He wasn't fooled by *that* either. "You're right. That was my mistake. I should have told you it was coming. And I should have given you some background on the whole . . . me and Eric thing."

"Damn right, you should have." Tony tucked the rag back into the pocket of his coveralls and leaned against the car behind him, his arms crossed over his chest, forcing his posture into something that wasn't quite as confrontational, but still guarded. "What's with you guys, anyway? I got this vibe that there's history. Were you like . . . together?"

"Me and Eric?" Janet laughed, but it wasn't a nice sound. It was derisive, condescending. It grated on Tony's nerves, made his ears twinge. He didn't understand how anyone could ever laugh at being with Marcelino like that. How they could see it as . . . what? Disgusting? Silly? Ridiculous? Below them? "Gosh no. But we were friends, once upon a time. Best friends."

"You don't seem too friendly now."

"No. We wouldn't." She shook her head but didn't expand on that at all, just took another step forward into his bubble, her too-bright blue eyes going sharp. "You need to get back in his good graces, whatever it takes."

"Hate to break it to you, sugar, but that shit ain't happening." Not because he didn't want it to. He did. He wanted to be all up in Marcelino's good graces. But he'd seen that look of hurt before, and he knew that it would take time for Marcelino to come off that, to forgive. He may never, if Tony's experiences with other people held true. But then, he didn't exactly know Marcelino, did he? Maybe if he—

"I don't care what you have to do." Janet stepped even closer, enough so the tips of her pointed blue shoes pressed down onto the toes of his boots, a small but not insignificant threat. "You protect him."

Tony opened his mouth to protest, to point out that maybe Marcelino didn't really need his protection—he was the longest living Venator they'd seen in centuries, after all—but Janet cut him off with a sharp look.

"There was a reason your sister was accepted into Moondale U so easily," Janet hissed, her voice just loud enough for Tony's sensitive ears to pick up, but also somehow ringing in the open space. If Lu heard it, she didn't react, and he hoped she didn't. He could see how stiff she sat out of the corner of his eyes. Ready for a fight. Good girl. "She can be kicked out just as easily."

"You can't—"

"Who do you think talked the dean into accepting a late admission? Who do you think helps keep that little program running in spite of how the other Huntsmen think it's a waste of time and resources? It doesn't matter that it's technically a Moondale-run school. If the Huntsmen wanted the Venator program shut down, it would be." Her eyes were wide now, over-bright and sharp, and they were fixed on Tony, keeping him still, keeping him silent as she flayed him alive. Because he would do anything in his power to protect Lu. Anything to make sure she had someplace safe to go, someone to look after her. Her acceptance into the Venator program at Moondale U had been a Goddess-send. A chance she wouldn't get anywhere else because it wasn't *available* anywhere else.

"And if one student is pulled"—Janet shrugged, unconcerned by the implications of what she was saying—"who's to say the rest of the program won't be shut down too?"

Tony gritted his teeth. He didn't like being threatened. Didn't care for the powerlessness that came with it usually, but it was something he understood all too well. Something he'd been raised to respond to. So instead of fighting back, instead of snarling and snapping and telling Janet to shove her offer right up her ass, he said, "I'll do what I can, ma'am."

"Good." Janet smiled again, her lips pressed together hard as she leaned back on her heels once more. "That's good. I want you to fit in here, Tony, to be a part of our community, and the best way to do that is for you to partner with Eric and make sure our prized Venator stays safe. Yeah?"

She said *prized Venator* like a farmer would say *prized hog*. Like they were fattening Marcelino up for the slaughter. It made Tony's skin crawl.

"Yes, ma'am."

"You ready to go, Jan?" a new voice called from the door to the garage, and when Tony looked over, he found a slim young man poking his head in through the big opening. With dirty blond hair and dimples in his cheeks.

"Just about, Dash," Janet called, and turned back to Tony, an assessing look in her eyes as she narrowed them. "Have you met my brother, Dash?"

"No, I haven't." Tony wasn't sure why this was important. Dash Chadwick wasn't going to take away his sister's spot at Moondale U. And besides, adding another guy to the fucked-up mess that was Tony's life probably wasn't the best idea.

Especially one who looked like Dash. Holy fuck. He wasn't as pretty as Marcelino, didn't have the fine features and speckling of moles that made Tony ache all over, but he was most certainly pleasing to the eye. Tanned and broad-shouldered, like some kind of beach god come down to earth to show them all how stupid they were. And there was this vague knowingness that settled in Tony's gut, like he'd met Dash before, known him all his life. Maybe he just had one of those faces.

"Dash, darling, come meet our new Venator, Tony."

Dash strode across the cement floor, hands in his pockets, a close-mouthed smile crinkling his eyes. And okay, so, he was even hotter up close. Hotter in that rugged-football-player way. Which yeah, Tony could get behind—or in front of—even if it was the complete opposite of Eric Marcelino.

"I'd shake your hand, but I'm a greasy mess." Tony offered his own crooked grin in return, and clocked how Dash's gaze flicked over his body, taking stock, and seeming to like what he found there if the way he licked his lips was anything to go by.

"A pleasure all the same," Dash said in a voice that was deep and smooth, much like his sister's. He tilted his head to get some of the blond hair back from his eyes where it was too long on the top, too short on the sides.

"Definitely," Tony agreed.

"Well," Janet said, breaking whatever moment Dash and Tony were having, "we've got to get going. So much to do, so little time."

"Of course. It was nice seeing you, Miss Mayor." Tony dipped his head in something he hoped Janet would see as respect, but she had to know he didn't trust her now. He might never trust her again. Even if she'd brought her brother to wiggle around in front of him like a fucking squeaky toy. Tony wasn't stupid.

Lu and Finn waited until the Chadwicks were gone before

they approached and took up residence leaning against the Honda parked in the neighboring bay.

"I don't like her," Lu said, biting into an apple.

Finn nodded her agreement. "She smells funny."

"That's just her perfume." Tony grunted as he turned back to the Impala, hunching over it. There likely wasn't much more he could do tonight, not with how Janet had come in to throw his brain for a loop. There would be no focusing, absolutely none. "Why are you here anyway, Finnley? Shouldn't you be with Marcelino's brat pack at the school?"

"Finn," she corrected, tilting her dark head, big brown eyes staring hard at the back of his neck, making the hairs raise there. He could see her in the reflection of chrome cylinder head cover. She looked so much like Marcelino, it was fucking scary. Tony wondered if they were related in some distant way, but he didn't ask. She'd also gotten real fucking sassy since hanging out with his sister. Good for her.

"Question stands."

"They're all locals," Lu supplied when it didn't seem like Finn was going to answer.

"She's local too." Or at least from what Tony had heard. Finn was from one of those old-school Huntsmen families that raised their children to be warriors from the time they were big enough to hold a stake, just like his father had with him. Poor kid.

"Homeschooled," Finn said, as if Tony didn't know that already.

"That explains *so* much," Tony teased and ducked out of the way when Lu chucked her apple at his head, snickering softly at the look of irritation from both girls. "Go get your shit together. We're heading home. I need to get some food in me before patrol."

"Pizza?" Finn asked hopefully.

"You're gonna turn into a fucking pizza. And who said I was feeding you, anyway? You're not my kid." The hood of the car slammed closed, and Tony whirled to fix them both with a raised brow.

"Fuck yeah, we're getting pizza," Lu said. She'd already made her way back to the bench where they'd been working on homework to pack up her and Finn's bags. "You don't have time to cook."

With a quick look up at the clock ticking away behind a cage near the ceiling, Tony groaned. She was right, he didn't have time to cook. Not if he wanted to make it out before sunset. "Lu, you're in charge of calling it in."

Lu gave a lazy salute and pulled out her phone as she shouldered on her backpack, and both girls headed through to the office while Tony closed up shop.

Chapter 14

THE QUIET LINGERED. The stillness leaving Eric unsettled and itchy. He had never, in his life, gone this long without a vampire showing their face. Almost two weeks. Two fucking *weeks*. Thirteen days, to be exact. And no vamp activity. No dead freshman. No exsanguinated twenty-somethings who had just been out clubbing and clearly gotten mixed up in "something nasty," as the police would say. Not even a missing cat, for crying out fucking loud. It wasn't right.

And he was losing his fucking mind with it, itching out of his skin for a slay. So much so that he couldn't go on patrol alone. Well, he *could*, but Ava and Hunter weren't going to *let* him. Because they were worried—and rightfully so, honestly —that he was going to get himself into something he couldn't get himself out of. Like fighting a fucking bear in the mountains or something. He wasn't going to fight a bear, but honestly? If someone asked him? He'd thought about it once or twice over the last couple of weeks, if only to get the buzz under his skin to die down for a fucking second so he could focus.

Which is how he found himself trudging down the frozen sidewalks of Ironport with Ava at his side, twirling a stake between her fingers like she would a crochet hook or a pen. They'd already been by the graveyards where there were nests to check if there was any movement. There wasn't. Thus, they were headed back toward the clubs in the hopes that something would set off his undead radar. Or he'd get roaring drunk, whichever came first.

"So," Ava said, her hands going behind her back to clutch at the stake there, like she was trying to make herself look as casual and unassuming as possible. It wasn't working. She was six feet tall with forest green hair, and she'd chosen tonight, of all nights, to wear one of her garishly bright neon jackets. One of the ones that looked like she should be a crossing guard, not a craft store owner. She stood out in a way not even Eric thought possible. But he was grateful to have her beside him, even still.

"So what?" he asked when she didn't push forward with the sentence—she was trying a little too hard to look casual, really. And he knew, beyond a shadow of a doubt, that he wasn't going to like whatever came out of her mouth next. Because he'd been friends with her since he was fucking eighteen, and it was kind of hard to miss the signs of Ava gearing up to say something Real.

"Why didn't you bring your uh . . . your boyfriend?" She wouldn't look at him, bright blue eyes fixed on the sidewalk up ahead, which was crowded from everyone waiting to get into the bars.

"My boyfriend?"

"Don't pretend you two haven't gotten all . . ." She wiggled her fingers to indicate whatever they'd *gotten all*, her nose wrinkled in distaste. Ava was the kind of person to make jokes about safe sex, and wearing protection, and *oh, Ricky, do you need me to go over proper procedure?* But she was also kind of a prude sometimes.

"You can say *sex*, Ava." Eric sighed heavily, but he wasn't looking to meet her eyes either. It was less weird to talk about stuff like this when he wasn't looking at people's faces. When they couldn't see the heat crawling up his neck and making his thick winter jacket too hot. "Yes, we had sex, sorta. Oral. Once. But he's not my boyfriend."

"Eric," Ava said, in that tired way of hers. Like she was very Done with their conversation. Which was super rude because she'd started it. But Eric had learned a long time ago that Ava was almost always Done with everything.

"Ava," he replied in the exact same tone; he was Done with this conversation too, actually. He was Done with *every-thing* involving Tony McMahon, if he was perfectly frank. Because Tony McMahon had shown exactly what kind of person he was, and Eric didn't have time to fuck around with that whole *thing*. Not when it felt like Ironport was holding its breath, waiting for the water to boil over. He'd wondered a lot over the last few days if this was what crabs felt like as they were cooked alive. Is this why they fought like they did? The constant knowing that something bad was coming, but not being able to stop it, and not knowing what *it* was? Of being trapped, trapped, trapped, the lid held down by someone who was thinking of how tasty crabs were. It was enough to make him swear off shellfish. Almost. It was kind of hard to be a Marylander who didn't eat crabs at least occasionally. Plus, they were fucking yummy, all right?

Ava had stopped walking, reaching out to grab Eric's wrist, and she finally looked at him. Her blue eyes too blue, too wide in the glare of the streetlight over them. Whatever she saw in his face was bad, because instead of some snide "King Ricky" comment, she said, "Oh. Eric. Honey, what happened?"

"Nothing. Nothing happened." And if it sounded like a lie, that was because it was. Everything had happened. Too much had happened. And Eric didn't particularly want to lay the whole sad tale at Ava's feet. Not when there was too much else to worry about. Not when he still felt sorry for himself for falling for Tony's whole doting-guardian act. He had seemed like such a good guy. Someone maybe Eric could fall for, eventually. Someone who could become a partner in a way Eric had never had before. And now . . .

And now . . .

"Eric," Ava pressed again, giving his wrist a firm squeeze.

He should wait to tell her this. He should wait until he had Hunter, Ava, and Britt all in a room together, so he could lay himself bare one time, and one time only. So he could put this problem at their feet and not have to retell the story over and over. But . . . well, here was the thing. Ava was his best friend in the entire world. He loved her dearly. And Hunter was . . . Hunter was complicated. Eric loved him just as much as he loved Ava, but the love was different, and there was a self-imposed distance between them. Because . . .

Because when Eric had been fresh off the Kalla Regan train, rebounding *hard*, he and Hunter had kind of messed around a bit. Nothing serious. Nothing that would ruin their friendship, because fuck all if Eric was going to spoil that. But it had left things strained between them. And Eric had thought, for about half a second there, that he'd get with Hunter. That Hunter would be it for him. The inevitable friends-to-lovers thing Ava wrote about sometimes in her novels. But then Hunter and Britt had become a thing, and Eric had been heartbroken all over again. So yeah, there was distance there. And Eric didn't particularly want to show Hunter what a fucking failure he was at the whole relation-ship thing, *still*.

So, instead, he laid it all at Ava's feet and hoped to what-ever gods looked after bisexual disasters that she—in all her wizened lesbian glory—would have some kind of answer for him. Some kind of way to fix this. He really was pathetic, wasn't he?

"Tell me I'm being an asshole," Eric said, hands stuffed so far into the pockets of his coat that they were inside up past his wrists. It would be easier if Ava said he was being an asshole. If he could simply apologize for what happened and make everything right again. That's what he was good at: apologizing. Placating other people so he didn't have to feel this . . . this unmoored, lost thing in his chest when people inevitably cut him loose. He'd spent so much time apologizing to Kalla while they were together that eventually she'd started saying *no you're not*, every time, and it landed like a blow.

"No." Ava shook her head. The stake had disappeared, likely into her pocket, so she could give him her full attention. Which was, arguably, terrifying. Ava was one of those people who you never wanted their full attention pinned on you. Hunter was another, but for entirely different reasons. With Ava, it was like she could see all the fucked-up shit, and trauma, that sat just under the surface, like some therapist who also happened to be a kindergarten teacher for whatever reason. And she was ready to make you hug it out. Fuck, Eric did *not* want to hug it out. "No. That was 100 percent a dick move on his part, you're right."

Eric's steps stuttered a little, his shoe catching on a crack in the pavement. Had Ava just said he was *right*? He was going to have to put that in his calendar. It would likely never ever happen again. He should celebrate such a momentous—

"But, Ricky, buddy . . ." She sighed, rocking back on her heels. A terrible fighting stance, he'd told her numerous times, but she was too old to have bad habits trained out of her now. And besides, she wasn't a Huntsman, she wasn't a Venator, she was just a witch who happened to be besties with Eric Marcelino. She wasn't supposed to be out there with him, hunting vamps. "To be fair . . ."

The moment hung too long. The silence broken up only by the bass of the approaching strip of clubs. He hated when she did that. It was all for dramatic effect. To keep him guessing and on his toes. And it was fucking annoying that everyone who surrounded Eric seemed to have a high base level of dramatics, himself included.

"What? To be fair *what*?" he hissed, resisting the urge to reach out and grab Ava by her shoulders. To shake her until all her secrets spilled out like coins from a piggy bank. Because what the fuck? How was she a year younger than him and so much smarter?

"To be fair, Tony doesn't know your history with Janet like I do." Ava shrugged and scuffed her shoes against the slick sidewalk. She was doing her best to sound and look casual, because she knew the heaviness of this conversation. Knew what Janet Chadwick meant to Eric once upon a time. Not that she'd been there to witness it, not really. They weren't friends then like they were friends when the whole Kalla thing happened. But some wounds didn't heal over quite right. Some wounds left scars, emotional ones especially. And Eric was littered with them. "He doesn't know how deep a betrayal that was. How it would hurt you. Plus, you know, he doesn't know how fucked up your relationship is with the council. He's not from here, dude, remember that."

"So?" Eric huffed, all righteous indignation.

"So, let the guy apologize." Ava pulled up to a stop at the end of one of the club lines, her gaze fixed ahead of them on the row of twenty-somethings all stomping in their too-thin club clothes, trying to ward off the late winter chill. "Talk your shit out, for once in your fucking life. Don't let it end up like you and Hu—"

"We aren't talking about that. We both agreed, we were never talking about that again."

Ava shrugged, unbothered. She'd never actually agreed to that, but Eric was going to hold her to it anyway, because poking at his scars wasn't going to make them ache less. They'd already healed over in the most fucked-up way imaginable. Poking at them would only make matters worse. And she knew that. But she seemed to think that *talking* about things was the way to heal emotional wounds. Pfft. What did she know.

"I'm just gonna have Kalla come out with me tomorrow." He wasn't. Kalla made for decent backup. She was a good fighter and would have made a half decent Venator if her gene had ever shown itself, which it didn't. But she also talked too fucking much and got real judgmental sometimes. And wasn't that exactly what he needed right now? His ex-fiancée looking at him with sympathy and something like disappointment? No. No, it was not.

Ava groaned, bumping her shoulder into him hard enough to send him stumbling toward the building on his left. "That is definitely the stupidest shit you've said in like the last month, at least. If not ever."

"Rude."

She was right though, it was stupid. This whole thing was so stupid. But he couldn't think of a smart way to handle things. Because he was not—*not*—talking to Tony about this. Not unless the guy came groveling, and—

A shiver crept up Eric's spine, raising every hair in its wake. Something was watching them. He tilted his head a little to one side, trying to catch the scent on the air, but he couldn't. There was just the feeling, the vague unease of a dead thing paying too close attention to him. A predator stalking its prey.

"What is it?" Ava asked, noticing his sudden stillness, her hands at her sides already glowing softly with the pale light of her magic. Yellow, like a sunflower. Like buttercups. Like dandelions. Like wishes in summertime. Ava always said the color a witch's magic manifested as was a peek into their soul. And Ava was all these soft things, but she was also brutal sunshine, scorching hot enough to burn the crops dry if you tested her.

"We're being watched." Now if he could only pinpoint the source of the feeling. "Anything on ye olde magic radar?"

A soft hum left Ava as she closed her eyes and focused, reaching out with her magic. Eric felt it brush against his senses, warm and inviting, but it didn't do more than glance against his skin then move on before Ava concluded, "Just normies."

"That's not right." He shook his head, focusing on the prickle of unease at the base of his spine, like the pins and needles of skin about to break into a sweat. Sweltering and terrifying all at once. But he still couldn't smell anything other than sweat and the stink of alcohol on the people around them. Nothing magical—aside from Ava's fresh-cut-grass smell. Nothing undead.

Ava shifted at his side, looking around them in a move that was way too obvious. But if he told her to stop, that would draw even more attention to them. No, he had to play it cool. "Approximately," she said, her tone low and a little scared, "how many times has your freaky-deeky Venator radar been off, King Ricky?"

"Never." Of course, it had also never told him there was something dangerous nearby when he couldn't smell it, but Eric wasn't going to think too hard about that, because it wasn't the point. The point was—"Why is it just watching? Why isn't it *doing* anything?"

"Can you tell where it is?"

"Across the street. Probably in one of those apartments above the restaurants."

"Or like . . ." Ava's voice went up an octave, real fear tinting it now, and her magic swirled faster around her hands, the tang of freshly cut grass souring. "In the parking lot?"

"What're you talking about, Ava? They wouldn't stand right out in the—" He turned to see the dark-clad figure standing under a streetlight in the parking lot across the way, unmoving and obviously facing their direction even though it was hard to tell where they were looking. "Open."

"You sure it's a vamp?"

"Positive." Living things couldn't fake the unnatural stillness that came from not having to breathe, from an unbeating heart. Living things were a myriad of tiny movements that maybe the human eye wouldn't see, but his Venator senses sure as fuck did. "You stay here, in the crowd, where it's safe."

"Eric, I really—"

But Eric didn't give her a chance to finish before he raced across the street, ignoring traffic and heading for the figure, which started moving the moment they noticed Eric pulling away from the crowd. This close, he was finally able to catch the scent of the creature, whatever magic it used to hide itself not strong enough once he was within range.

Death. And blood. Blood. Blood.

Definitely a vampire.

"Hey buddy, I just wanna talk!" But the creature was running, not even glancing back to see if Eric was following. Which he was. His feet slapped hard against the pavement, and he was grateful he'd worn sensible shoes instead of something obnoxious to go out with Ava tonight.

The vampire didn't slow but pushed themselves harder, running for the edge of the entertainment district, into the part of town where the warehouses resided. All closed up and dark for the evening. A labyrinth of cube-like buildings. One the same as the next, and the next, and the next.

They turned a corner, their hood falling from their head, and Eric had just enough time to catch the sight of blond hair before they disappeared down an alley. Eric pushed himself harder, the muscles in his legs burning, instantly regretting the big dinner of pasta he'd made for the kids, to try to reach the alley in enough time to catch up with the vampire. But . . .

But he turned the corner, and the alley was empty. Not even a trace of the dead thing's scent left behind. Leaving him with nothing at all to track. He could follow, run down the pitch-black alley and hope it turned up something. But without backup . . .

Well, Eric probably would have done just that maybe half

a decade ago. But he wasn't so stupid now, and he knew better. Instead, he pulled out his phone and marked his location on a geo-tagging app. He'd come back when he was better prepared to investigate. For tonight, he needed to get back to the dorm and figure out what the fuck this meant.

CHAPTER 15

THERE WAS TOO much at stake here. Too much on the line. Tony didn't like it. His life being at risk was normal, acceptable, *expected* even. He knew that's what he was getting into when his Venator gene activated because there was no way to *not* know. Not with how their mother died.

But Lu's safety? Her education? Those were never supposed to be up for debate. Never supposed to be in question. Tony worked hard to make sure Lu had someplace soft to land, someplace safe. He fought tooth and nail to gain custody of her after their father died. Budgeted himself until he was blue in the face, making cuts and sacrifices until the insurance money came through for them. It was why he'd put off his top surgery for so fucking long. Why he had driven a car to the brink of breaking down until it finally left him stranded at the grocery store one day. Why they'd stayed in that fucking house with the ghosts and the memories for so long. Because he took his guardianship of his little sister seriously, damn it.

Always had. Always would.

And yeah, objectively, doing whatever it took to get back into Eric Marcelino's good graces wasn't exactly a hardship. Because he did *want* to be in them. Their quick romp in the kitchen had done nothing to satiate the desire burning low in

Tony's stomach, as it might have for some of his other flings. Instead, it had set it ablaze, made it burn through most of his common sense. Which was never, ever, a good thing in Tony's experience.

Still, it was why he was up at bumfuck thirty on Thursday to pick up breakfast and drive Lu to Moondale U even though she didn't have class until that evening, and even though he didn't have to be in to work until after noon. Because apologies were usually good for getting back in people's good graces, and food—in Tony's experience, at least—was great for getting back into someone's pants. Which, you know, wasn't his goal, but would be an added bonus.

"Stop thinking with your dick," Lu muttered, glaring at him from the passenger seat. He didn't know how she could tell what he was thinking; she probably just knew him that well, but he didn't appreciate it.

"I'm not."

"You are."

"Am not."

"Are too."

"Am—" Tony cut himself off, biting down hard on the inside of his cheek. The argument wasn't going to get them anywhere, least of all get her the fuck out of his car so he could head over to the dorm without her. Which was numero uno on his list of priorities at the moment. "Look, you don't want to flunk out of Marcelino's class, do you?"

"He wouldn't flunk me just because my brother's a piece of shit." But she didn't look entirely certain about that. It had only been a couple of weeks, after all. How could she know that Marcelino wasn't a vindictive asshole? He wasn't. Tony was pretty sure about that. Almost positive, in fact, that anything he did to fuck up his relationship with Marcelino would have absolutely zero effect on her grades. But there were other problems to handle, and it'd be easier to lay it on thick without his kid sister gumming up the works.

He would have let her hang there, uncertainty creeping into her belly, making her uneasy, if he wasn't such a damned softy and didn't cave the moment she asked, "Right?"

"No," Tony said, blowing out a long breath and wishing he could be less sober for this entire thing. But honestly, being high would probably make it worse, would make him seem less genuine about his apology. Sober it was. "No, he probably wouldn't. But still, you don't want to be there, do you? It's probably gonna be gross as fuck watching me drool all over your prof."

"Ew. Don't say shit like *prof*. That's so fucking weird. Who does that?" Lu blanched and reached for the door handle, already pulling her scarf up to her freckled cheeks to shield herself from the early morning chill. "Are you a frat bro now?"

"What if I am?" He licked his lips, biting back a laugh as he leaned back in his seat, puffing out his chest. "Maybe I pledged to Beta Alpha Phi? You don't know my life, Lu. Maybe I'm all up in that frat-bro jam. Maybe—"

"Stop saying words. Right now. It's too early for this shit." And then she scrambled from the car, but not before snagging the extra coffee and breakfast sandwich he'd bought for himself.

He opened his mouth to argue.

Lu shot him a stony look. "I need sustenance, I'm a growing girl." She slammed the door in his face and trotted toward the library without a backward glance. Little shit.

He revved the engine of his car, loud enough for a couple of the professors heading into one of the buildings across the lot to turn. He resisted the urge to flick them off for the stink eye they shot his way. It would probably not help his case with Marcelino if he was caught stirring up trouble on campus. So he gave a cheeky wave instead and waited until he knew Lu was safe inside the library before peeling away from the curb to head toward on-campus housing.

Through the mist that lingered from the early morning, Tony could see a light on in the kitchen window, a shape moving around inside, likely Marcelino making breakfast for his pack of gremlins. Tony flipped the visor down to give himself a once over in the mirror before he got out of the car. He'd spent extra time on his hair and makeup that morning, adding extra fluff to the mane of curls, and making the winged eyeliner thicker at the corners than might otherwise be deemed appropriate for a morning visit. It was a look he wouldn't have tried a few years back, before his father died. A mix of feminine and masculine that he hadn't been able to fully embrace until his Venator hormones and the T decided to play nice and make his hips a little less full, his jaw a little more cut. But now, after years of looking in the mirror, after buzzing his hair at one point, he liked what he saw when he looked at himself. Even before the top surgery, his face at least looked like *Tony*.

All he could hope was that either Marcelino wouldn't notice the effort, or he'd appreciate it and not see it for what it was: Tony leaning into his best assets in an attempt to hide the fact that he royally sucked at apologies. And like . . . words and shit.

His knuckles ached from the cold where he rapped on the front door to the 1106 Moonshadow Way, half expecting no one to answer. If the kids weren't up and Marcelino decided he didn't want to deal with Tony, then Tony might stand out on the front porch forever. Which would serve him right, honestly; he should have known better than letting Janet get into his head like that.

He fully anticipated Marcelino to either look out the peephole and not open the door at all or open it, take one look at Tony standing on the stoop with his too-thin leather coat, and hastily wrapped scarf—Lu insisted he needed one—then promptly slam the door in his face.

What he didn't expect was for Marcelino to open the door, hum softly, his eyes flicking over Tony quickly then up to the right as if deep in thought, then nod. "You may as well come in."

"I brought breakfast." Tony held up the bag and the coffee.

"Of course you did." Marcelino didn't take either, he just moved out of the way, letting Tony enter, and muttered a soft "Take off your fucking boots, man" before heading back to the kitchen.

Tony wasn't sure if it was the early morning, or something else, but he was more than willing to take advantage of the softness that lingered around Marcelino's mouth, the way his shoulders drooped in exhaustion, and the not-quite-awake tone to his voice. He toed off his boots, not even bothering to untie them, and followed Marcelino into the kitchen where the coffee maker beeped overloud in the silence of a still-sleeping house when Marcelino turned it on.

Readying himself to dive headfirst into the bullshit apology he'd practiced at least fifty times over the night before, Tony took a deep breath, and opened his mouth, and —stopped. Immediately. Sentence halfway through the filter between his brain and his mouth—which worked just fine, fuck you very much, Lu—when Marcelino held up a single finger, not even looking at him as he took the to-go cup and downed half of it without a single wince for the heat that still burned through the cardboard.

That done, Marcelino flapped his wrist as if to say "continue" and moved to the cupboard to pull out boxes of Pop-Tarts, donuts, and other various quick breakfast foods.

Tony waited till Marcelino's back was turned before he took the half-finished box of donuts and picked up every one of them to lick, staking his claim, because his impulse control was shit, and he hadn't had powdered donuts in what felt like forever. Marcelino turned around just in time to see Tony trying to wipe white powder off his chin.

"Did you just . . . did you just *lick* all the donuts?" Marcelino's hands moved to his hips. He looked like a disappointed mother hen, and Tony had to swallow a chuckle as he took one of the donuts from the box to start eating it.

He shrugged, unrepentant, getting crumbs all over the fucking place. And sure, yeah, this probably wasn't the best way to get Marcelino to forgive him, but Tony thought he heard Marcelino choke back a chortle, and honestly, he couldn't be fucked to bother with much else.

"Those are for the kids." Okay, Marcelino was definitely laughing now. His eyes crinkled with it, even if he seemed to be trying to speak through it, keeping his tone level. Tony could still hear it.

"The gremlins can get their own donuts," Tony said around a cheek full.

Marcelino barked a laugh, his eyes going wide and startled like he hadn't meant to release it, to let it past his throat. Then he leaned over, holding his stomach as he giggled like an absolute fucking maniac, all snorting and gasping for breath. While Tony just stood there, blinking at him, his heart pounding hard in his chest because that—*that* had to be the most beautiful sound he'd ever heard in his life. And suddenly he wanted to dedicate the rest of his days to hearing more of it. To letting it echo around him clear as a bell, chasing away all other possible sounds. He'd never get sick of it. He just knew it.

Get it together, McMahon. It's just a laugh. Kind of a dorky one too.

"So . . ." Tony said, letting the words fall off as Marcelino got himself together enough to wheeze in a breath and stand upright once more. "Does that mean I'm forgiven?"

"Yeah. Yeah, I guess you are." Marcelino shook his head, the smile still twitching at the corner of his lips like he couldn't help it, and gods if that wasn't the most breathtaking thing Tony had seen in all his life, he didn't know what was.

Buddy-boy, I think we're fucked.

"Come on," Marcelino said, picking up his coffee and grabbing the paper sack carrying his breakfast, "bring your donuts."

"Where are we going?" Tony scooped up the donut box and followed Marcelino without an answer as he led him through the living room to a door at the back of the house that seemed to be a large study. Marcelino flopped down, patting the couch next to him as he settled with one leg curled up beneath him, his coffee still in his hands.

"We're getting out of the way so when the gremlins wake up, we can still chat in peace." He waited for a beat, head tilted to the side as if listening, and Tony caught the telltale thump of someone's feet hitting the floor. "That'll be them now."

Tony opened his mouth to speak, but Marcelino shushed him before getting up to shut the doors to the study and settling in again. "They'll think I just went to my office early."

"They won't come in here?"

"A bunch of twenty-somethings study before ten?" Marcelino snorted. "Not a snowball's chance in hell."

"Right. So . . . Uh . . ." Tony set the box of donuts on the table in front of them, brushing his hands on his jeans and leaving behind a smear of white sugar. "Why the privacy?"

"Hmm?" Marcelino asked around another sip of coffee, then his still slightly hazy eyes seemed to sharpen, and he frowned. "Ah. Right. That. I wanted to give you some background on me and Chadwick."

"She said you guys were best friends back in the day." *But it felt like there was more to it than that,* he didn't say.

"Yeah, I'll bet she did." Sucking down the last dregs of his coffee, Marcelino set it down on the table and turned to face Tony fully. He took a deep breath, his hands slapping against his thighs for a moment, fingers flexing, then he lifted his head. That same stubborn, determined expression on his face again. The beautiful one that made him look like a general going to war and sent Tony's heart skittering into his throat.

"Did you love her?" Because Tony needed to know that before they dove too far into this thing between them, whatever it was. Whether it was strictly physical or something more, he had to know. He had to go into it with his eyes open.

Not that it matters. You're fucked already, remember?

"No." Marcelino laughed, shaking his head. "Not . . . not in the way you're thinking. But when you grow up like we did, raised for politics from before we could talk, given everything and nothing at the same time . . . It's tough to find other kids who understand you. Who get it. And we understood each other. And that can be its own kind of love sometimes. Especially when you're practically raised in each other's pockets the way we were."

Marcelino took another deep breath, straightening his spine further and lifting his chin. Tony didn't know what Janet Chadwick had done to Marcelino, but he had a feeling it went much deeper than Marcelino would ever be able to express with words. And maybe it was more to do with what he'd said about his parents, about being given everything and nothing, than to do with Janet at all. But Tony didn't go to college, and he sure as shit didn't know anything about psychology. He was taking a stab in the dark.

"And it was no big secret," Marcelino continued before Tony could even formulate a response to what he'd heard so far—which might be better, honestly. Whatever he was going to say would probably sound trite in comparison to what Marcelino was trying to share with him. "That our parents thought one day we'd get married. I mean, that's what influential families do, right? They sell their kids off to each other to power their ever-expanding empire, or some shit."

Tony didn't know what influential families did. He came

from the Brenners and the McMahons, and neither of them had ever been big names in the Huntsmen community, not even when they weren't foot soldiers for the fight against the undead. But he didn't say as much, because Marcelino wasn't finished.

"Then her parents up and died in that car accident, which kind of made things weird between us. And lo and behold, a year later my Venator gene suddenly activates, and you know what? No one in my family had ever even tested positive before. So it came totally out of left fucking field.

"And high school started. And word got around about my gene in the Huntsmen community. And suddenly, I didn't exist to her anymore. I walk in, go to say hi to the girl I've been best friends with since we were eating boogers, for fuck's sake, and she looks right through me. Like I'm nothing. Like I don't matter. I—like . . . I don't even . . . even *register* on her radar." Marcelino's face had contorted into something Tony could only identify as grief-stricken, even now, even years later.

Fucking hell. He'd been so fucking stupid. Was *still* fucking stupid, really. How did he get himself mixed up in this mess? Drama was so not his bag; that's why he avoided people as best he could. And yet, here he was, all tangled up in Marcelino's drama with Chadwick when all he wanted was to kill some leeches and get laid. Damn it.

Marcelino let out a long breath again, his shoulders sinking as he slumped back against the arm of the couch. "Fuck, man. I'm sorry. I didn't mean to just, like . . . unload on you like that. But I need you to understand—to *get*—why what you did hurt me so bad." He shifted, his fingers toying with the tie on his sweatpants for a moment, fidgeting, like Tony was going to judge him for this. Which maybe he could have, would have, if Tony didn't see what an utter fuckup he himself had been in all this. "I dunno, Ava said I needed to be honest with you. She says I need to start talking about my shit more, or it's all gonna build up inside me and I'll die."

"I don't think you can die from emotional constipation," Tony blurted, because what the fuck else was he supposed to say?

It maybe wasn't the right thing, but it eased the tension, made Marcelino snort with laughter then double over wheezing again as he held his stomach.

And oh. Oh shit. Tony could *really* get used to that sound.

"No. I don't suppose you can." Marcelino swiped at his eyes, but the smile didn't go anywhere, and it left Tony warm all over.

Yup. Deeply fucked. Way to go, Tony!

"So. Can I go out on patrol with you tonight, pretty boy? You know, watch your back and all that. I do really enjoy the view." He winked, his tongue between his teeth.

That's right, Ton, cover it with vulgarity. Nice save.

"That's really not necessary." Marcelino shook his head, reaching for his empty coffee cup as he stood, but there was something less open about his posture now, his shoulders curling in on themselves slightly. Was he lying? Was he hiding something? Or did he not trust Tony yet? Janet was not going to like this. "I think I've got things covered, at least for a couple more nights. Why don't we trade off this weekend? Then I'll get, like, a break?"

Tony's eyes narrowed, following Marcelino to the door. "Yeah, sure. We can do that." There was chatter from the kitchen, a clattering of dishes, as the kids milled about getting ready for their day. Tony grabbed Marcelino's wrist, stopping him right before he could open the door and let all that noise into the calm they'd found together in that room. "What about another date?"

Marcelino turned to smile at Tony over his shoulder, his eyes dancing with mischief even as he said, "Don't push your luck, handsome" in a tone so low and rumbling that it made Tony's toes curl.

Fuck.

Then he was out in the main room again, and all the noise of his horde of gremlins came rushing in, effectively ending the conversation.

CHAPTER 16

"SO," Hunter started, and Eric could see him out of the corner of his eye, his hands in his pockets, his shoulders slumped in that fairly casual way he looked sometimes when he was gearing up to say something that might get him punched as he elongated his steps on the sidewalk. Eric swallowed the sigh that sat heavy on his tongue, knowing there would be no stopping Hunter even if he tried. Best to let him say whatever asinine thing was going through his head. "Why did you bring me out tonight on patrol? Why not lover boy?"

Asinine: check.

"He's not my *lover boy*." The term was so weirdly dated, like something out of a Swayze film. And sure, Eric's hair did look a little Swayze-ish . . . sometimes, but that didn't mean his friends had to be all weird about it. And it sure as shit didn't mean he was going to use terms like *lover boy*.

Hunter turned to look at him, his head tilted to the side when he deadpanned, "He made you tacos and gave you a BJ on your kitchen table."

"So?"

With a sigh, Hunter raked his fingers through his long dark curls, which he'd left down that evening in spite of Eric telling him how stupid that was. Hunter's response had been to hold up one tatted wrist that sported no less than five hair ties and raise his brows. Eric had no arguments after that.

"Hon," Hunter said in that soft, sweet way of his. The one that always made Eric's belly warm a bit, because he'd never heard Hunter call anyone else *hon*. Hunter and his bio dad were from Baltimore, and he'd spent most of his life there before moving to Ironport when his mom remarried Chase's dad when Eric and Hunter were in high school. So he carried markers of his life there with him. Still, *hon* was reserved for Eric, always had been. "Food is a love language unto itself. Then add oral right after? Phew, lover boy may as well have proposed."

"Stop calling him that."

"You know I'm right." Hunter nudged Eric with his shoulder, jostling him where they walked down the streets of Ironport, the cold licking at their skin.

"You're not." Because who in their right mind would propose to Eric Marcelino? And even if Tony weren't in his right mind, the question still stood. No one, was the answer. "He's just—he's just some guy I slept with. That's all. It didn't mean anything."

Hunter's steps stuttered on the sidewalk, his shoulders stiffened, and his face twitched into something complicated that Eric couldn't decipher because by the time he turned his head to look, the expression was gone. It left him wondering what it'd meant, what Hunter had felt. But Eric shook it off. He needed to focus on the task at hand, on the patrol.

"Question stands," Hunter said with a small sniffle.

"Because." Eric looked around them, the feeling of eyes on his skin raising the hairs on the back of his neck. He couldn't tell where it was coming from, not yet. But they were getting close to something. Which made sense, since the warehouse district was coming up and that's where he'd lost the vamp the other night. "Because I don't know if I can trust him yet. That's why."

"Okay then." Hunter rolled out his shoulders, tilting his head from side to side as if he was preparing for a fight. Which was hilarious because he'd never actually been in a fight in his life—not that Eric knew of, anyhow. Hunter was the type to say, "Look, a UFO," point behind the person, and run the other direction. And that was fine. He didn't need to be a fighter. He had Britt, who was pretty damn kickass for a normie. "Why me, though? Why not Ava?"

"One," Eric said, holding up a single finger, "because Ava keeps asking stupid fucking questions about my love life. Two"—he held up another—"because your stunner spells are better. I want to catch a vamp, not dust 'em."

"I'm better than Ava?" His tone went up higher, leaning into the dramatics as he stumbled back a little. "Be still, my beating heart. Big Ricky, you really know how to sweet talk a guy. Watch it, you'll make my wifey jealous."

"Shut up," Eric mumbled, and he hoped Hunter couldn't see the heat that had begun to crawl up his neck and into his ears with how few streetlights were actually lit in this part of town. It was like someone had decided that once the businesses closed up shop, the warehouses could go full dark. Which was really fucking stupid considering vampires weren't the only issue Ironport had; there were also a fair few break-ins. "Remind me why I brought you."

"Because my stunner spells are top notch," Hunter teased, bumping Eric gently again. "And because I'm the man with a plan."

"What kind of plan?" He already didn't like where this was going. Hunter was notorious for his bad ideas. Like slaying while high, which had only happened once because they'd almost been fucking eaten. *Three times! In one night!* And would have probably died had Kalla not found them and pulled them out of the nest they stumbled onto. Never again.

"Well. Why don't you set Ava up with someone? It's what you did with me and Britt, and look how that turned out!"

Eric's stomach churned. He didn't have the heart to tell Hunter that setting up him and Britt had been 100 percent unintentional. That Britt was brought to the group hang for Ava, actually. He hadn't thought for a second that Britt and Hunter would hit it off like they did, much less that they'd wind up married a year later. The main reason he wouldn't admit that out loud was that it'd mean exposing the fact that Eric still held a flame for Hunter. That even though he'd told Hunter he was a rebound and not to think much of it, that had been the biggest fucking lie he'd ever told anyone, including himself. Hunter wasn't just a rebound. He was also Eric's best friend—aside from Ava. One of two people who had seen him at his lowest and stayed, and that meant something huge to Eric. So huge, he couldn't find words to describe it.

But—but what if things had gone sideways? What if Eric and Hunter had gotten into it, and things hadn't worked out? What if their breakup had been as epically bad as Eric and Kalla's was? What if it was worse? What if Eric lost Hunter entirely? It hadn't been worth the risk, hadn't been worth the risk, hadn't been worth the risk, and then he'd lost his chance. The window had closed. And Hunter found Britt, and as the stories go, they'd lived happily ever after.

"Who would I even set her up with?" Eric asked, swallowing the rise of bile in the back of his throat. There wasn't time enough for him to get emotional now. Not as more hairs raised on the back of his neck. Why were they even talking about this? They should focus. Hunter shouldn't get Eric all twisted up inside when there were vampires lurking somewhere close. Not that Hunter knew that's what he was doing, but still.

Hunter hummed, his fingers laced behind his head like they were holding his head up. Then he snapped his fingers and turned to fix Eric with the full force of his brightest smile as he asked, "What about the dean?"

"The dean? You mean like . . . the dean of Moondale University? Vanessa Cochburn? That dean?"

Hunter nodded eagerly.

"That is such a shitty idea, Hunter, I can't even put it into words." And not just because he couldn't possibly imagine the straitlaced, uptight, bookish Vanessa Cochburn with someone as spunky, loud, and outspoken as Ava Franklin. Second thought, that had the potential to be hilarious.

"Why not? I'm pretty sure Dean Cochburn is into women."

Eric snorted, rolling his eyes. "Sure, but do you know how many deans Moondale U has seen since I started working there?" He shook his head, brushing a hand through his hair. "I'm not setting Ava up with someone the Moondale Board of Magic is going to drive off in under six months."

"Ah, but that's six months of freedom, hon. Six months of Ava not sticking her nose into your love life."

"Tempting as that sounds . . ." And it did sound tempting because as much as Eric loved Ava, she could be nosey as fuck when she wasn't busy with something else. Maybe he should get her started on another story idea. Maybe that'd keep her out of his business. Not likely, but he was willing to try almost anything at this point—anything apart from setting her up with the Moondale U dean. "Not gonna happen."

"Suit yourself." Hunter shrugged, returning his attention to the buildings that loomed around them.

The feeling of someone watching still lingered at the back of Eric's neck, growing more intense the deeper they went down the main road through the warehouse district. There were parking lots on both sides, small when compared to some of the ones at the heart of Ironport where the bigger businesses resided, but large enough for a box truck to turn around in. A few trucks sat empty in front of squat buildings with large bay doors and darkened windows. Eric squinted, trying to see if there was anyone in the windows, but he couldn't tell. Whoever was watching them could be anywhere, hiding in the dark between buildings, behind drawn shades, lurking around the edges of the few box trucks sitting at bays waiting to be unloaded.

Fear crawled across Eric's skin. He didn't like this. Didn't like the stillness, and the quiet. It wasn't right. Vampires didn't wait like this. They didn't hold back. They were always too hungry for that. And Eric had brought a meal with him between him and Hunter; their magic should smell tantalizing in a landscape otherwise barren.

"What're they waiting for?" Eric muttered to himself, his fingers tightening around the stake in his pocket.

"Maybe word finally got around about how big and scary you are, big boy." Hunter winked. Normally the flirting would have made Eric blush and duck his head, laugh nervously, but he was too keyed up now. Too in tune with everything around them to focus on what Hunter was saying, much less the lilting tone he used.

"Doubtful. This is—It's like they're under orders." Which was exactly why he'd brought Hunter along. Because if the vamps of Ironport were answering to someone, he needed to know who, and the quickest way to do that was to catch one and question them.

Something flickered out of the corner of his eye, and Hunter muttered, "On your right" just before a shape took off, running full speed across the parking lot. They were joined by not one, but a dozen other swiftly moving shadows.

"Slow them down, Hun!" Eric barked and started after them, boots slapping against the cracked cement as he put anything and everything he had into catching up to the pack of vampires. He prayed to the Goddess that they wouldn't circle back around for Hunter. Because that was a very real possibility.

"One stunner spell coming right up." Hunter cackled, his magic flickering to life in the dark, jumping like lightning from one spread finger to another to another to another, like touching a static ball. Only it was multicolored and black to match the plethora of tattoos Hunter had drawn into his skin, and it smelled of black licorice.

It took one beat, one breath, for the magic to heat up, Hunter murmuring words under his breath that Eric couldn't have hoped to understand even if he was close enough to hear them. Then Hunter clapped his hands together in front of him, and the magic expanded outward from him like a bubble. It started slow. Eric could see the reflection of it in the windows as he ran past, then the magic picked up speed, chasing Eric, chasing the vamps, until it engulfed them all.

Eric felt the spell tingle at his skin, drag on his muscles like he was running down the beach, but then it seemed to register who and what he was and released him, moving on to swallow up the vampires instead. They slowed first, their legs moving in slow motion, then stopped entirely, glued to the spot by Hunter's magic.

"Do what you're gonna do, I can't hold them for long!" Hunter grunted against the strain of the spell.

With a nod, Eric pulled the restraints from the bag over his shoulder and made his way toward the vampires. But just as he reached them, something shifted, a *thud* followed, and Eric looked back just in time to see Hunter hit the ground where something had slammed into him.

"Hunter!" Eric spun, already ready to go back and save his friend, but a hand grabbed his shoulder, and he was yanked back into the horde of vamps with too many teeth and too many clawed hands. He pulled the stakes from his pockets so hard he ripped the seams, and started dusting, because there was nothing else he could do. He had to get back to Hunter, had to keep him safe. And he had to be quick about it, before—before—before—

"Come here often, pretty boy?" Tony said, his smile sharp and dangerous as a vampire turned to ash between them, revealing strawberry-blond hair and a hint of stubble on a sun-kissed face.

"Where did you come from!" Eric shouted. The herd was thinning, one by one the vampires were going down, settling into piles of dust and fangs at their feet. Eric looked back, searching for Hunter, and found him sitting on the sidewalk, a hand wrapped tight around his neck, a little pile of dust beside him.

"What's that matter?" Tony shot back. He was a riot of movement, of killing blows and graceful dance-like steps. Like this was a game. "Point is, I got here in the nick of time."

They were down to one vampire before Eric knew it—maybe having a second Venator around *would* help with their infestation—and Eric dropped to the ground to look for the magical restraints Ava had given him. They'd slipped from his hands somewhere in the scuffle. He just needed—*There!*

The knees of his jeans scraped against the sidewalk, probably leaving scuff marks behind, but that was fine because the restraints were right—

The vampire exploded into ash, falling like snow around Eric, in his hair, in his eyes, up his nose. "What the fuck, man?"

"What?" Tony asked and sneezed as he tucked his stake into his back pocket. "You good, pretty boy? What're you doing down there?"

"I was trying to catch one of them, you idiot!" Eric lurched to his feet, his hands on his hips as he glared down at Tony, who was only about two inches shorter. "I was going to question them."

Tony frowned, gaze flicking to the piles of dust around them. "Oh . . . sorry."

"Can you two flirt *later*? I'm bleeding over here!" Hunter shouted. Eric turned and found his friend's face drawn, blood dripping from between his fingers where they were wrapped tight around his neck.

"Fuck." Eric dropped the restraints and ran back toward Hunter, already pulling his phone from his pocket. He tossed it to Tony, who caught it on instinct. "Call Britt! Tell her to be at the house when we get there!"

Tony didn't ask questions, just started dialing.

"All right. All right," Eric soothed, dropping to his knees beside Hunter and pulling a towel from the backpack on his back. His fingers shook where they latched on to Hunter's wrist, carefully peeling Hunter's fingers away from his neck. "Fuck. I've got you, Hun. You're all good. I've got you. Just apply pressure, all right?" He turned back to Tony. "What'd she say?"

"She's on her way. My car is just down the block in one of the lots. I can get him back to the dorms quick."

Eric shifted, his gaze flicking between Hunter and Tony. He hadn't trusted Tony enough to bring him out on patrol, enough to go on another date. Could he trust him with this? With a member of his family?

"I'll get him there safe, Eric," Tony said in a voice so firm, so soft, that Eric felt the vow all the way down to his toes. "I promise."

Eric nodded and helped Hunter to his feet. "I'll be right behind you."

Chapter 17

TIRES SCREECHED across slick pavement as Tony took a turn a little too fast and Hunter slammed into the door. Arguably, probably not great for his injuries, but Tony was in a hurry, damn it. He wasn't about to waste time slowing down for a turn he knew perfectly well he could make at speed.

"Dude! Slow *down*!" Hunter shouted from the passenger seat once he'd righted himself again, his fingers so tight around the towel Eric had given him to hold to his wound that his knuckles were going pale. Or maybe that was the blood loss. Tony didn't really know enough about medicine to tell. They probably should have brought Eric in the car with them, then he could have monitored Hunter's condition. But then Tony would have Eric in the back bitching about his driving and asking if he drove like this with Lu in the car, and honestly, it was better to not deal with that when he was trying to focus on slick roads.

"No can do, handsome. Gotta get you to the dorm so your wifey can patch you up." Tony licked his lips as he shifted hard into the next gear, the engine roaring.

"I'm not gonna die if it takes us five whole extra minutes!" Hunter pulled the towel away, flailing his hand in Tony's face to gesture toward his neck. "See? It's already clotting!"

It was, partly. But there were still dribbles of blood,

enough that it was a concern. Besides, there was the issue of the other damage that could be done in a vampire mauling like that. Deep nerve damage. Anemia. Add to all that the toxins that a vampire bite produced. Tony had experienced the hangover-like symptoms enough times to know they weren't exactly kind. And he was a Venator, he was built for this. Hunter wasn't. He was a witch, making him more susceptible to a vampire's venom. The fact that he wasn't feeling any pain probably had more to do with the loopy high of vamp toxins than adrenaline.

"Sorry buddy, Eric entrusted me to get you to your wifey before you passed out, and that's what I'm gonna do." Tony's smile stretched into something manic, and his toes pressed down harder on the gas pedal.

"Yeah! Well! Getting into a car accident isn't going to get you into Eric's pants again!" With the towel wrapped tight around his neck once more, Hunter braced himself on the ceiling to keep from slamming into the window as Tony took another turn too hard.

He was being a little reckless, he knew he was. But that wasn't going to stop him. Because there was something desperate in Eric's face when he'd looked at Hunter sitting there on the pavement, bleeding out. Something like loss that Tony didn't quite understand and didn't think he wanted to. Loss, and guilt, and longing. It made Tony's gut twist. Because—because why couldn't Eric look at *him* like that? Why was he looking at this *married* guy like that? And yeah, okay, he was jealous. So sue him.

"Yeah? And how would you know?" Tony asked, hands gripping the wheel harder to maintain control of the vehicle as they swerved along the winding road that led to Moondale U.

"Cause I've tried it!" Hunter laughed, the sound all forced brightness, and when Tony looked over at him, he didn't see a hint of a lie on his face. No tell in the twist of a sardonic smile. "Well"—Hunter shrugged—"I didn't get into the accident on *purpose*."

"You've got to be shitting me," Tony muttered. It took every bit of willpower he had to return his gaze to the road ahead of them and not watch Hunter squirm in his seat. Was there anyone in this fucking town who didn't want to get into Eric's pants at one time or another?

"Cross my heart. Scouts honor. All that shit." Hunter held up one hand, his fingers pressed together in a way Tony assumed Scouts would make a promise. He didn't actually know, he'd never been a Scout. Not a Boy Scout. Not a Girl Scout. Not a scout of any kind. But he'd seen people do that in movies before, so it must be right, right? "Even got the scars to prove it. Wanna see?"

"Nah, I'm good." Getting the hots for Eric's best friend/old flame/current flame/whatever-the-fuck-they-were didn't really sound like the best idea, and Tony was the king of bad ideas. So, seeing Hunter's bare chest was definitely out of the question. Tony didn't need that visual on top of the adorable face he'd already seen. "You keep that shit on and sit still. We're almost there."

"Suit yourself." Hunter wriggled in the seat again, as if he'd been preparing to lift his shirt before Tony turned him down. "Point being, don't get us hurt, yeah? As much as you might think it, Eric isn't into the whole mortally wounded thing. Doesn't get him hot, just makes him worried."

"Noted," Tony said, and bit down on his tongue to keep from saying anything more. It'd be better if he didn't get himself going, if he didn't start asking Hunter what the fuck that whole ramble meant. Was it the blood loss talking? Or the venom? Or had there actually been something between them at some point? Well. If the way Eric had looked when he whirled around and found Hunter bleeding was anything to go by, there *had* been. But then why hadn't it—

Britt ripped the door open, and suddenly her hands were

everywhere. Checking Hunter's pulse. Looking at the wound. Holding a flashlight up to his eyes. If Tony didn't know any better, he'd think she was some octopus-like creature with a million fucking arms.

All the while, Hunter leaned back and let her work, even as he said, "I'm fine, baby. I'm all good. I'm fine. Really though, I'm okay." He didn't sound terribly convincing, but Tony could see him trying.

Eric pulled up into the spot next to them, his breaks squealing in the wet and the muck as he slammed the car into park. Tony winced. He knew exactly what kind of damage that could do to the brake pads, and they already didn't sound so hot. He'd have to look at Eric's car in the morning to make sure it was still safe to drive.

"Help me get him into the house," Britt ordered. Not knowing who she was speaking to, both Tony and Eric moved as a unit around the hood of the Mustang.

"I can walk. I'm fine! Stop it! Eric! Make him stop!" Hunter swatted at Tony's head as he manhandled Hunter out of the car. The hair tie slipped from Tony's curls so they fell around his face, getting tangled in Hunter's flailing limbs.

"Knock that the fuck off," Tony growled. By the time he stood again, Hunter's long lean frame in a bridal carry, Tony was panting from the struggle. "Wiggle, and I'll drop you on your ass. I promise it'll hurt just as much as you think it will."

"You're a complete brute." Hunter scowled, but he'd wrapped his free arm around Tony's neck and ceased his struggling.

"Yeah, I get that a lot. Someone get the door." He didn't really have to say it. The kids already had the door propped open, light streaming out into the murky darkness. Britt marched up the walk with only a single backward glance to make sure her husband was secure in Tony's arms, her head held high. Eric scuttled along in the grass, keeping pace, his arms outstretched as if he could catch Hunter if Tony dropped him. "Cut the shit, Marcelino, I got him."

"I'm here just in case." Eric's shoes caught in the grass when he wasn't looking and only some miracle of his Venator reflexes kept him from face planting and likely busting a tooth.

"Chill out, hon, the big guy's got me. Don'tcha?" Hunter asked and tilted his head back to fix Tony with the second-most brilliant smile Tony thought he'd ever seen in his life— only outshone by some of the ones he'd seen on Eric's face. It made Tony's heart stutter in his chest, the toe of his boot scrape oddly against the sidewalk, as if he might stumble over himself. But he caught the reaction before it could get him into trouble and send them both reeling. "Look how he blushes. I like this one, Ricky. I think we should keep him."

"Hunter, shut the fuck up," Eric groused. It was hard to tell in the blue-gray of nighttime, but Tony thought he saw Eric blushing. "You're high out of your mind from all that venom."

"So? What's that saying about drunk lips telling truths?"

"I'm pretty sure it's loose lips sink ships," Bert called from the porch where he leaned beside the door as he watched the whole scene with crossed arms.

"No one asked you, Humbert!" Hunter glared at him as Tony turned to slip into the house, walking sideways so that he wouldn't bang Hunter's head on the doorframe. "Isn't it past your bedtime, little boy?"

When Tony looked back to raise a brow at Eric, Eric shook his head, smiling fondly at Hunter and Bert's antics. He glanced to Britt, but she too watched them with a smirk twitching at her lips, like this was exactly what she'd expect from her husband. Goddess, these folks were weird.

"He's right, I distinctly remember telling you that all of you needed to be in bed before midnight. And here we are."

Eric pulled his sleeve back to reveal an *actual* watch, like an analog one, like an old man. "Two twenty-six."

"Britt called us and woke us up, to make sure we had supplies," the girl who wasn't Finn called, her nose curled in distaste. She was the one who'd answered the door a few days back when Tony brought tacos. Tony wished he'd caught more of the kids' names, but there were other things to worry about, and honestly, he didn't think he liked any of them. Least of all Eric's original brats.

"Everything's on the table in the living room. You can set him on the couch," the other boy said. His pajamas were hopelessly wrinkled at the front like he'd been bunching the too-big T-shirt into a ball and letting it go again in anxiety, the shirt neck stretched and hanging awkwardly around the tawny-brown skin of his throat. "Hunter's gonna be okay, right?"

"Of course he is, Nik." Eric patted the boy's shoulder as he passed, then moved to help Tony settle a loose-limbed Hunter onto the couch. At first, Hunter didn't let go of Tony, his long fingers twisted in Tony's strawberry-blond curls.

"All right, you're gonna have to let go, handsome. You're tearing the goods," Tony murmured, gently trying to unwind Hunter's fingers from his hair.

Hunter blinked for a moment, confused, then smiled dazedly up at Tony as he pulled his hand free, running his fingers along Tony's neck and eliciting a shiver that Tony hoped no one else saw. He needed to get laid. He *definitely* needed to get laid. It was all the adrenaline from fighting vamps side by side with Eric. He was pent up. He just needed to—

"Where's my bro-sef?" Hunter asked, turning glassy eyes on Nik before they darted away, bouncing from one face to the next, to the next.

"We didn't wake him up," Bert said, shifting from foot to foot.

"He would have completely wigged," the girl cut in.

"Like last time," Nik muttered, scuffing his slippered foot on the ground.

Hunter pouted but didn't say anything, not that Britt seemed intent on giving him time to as she pulled out a suture kit and got to work. To his credit, Hunter only winced a bit.

"For crying out loud Hunter, this is *torn*," Britt muttered, shaking her head in exasperation.

"Heh, you should see the other guy." Hunter's eyes were closed where he tilted back over the arm of the couch, his jaw clenched against the pain of Britt's work. Her hands moved quickly and efficiently, but there was a gentleness to her movements. A care Britt may have not shown any of her other patients.

"I'll bet I should." And even if she clicked her tongue and shook her head, she sounded fond. Warmth layered in her tone that Tony decided almost abruptly he should probably not bear witness to.

"He's dust," Hunter bragged.

"Yup. Figured." Britt nodded. She reached back into her bag for a bottle of pills and took Hunter's hand to shake two into his palm, watching as he diligently swallowed them dry. "Did Eric dust them, or was it Tony?"

"Britt! Britt! Britt!" He swatted at her, smacking lightly against her face. Britt nudged his hand away. "It was me! I did it! I dusted them!"

"Uh-huh. Sure."

Hunter let out a long loud whine, which made Eric snort. He had been puttering around the kitchen, heating up something, and had just returned with a bowl of white rice that he set in Hunter's lap. "To soak up the shit in your stomach."

He caught Tony's attention over everything and tilted his head toward the still-open door, saying, "All right you miscreants, to bed with all of you" to the kids who had been watching slack-jawed. "You have class in the morning, and I don't need your professors coming to me bitching when you fall asleep. *Again.*"

"But Eric," they whined in unison then devolved into a million different excuses, all talking at once, so fast and so loud that Tony couldn't pick them apart.

Hunter groaned behind them, holding his head with his free hand, and Eric shushed them so aggressively, Tony saw a bit of spit fly from between his teeth. Then he shooed them toward the steps, and Tony slipped out onto the porch to give Hunter and Britt some privacy and wait for Eric. He reached for the blunt that usually lingered in his pockets without thinking about it, and came up empty, cursing softly.

"About that date," Eric said, poking his head out the still-open door. Tony could hear Hunter and Britt speaking softly to one another, something low and intimate. Their voices combined with the stillness of the night loosened his shoulders, and he slumped back against the building.

"What about it?" Tony asked. He'd pulled his lighter from his back pocket, flipping it open and closed, open and closed, to keep his hands busy when he had nothing else to do. He wasn't going to get his hopes up. Not after what he'd seen tonight. Eric was clearly still hung up on Hunter. And Hunter was . . . whatever he was. Married? But also still kind of goo-goo-eyed for Eric. How did that even work? Had Hunter cheated? No. He didn't seem the type. And Eric didn't seem the type to let it happen either. So that was out. Then what was their deal? Did Britt and Hunter have an open relationship?

"I was thinking." Eric produced a little blown-glass pipe from somewhere on his person. He lit the dried weed in the end and sucked down a mouthful of smoke before offering it to Tony, who took it gratefully.

"You were thinking?" Tony pressed and took his own hit off the pipe.

"I was thinking," Eric repeated, the smoke curling from his chapped lips, "that we should try the date thing again. Just one though. Cause, like, there's too much else going on."

"You think one is gonna be enough to get me out of your system, pretty boy?" Quirking a blond brow, Tony leaned his head back against the side of the building and smiled at Eric, sharp and sly. The light from inside the house cast half of Eric's face in shadows, hiding it, but what Tony could see of it was just as beautiful as that first night in the graveyard. And yeah, okay, maybe something had gone down between Eric and Hunter, but whatever it was, whatever feelings lingered, they weren't going to stop Tony from trying to slide in there.

"Don't push your luck, McMahon."

"Oh baby, that's what I do best." Tony grabbed Eric by the wrist and yanked him in close, his hand slipping into his back pocket to grind their hips together as he pressed his lips against Eric's, aggressive and biting.

Eric laughed into the kiss, the sound spreading warmth through Tony that chased away the cold in his fingertips, still clutching the pipe. "All right. All right," Eric murmured, pulling back in spite of the soft whine from Tony's lips. "I've got to go look after Hunter and Britt, and you need to head home to your sister. We'll uh—we'll continue this later. Yeah?"

"Yeah." Tony swallowed roughly, pressing the pipe into Eric's hands as he slid away from him and toward the stairs. "Tomorrow. I'll pick you up at eight?"

"Make it five."

"Are we eating at grandpa times now?"

"Nah, I just want to get out on patrol before it gets too dark. That cool?"

"Yeah. Cool." Tony shook his head, laughing to himself.

"He's asleep," Britt said from where she was in the door all of the sudden. Her face was drawn, blond hair a tangled mess, but her hands were steady where they gripped the doorframe. "You should come in and let me check you out. Tony?"

"Nah. I'm good. Just a couple scrapes and bruises." Tony shrugged her off. "I'll have Lu look me over when I get home. It's good practice."

Britt nodded and turned to head back inside.

"I'll see you around, pretty boy." He loped down the steps, turning once to blow a kiss to Eric over his shoulder before he raced to his car.

CHAPTER 18

A HEADACHE POUNDED in Eric's temples and made it feel like his brain was pressing out against his skull, threatening to pop his eyes out of the sockets. He pressed the heels of his palms into his eyes, trying to hold them in, but it did little good to relieve the pressure. It just made him groan more.

"Definitely didn't smoke enough last night." He should have learned his lesson a long time ago—any tiny nick of a vamp's teeth was enough to send the venom rioting through his veins. And of course, he never got the fun loopy bit, like Hunter had—gotta love that Venator gene—just the hangover. Just the rolling of his stomach as he smelled someone frying eggs downstairs, and the throbbing in his head. All the after-effects, none of the fun. Because wasn't that the way? Britt posited it was a byproduct of his chronic migraines, which were a byproduct of too many knocks to the head in his teen years, which were a byproduct of being a vampire hunter. So . . . "Fuck this."

Eric rolled to look at the clock on his nightstand and groaned at the time that glared back at him. He'd slept in by two whole hours. The kids would be up and off to class already. But then . . . who was cooking downstairs?

Dishes rattled, and he could make out someone's voice, lighter and higher in tone than either Britt or Hunter ever boasted, even when Hunter was high off his ass and being theatrical as fuck. "Fucking Kalla." Because who else could it be? Ava didn't usually come by the dorm if she could help it; she said the wards of Moondale U gave her the wig.

With *another* groan, Eric practically slid from the bed, only pushing himself to his feet at the last minute, saving himself from collapsing onto the floor among the clothes he'd shucked off last night right before throwing himself into bed. Last night's jeans caught on his foot as he made his way to the door, and he had to stop and hop about on one leg to kick them away before continuing.

He stumbled only slightly on the stairs as his vision swam dangerously. *Maybe I should have taken Britt up on the antidote.* Not that he'd ever needed it before. And besides, he couldn't take any other substances when he took it. With how little sleep he'd been getting over the last few days, that was out of the question. He couldn't afford for the nightmares to keep him awake.

Still scrubbing at his eyes, he shuffled toward the kitchen where Britt, Hunter, and Kalla sat around the table.

"All I'm saying is, I don't think it's a good idea to let McMahon keep hanging around Eric," Kalla said. Her back was to him, so she hadn't seen him yet, which probably wouldn't have changed anything. Kalla, like Ava, had absolutely zero brain-to-mouth filter. Why did Eric surround himself with women like that? The world may never know. Except in Kalla's case, the stuff that came out of her mouth wasn't spunky or sarcastic—it was usually laced with a hint of judgment. And not the fond, fun kind Ava liked to direct toward Eric. No, this kind made his stomach churn threateningly.

"No one's *letting* him or me do anything," Eric said as he made his way across the kitchen toward the far corner. He needed coffee if he was going to put up with Kalla this early in the morning. He needed coffee period. But, like, especially when Kalla was involved. Fuck. And he'd thought he was going to marry her once upon a time. Although, granted, he'd always had a thing for women with ambition, and Kalla had made sheriff at a young age.

"Eric," Kalla sighed, and although Eric wasn't facing her, he could imagine the way she had lifted her head higher, preparing to take whatever he said next on the chin. "I'm just—"

"Worried about me." She'd said it enough that Eric could almost repeat the speech from memory now. It'd been five years since they'd broken it off, but she still worried about him. Which would be sweet if it wasn't so frustrating, if it didn't make him feel like on some level, she thought she was more mature than him, better qualified to make these decisions *for* him. Maybe she was. She'd always been smarter. Gotten the grades to go away to a *good* college. "I know."

"It's just because I care," Kalla insisted, but when Eric turned around, he saw Hunter and Britt share a knowing look, and he was glad Ava hadn't made the trip over with them. She hated when Kalla said shit like that, and to be fair, so did Eric. Five years wasn't enough to take the sting out of the thought that Kalla cared, just not *enough* to stay with him.

"Right." Eric took a sip from his scalding coffee, let it burn all the way down, settle in his stomach along with the acid and the bile from the night before. He was definitely going to be sick before his classes later. Damn it. Today was gonna suck. "But believe it or not, Kalla, I'm an adult."

He saw Hunter wince out of the corner of his eye, open his mouth to maybe say something, and be kicked into silence under the table by Britt. Good. It was better they not get involved if he was going to face off against Kalla and her pissiness. They didn't *all* need her mad at them. Although, knowing Kalla, she'd probably take her mood out on all of them anyway. She was like that sometimes. Even when she actively tried not to be. Which she did, these days, after Ava pointed it out to her one too many times. Didn't change her base nature, though.

"Well, I know that." Kalla huffed, shifting in her seat. She was fighting it, railing against the urge to tell him off, to say something else cutting. Eric was proud of her, really, and maybe he'd have told her so if he wasn't so fucking tired.

"Good. Then you know that trying to tell me who I can and cannot date—"

Kalla opened her mouth, her eyes gone wide in something that almost seemed like panic.

"—would be a gross overreach of our current relationship," he continued, not giving her a chance to voice her protests, repeating exactly what Ava had said to him the first time Eric had gone out on a date post–the whole Kalla/Hunter fiasco. Of course, Kalla had been right about that girl; she was just trying to see how much money was left in his trust fund, but she didn't have to say as much. "Don't you think? All things considered?"

Kalla's nose curled, and she looked like she was biting down hard on her tongue, but she nodded anyway.

"Toast?" Britt asked when the silence stretched on for too long, offering Eric a plate of soggy-looking toast. "To soak up all that crap in your belly."

"No solids. Not yet." Eric shook his head and took another long slurp of coffee.

Hunter stood from the table, grabbing a piece of toast on his way, and paced across the kitchen with long strides, ignoring the way Eric tried to curl back into the counter. He knew exactly what was coming, he wasn't stupid. And besides, Hunter had telegraphed his movements perfectly, giving Eric the chance to pull away and hide if he wanted to. Which they both knew he never would, because he didn't back down from a challenge.

"Doctor's orders," Hunter said, voice slightly raspy from the cotton mouth left over by the venom antidote Britt had shoved down his throat the night before. He wriggled the piece of toast in front of Eric's face, making soft airplane noises until Eric took a begrudging bite and swallowed it in spite of the slight gag. "Good boy."

A shiver raced up Eric's spine, and he took another big bite of toast to keep anyone from noticing, then he snatched what was left of it from Hunter's hand to stuff into his mouth. Fuck. This was going to be a long day.

"I'll get you some meds," Britt volunteered, a look of sympathy on her features as she pushed back from the table. "You should head out, Kalla. You're already running it close."

It was a total ploy, and the look Britt shot him told Eric she knew it was, but it got Kalla out the door with a soft curse, and Eric was so delighted he could have kissed Britt.

———

It only got worse from there. The kids were loud and rambunctious as they filed into his classroom hours later, their voices echoing off the inside of Eric's head. The pounding had dulled for a little while, thanks to the food Hunter and Britt force-fed him, Kalla fucking off to go to work, caffeine, and some truly impressive pain killers from Britt's med kit. Only to return if not in full force than at least with double the intensity when Bert's voice went up two octaves as he argued about something with Kate and Nik.

What about? Eric had no fucking idea. Some science-y shit. Could be nuclear physics, for all he understood.

"Sit down and shut up," Eric grumbled, rubbing at his temples and adjusting his glasses. He'd had to forgo his contacts because of how dry his eyes felt, but the arms of the glasses dug in above his ears, and honestly, fuck this shit. He wanted to go back to bed. But *nooooo*, he had a date, and patrol, and *responsibilities*.

"Mister Marcelino," a soft voice said to his right, and he

looked over to see Lu standing at his side, Finn hovering near her shoulder as if Lu needed moral support or some shit. And while that was adorable, it was also kind of upsetting. Eric didn't like to think that his kids were afraid to talk to him.

"Just Eric is fine, Lu." With another rub at the bridge of his nose, Eric lowered his glasses and fixed the two girls with a tired smile. He didn't usually tell the kids to call him Eric; usually he tried to get them to call him Mister Marcelino, out of respect. But Lu and Finn were good kids. Hadn't caused him any trouble. Yet. And besides, if he let the other little shits get away with it, he kind of had to let them all get away with it, didn't he?

"Right," Lu said, licking her lips, "Eric."

"What's up, Lu?" Her eyes flicked to the rest of the class, and Eric glanced over to them as well; the others were too entrenched in their debate to even notice. Which was probably good if the antsy way Lu shifted from side to side told him anything.

Finn gave her a nudge, and Lu scoffed, rolling her eyes. "My brother said he's not picking you up tonight."

Eric quirked a brow. "Why not?"

"Cause he wants you to bring your car by the shop. Something about brake pads, I don't know. But tell him I'm not your messenger pigeon." She slid a torn-off slip of paper across his podium to him with a number hastily scrawled onto it. Her cheeks were a ruddy shade of red, and Eric couldn't tell if she was angry at Tony for making her ferry his message to Eric, or if she kind of liked being involved that way. It was always a toss-up with teenagers, Eric knew from experience.

"I'll let him know." But Eric couldn't fight the small smile that tugged at the corners of his lips. It was kind of cute, actually, the thought of Tony talking about him over the breakfast table with his sister. It was . . . cozy. Enough that Eric could almost—*almost*—forget the headache pressing at his temples threatening to become a full-blown migraine.

"You do that." She nodded once, sharp and curt.

"Thanks for ferrying it along, this time." Although he wasn't sure what "something about brake pads" meant? What even were brake pads? Were they like regular pads? He shook himself; there was no point trying to understand car guys. That way lay madness.

"Sure." Lu's lips twitched, like she was losing the battle against her own smile, then Finn nudged her again. "And you need to like, be nice to him and shit. Okay?"

And wasn't that the cutest fucking shovel talk *ever*?!

"I'll do my level best. I promise." He held his hand up to her, pinky out as if to pinky swear.

She scoffed, rolling her eyes again—because fucking teenagers, man—but took his extended pinky, gave it a quick shake, up and down once, then spun on her heel to take her seat between Finn and Chase as if nothing at all had happened. There was a beat of awkwardness before she and Finn—as a fucking unit, like something out of a fucking horror movie—reached into their bags, pulled out the exact same neon purple notebook, turned to a page, and fixed him with mirroring expressions of *Well? We're waiting*. Because sure. Why not. Eric needed that creepy-as-fuck mental image in his brain for the foreseeable future.

"All right, shitheads." He clapped once, sharply, to break up the argument that seemed to be heading toward a fight in the back of the classroom. "Everybody take your seats. It's time to get started."

Chapter 19

WHEN ERIC PULLED up to the garage a couple of hours later—after having to chase off his kids and lie to their faces because he wasn't dealing with the level of judgment he'd get out of Bert for going on a date with Tony when Bert had actively decided he despised Tony—the front office was dark. The place had probably been closed for at least a half hour, since it was almost six, and businesses in Ironport tended to roll up their welcome mats long before it got dark during the winter.

The normies might not have *known* about vampires, but they knew that the rate of deaths and disappearances was high in the winter, and they weren't taking any chances. Plus, it was like instinct to fear the undead—and dead, if he was honest. That's why necromancy was so frowned upon. It was built into every humanoid being—folk and mortal alike. You know, right up until they were faced with a vampire oozing charm, charisma, and a whole lot of sex appeal. Then they couldn't get to a dark alley fast enough. Eric would never understand humans.

One of the bays down at the end was partway open, light and music with a heavy bass spilling out from below the door into the night. Eric shut his car door, wincing when it slammed, and the sound bounced into the mostly quiet night. In his pocket, he tightened his grip around a stake. Not that he actually thought he was going to be attacked out in the open like this, but there were so many weird things going on lately, it paid to be cautious.

"Hello?" he called, steps slow and measured as he paced toward the open bay. Tony was supposed to be there, waiting for him, but that didn't mean something hadn't gone wrong in the meantime. That didn't mean a vampire hadn't attacked and left a bloody mess for Eric to find. It wouldn't be the first time—memories of his grandmother swimming in a pool of her own blood, wasteful, but a clear message, flashed through his mind—and he doubted it would be the last. Vamps were like that.

He held his breath, readying himself to swallow whatever noise of terror he might make, as he shifted close enough so the light from inside bathed his sneakers in warm yellow, chasing off the cold gray-blue of twilight.

"Hello?"

"Hello!" Tony shouted from inside, then his head appeared in the crack between the garage door and the ground, stray bits of long curly hair falling into his face. A smear of grease across his cheek seemed to make his eyes sparkle even more. *Unfairly hot is what that is.* "You gonna stand out in the cold, or are you gonna bring 'er around and let me take a look at her?"

"I—What?" Eric frowned.

"The car." The bay door was loud as Tony pushed it open further to reveal the rest of him. He was in a pair of olive-green coveralls—a color a lot of people couldn't pull off, but seemed to work *really* well for Tony McMahon, too well—with the sleeves tied around his waist to show off the tight fitted tank top he had on beneath. All of which were covered in grease smears. Which was, again, unfairly hot.

"I thought this was a date." Eric's stomach did an annoyingly familiar swoop toward his feet. Disappointment scuttled awkwardly across his nerves, doing a crab walk to his spine where he curled in on himself a little, hoping to look casual when he felt anything but. Goddess, he was so fucking stupid, wasn't he? Of course it wasn't a date. Of course it was just—

"It is." Tony blinked at him for a moment in confusion, then a smile split his face, and he licked over his lips. "What? Did you think I was just gonna fix your car for free?"

"I—What?" Eric asked for the second time, like an idiot.

Tony laughed, his arms curling around his stomach like he could hold the sound in by hugging himself. He couldn't. It was a full-bellied laugh, loud and bouncing off the walls of the garage. Obnoxious. It made Eric's toes curl in his shoes. He didn't think he'd ever seen Tony so open, so free. Although, they hadn't known each other long, so maybe that wasn't saying much. Maybe he'd open up more once they—

"Just pull that beat-up mom-mobile you call a car into the bay, and let me take a look at her," Tony said when his laughter had eased off, although it still shook the words a little. "I might not be able to deal with the dent that vamp put in it yet, but we'll see."

Eric wasn't sure what to say to that, so he turned and headed back to his car to follow directions. Tony was waiting for him in the middle of the bay, his tongue poking out between his teeth as he waved Eric through onto the lift and held up his hands to signal for him to stop once the car was in position. With the engine shut off, Eric climbed out and went around to stand by Tony as he popped the hood.

"I've got pizza coming. You're good with vegetarian, right?" Tony said from where he'd leaned over the car to get a look inside, careful not to touch anything while the engine was still hot.

"Is that your idea of a date?" Eric teased, prodding Tony's calf with his toe as he took a step back to cross his arms over his chest. "Pizza and a tune-up?"

"What? You aren't having a good time ogling my ass?"

Tony bit back, wriggling his hips for emphasis. And yeah. Okay. So maybe Eric was totally all right with spending the night eating pizza, listening to chill music, and ogling Tony's ass. Yesterday had been a long-ass day, and maybe this was exactly what he needed out of life right now.

"I didn't say that." Eric shrugged. He turned on his heel and went to drop down onto the bench that someone had dragged into the center of the empty bay beside the one where Tony was working. "What's with the music? This wasn't what you were listening to when I pulled up. I didn't think you were a jazz guy."

"Hm?" Tony asked, his head popping up from where he was half hidden by the hood to raise strawberry-blond brows at Eric. "Oh. Lu said you had a headache earlier, so I thought maybe you'd like something a little more . . . I dunno, relaxing?"

And wasn't that the sweetest thing? Eric hadn't noticed when the music changed after he pulled up, too keyed up trying to make sure he wasn't about to walk in on something nasty, but Tony must have swapped it shortly after he heard Eric's first hello. And that was . . . that was so fucking considerate, it almost made Eric want to cry. When was the last time one of his dates had done something nice like that for him?

"Don't let it go to your head, Marcelino. I just know guys like you aren't up for bangin' if they don't feel well." Tony was back beneath the hood, hiding his face among the metal. Eric wondered if he was trying to hide a blush, or if he actually meant the crude words coming out of his mouth. It was kind of hard to get a read on Tony. Especially when most of the time they spent together was either fighting or fucking. In fact, this might have been the longest running conversation they'd had so far without any bodily fluids being spilled. Aside from the one they'd had about Janet.

"You have a type then." Eric curled his legs up on the bench, folding them into a careful lotus pose as he shifted around, trying to get comfortable. It wasn't working. The bench was hard. His ass was going to wind up going numb long before the pizza ever got there. And he'd probably have lower back pain the following day if he wasn't careful. Ah. The joys of being in your thirties. "Good to know."

A soft choking noise came from somewhere under the hood, and Eric couldn't swallow the smile that overtook his face. It was cute how flustered Tony got. Although he always tried to cover it with some kind of crude—

"Yeah, I guess I'm into MILFs in fuck-me jeans."

—comment.

"These are not fuck-me jeans!" Eric gasped.

"Tell that to your ass."

Eric stood from the bench to spin around in a circle like a dog chasing its tail, trying to look back at his ass. "They're just *regular* jeans. I got them from the Gap."

"Of course you did, Mama Bear." Tony laughed as he pulled himself from beneath the hood and wiped his hands on a rag that he'd had tucked into his back pocket. "Well, looks like you need an oil change, your windshield wiper fluid needs to be refilled, and you need new spark plugs. So I guess I'll be getting to the brakes and the dent another night."

"I told you one date, one date only. We aren't—"

"Sure we're not, baby." Tony shot him a wink, his tongue between his teeth. Boots thudding against the ground, he made his way over to the towering tool cabinet to pull out what he needed. "Good thing for you, we've got most of what you need floating around here. Miracle really that Ralph keeps such tidy stock. You come here often to get 'er serviced?"

"I usually go to a place out in Moondale." Not because they were cheaper—they weren't. But he felt safer not having a car when he was behind the wards of the town to the east of them. The beamer up on a lift with pieces taken out of it— unusable for a quick getaway—always made him itchy in his skin, like it was too tight. And even now, knowing that Tony was there and would have his back didn't help much at all.

"When was the last time?"

Eric shrugged, even though Tony wasn't facing him to see it. "It wasn't making any weird noises yet."

Tony stopped what he was doing, his hands deep in a drawer, and turned to look at Eric over his shoulder. "You're telling me you only bring your car in to have it serviced when it starts making noises?"

"Yeah. Or when the check engine light comes on." Now that he said that out loud, Eric could see how that might be potentially problematic. He relied on his car not just to get him where he needed to go, but also as an escape, a weapons cabinet, and a safe haven all rolled into one. His car had saved Hunter's life, with the wards scrawled into the doors to keep dead things out. So yeah, shame on him. "Fixing the dent . . . is that going to require a new panel?"

Tony's eyes narrowed, but he let the subject be changed. "No, I should be able to pop the dent out and buff the paint. Why?"

"I'll have to swing by Ava's afterward, to make sure the warding marks are still working after you've done that. Hunter said it was good for now, a little weak but still enough to keep most vamps out." Ava would probably only grumble about having to repair the wards, especially as the attack had happened outside of her business. Which he wouldn't hesitate to remind her of.

Another set of headlights pulled up outside of the garage, and Tony tilted his head as if listening to the car. Eric did the same, sniffing the air and looking for the telltale smell of death, decay, blood, blood, blood.

"That'll be the pizza," Tony said after a minute. "You make yourself comfy, princess. I'll go grab us some sustenance." Then he was gone, long strides eating up the space between the toolbox and the bay door. When he came back, he had a big brown box in his hands and a smile on his face. "I got extra cheese."

"Oh baby, oh baby, you really know the way to a man's heart." Eric laughed, shaking his head. There was a smile on Tony's face, sharp and feral, and Eric vowed that before the end of the night, he was going to find out what it felt like pressed against his skin. But first . . . pizza.

Chapter 20

"COME ON, PRETTY BOY," Tony hummed against the skin beneath Eric's ear, his voice a low, drawling murmur, "let me fuck you. You know I'll make it good."

"You said you didn't have everything we'd need." Eric stuffed another big bite of pizza into his mouth where he sat in front of Tony on the back bench seat of his beamer. The handle for the door dug into Tony's back, which sucked, but Eric was a line of lean muscle against his chest, ass pressed into his hips. Tony didn't see where there was anything to complain about.

"We'll make it work." Tony had given up any pretense of eating dinner a long time ago, instead splitting his attention between chasing Eric's moles down his neck with his teeth, and running his fingers along Eric's stomach under his shirt. Fingers tracing ever closer to Eric's nipples. Tony wondered how long it would take before Eric noticed that's what he was doing. "Please, I've always wanted to fuck against a BMW."

"Good Goddess, fucking car guys," Eric huffed, but there was fondness in his tone. "I suppose you want to bend me over the engine block or whatever?"

"Fuck. Who taught you the words *engine block*?" Tony hissed, his hips shifting a little to grind against Eric's ass where it was pressed into his crotch. Whoever had taught Eric that phrase ought to be given a winning lotto ticket, or a

Nobel Prize, or something. That hadn't been what he'd had in mind, not originally, but now that he was thinking about it . . . Yeah. He could probably make that work.

"I know things about cars," Eric said. He sounded defensive, but Tony would swear there was a laugh in the words as he leaned over to wipe his greasy hands on Tony's coveralls. Little shit.

"Sure, you do, sweetheart," Tony agreed warmly, his hands moving to fiddle with the button on Eric's jeans now that the pizza was gone. He wondered if he could get Eric to talk car to him . . . Later. That was a thought for later. "So, what do ya say?"

"That means we have to get up, doesn't it?" Eric groaned, turning his face to press it into Tony's neck. Tony had managed to get his jeans undone and was wriggling his hand beneath the fly to brush against Eric's slowly hardening cock.

"Yes, it does. Unless you wanna fuck around in the back seat of your car like we're sixteen. I'm game for whatever." Tony shrugged. He would prefer they not do it in the back-seat—his hip would make him pay for it later if he did—but if that's where Eric was most comfortable, far be it for Tony to make him move. Besides, he kind of liked the idea of getting Eric off from behind like this, his ass wriggling against Tony's crotch, the seams of his jeans rubbing Tony through the thin coveralls.

"Fuck that. C'mon," Eric said, scooting for the door and out of Tony's reach. "But you're letting me get you off this time."

"Aye, aye, Princess." Tony gave a little salute and followed him out of the car. They didn't make it far though before Tony had grabbed Eric by the belt loops and spun them around, pushing and shoving until Eric was pressed against the door. "You can get me off after, yeah?"

"Yeah," Eric mumbled. He was already wriggling, his hips pressing forward into the metal as Tony worked him out of his jeans. He leaned through the window of the front and dug around for a moment until he'd pulled a packet out of the glove box to flap over his shoulder at Tony.

Lube. Tony grinned to himself, licking his teeth. "Maybe I should start calling you a Boy Scout. You're always prepared."

"Not now, I'm not. Hence the lube." He shimmied his hips, those fuck-me mom jeans sliding down his legs along with the pair of boxer briefs he had on underneath to show off his pale rounded ass, also littered in moles.

The sight brought Tony up short, his movements—which to that moment had his coveralls and boxers halfway down his thighs—stilling as his throat ran dry. Eric leaned forward more, braced his hands on the open window and wriggled his ass.

Fuck. He's going to send me to an early grave with all that.

"You good back there?" Eric asked, a smile in his voice. He knew exactly what he was doing to Tony. Asshole.

Tony growled, ripped open the packet of lube, and spread it between his fingers quickly before he shuffled forward, kicking his coveralls off in the process. He leaned in, his hips pressing against Eric's ass, grinding against him as his fingers slipped between Eric's cheeks to brush over his rim. "Shut up."

"Make me." Eric arched further into him.

"You asked for it." Tony bit Eric's earlobe, savoring the shudder that wracked through him as he slowly pressed a finger into him, stretching his rim little by little. "Relax, sweetheart, I got you."

Eric made a soft sound, a cross between a moan and grumbled agreement, but Tony felt Eric's rim give a little more, and his finger slipped in to the knuckle.

"Good boy," he murmured, earning a strangled whine from Eric, and Tony made a mental note to come back to that as he continued to work Eric open with his fingers.

Twisting, and turning, and working up to two fingers, then three, before Eric's hips were jerking back against Tony, fucking himself on Tony's fingers. Until Tony curled them, brushing against Eric's prostate, and Eric went limp against the car, held up only by the fingers inside him and where Tony had plastered their bodies together, pressing Eric into the metal.

"You gonna get off on this, baby? Just this?" Tony asked, his breath coming in hard pants as he rubbed his thighs together to try to relieve some of the pressure building there. It'd be better if he could touch himself, but he'd promised Eric, so he waited. Kept winding Eric up, and up, until he pressed down hard on that bundle of nerves and ripped a moan from Eric's throat, sending him over the edge, the sound almost enough to get Tony off.

They stayed for a while, pressed against the car, Tony's hips rubbing idly against Eric's ass, metal now splattered with Eric's spend, until Eric got his legs under him again. Then he took a deep breath, pushed off from the car with a breathy "Your turn" and grabbed Tony by the hips, pressing him back, back, back, until his calves hit the bench and he flopped down on it.

"How can I touch you?" Eric murmured, dropping to his knees, big doe eyes pinning Tony in place, making his breath lodge in his chest. When was the last time someone had asked him that? When was the last time someone had given two fucks about him getting off? He couldn't . . . he couldn't remember.

"Just . . ." Tony breathed, trying to get his wits about him, but it was hard to do with the way Eric stared at him. His cheeks still flushed, his eyes shining bright from his own release. He was so fucking beautiful, and earnest. "Just no— no penetration. Not . . . not there."

"I can work with that." Eric nodded, once, firmly. No questions asked. He started with a kiss to the inside of Tony's knee. Whisper soft. A whine crawled up Tony's chest. He wasn't . . . he wasn't going to last if Eric kept treating him that way, soft, with kid gloves, like he fucking *mattered*. But fuck off, he wasn't going to stop him either.

Eric traced a line up Tony's thigh in kisses and nibbles so soft, they made Tony break out in shivers, his skin raising in goosebumps. Made the fire in his belly bloom hotter. A blazing inferno by the time Eric's mouth and fingers got to where Tony really needed them. Tony leaned back and almost toppled off the bench at the first brush of Eric's tongue against him, close enough to a head injury that Eric grabbed him by the hips and turned him so he was long ways on the bench instead.

"Lay back, baby, let me take care of you," Eric murmured, gently nudging Tony until he was braced on his elbows on the bench.

"Yeah. Yeah. Okay." Tony let Eric spread his legs wider, Eric's nails digging in a little, the gentle bite of pleasure-pain making all of Tony's nerves buzz, before Eric leaned forward and put his tongue back to work.

Wet, and warm, and so slow, Eric took Tony apart, putting that pretty mouth of his to good use. All the while brushing his fingers up and down Tony's thighs, massaging the muscles, raking nails gently down the skin. His teeth grazing Tony, making him twitch one moment then lurch forward the next with a soft suck. Until Tony's arms gave out beneath him, and he flopped back against the bench, his legs jittering.

It took a while—maybe longer than it would have before the hormones—but Eric didn't let up, not until Tony came with a cry, turning to absolute putty against the hard surface of the bench, his throat dry, spots dancing before his eyes.

———

They wound up sprawled together across the floor of the garage post-sex and spark plug repair. Which was super unsanitary, Tony recognized, but it wasn't the first time he'd had sex in a garage, and it wasn't going to be the last. Not with the way he and Eric were going. Already, he had a list of things he wanted to do to Eric's car—and to his person. There was no replacing the car, he knew that. Eric wouldn't allow it. Even if he did have the disposable income to do so. But he could do with a remote start, some new tires, maybe even a paint job. Tony was thinking racing stripes. Silly, but fun. Then there was *lots* of sex stuff. A list that went far beyond the car stuff, half of which he probably couldn't name without blushing.

Tony was . . . well he was going to do everything in his power to make Eric as comfortable as possible. Even if the only things he could do were work on his car and fuck him into a state of calm.

"You know," Eric said, brushing his fingers across Tony's bare collarbones from where he lay beneath him. "We probably should have saved some of that energy for patrol."

"Bullshit." Tony pressed the word into Eric's neck, worrying the skin into a bruise he'd started somewhere around the time he got Eric out of his fuck-me jeans. Which were really just mom jeans. Tony was into male MILFs, what of it? Okay, maybe he was just into Eric. It was kind of hard not to be with the way he looked. All big doe eyes and floppy hair, coiled like a spring ready to release and kill anything and everything in his path to protect the people he loved. Goddess above and below, if Tony didn't have a type before, he sure as fuck did now. "This'll mean your head is clear when we get out there. You're all fed and sated. We'll be at the top of our game."

"If you say so." Eric shrugged, but he didn't push Tony away as he wriggled his hips against him again.

"I do say so." There was still work to do on Eric's car. Oil change and brake pads. The brake pads were a genuine concern. Maybe he should have started with that. "You're leaving your car with me tonight. I'll drive you home, and you can pick it up tomorrow evening."

"Is that how you're going to ensure a second date? You're gonna hold my car hostage?" Eric poked at Tony's side, making him squirm a little when his bony-ass finger dug into his ribs.

"Is it working?"

Eric's head flopped back against his rolled-up coat that they'd been using as a pillow, because *Proper neck support is important, Tony. What the fuck, do you expect me to just lie here on the hard ground without any kind of comfort? I won't be able to fucking walk tomorrow. And not in the good way.* His neck stretched out long and inviting, the moles like constellations on his skin, but in reverse. If Tony were a vamp, he'd probably have had a bite by now. Hell, he didn't drink blood, and Eric's neck was already littered in little marks. Most of them would go away by the following day, but not the purpling bruise Tony had been working on beneath his ear. That made something possessive and feral settle low in Tony's belly. Which was probably a bad thing. Eric arched a little more, stretching out his back. *Definitely a bad thing.*

"You're going to spoil me with all this," Eric complained, but he didn't sound bothered about it. "Fixing my car, and pizza, and sex. What's a guy supposed to do with all that?"

Tony didn't have an answer, so instead he said, "I'm gonna look into getting you a remote start. It's too fucking cold here to not have one" as he stood and pulled his jeans back on.

Eric swatted at him, shooting him a baleful glare, but he didn't argue. Just rolled onto his side to start looking for his own pants. Then asked, "Patrol?"

With a glance outside at the dark that had settled over Ironport while they'd been too wrapped up in each other to give a flying fuck about vampires, Tony frowned. "We should probably go back to those warehouses and see what the fuck that pack was about. It was too many to be one nest."

"Yeah." Eric was on his feet, hopping on one leg and then the other as he yanked his jeans up. "And they ran away when they caught sight of me and Hunter. It was *weird*."

Tony nodded his agreement but didn't say anything else as he finished getting back into his clothes, the coveralls hung up on the rack in his locker. He was spinning his keys around his finger, his jacket already on by the time Eric got himself together. "You ready to go make some dead things a lil bit deader, sweetheart?"

"I thought you'd never ask." Eric pressed a kiss into Tony's jaw and followed him to the cherry-red Mustang parked out in the lot.

CHAPTER 21

OVER THE WEEKS that followed there were other dates, other repairs to Eric's old beamer. New brake pads, sure, but less safety-focused things too. A remote start, which was great; Eric could push the button in the morning while he was enjoying his coffee on the couch, and the car would be perfectly heated up by the time he made his way out to it for class. And Tony had decided to replace the speakers, solving the issue of Eric not being able to use his radio. And a million other repairs Eric didn't fully understand.

They didn't spend all their time at the garage either. It seemed like Tony had made it his mission to do all those weird little things people usually did on first dates. Dinners and bowling. No long walks on the beach—it was too damn cold for that, and besides, the beaches in Ironport were notoriously small and kind of grimy until they got cleaned up in spring. But there was one very awkward instance of milkshake sharing that turned into more of a competition and ended in them both getting brain freezes, and that was fun. There was also plenty of cuddling and fucking, which . . . *nice.* Eric hadn't realized exactly how touch starved he'd been over the last couple of years, not until Tony's fingers settled warm on his wrist over-long while he was showing Eric how to change his own spark plugs, and Eric had felt a tingle go up his arm, a rush of endorphins settling into his brain.

But that wasn't all there was. It wasn't just the physical. Eric was . . . he was having *fun*.

When was the last time he'd been able to say that about a date? Sure, he'd been on plenty of them since Kalla broke it off. Because he was a glutton for punishment it seemed, or maybe Ava was right about him and Eric just couldn't be by himself. He wasn't built for it. Some people weren't. He needed to be in a relationship. Having his friend group helped—he and Ava were ridiculously co-dependent—but it wasn't the same, would never be the same, as having a significant other in his life. He had "abandonment issues," or so Ava said anyway.

Still, it had been a nice couple of weeks. And as much as Eric knew it wasn't a good idea, he was getting used to having Tony around. To hearing the rev of his car as he pulled up just after classes let out, ready to take Eric out on another date before they had to hit patrol. It was almost like having a family again.

That same growling, churning sound was what pulled Eric to a stop when he was putting the lasagna in the oven for the kids. Three pans, because leftovers made the world go round. He peeked out the kitchen window to see Tony and Lu climbing from the Mustang, a reusable grocery bag slung over Tony's forearm.

Eric beat him to the door, ripping it open before Tony even had a chance to knock, a bright smile splitting his face. "What's this?"

"I heard you were making your famous lasagna for the kids, so I thought we could do a date night in. I brought wine." Tony held the sack up to let Eric make out the shape of two wine bottles in the porch lights.

"A bottle for each of us, I see." Eric stepped back from the door, letting Tony and Lu inside. Lu hardly took the time to remove her shoes before she was running into the house to tackle Finn in a tight hug. Eric didn't know when it had happened—he'd been so busy with other things lately—but the two seemed thick as thieves these days. "What about patrol?"

"You'll burn it off quick. I'll make sure of that." Tony moved onto his toes a little so he could look down at Eric as he pressed him back against the wall of the hall where everyone kept their shoes. His free arm resting against the paneling, looming over Eric. Making him feel small . . . prey more than predator. His toes curled in his bunny slippers. There was a beat, a breath, where Eric's eyes flickered over Tony's face, wondering if he'd pull back, play tease like he did sometimes, or press his body so firmly against Eric's that they left a fucking dent in the wall.

But Tony didn't leave him waiting long. He tilted his chin just so, dipping down to meet Eric where he'd slid down the wall, and captured Eric's lips in a biting, bruising kiss that had too much teeth and not enough tongue, but was somehow really fucking good all the same. Something fell in the main room, drawing them apart. Eric just managed to choke back a whine.

"Plus," Tony murmured, nudged at Eric's jaw in a little nuzzle before he completely extricated himself, leaving Eric's front feeling too cold too suddenly, "with all the carbs? We're fine."

"Hmm . . ." Eric patted Tony's chest, nudging him back so he didn't trip over the shoes left behind by the kids on his way to the kitchen. "Well, if I'm eaten I think we both know who people are gonna blame."

"If you're eaten, I'm going to be doing the eating," Tony muttered, following Eric as he went to open the oven and check on the trays of lasagna. A few more minutes yet.

"Maybe later, big guy. For now, you need to open one of those bottles of wine, and then go check to make sure the kids didn't break anything while they set up for movie night."

There was much grumbling, some tugging at Eric's hips as

if Tony were trying to make Eric follow him upstairs, their dinner be damned. But Eric held firm, and in the end, Tony headed into the living room to make sure the kids hadn't caused too much trouble.

Dinner was dished out shortly after. They all settled into the living room with their bowls and a piece of garlic bread each. The kids took the floor, dragging cushions from the furniture in the study and the other couch to build one massive pile of pillows and blankets. While Eric and Tony curled up together on the couch, Eric's feet tucked under Tony's thigh to keep them warm.

"I don't want to watch *Iron Man* again," Kate hissed, pinching Bert with her toes when he refused to give up the remote.

"I didn't ask what you wanted," he fired back, moving his leg out of her reach. "It's my turn to pick the movie, you don't get a say."

"Okay, but Robert Downey Jr. isn't even cute," Nik complained.

"He is *so*," Lu argued.

"It doesn't matter! I'm in control of the remote!" Bert waved the device around, crowing like the victor in some kind of huge battle when really it was just his turn in the rota-tion—which Eric had set in place to solve issues like this, because fuck all were these kids annoying.

"Whatever, just turn it on," Kate grumbled. She had stuffed half of her garlic bread into her mouth, dry, no sauce —sacrilege if you asked Eric, but he didn't want to get into a debate with her about proper lasagna etiquette. They didn't have all night.

Bert saluted using the remote, knocking it a little too hard against his forehead with a *thunk* and a soft "ouch" before he hit play, and the movie started up.

Eric lost the thread of it a quarter of the way in. The kids enjoyed it though, which was all that mattered really. And

Tony didn't seem to mind the chaos that was movie night, didn't even put up a token protest about joining them. Maybe because he was already sort of a parent to Lu. It was nice, though. Most of Eric's dates didn't care much at all for the kids. Got real shifty when they found out he was a dorm parent. Like oh, you're responsible for the well-being of six kids? I didn't sign on for being a mom. Like that was even a *thing*.

"All right, assholes, upstairs. You've all got homework, and it's getting close to bedtime." Eric rose to collect the dishes and nudge a half-asleep Chase with his slipper to rouse him.

"Lu, you can bunk with Finn for the night." Tony scrubbed at his face, brushing errant curls back so he could watch Eric with lazy, heavily lidded eyes while Eric shooed the kids upstairs. Once they were all gone, Tony grabbed at Eric's waist, giving his belt loops a tug. "You wanna make out?"

"I thought you'd never ask." Eric laughed, setting the dishes he'd collected onto the coffee table and flopping down into Tony's lap.

It was the kind of slow, lazy make out session he'd always loved. All languid grinding of hips and breathing in each other's air, with half formed kisses pressed along the moles on his neck. Eric didn't know how else to explain the careful attention Tony showed him sometimes, the way he seemed to read Eric's body language and mood so easily, but he felt . . . *cherished*. Which sounded sappy. And fuck off if you thought you'd catch him saying that out loud.

"So I was thinking, would it be better to use ash wood instead of—" Bert stopped, his blue eyes bright and wide behind his glasses. "Oh. You really *are* dating Lu's brother."

Eric leaned back but Tony wouldn't let him go too far, his hands still tight around Eric's waist. Not that he was really trying to. Fingers still fisted in Tony's shirt, wrinkling it beyond recognition. "I thought that was kinda obvious, buddy."

"Kate said something about it." Bert wrinkled his nose, his brow creased in thought, and Eric could practically see him doing the calculations in his head. Adding up all the moments and glancing touches to make a full picture. Tony stayed eerily still where he sat between Eric's thighs, as if afraid to intrude. "But you know she lies."

"Is that a problem?" He didn't know what he'd do if it was. Bert was his first kid, and kind of his favorite, although he'd never admit that on pain of death. Eric had been there when Bert's dad left just after he tested positive. He'd taken Bert under his wing, made himself into a surrogate big brother. Bert meant the fucking world to him.

"That she lies? Yes. That you're dating Lu's brother? Nah. I just didn't realize you were like . . . into guys." Bert didn't sound offended by it, just kind of curious. It was the exact same tone he used when Hunter guest lectured sometimes, and Bert learned something new about the science behind hunting vampires. Like he was adding it to his mental Rolodex, adjusting his perception of the world based on this new information. Which was kind of . . . nice, actually.

"Both. Guys and girls." Eric nodded. He felt Tony's fingers flex on his waist a little.

"Huh. Okay." Bert shrugged. "So like I was saying, I was experimenting with ash wood earlier to make some new stakes and I think . . ." and he was off, Bert's mind moving much faster than Eric could ever hope to keep up with, but he sat back on his heels and listened, because it didn't look like he was going to be getting anymore making out in before it was time for patrol anyway.

"Ash only has a Janka hardness rating of about 9.1," Tony said, and Bert's brows lifted, his eyes shining suddenly. "It's pretty good, better than pine, oak, or birch, which are about 5.5, but nothing beats pockhout."

"Yeah, but isn't that like . . . super rare in this part of the world? Those trees are indigenous to South America and the Caribbean. And yeah, I mean you could get it imported, but finding a supplier is kinda—"

"I've got someone." Tony licked his teeth and winked at Eric, who was following the volley of conversation with rapt attention. Honestly, what the fuck were they talking about? And who the fuck knew the hardness rating of different woods off the top of their head? Tony McMahon apparently. "I'll bring some samples by tomorrow for you to play with. That's what I make all my stakes out of. Nothing beats it in terms of sturdiness."

"Really?" Bert asked, tone going up a few octaves, and Eric could practically see him bouncing in his excitement. "That'd be amazing! Thanks, Tony."

"Sure, kid," Tony murmured. Bert bounced one more time on his toes, as if maybe he wanted to hug Tony, but then he thought better of it and spun to head back up the stairs. Once he was gone, Tony turned to find Eric staring at him. "What?"

"I think you just made like . . . his entire semester. Maybe his entire year."

A shrug lifted Tony's shoulders, but they couldn't hide the red heating the tips of his ears. "We should be getting out on patrol, yeah?"

Eric leaned in to plant one last kiss on his lips, then pulled back again. "Yeah, I think we should."

He rolled back off the couch, onto his feet, and finished gathering the dishes while Tony cleared away the leftover pillows and blankets. Once that was all done, they just had to grab their coats, put on their shoes, and go.

———

After a night full of bickering brats, a movie with too many fucking explosions, and not near enough getting off—in

Tony's honest and *correct* opinion—it was nice to be up and moving. Nice to be on patrol.

He hadn't realized it until they were out in the crisp night air, the bitter wind biting at his cheeks, but he needed this. He needed to run. Needed to move. Needed to *fight*. To escape the feeling of . . . *something*, nipping at his heels. Something he hadn't experienced since—since before their mom died. Since before Lu was born. Something warm, and inviting, and domestic. Something *dangerous*.

Only—only the vamps weren't out. Every usual spot they checked turned up empty. The hospital. The cemeteries. The entertainment district. Even the warehouses where Hunter had been attacked. All duds. Just like every other night over the last couple of weeks.

It set Eric's teeth on edge, Tony could see it. He was jumpy. Jittery. Eyes darting all over the place. Hands fidgeting and spinning his stake like a baton. All that adrenaline building up and up and up with nowhere to go. They'd had sex about it a couple of times, but it wasn't enough. Would never be enough. Not for someone who had been at this as long as Eric had.

And honestly? Tony wasn't much better. His muscles tightened, and coiled, and spasmed like a spring waiting for release, but there was nothing to pounce on except Eric.

It wasn't right. None of this was right. Tony had never gone a day in his life without some kind of vamp activity until he came to Ironport. Ironport was smaller, less densely populated, sure, but it was practically sitting on a nexus with how close it was to the one in Moondale. There was no reason for it to be this quiet for this long. No. They were planning something. Something was coming. He just didn't know what.

"Hunter thinks we should set Ava up with the dean," Eric said out of nowhere once they'd loaded into Tony's car and were on their way back to Moondale U. But he hadn't stopped moving since he buckled up. His fingers tapped against the door handle. He bounced his leg. He chewed on his lip. Every bit of anxiety worn on his skin.

"The dean?" Tony shifted smoothly, taking the turns slower now that he wasn't trying to keep his passenger from bleeding out. "Like of Moondale University?"

"Yes."

"Well . . ." It didn't seem like a bad idea, but then, Tony didn't know much at all about Ava. And he knew nothing at all about the dean. "Is she Ava's type?"

"I don't know."

"You don't know." Tony frowned, but he didn't turn to look over at Eric, who was shifting around more in his seat now. He had a feeling this conversation was less about Ava and more about keeping their minds off the anxiety creeping along their spines from a night determined to be too quiet. "Is that because you don't know what type the dean is, or because you don't know what type your best friend is into?"

"Ava doesn't really have a type. She's gone out with a lot of different women." Eric shifted again, the leather creaking beneath his legs. They were getting close to the school now, and Tony could tell Eric was tired even though they hadn't fought any vampires. The constantly being on edge was worse than an actual fight. So he decided to lean into this, to hopefully make Eric smile, if nothing else.

"Baby." Tony lifted his hand from the gear shift so he could give Eric's thigh a squeeze, stilling him where he'd been bouncing it still. "Everybody's got a type. You're just not seeing it because you aren't a woman, and women have different parameters than men."

"I've dated women." Eric sounded like he was sulking, but there was a playful lilt to it, and that was better. So much better than the jittery edge Tony had heard in his voice before. He glanced out of the corner of his eyes and saw that Eric had relaxed back into his seat finally.

"Okay, and?" A smile lit Tony's face, his tongue poking out through his teeth as he turned his head for a moment to shoot Eric a flirty wink. "I dated a heart doctor once. That don't mean you want me performing cardiovascular surgery on you."

Eric hummed, accepting that as an answer as Tony turned onto campus. Unease crept along his nerves again in the silence that followed Eric's soft noise of assent. The reminder that something was deeply wrong here in Ironport.

"What about you?" Eric asked after the silence had stretched on too long, lighting every one of Tony's nerves up with buzzing energy.

"What about me?" His turn signal clicked loud in the stillness of the night. It was *too* still, wasn't it? And there were . . . did the lights always go off in the parking lot like this? Was it to conserve energy in parts of the campus that weren't frequently used at night?

"You're not really . . . *my* type." It took everything Tony had not to slam on the brakes and rip Eric from his seat so he could make good on the taunt in Eric's tone.

"Oh, baby boy, I'm *everyone's* type," he said instead, turning his head so he could waggle his tongue at Eric as he pulled into a parking spot. Eric's cheeks flamed hot. And delight replaced the unease. "Apart from lesbians. For obvious reasons."

"Right," Eric said, the teasing lilt still present as he all but rolled from the car and took off toward the dorm.

Tony barked a laugh and killed the engine. "Get back here, you little shit!"

His feet slapped against the pavement, eating up the ground, his hands outstretched, ready to grab Eric up into his arms and spin him around, laughing and cursing and freezing in the cold, but warm and bright with happiness.

And then something ripped through the darkness that

surrounded them and tackled Eric to the ground. Eric let out one startled, pained yelp, before the creature had him pinned.

There was a flash of something, a knife maybe. Which didn't make sense, did it? Since when did leeches use knives?

And this campus was warded, wasn't it?

And everything was moving in slow motion.

So slow.

Even Tony, who felt like he was running through sand to get to Eric in time. To stop the creature before it could do more damage to Eric than it already had. There was a wet gurgle, and the sharp, metallic scent of blood filled his nose so much, he was sure he'd be smelling it for days to come.

His body finally caught up with his brain, and he was moving. Ripping the thin chain he'd worn on their date from his neck and stringing it around the creature's throat. The silver burned. Sizzling hot. The leech screamed, flailed, wailed. Tony didn't let up. Couldn't. Not with the blood coating the sidewalk and Eric lying too still, barely breathing, silent.

He pulled, and yanked, and tugged, until the chain cut all the way through the brittle dead skin, and the brittle dead bone, and clean through to the other side. Its head popped off, eyes wide and still blinking for a minute, long enough to bounce once against the ground before it caught up with the rest of the leech's body and turned to dust.

Then Tony bent down and scooped Eric up into his arms, ignoring the way that he felt too heavy and his head lolled against Tony's shoulder, and practically kicked the door to the dorm down.

"BERT! BERT!" Tony screamed, his throat aching. Had he been screaming this whole time? He wasn't sure. It felt like it. It *burned* like it.

The kids tripped over themselves to run down the stairs, Bert at the head of the pack. All of them sleep rumpled and in pajamas. They took one look at where the blood *drip, drip,* *dripp*ed from Eric onto the big rug laid under the couches of the living room and paled.

"Call Britt and Hunter. And . . . and . . . Ava. And that other one. The bitchy sheriff one. All of them. Call all of them. Get them here. Get them here. Do you hear me, Bert? Get them here!"

Bert nodded once and whirled around to run back up the steps to find his phone, but the other kids were already in motion. A buzzing, swirling hive of activity. Getting a towel to press against the deep gouge in Eric's stomach, the bite mark on his neck. Finding a wet cloth to clean up the blood. Moving around Tony carefully, so carefully, to shut and deadbolt the door. Standing watch over their unconscious teacher and the bloody man who had brought him home.

Chapter 22

THE WORLD WAS a blur of pain and sound. Everything was too loud and ached too fucking much. And Eric was sure this is what it felt like to die. He was sure it started with the cold bite of numbness, with the shiver of shock along his spine, with the feeling of drowning while on land. The world going murky and dark, like that time he'd swam to the bottom of the bay just to see if it was the same muddy texture at its depths as it was near the shore. A grungy haze yellowing everything around him.

Yeah. This is what it was like to die.

He shut his eyes, preparing himself to slip away into the darkness. The place beyond the veil, the place that would finally bring him peace.

Only.

His eyes didn't stay shut. Instead, his movement became a long, slow blink, as if he were fighting against sleep and winning. Eric didn't think he actually *wanted* to win this particular battle. He was so tired. The world was so hard, and sharp. It would be easier, gentler, if he went like this. If he let the darkness take him now.

But something made him raise his lids and . . .

Oh. Maybe he *was* dead after all.

An angel hovered over him, long strawberry-blond curls

falling into his cherubic face, green eyes shining in the low light.

Another angel jostled up beside the first. This one was Black and had dark curls that hung down past his shoulders, and eyes so brown they were almost black peering through a pair of rounded glasses made of metal.

"Angels wear glasses?" Eric croaked, his throat raw and dry.

The blond angel snorted, rolling his eyes, but the dark-haired one just smiled at Eric, his gaze bright with mirth. "You think you went to heaven, big boy?"

"Gotta be." Was there any other explanation for the two beautiful people hovering over him? Light shining behind their heads like halos.

"For fuck's sake, Britt, what did you *give* him?" another voice asked, and a third face pushed its way into Eric's view. Shoulder-length green hair, fierce blue eyes. Ava.

"Nope, this is hell. Do not pass go. Do not collect two hundred dollars. Straight to hell for Eric Salvatore Marcelino." He flopped his head back against the arm of the couch. As reality filtered back in, so did the memories and the pain. That vampire had stabbed him. *Stabbed* him, of all fucking things. Since when did vampires carry *daggers*?!

"That's because of all your stupid dad jokes," Ava bit back, not pulling her head away from where she wasn't even blocking the light glaring into his eyes, because she was a bitch like that.

"Okay, you know what—" He sat up and groaned when the movement pulled at the stitches in his abdomen, irritating the stab wound and making his head spin.

"Don't move, you idiot," Britt grumbled. "You're gonna tear your stitches. I just got done putting them in!"

"Sorry. Sorry." Eric held up his hands and leaned back against the arm of the couch again. Tony had moved from where he was hovering over Eric to pace across the opposite end of the living room, his hands fidgeting and fiddling with the blood-stained shirt hanging oddly from his shoulders, as if it'd been stretched out by his nervous actions. "So what do we know?"

"We know *fuck all*, is what we know," Tony growled, his fingers running through his hair and getting caught in the tangles, which made him growl more and rip his hands from the curls, taking strands with them that he plucked away and dropped on the carpet.

Eric would have to vacuum later. No. Not just vacuum, Eric realized as he finally caught sight of the rug in the living room. There was a big patch of red on it, splatters leading from the corner all the way to the couch. Someone had made the valiant, albeit not very well done, attempt to wipe off the blood on the hardwood. Eric was sure the smears would stain the scuffed floors. They were in desperate need of refinishing as it was, but there was likely no point at all now. He didn't think a sander would be able to buff away the red. And the rug was a lost cause completely.

"Stop pacing, you're making me nauseous," Eric pleaded. He swallowed back bile, saliva thick in his mouth at the threat of vomiting up lasagna and garlic bread. The mere thought of food made his stomach give another sickening roll.

"The *blood loss* is making you fucking nauseous," Tony spat, and no one argued with him. Eric looked around to realize that the women had fled, leaving him alone in the room with Tony and Hunter. He wasn't sure why, or when it happened. Maybe they needed to escape the smell of blood for a while. Or maybe they were trying to sort this thing out on their own, far enough away where he, Hunter, and Tony couldn't hear. Although he wasn't sure what purpose that would serve. "From a knife wound. A *knife* wound. What kinda vamp runs around with a knife!"

"I still think we should take him to the hospital," Hunter said, fidgeting with his long hair, tugging at the ends and then releasing the curls so they sprang back. "Britt can only do so much. He probably needs a transfusion."

"And tell them what?" Eric pushed the blanket from his legs, taking in a deep breath through his nose to quell the feeling of vomit crawling up his throat again when the room spun from the movement. He needed to find Britt, Ava, and Kalla. He needed to get his people together and figure out the next step. "That I got mugged? Then they'll want to file a report. And *then* what will they do when I make a miraculous recovery in a matter of days?"

Hunter shot him a pleading look when Eric swayed to his feet, his hands shooting out to catch Eric should he stumble toward any sharp-looking furniture. "Eric."

"It's fine. I'm fine."

A pointed look from both men had him rolling his eyes—which, fuck, that hurt. Stars swam in front of his vision, but he blinked them away. Note to self: never do that while dealing with a concussion and blood loss.

"I'll be fine." He brushed them off, decidedly ignoring the way Tony had come over to hover on the opposite side of where Hunter still held his hands aloft, ready and waiting for a stumble. "Where are the others?"

"The library." Hunter grabbed at his forearm when Eric's steps stuttered as he stepped down on squelching carpet. He hadn't been out long enough for it to dry then, only long enough to wrangle the kids back into their beds, which might not have been that much of a chore considering how terrified they all were of Kalla. Something about the sheriff unsettled a group of kids who were under legal drinking age. Which probably meant that Eric should search their rooms for fake IDs. But hey, who was he to judge? He'd been drinking when he was fourteen.

"They won't find anything there." Although his pride wanted him to, Eric wasn't stupid enough to try to shake off Hunter's hold or Tony's steady presence on his other side.

"I grabbed the dagger it used. It looked ritualistic." Hunter's grip tightened around his arm, ebony fingers digging into the skin in a way that hurt and was comforting all at once.

Eric was glad Tony and Hunter had been the ones to stay with him. Even if he did love Kalla, Britt, and Ava like family. Their energy was too . . . erratic for this kind of thing. Kalla and Britt both tended to be rather militant, hard-nosed, and unlikely to baby him. And Ava would have poked fun at him in that gently snide way of hers. It's how she dealt with things. She didn't do feelings very well, and he got that.

But Hunter and Tony were different. Both of them had such intense energy normally. Hunter bounced about like a ferret on coke half the time, flip-flopping between one project and the next, and the other half he was being so over-the-top dramatic that even an improv teacher would kick him out of class. Tony, on the other hand, was usually all hard edges and fury, ready to fly off the handle at the slightest provocation. But now? Now they were both gentle—not calm, but it was like they'd focused all that intensity on helping Eric make it to the library safely and had no room in their minds for anything but that task. It'd be sweet if it weren't so fucking confusing and didn't make his chest ache in a way that had nothing at all to do with the huge muscly vamp who'd barreled into him not more than a couple of hours ago, likely cracking a few of his ribs, or at the very least bruising them.

"Find anything?" Eric asked, nudging the door to the small library open more. All three women were huddled together over one of the tables strewn in books. Their movements frantic in their search, and Goddess, he loved these idiots. Each and every one of them.

"Nothing." Kalla frowned. Her upturned nose was curled in distaste, her lips pursed. Unlike the rest of them, Kalla was dressed in a pair of jeans and a T-shirt instead of loungewear or pajamas. Either she'd been out when she'd gotten the call, or she'd decided to take the time to get dressed versus coming over in her jammies. Probably the latter. Eric was on the fence as to whether he should be hurt by that.

"The markings on it aren't anything I recognize." Ava scrubbed at her face. Her glasses were perched high in her messy hair, no doubt getting tangled up in the thin strands. She'd bitch about it later, but by then it'd be too late.

"Has Hunter looked at it?" Easing himself down into a chair, Eric looked up at Hunter, brows raised.

"I glanced at it, but nothing clicked off the top of my head." Hunter continued to hover over him for a moment, his hands brushing against Eric's shoulders until Tony nudged him out of the way so he could push Eric's chair in closer to the table. Not that he'd be much help. His vision was already swimming, his head pounding. Looking at words right now was a no go.

"Look again." It would be easy to stay curled up in his chair and let the others do the research end of things. Simple, really, to let the brains do their work. But Eric knew this town and these vampires better than anyone, and he was the Venator leader. He was there to give direction. To delegate to the best of his ability. "Was there anything else about the vamp who attacked me?"

"It got through the Moondale U wards," Britt whispered, her voice raspy either from upset or from not talking for an extended amount of time. The panicked way her gaze flitted from one text to the next told him all he needed to know. This attack had shaken more than just him, more than just Tony. They'd thought Moondale U was safe. They'd been wrong.

"I'm going to talk to the dean about that," Ava volunteered. "It shouldn't have happened."

"We need to find where these fuckers are hiding out." Tony gripped the chair behind Eric's shoulders tighter, the wood creaking under his hands. "Wherever that thing came from, it's the same place the ones who attacked Hunter came from. And I'd put good money on it being a huge fucking nest."

"Vamps don't usually cluster like that," Hunter said. He pushed his glasses up further on his nose, a nervous habit when he felt like there was going to be a confrontation. But the fact of the matter was, he was their expert on vamp behavior. He would know almost as well as Eric what these vamps would do.

Eric heard Tony open his mouth to protest, and held up a hand to silence him. Which worked, surprisingly, and gave him room to talk. "Hunter's right. Transient vamps don't cluster like that. But we aren't dealing with transient vamps. Not anymore. If what we've seen this last month is true, then Tony's also right: We have a big nest somewhere in Ironport that's *been* here, lying low. And we need to find it before it does more damage to the community."

"Or to you," Tony muttered under his breath.

There was no point in dignifying that comment, or even addressing it, but Eric waited for a moment, his lungs burning with a held breath, for the others to try. It was a nice sentiment. The idea that they could search these creatures out. Get to them before they got to Eric. But his safety was never, and never would be, their first priority. Ironport was.

"He's not wrong." Kalla was the one to break the silence with that tone that always made Eric want to grind his teeth, like she was better and smarter than everyone in the room. He knew she didn't mean it that way—it was just in her nature, but it still grated on him. "This was targeted. And it's the second time."

"I know that." Eric flexed his hands against the armrests of the chair, forcing himself not to otherwise outwardly show the nerves lit within him. He needed to be calm, collected. He couldn't let them see his fear.

"Even more reason to find the nest quickly," Ava said, and when Eric looked at her, she gave him a tiny nod. Like she'd read what was going through his mind and provided the out he needed. Goddess, his bestie was the *best*.

"What about that thing you were showing me the other day, Kalla?" Hunter asked.

It was such an obvious ploy to distract Kalla, to get her away from something that they all knew she wouldn't drop unless she had to, that Eric was a little surprised when she turned to Hunter and said, "What thing?"

"The thing that witch over in Moondale is working on. The negative energy tracker?"

"Ghost Tracer," Ava supplied, her eyes lighting up with enthusiasm and a little amusement.

"That." Hunter snapped, pointing at her.

"The what now?" Tony grumbled, leaning over Eric's shoulder, his hair brushing Eric's cheek. He smelled mostly of the coppery scent of blood, but beneath that sat leather and grease, cedar wood, and a hint of lavender.

"The Moondale sheriff, Greer, showed it to me." Kalla pulled out her phone, tapping against the screen to unlock it. "There's a witch in Moondale creating an app that would allow us to track spikes in negative energy. It's already proven effective at ferreting out a soul eater."

Ava held out her hands, her fingers wriggling in a gimme gesture that Kalla reluctantly obliged.

"But it's only for Moondale right now, isn't it?" Hunter asked. He'd moved to peer over Ava's shoulder, the ghostly blue glare of the phone reflecting in his glasses.

"Well, it looks like she has it attached to a weather balloon." Ava's fingers drummed on the back of Kalla's phone, her head tilted in thought, but there was a twitch at the corner of her lips like she was impressed by all of this. "Theoretically, it might pick up data that reaches further out."

Hunter reached over her shoulder and pinched at the screen. "The map goes all the way to the west end of Ironport."

"So we can use this?" Hope tinged Eric's tone, and he did his best to stomp it down, to try to calm himself. He couldn't afford to get ahead of himself.

"I can't tell if it's picking up any readings in our area. Not that I'd know what vamps even *looked* like on this thing. But we're on the map." There was a thoughtful, almost restrained note to Ava's voice. Like she was holding back her excitement. She'd probably decided it wasn't appropriate. Which was a far cry from the girl Eric met when he was sixteen and working at the local McDonald's, who probably would have jumped around on the table at this discovery.

"I can check with Rus, see if we can get her to include the readings for Ironport. It might take a bit, though." Kalla reached out to swipe her phone back from Ava, already tapping away at it, likely to text the witch.

"If she's already getting the readings, pushing it to the app should be simple enough." Hunter shrugged. "But don't . . . you know . . . do that thing," he said, flapping his wrist in Kalla's face.

"Do *what* thing?" she snapped.

"You know what thing," Britt chimed in.

Kalla huffed, blowing hair away from her face, and returned to her phone with a sullen expression. "I'll be nice."

"Atta girl!" Ava crowed and clapped Kalla on the back hard enough to make her nearly drop her phone.

"For the time being," Tony said, his hands warm on Eric's shoulders, "we need to get this one to bed. The Venator healing can only do so much. You need to rest."

Eric groaned, but he let Tony pull him gently to his feet and guide him to the stairs, his big hands soft on Eric's waist. He also let Tony bully him into pajamas, then into bed, and pull the blanket up to his neck.

"I'm all right," Eric protested weakly.

"You will be." Tony nodded. He sat on the edge of the bed, fingers gentle where they brushed through Eric's hair. Eric hummed, leaning into the touch. "You scared me back there, pretty boy."

"Didn't mean to," Eric mumbled through a yawn. "You going home?"

"No. I'm going to hang out here. Keep an eye on you and the idiots downstairs."

Eric nodded weakly. He wanted to say something else. Maybe to tell Tony that they weren't idiots. Or maybe to protest that he didn't need a babysitter. Or maybe to ask for some water. But between one slow blink and the next, he was asleep.

CHAPTER 23

HEALING from a stab wound to the gut was a slow, painful process, even for a Venator. Even for one like Eric who had a personal nurse and two witches looking out for him.

Hours turned into days of Tony helping Eric stand, make it to the bathroom, and redress his wounds as Eric's insides slowly knit back together—a process that not even magic could speed up. Tony went home for a couple of hours to shower, check in, and get some clothes, but then he was right back at Eric's side. Unable to leave even if he wanted to because . . .

Because he saw too much of Eric Marcelino, knew too much of him. Tony didn't know when he'd picked up on it. Maybe it was when he saw how Eric took care of those kids. Or maybe it was the morning after the stabbing, when Eric was up cooking breakfast for the others, in spite of how he'd struggled to get out of bed. Eric wouldn't even wince where the others could see him. Wouldn't let the others see how much pain he was in.

He was just like the Happy Prince. Giving bits and pieces of himself away over and over again to the people around him, as if they were better, more deserving. How long before there was nothing left of him to give? How long before someone came and melted him down because he was no longer beautiful or useful to them?

Tony couldn't stand it. Couldn't deal with the thought that one day there might be nothing of Eric Marcelino left for him to even hold. So he stayed.

He stayed, and he hovered, and he took every comment of being a "helicopter parent" and "fuck, Tony, I'm not a child" in stride. It seemed the only way to ensure that Eric didn't slip away entirely. And . . . and . . . and . . .

What did that mean? Tony didn't know.

He shook himself, blinking the sleep from his eyes and scrubbing at his face to try to clear away the vestiges that clung to his mind. The nap had been necessary after pulling double time for nearly a week between taking care of Eric and running patrol with only one of Eric's idiot friends for backup. It left Tony with a crick in his neck, an ache in his hip from the lumpy couch cushions, and a low-level headache.

Fuck. He felt hungover.

But with none of the bleary-but-fun memories attached to it. Shitty.

The house was quiet around him. Too quiet. The kids had been in class for hours by the time Tony laid down for his nap, but Eric was still piddling about. Tidying up and prepping something for dinner. None of those noises filtered in through the oppressive pressure of a house too empty around Tony.

"Fuck me, where did he go now?" Pressing to a seat, Tony lifted his hands above his head and stretched, his shoulders popping from the motion. He tilted his neck from one side to the other as he cracked his knuckles. All of it relieved some, but not all, of the pressure that built up while napping on a piece of furniture that was probably older than he was.

Maybe he should have taken Eric up on the offer to sleep in his bed after all. It certainly would have been nice to lie down wrapped up in the scent of him, in the musk and the fruity hair product smell. To surround himself with the vanilla incense Eric used after he smoked in his room, thinking stupidly it would cover the scent of weed on his sheets. It didn't. The smell clung to the walls and the carpets. But all of it added up to a lingering trace of Eric in the room, even above the alcohol-like tang of air fresheners. Something Tony could get used to. Could roll himself in over and over and never get sick of.

Which was exactly why he *hadn't* taken Eric up on the offer. Because this? It was just temporary. It wasn't permanent. Tony would move on soon enough, leaving Eric behind. And even if he didn't, he knew enough of Eric's type to know he wouldn't want to keep Tony around for long. Settling down had never really been an option for him, and it wasn't one now. Even if he did—

No. He wouldn't think about that.

A feeling he refused to give name to—because that would give it too much fucking power—churned low in Tony's gut in spite of him trying to ignore it, and he pushed to his feet, heading for the kitchen to keep himself occupied. He knew better than to eat when he was bored or upset, but fuck it. No one was there to see him anyway. And he knew for a fact that Eric kept the pantry stocked full of snacks for the kids. Chips and crackers. Cookies and pudding cups. Everything they could so much as dream up, shelves stuffed so full it would put a grocery store to shame.

A slip of paper sat on the counter, untidy letters crowded so close together they were almost on top of each other. Tony blinked at the note for a moment, trying to decipher what the fuck it said, then he growled softly.

Tony,

I needed to clear my head. Went to the batting cages across campus. Left the car. There's lunch in the fridge if you're hungry. Don't make a mess of my kitchen.

Eric

"That absolute dipshit." Tony scrubbed at his face and tossed the note into the trash with so much force, it made the bag rustle in the quiet of the house. Grabbing his keys from the bowl near the door—because of course Eric had a little table with a bowl for everyone's keys, even if he was the only one who owned a car who lived there—he tugged on his jacket.

In the cold watery light of winter, Moondale U felt like it lived in a perpetual state of twilight. Tony had to turn on his headlights to make sure he didn't hit any of the idiotic students running across the parking lot like absolute hooligans. Tony wasn't sure if that was a normal college campus occurrence or if it was just Moondale, but he swept his eyes around the area behind the kids every time, just to make sure they weren't being chased.

No one seemed to realize the danger they were in. No one seemed to know that the wards of Moondale U had already failed once, could fail again. Maybe the dean hadn't told them. Maybe she was trying to keep the population from panicking. Or maybe it was just the hubris of youth, the arrogance of an early twenty-something not knowing any better. Or worse yet, the ignorance of a magical child who had spent their entire life at the top of the food chain, far above the normies.

Tony made a mental note to add a patrol of the campus to his rotation as he followed the signs on the east end of campus near the football stadium to the batting cages tucked behind the abandoned baseball fields.

Once the engine cut, Tony could hear the sound of a bat cracking against ball after ball, breaking the silence of an area of campus left empty during the colder months. They hadn't even properly salted the sidewalks. Which was a fucking hazard, not just to the kids, but to the still-healing Venator who'd decided to walk there all on his own for batting practice on a cold February afternoon.

With his hands buried deep in his pockets, Tony approached the wire fence that made up the walls of the batting cages. They were outdoors, which didn't make sense to him considering how far north they were, but he had spent the last few years in Florida, so he wasn't exactly a good judge of what could be considered moderate temperatures.

Tony watched as Eric twisted one sneakered foot in the damp ground at the far end of the cage—his back facing Tony —planting his feet and readying his stance. The machine made a soft sucking sound as it pulled up another ball, then a *thwap*, launching it Eric's way almost too fast for even Tony's enhanced eyesight to catch.

It looked for a moment like Eric wouldn't hit it. Like he'd waited too long to start his swing. But he moved, swift and sure, the bat cracking against the ball, sending it careening back toward the top right corner of the cage.

"Fuck, Marcelino, you could go pro." Tony wolf whistled, licking his teeth as his stomach heated. There was something sexy about a man who could swing like that—not that Tony had ever really had an interest in baseball before, but he sure as fuck did now. Probably helped that Eric had an unfair advantage in his Venator abilities. Preternatural strength, speed, eyesight, and the training to kill something at least doubly strong and three times faster than even a pitching machine could launch a ball.

Eric grunted like he wasn't surprised by Tony's appearance. Which was good. Tony didn't want to fight if he found that Eric was still out of it enough to let Tony sneak up on him. Especially as he hadn't exactly hidden his approach.

Another ball came whizzing toward Eric, and he settled in just quickly enough to send it sailing before he spun to smack the bat against the red button along the cage wall, shutting off the machine. "I was on my high school team," Eric said, turning to face Tony finally, his bat slung over his shoulder, hip cocked. "I loved it. Liked the teamwork of it."

"I can see that." Tony had heard tell that baseball was much more of a team sport than some of the others. Personally, he'd never been much of a team player, never wanted to be either. He liked going at it solo. Liked having to watch only his own back. It had its drawbacks, sure, but it was preferable to having someone fail him. From what Tony knew of Eric, he was the opposite.

It seemed to Tony that Eric Marcelino had never wanted anything so much as he wanted to not have to be alone. Which explained absolutely everything about him from the mom-mobile to the house full of kids.

"Coulda gone pro probably, like you said." Eric shrugged. He lifted a hand to scrub at the back of his neck almost like he was embarrassed. "My coach thought so, anyway."

Tony wanted to ask what happened, but he knew better. Out of anyone in the world, he was probably the most intimately aware of how little room was left in a Venator's life for things like a career—a life at all, really—after vampires. Especially when a person took into account how young the average Venator seemed to die. It had never bothered him before. But something inside of his chest ached at the look of heartbreak Eric didn't wipe off his face quick enough for Tony to miss.

"Another person's dreams I couldn't live up to." Eric shrugged again, lifting the neck of his shirt up to his face so he could wipe away the thin sheen of sweat that gathered on his forehead in spite of the cold. "What'd you want?"

Tony blinked for a moment, his eyes tracking a bead of sweat Eric missed that trailed down along his jaw. Goddess, he wanted to lick it off. He shook himself. "You're supposed to be resting, you dipshit."

"I'm fine. Britt removed the stitches earlier. All healed." He patted the place where Tony had meticulously cleaned and reapplied bandages over and over the last few days. Then winced.

"Not *all* healed up, it looks like." Tony lifted a brow and waited for Eric to argue, but he didn't. He just looked vaguely guilty and headed for the door to the batting cages.

"I needed to clear my head." He didn't provide any other explanation, stepping over to the bench at the back of the cage to grab a towel and wipe off the back of his neck.

"You're gonna catch cold running around like that without a fucking coat on. It's fucking January."

"February, actually," Eric corrected. Exhaustion clung to him, making his movements seem sluggish, but he didn't stop. Drinking water. Wiping the sweat away some more. Spinning the bat lazily in his hand like Tony had caught him doing with a stake on slow nights. "You didn't answer my question."

"Didn't I?"

Eric's lips twisted into one of those disapproving scowls, and he opened his mouth—no doubt to tell Tony off for being a shithead—but his phone rang before he could get the words out, and he spun to dig it out of his coat pocket. His eyes widened, breath stilling for a moment before it picked up too quick, too close to panic.

"What is it?"

"Kalla thinks they found the nest." His thumbs tapped against the screen, likely replying to Kalla, and Tony tried not to feel a jealous twist in his belly at the way Eric focused his attention on the task. He'd never gotten the full story of what happened between Eric and Kalla, but he could see the way feelings lingered. The way Eric would look at her sometimes like she was the one who got away, and she wouldn't look at him at all. It made Tony so irritated, he wanted to make them both choke on his feelings. "I've got coordinates."

"Then what are we standing around here for?" Tony asked, straightening from his lean against the fencing so he could tug his leather jacket back down into place where it had crept up to let a chill settle into the skin at the small of his back. "Let's go hunt some leeches."

"I thought I wasn't all the way healed up?" Eric tilted his head, a bit of soft brown hair falling into his eyes. There was a sardonic twist to his lips, and if there wasn't a chain link fence between them, Tony might try to bite it from his mouth.

"Fuck off." Tony tsked and spun on his heel. "Just get in the fucking car, Babe Ruth. We've got some vamps to kill."

He smiled to himself when he heard Eric mutter a soft curse then scramble to follow him toward the car.

CHAPTER 24

THE HOUSE LOOMED over them where Tony and Eric sat in Tony's Mustang parallel parked across the street.

Loomed. What a strange way to say it sat there looking terrifying and a little run down. Tony didn't think he'd ever used the word *loomed* before. Had never had cause for it. But the two-story colonial-style monstrosity Kalla's coordinates led them to *loomed*.

It was on the outskirts of Ironport. On the east side of town, too close to the border that separated Ironport from the land beyond, the land that led to Moondale U and Moondale itself on the other side of the mountains. Leather creaked under Eric's thighs as he shifted, no doubt thinking the same thing.

It had been so close to them this whole time. If Tony didn't know better, he'd think maybe this was why the leeches had ended up on campus. That they'd just followed their noses to the nearest available blood source. But he *did* know better.

The location of this nest wasn't an accident. It wasn't about convenience or how the house was tucked deep in a neighborhood littered in old houses, many of which were much better kept than this one. It was intentional.

His only question was—

"Why hasn't the HOA torn this rat trap down?"

"Maybe they don't have one?" Eric leaned forward to get

a better look at the place through the windshield. His fingers were tight on his knees, body held still like a spring about to pop.

"Bullshit." Tony sniffed. It didn't sit right with him. Neighborhoods like this one? With historic houses that had been kept up, maintained, and rejuvenated regularly? They didn't just not have Homeowners Associations. They didn't just let the places around them go to pot. There was a reason this place sat empty. A reason it hadn't been leveled or touched in Goddess knew how long.

"Maybe it's protected under some kind of historic landmark status." Eric shrugged. He didn't look like he wanted to get out of the car yet, and Tony didn't really want to either. Even with the heat blasting on high from the vents, a chill had settled into the base of his spine. A strange foreboding. This wasn't right.

"Then why not fix it up?"

"Lack of funds? Or maybe it's haunted." Eric shook his head, dark hair falling into his face as he reached for the door finally—and too soon for Tony's liking. "Doesn't matter. Let's just go."

The passenger door opened, letting in a biting wind that added to the shivers creeping along Tony's spine. Eric stepped out, his fingers tapping against the inside of the car door for a moment before he leaned back in to peer at Tony.

"Don't tell me you're afraid of a couple of ghosts." The words were teasing, but the tone was anything but. Whatever instinct screamed at Tony not to go into that house was at least whispering in Eric's head too.

"I ain't afraid of no ghost," Tony grumbled back, then narrowed his eyes on the house again, ignoring the startled laugh that left Eric at the joke. It was a nice laugh. It eased the tension threatening to hitch Tony's shoulders up to his ears. Still. "Don't you feel that?"

"Yeah." Which was a relief, but then Eric stood again and

turned back toward the house, his hands on his hips. "But we're going in anyway."

"Right." Swallowing the slithering traces of unease, Tony cut the engine and climbed out, following Eric around to the trunk to dig through his cache of weapons. Tony slid a silver dagger into his boot while Eric tucked a stake into every pocket he had on his person then reached for the bat he'd left in the trunk after going back to the house to change.

With a brow raised at the way Eric spun the bat in his hand, Tony stuffed his copy of *The Happy Prince* into his breast pocket.

"What?" Eric asked. The trunk slammed, the sound echoing around the quiet street. It was too quiet. Tony didn't like it. Didn't like anything about this, really. It felt like a trap. Or at least what Tony thought a trap was supposed to feel like. Too easy.

"You know you can't kill a vamp via blunt force trauma, right?" Tony zipped up his leather jacket against the biting cold.

Eric tilted his head, the bat swinging lazily at his side as they made their way across the street. "You've only seen me hit a baseball." Then he moved closer to Tony where they stood at the end of the cracked, crumbling walk that led up to the house. He leaned the bat against his hips, his hands lifting to flip the collar of Tony's jacket up to shield his neck. A sweet but no doubt fruitless gesture. With his breath ghosting warm over Tony's cheeks, there was only a second to think before their lips were pressed together. Tony wasn't sure who moved first, who initiated it, but he felt the heat of it all the way down to his curling toes where they rested in his boots. Eric hummed into the kiss, the sound content and warm.

Then he pulled back, shot Tony a lazy wink, and said, "Watch and learn, sweetheart" before grabbing his bat and starting up the walk again.

"Oh, I'm watching," Tony mumbled, licking his lips, his eyes following Eric's ass as it swayed. "Try and stop me."

The lingering traces of fear burned away by Eric's kiss, Tony ran up the walk to join Eric at his side, so they could enter the house together. Sagging porch steps creaked under their weight on their way to the door, and Tony nodded when Eric motioned for him to move off to the left, flanking the entrance.

They waited a beat, the wind howling through loose shutters and crumbling siding. But no other noise came. No creak of floorboards. No intake of breath. Nothing to signify that anything waited for them on the other side.

Eric held up three fingers, his gaze fixed on the door. It looked like once there had been a screen door in front of it— an extra set of hinges remained—but it'd been ripped away at some point.

Two fingers.

Tony gripped his stake so tightly, he felt splinters biting into his palms. But instead of causing pain, it relaxed him, made him feel safe. Eric shifted the wooden bat from where it was at his side to lean it against his shoulder, fingers deceptively relaxed around the grip.

One finger.

The wind shifted. The house creaked. The smell of decay and death tickled Tony's noise. The sharp, metallic tang of blood burned with every inhale. That was too much blood. Too much. *Too much.* And not enough all at the same time. Fear crept along his spine again, chilling his skin, making his fingers go numb around the stake. Something wasn't right. This wasn't right. He needed to—

A fist, and Eric sprang into action, spinning in front of the door and kicking it inward so it slammed against the wall to the left of it, making the whole house shudder with the force. Inside was pitch black, the shadows writhing with movement, and before Tony could grab Eric's wrist, could rip him away from the danger that lurked beyond the threshold, Eric entered.

Sweat gathered at the base of Tony's spine, unease threatening to make him immobile as he waited on the stoop for Eric's signal.

It never came.

What did come was the crack of a bat. The thud of something bouncing off the floor then rolling across it. And Tony had only a single *thud-thud* of his heart to recognize the head of a vampire, the edge where it'd been severed from the leech's body ragged like it was ripped off, right before it burst into dust. Leaving behind only two thick fangs.

"Home run!" Eric whooped from inside, and a manic laugh burbled up Tony's throat as he stepped over the threshold, excitement burning away his fear.

His eyes adjusted quickly, and when they did, what he saw before him stole his breath. Eric Marcelino surrounded by a ring of vampires, knees bent, baseball bat resting on his shoulder, lined up just like he'd been in the batting cages not but a few hours ago. The vamps were holding back, looking uncertain, maybe waiting for an order? Tony didn't know. But there wasn't time to find out because a second later another vampire lunged at Eric, and he swung.

The crack of the bat was so loud, it left Tony's ears ringing, and he didn't even hear it when the vampire's head bounced across the floor, landing at his feet, its eyes rolling into the back of its head.

"Come on, buddy, pitch me another soft one. Low and slow." Eric glanced at Tony for a second, shot him a wink that set every single nerve in Tony's body on fire, coiling hot and low in his gut. He was definitely going to bend Eric over the hood of his car later. Fuck the cold.

A hiss drew Tony's gaze down to the leech at his feet, and he snorted, kicking the head away as it turned to ashes. But the sound was enough to draw the attention of the horde, who all spun to see him, their focus momentarily drawn away from Eric. One of them shouted something in a language Tony didn't understand, and they all sprang into action at once, half lunging for Tony, half for Eric.

He took the first down easily, but by the time he'd pulled his stake from its chest, there were three more on him. Shoving him hard, backing him into a room off to the right. He tripped over a piece of furniture, not seeing what it was in the gloom. Rolling to his feet, he pulled a second stake from his pocket. The leeches gave him no room to breathe, no room to move, no room to even *think*. And there were more of them. Bleeding out of the shadows, becoming whole as they entered the limited light through the windows from the outside. So many more than he'd been expecting. At least triple the amount he'd seen when he first entered.

Ambush.

The word rang through his mind, but he couldn't give it the attention it deserved. Tony swiped with his stake, knocking one of the vampires and making it hiss, but he didn't push it back.

And they kept coming. Fuck. They *kept* coming.

One of them grabbed him from behind. Its talons dug into the skin of his shoulders, slicing through the leather of his jacket. He spun out of its hold, dancing across the floor in what limited space they'd left him. He needed to get out. He needed to regroup. He needed to get back to Eric. They were better together. Better working as a single unit. Better when they had each other's backs.

But the exits were blocked.

Well, if there was no way around, he'd have to go through.

One of the leeches said something he didn't understand again, and there was a collective nod of agreement as they pushed in further.

Tony's stake was knocked from his hand, and he dropped

the other, reaching instead for the silver hair pins holding his hair in place. They would be easier anyway.

The leeches circled. Tony side stepped, trying to size them up, get a feel for the numbers. Too many. There were too many.

Eric screamed from the other room, and Tony wasn't sure if it was out of fear, victory, or something so much worse.

He lunged into the fray, kicking one leech in the stomach. Jamming a silver hair pin through the eye socket of the other. Each movement a practice in desperation. He had to get to Eric. He had to. There was no other *choice*.

A jab up through the soft palette beneath another leech's chin. A right hook that sent a fourth reeling. Tony was making progress. Slow progress. But progress still. He just couldn't be too late. He couldn't.

The floor was slick, the air thick with the smell of blood. Who was bleeding? Was it him? Was it Eric? Was there a victim somewhere in one of these rooms slowly bleeding out? Dying while Eric and Tony fought for their fucking lives?

He wasn't quick enough. He wasn't going to make it.

The same adrenaline that had always worked for Tony in the past backfired on him now. Made his head swim. He stumbled. The side of his neck was wet. He reached for it. His hand came away bloody.

He'd been bitten. *When* had he been *bitten*?

Spots danced in his vision. His knees grew weak.

Tony slammed a hair pin into a vampire's chest, turning them to dust immediately, but his fingers were going numb. The piece of silver was too thin, slippery.

He lost his grip.

Pain pricked at Tony's uncovered wrist, there and gone, the vampire spinning away before he could swipe uselessly at it with the pin he still held, and realization dawned.

There was something in the air. Not just dust, cobwebs, and asbestos. Something else. They were being *drugged*.

Ambush rang through his head again.

The group of vampires that surrounded him parted for a moment, just long enough for Tony to see Eric standing in the middle of the open foyer, a broken bat gripped in his hands, swinging wildly. Eric stumbled and shook his head hard, likely to try to clear away the foggy feeling that was quickly taking over Tony's own mind, long dark hair falling into his pretty face.

Goddess. He's so beautiful.

"That all you got?" Eric shouted, his chest heaving with each panted inhale. He was taking in more of the drug, Tony realized as one of the vampires knocked into him. Too much of it. But it hadn't stopped him yet.

I think I love that idiot.

# Chapter 25

ERIC HAD to peel his tongue from the roof of his mouth, smacking his lips around the taste of stale and fuzzy unbrushed teeth. His throat was so dry, it felt like he'd been doing tequila shots all night. Which was funny because he hadn't had tequila since his twenty-sixth birthday when Hunter had to hold his waist so he didn't fall over the side of the dock they stood on, and Ava had to hold his hair when he threw up after.

The cold light of day flared harsh and cruel through the open front door. It burned Eric's eyes, and he blinked against it, lifting a hand that was too heavy and unwieldy, like it was still asleep, to his face to scrub at them.

When he pulled his hand away again, the sun remained. Shining not just through the door but through the windows as well. It lit up the front rooms like a crime scene, high-lighting the harsh details. It reminded Eric of how he had failed.

Failed—failed Tony.

The night before came back slowly at first.

Then all at once.

The crack of the bat as it finally splintered.

The wobble of his feet beneath him.

The dark.

And the stink.

And the bruises already littering his body from the fight.

And then Tony was lying on the floor, eyes open but unseeing. Not dead. But too still. Too still to be anything but unconscious.

"Tony!" Eric lost his grip on the piece of the bat he'd been using like a stake, the wood clattering uselessly to the floor. He took a step, the world tilting dangerously beneath him with whatever drug the bastards had pumped into the air. It had been slow acting, sneaking up on him. Settling into his lungs a little at a time until it was too late. Until the ground he stood on started to go soft and mushy like a ball pit.

In his distraction, a vampire grabbed him, sharp nails digging into the soft fleshy skin of his shoulders, pinning him to the spot for a moment. Just long enough for their fangs to pierce his neck in a tight pinch. The venom rushed into him in a wave, combining with the drug, swirling in Eric's head, in his blood.

He didn't know what was happening at first. Didn't understand the chemical reaction going on inside of his body. But he took one lumbering step, then two, his legs going numb on pins and needles every time his foot touched the floor. His arms hung limp at his sides. But no other vamp approached him. None tried to stop him. And even as he walked, even as he tried to eat up the distance between himself and Tony, he wasn't getting anywhere. It was like walking on a treadmill. The exertion was there, but no distance was covered.

Then on the third step, his legs locked up entirely, going stiff and unyielding. It took a second before his balance shifted just right, sending him toppling. He slammed hard against the wood floor, something in his shoulder cracking, but he couldn't even curl in on himself as the rest of his body had frozen up.

Even still. Even as Eric's body froze in place and he couldn't move, couldn't reach for Tony . . . He could see. He could watch as one of the vampires bent to scoop up Tony's prone form, blood seeping from wounds on his body that Eric hadn't noticed before. He was helpless. Useless. To do anything but watch.

Tony groaned, his lids fluttering, then whimpered as the grip around him tightened, likely irritating his injuries.

The vampire made their steps slow, measured, like they wanted Eric to watch as they carried Tony to the door. To see that they were taking him and there was nothing Eric could do to stop them.

"Tony! Sweetheart! Look at me! Baby! Tony! McMahon!" Eric hadn't realized he was screaming after them until his throat burned with the final word. Tony's lids fluttered again, and Eric felt like he was pinned to the ground by that green gaze. "Tell me you're okay," he begged, eyes burning, as the vampire and their precious cargo passed too close to Eric in the foyer. "Please be okay."

"Don't worry, little Venator," a voice slithered through the dark right before a face dropped into Eric's vision, blocking his view of where they were taking Tony. Their eyes burned bright in the darkness, so blue they were almost neon. And their lips were peeled back in the imitation of a smile, but they were showing Eric too many teeth. Teeth stained in blood. His? Tony's? He didn't know. "We'll take good care of your boyfriend."

They bent closer, their breath a putrid stink of death and blood and decay on Eric's cheek. Eric thought for sure they were going for the kill as they leaned in, their jaw unhinging like a snake readying to swallow down something too big for them. He cringed, but he refused to squeeze his eyes shut, refused to look away from where the other vampire still held Tony at the door, waiting. But they just ran their wet tongue along the bite wound on Eric's neck, pumping more venom into his system and sealing it shut.

"I'm going to make sure your boy is nice and sated," they whispered to him like a dirty little secret. Then they laughed, condescending and pointed, and patted Eric's cheek. "See you around, King Ricky."

Eric's lids grew heavier, his limbs melting into the floor. Between one blink and the next, the vampire who had whispered to Eric was across the foyer, cradling Tony's head in their hands, eyes on Eric as they pressed their fangs to Tony's neck and took a deep drink.

"I'm coming for you," Eric mumbled, his tongue thick and useless in his mouth. "I'm coming for you, Tony."

The venom caught up with him then, sucking him into the dark like the tide. He didn't even see them leave with Tony.

Small mercies.

But that couldn't stop Eric from berating himself, from banging his head once, twice, against the hardwood floor as he tried to shake feeling back into his limbs. Tried to clear away the grogginess and get his ass moving to return to the dorm.

Tony had been right. Eric's instincts had been right. And he'd forged ahead, ignoring the warnings. Why?

Did he think because he had Tony there, he wouldn't have to worry? No. Eric knew why. It was his own fucking pride, his own Goddess-damned arrogance. He was the longest surviving Venator in over a century. He was Eric Marcelino. He could take on a nest of vamps no problem, especially with Tony at his back. This would be a piece of cake.

What did he have to worry about?

What did he have to lose?

A soft whimpered whine ripped up Eric's still-raw throat.

Everything. He had *everything* to lose.

He pushed himself to his feet, groaning when the room swayed dangerously. He was going to throw up, probably. But he managed to swallow it down, at least until he made it out onto the porch. The crisp winter air cooled the still-damp blood that made his clothes cling to him.

He didn't remember being wounded during the fight, but then, he usually didn't. It was hard to pay attention to his own injuries when he was so deep in it, trying to keep track of too many teeth and claws all at once. Usually, the only time he recognized his wounds was when he stopped moving.

Hunter had told him once that it was another perk of being a Venator. That his adrenaline levels spiked way higher than a human's when he was in a fight-or-flight situation.

That also made the crash about a million times worse.

Which had never been more evident than it was right then as Eric's temples throbbed, his throat clicked on every swallow, and the world spun beneath him. *The drugs and the venom probably aren't helping.*

Shielding his eyes, Eric looked at the Mustang still parked across the street from the house. "Fuck me. Of course we had to bring his fucking car last night."

When he fished his phone out of the inside pocket of his jacket, he winced at the cracked screen and the pulling feeling in his shoulder. Gratefully, the screen lit up when he hit the lock button, although the battery was low. Enough to make a call. No explanations. Just an address and a request for a pickup. There was only one person Eric trusted with that, so he dialed Hunter.

Hunter's truck rumbled up to the curb about ten minutes later, and the man himself was out of the driver's side before Eric could hobble his way down the front walk.

"Fuck, Eric, hon, you look like death warmed over," Hunter rasped, his hands suddenly everywhere. Pulling the lapels of Eric's jacket back so he could peel the finally drying shirt away from his body and get a better look at the mottled flesh below.

"I'm fine." Eric shrugged Hunter off, but it made his shoulder twinge and he winced. Hunter didn't miss it, his dark eyes keen behind the glasses perched on his nose. "But they—" The words got caught in his throat, making it hard to breathe around them. He swallowed, another click of his throat bouncing around the hollowness of his skull. "They took Tony."

"Oh, hon, I'm so sorry." Hunter pulled Eric in close, curling his arms firmly but carefully around Eric's battered body, and Eric felt so small all of the sudden. Pressed in close to Hunter's chest, he let the tears in his burning eyes fall. Let his head rest there, away from the glaring sunshine and the truth of what that likely meant. He hadn't thought about it yet. Had avoided it on purpose.

Tony probably hadn't survived the night. And if he had—

"We're going to get him back," Eric said, pulling himself up to stand taller, ignoring the way it made his body ache all over. "We're going to get him back before—"

Hunter, Goddess bless him, didn't say that it might already be too late. Didn't point out that there was a very real possibility they might be retrieving a corpse. He simply nodded. "Of course."

With Hunter's help, Eric climbed into the truck and got himself buckled. He breathed through the pain in his body, the throbbing in his head, and grabbed Hunter's phone as Hunter climbed into the driver's seat. The password typed in, Eric's fingers flew across the screen to send out a group text to everyone—the kids included—telling them to meet him and Hunter at the dorm in an hour. Then he texted Britt and asked her to meet them there in ten minutes. He'd need fixing up before he let the kids see him.

That done, he leaned his head back against the headrest and closed his eyes, hoping to block out the world for a moment, to regain his bearings. All it served to do was dredge up the memories. Blank green eyes staring back at him, unblinking. Nausea roiled in his stomach. "I'm gonna be sick."

Hunter swerved, pulling to a stop at the curb again in time for Eric to open the door and vomit into the grass. It was mostly bile, tasted like acid and ear wax, and once that was done, he was dry heaving. Gasping around every choked sob of breath. Hunter leaned over to rub his back, hands gentle as they brushed soothing circles into the skin.

When Eric had control of himself again, he lurched back into the seat where Hunter was waiting for him with a bottle of water and a sympathetic look.

"You need to tell me what happened, Ricky. Now." It was

an order, but not an unkind one. Eric nodded before uncapping the water bottle and taking careful sips in between his words as he laid it all out in front of Hunter. Laid himself bare, ready for Hunter's judgment, for his disgust. Hunter would look at him like he was a failure. Would blame Eric for Tony's disappearance. And he should. Because Eric *was* a failure.

When it was all done, Eric felt rung out, every inch of him even more weak and shaky than after he'd vomited. He chanced a look at Hunter out of the corners of his eyes, afraid of what he'd see there.

No anger, no disgust, marred Hunter's handsome features. He just looked very, very sad. "Oh Eric," he sighed, pulling up to park in front of the dorm house then yanking Eric across the center console into a tight hug. "There was nothing you could have done differently."

"I should have saved him, I shouldn't have let us get separated, I shouldn't have made us go in there at all, I should have—I should have—I should have . . ." The words petered out after the initial rush, and Eric's mouth moved, gaping like a fish as he tried to think of all the ways he could have made things go differently, but no sound came out.

Hunter didn't give him time to stew. "I do wish you'd told me before we left that they'd drugged you. I should probably go back and get samples."

Eric made a sound like a deflating balloon, the whimper completely involuntary, and Hunter gave him another tight squeeze, pressing a kiss to his temple that lingered probably longer than it ought to, considering their circumstances.

"Britt and I will check it out this afternoon." Hunter pulled back, detangling himself from Eric so slowly, Eric could almost fool himself into thinking Hunter didn't want to let him go. But really, Hunter was probably worried that once he wasn't holding Eric together anymore, he'd fall apart.

Eric chewed on the inside of his cheek and pulled himself

back into his own seat, straightening his spine. He needed to be Eric Marcelino, Venator, now. There was no time for anything else.

"For now, let's get you in the house. Britt needs to look you over before the kids see you."

Then they were out of the truck and heading toward the house, Eric refusing to let Hunter help him across the cracked sidewalk, holding his chin high. He knew without a doubt that the kids and his friends would fight him on what was coming next, and he needed to be ready for that battle. Because he wasn't leaving Tony, not for one second longer than he had to.

Tony McMahon was too important.

Chapter 26

ERIC'S EARS ACHED, cringing away from the loudness of the room around him. Britt had treated his wounds, but there wasn't much she could do for the hangover and the headache aside from pump him full of painkillers and water. She'd threatened to give him an IV, waving a needle around like it was nothing, and Hunter had to excuse himself before he passed the fuck out. Which would have been funny, considering the tattoos that littered his whole body, but wasn't because Eric had been on the verge of fainting himself and *he* wasn't afraid of needles at all.

Now, he was surrounded by the people he loved the most. The ones he had fought tooth and nail to protect for these last nineteen—nearly twenty—years. And as he watched them argue over what to do and how to do it, something warm and weighted settled into his chest. Something like—like—like *knowing*. Like understanding for the first time.

Bert was red faced, his curly hair sticking up in all directions from where he'd run his hands through it so often, the curls had been stretched to their limits.

Kalla and Kate wore twin expressions of determination, brows creased, lips pursed, hands clenched tight into fists at their sides.

Nik sat close to Lu, Finn on the other side, their shoulders pressed into hers for support, holding her up as she watched the commotion with eyes that seemed unable to focus on a single subject for long. She'd been quiet since Eric told everyone what happened, but Nik's voice was loud enough for the both of them.

Hunter and Ava had come to flank Eric on the couch at some point, their bodies crowding so close to him, there was hardly room for his hips much less his shoulders. Britt sat on the arm of the couch, holding Hunter's hand in her lap so tightly that Eric was sure she was grinding the knuckles together.

Chase sat by himself in the chair closest to the fireplace, looking like a ship out to sea with the way his face had grown paler with every second that passed. Poor kid. Out of all of Eric's students, it was Chase who wanted this the least. Chase who was the least ready to be a Venator. He was just a baby.

They were *all* just babies, even the adults. None of them truly understood what they were signing on for. None of them truly knew the danger that Eric faced every fucking day of his life. But it was time for him to share that burden. Time for his friends—his family—to shoulder some of the load. He couldn't keep doing this by himself, not if his instincts were correct about what was coming for them.

Their voices were too loud in his ears as they argued, every one of them trying to shout over all the others. It would be sweet how all of them had a plan, all of them wanted to help, if it weren't making his head throb. Eric lifted a hand to rub at the bridge of his nose, pinching it and letting out a long, slow sigh. He didn't open his eyes again until Ava reached down and gave his thigh a squeeze.

With a pat to the hand still holding his leg, Eric rose from the couch, and the entire room fell into silence. Sweat pricked at the base of his spine, nerves chasing it down his back to rest there. Eric Marcelino had spent his life as a lone warrior. A solitary sentinel standing against the tide of the undead in Ironport. But as he straightened his spine, his eyes sweeping around the room to take in his small army, he felt more like a general on the brink of war.

And he needed a plan. *Fuck.* He needed a plan.

"I would like to provide backup," Finn said, her voice quiet and sure.

Eric's heart gave a sick twist of gratitude; it clenched then beat again double time. These kids. These fucking people. All of them were ready to fly into battle, no questions asked. They'd accepted Tony as one of them. Brought him into the fold, even if they didn't know much about him, even if they hadn't seen much of him, even if—in Kalla's case—they didn't trust him. Eric cared about him, and that was enough.

"No." Eric cleared his throat around a well of emotion and lifted his chin. "No, the kids will stay—"

"But I have training," Finn argued. She had been so quiet up to this point, so subdued. She hung around Lu, sure, but when they were causing trouble, she usually let Lu do the talking. "This is what my family raised me for."

"Maybe that's true." Eric licked his lips, a plan already forming, his mind working over the best way to utilize their assets. "But you're still barely nineteen, Finn. I'm not putting you in the line of fire like that. No. I've got a better idea."

He paused and everyone around him leaned forward.

———

Everything hurt.

Everything hurt, and there was a throbbing behind Tony's eyes.

No. Not a throbbing. Piercing. Stabbing. Slicing.

He thanked the Goddess for the dark, but not for the stench that burned in his nose, made his mouth thick with saliva, bile crawling up his throat. Fuck. Fucking *fuck.* Maybe dying would have been better?

"Wake up," someone whispered in the dark. Cold fingers

traced the sore places on his neck, making him wince and jerk back. "Sorry. Sorry," the voice murmured, soft and kind. "I think they're infected."

"Vamp bites can't get infected." Or at least, Tony didn't think they could. He'd been bitten plenty of times and never had that issue. But then, he'd always been able to go home and have them treated by either himself or Lu. There was always disinfectant and bandages until the bites closed up. And he'd never taken on so much venom before.

"They're swollen."

Tony peeked his eye open and groaned as the bit of light from the crack under the door burned his sensitive retinas. Still, he forced himself to focus on the face hovering over him. Blond hair. Bright blue eyes. A long elegant nose. Dash Chadwick.

"The fuck is the mayor's brother doing in a shithole like this?" He tried to push himself up to sit against the wall, but his elbows gave out before he'd even lifted his torso an inch off the ground. Hitting the floor again hurt, jarred every aching bone in his body, and that's when he noticed the trembling. The way his form shook with shivers, cold sinking deep into his skin. "Do these fuckers not believe in heat?"

Dash reached for him, carefully telegraphing his movements until he had scooped Tony's shoulders off the floor and pressed them into the wall. Then he settled next to Tony. "That's the venom talking."

"What?" The words took a moment to register, Tony's brain having to work double time to fight off the fuzzy feeling that clung to it. Every thought was slow and syrupy. The venom. "How many times have they bit me?"

Dash winced at the question, and in the light from the streetlamp outside, Tony could see how his brow creased, his lips thinned to a tight line. He didn't want to answer, and Tony didn't think he could blame him. No one liked delivering bad news.

"How long have I been here?" It felt like it had only been a few hours, but if he'd been fed on as many times as it seemed . . .

"A few days? Maybe a week? I—" Dash swallowed, his throat bobbing with the motion, and he leaned away from Tony as if he were afraid of him. Had Tony been violent the other times he'd been lucid enough to react at all? Dash reached for his neck, palm covering several overlapping bite marks of his own, all in various stages of healing. "I've lost track."

Tony swallowed around the question *How long have you been here?* and nodded. There were other questions: *How many are there? Do you know where we are? How long was I out? Do you think anyone's coming for us?* But he forced those down too. He didn't think he wanted to know the answers, especially not for the last one. Because who *would* come for him? Who would bother? Other than maybe Lu, but Eric would keep her from doing anything rash or stupid. Hell, they probably thought he was dead already.

"Don't you remember the bites?" Dash asked.

He didn't—

He *did*.

They pounded through him, making his head spin.

He was dragged from the dark room by his arms, his shoulders screaming from the pressure of nearly being pulled out of their sockets. Feet kicking at the ground uselessly. And a sob, choking off his breath, making his eyes burn.

They strapped him to a chair. The leather tight, cutting into his forearms, his shins. Legs spread wide. A metal bit between his teeth to keep him from snapping at the creatures writhing around him like a single massive shadow, waiting for their turn to feed.

Then too many teeth in too many places.

His wrists.

The crooks of his elbows.

Each side of his neck.

His inner thighs.

Panic settled in first. His heart rate ratcheted up so high, it made him lightheaded.

Bliss followed after. The venom pumping through him so fast, it made him moan. Every inch of his skin tingling in a way that far outweighed the tender kisses of Eric's lips. Had him coming untouched and unashamed.

Then a voice would say, "Not too much, make him last" from the darkness, and they would all pull away as if tugged by an invisible leash. Leaving Tony bereft, free falling through space and crash landing back to earth in a jolt that jarred every bone in his body, left him aching hours later.

"He's not coming for you," Dash said, so soft and sure that it felt like a mercy killing when it dashed all of Tony's hopes.

"Who?" Tony shifted uncomfortably in his soiled clothes, his fingers shaking where they gripped the hard floor, trying to gain purchase where there was none to be found. He didn't think he'd said Eric's name out loud. Didn't think he'd begged and pleaded for Eric to save him. But maybe he had. Maybe he'd whispered the name in his venom-hazed state like a prayer, like a wish, for his avenging angel to come to him, to get him out of there. There was no way to tell.

"Eric Marcelino." Dash reached down to take Tony's hand, and Goddess above and below, Tony let him thread their fingers together. Let Dash feel the way his nerves trembled, his muscles jumped. "Even if he does come," Dash said, almost casually, lifting Tony's hand from the floor, his wrist pulled close so Dash could rub his stubbled chin against the still-aching bite marks there, "he can't save you now. Only I can."

"What?" Tony's eyes opened again—when had he closed them?—to watch as Dash peeled back his lips in a feral smile, the light from outside the window glinting off a sharpened fang. "I saw you—I saw you in the—"

In the sun. The rays shining golden in Dash's hair making him even more handsome, Tony remembered. Sunglasses perched on Dash's nose like any other human who'd just rolled into the garage after having been outside.

The sun. The third and only way to kill a vampire. A wooden or silver stake to the heart. Beheading. Or the sun.

"Oh that?" Dash laughed, and it sounded like bells. Beautiful and tinkling. His eyes glittered with it in the moonlight, and Tony wondered what he'd look like laughing in the sunshine, his head thrown back, his blond hair glistening. "Little trick I learned centuries ago."

Centuries echoed in Tony's mind for a moment, but he shook his head and forced himself to focus.

"Magical creatures—folk, I believe is the term they use—aren't nearly as tasty as humans, but they sure get the job done, don't they? You thought I was just another normie, didn't you?"

Tony nodded, open mouthed, in awe of the creature before him. A viper hidden beneath the skin of a harmless garden snake.

"Oh, sweet boy," Dash cooed, bending down to bite into Tony's wrist like an apple, sending Tony plummeting through the dark, dropping to the depths, his stomach in free fall, "you have so much to learn about our kind."

When he said *our*, it sounded like he meant Tony too. Like he was one of them now. But that couldn't be right, he hadn't—

Blood coated his tongue, thick and metallic, then he was soaring.

CHAPTER 27

HUNTER DELACROIX WAS the kind of witch who had never learned patience. The kind who rushed results and had to walk away from potions that took too damn long because he got bored. It was half the reason he'd never excelled in his craft the way so many others of equal intelligence had. Why he had to rely on the magic etched into his skin with a tattoo needle or a piercing gun. He couldn't sit still. The fact that he wasn't exactly powerful—likely never would be so long as he remained covenless—created the perfect storm for a witch who never specialized, never settled, always hopped from one thing to the next.

Still, he tried for patience for Eric's sake. He aimed for it, like Diana notching her arrow and targeting a stag. But even with that, he could tell that finding the new nest was taking longer than any of them would have liked.

Every second that ticked by sent another bead of sweat down between Hunter's shoulder blades, another painful lurch in his chest as he watched the tick of the clock strike Eric like a blow. Another tock, and Eric's face shifted into something like a wince, his shoulders hunching in a little more.

Hunter tapped the screen, refreshing the map again. Even with all the times he'd done it, and the tweaks he'd made to the back end—under threat of death from the witch who'd created it should he break it. Goddess, when this was all over, he was going to see Icarus Ashthorne in person and beg at her feet for her to take him as a pupil. Under a month. She'd made this app in *under a month*. What the fuck? There was still nothing.

"Nothing yet?" Eric asked for the fifth time in as many minutes. His skin had gone paler than usual—the moles along his cheek, his neck, in glaring contrast to the rest of him —and it had nothing at all to do with his injuries. It was the wear of waiting.

"They have some kind of cloaking magic," Hunter said, running his thumb and pointer finger under the nose pads of his glasses so he could pinch the bridge of his nose where a headache was forming. Britt nudged his knee with her own under the table, soft and easy comfort. Because she saw him, because she understood him. A little went a long way with them, and her touch settled some of the thrumming, buzzing nerves under his skin. "They have to be. You even said it yourself: your Venator radar wasn't working on them."

Eric shifted in his seat, his fingers clenching and unclenching where they rested on the table between him and Hunter. Hunter almost felt bad for bringing it up; he knew it made Eric uncomfortable to admit his failings. Especially as this one in particular might be what led to Tony being taken. But Hunter had never been one to pull punches, not with Eric, not in a situation like this one.

"You think they have a witch on their payroll." Britt frowned over at him, her thumbs *tap-tap-tap*ping against the table, the thumb ring on her right hand making a soft echoey sound that soothed Hunter's rattled nerves. It was a noise he'd heard so often over the years since they'd married, it was hard not to find solace in it.

Britt was so much like him sometimes, it scared him. The same, and yet different. She had to be moving constantly. Was never the sit-still type. Didn't deal with it well when there wasn't someone to fix in front of her. It was one of the reasons they worked. She was forever dragging him out on hikes, kayaking on the bay, riding bikes through the mountains to Moondale, something. Keeping his energy levels managed enough so he could focus on his work. On ancient texts, and new tech, things she herself found no interest in but appreciated because he appreciated them. It was true what they said: opposites did attract.

Goddess, he'd gotten so lucky with her.

"Of course, they do!" Kalla slammed her hands on the table, making Bert snort once loudly in his sleep, then grumble as he rolled over where he was pressed into the back of the couch by Chase, who'd curled up next to him seeking comfort. The kids had passed out in the living room at some point after Eric told them all to go the fuck to bed and they hadn't listened. Now they were scattered on couches, the floor, in chairs. The only one not sleeping was Tony's younger sister, who sat with Finn's head on one leg, Nik's on the other. Lu looked about two seconds from falling over but had managed to only flinch at the loud noise, not waking the others.

"Kalla," Eric hissed, a warning in his tone as he narrowed his eyes at her.

"Sorry. Sorry." Kalla held up her hands and moved away from the table to lean against the island, but it did nothing to release the tension that seemed to linger in her shoulders. Coiled and ready to spring. "I'm just saying, if they've been under our noses this long, someone must be helping them."

"Okay," Ava mumbled tiredly, wiping the sleep from her eyes. She'd leaned forward on the table, her head pillowed in her arms, and Hunter was sure that for a while there she'd been asleep. A long-ass day of mission prep could do that to anyone, but especially a witch who'd been tasked with making sure their air was breathable once they went in. "But who in their right mind would work with vamps?"

When Hunter looked to Britt to check in with her again, she was sitting straight backed, her eyes wide. Years of working at the hospital in Ironport and taking shifts that sometimes stretched closer to seventy-two hours than twenty-four had left her much better suited for this than the rest of them. Goddess, she was a marvel. While the rest of them were worn thin as the minutes turned into hours, she stayed upright and alert.

"It's gotta be about the money," Kalla muttered, already on her way to the coffee pot to start them all another round. She sounded hilariously like a cop. "It's always about the money."

"Either way," Eric said. He had taken to rubbing at the scabbed-over bites on his neck, Hunter noticed, and it took everything in him to keep from reaching for Eric. If he could, he'd thread their fingers, he'd hold all the pieces of Eric tight while Eric glued himself back together, just as he'd done on the sidewalk in front of that damnable house. He didn't though, because he knew better. That way led madness—Hunter was intimately aware of this fact. Eric didn't want him like that, and Hunter loved Britt. But before Britt, there was Eric Marcelino, and try as Hunter might, he'd had to come to terms with the fact that there was simply no getting Eric Marcelino out of one's system, not once he was there, not for Hunter. Oddly like a vampire once they'd been invited into a person's house. Even when his love for Britt settled warm into his veins, making him cozy and comfy. "When they finally uncloak themselves, it will be because they want to be seen."

The words landed like a blow, a death rattle, in the quiet between them.

And they all sat with the implications of what Eric said for one beat, two, before Britt said in the most matter-of-fact tone possible, "Another trap."

Hunter's breath caught in his lungs, threatening to turn

into a sob, but he looked across at Britt and found her staring back at him, her gaze steady, and he calmed. She wasn't even bothered by this, not nearly as much as Hunter thought she ought to be, not being born of their world. Britt was a normie. Just a girl who'd fallen in love with a witch and became friends with a Venator. But she was so fucking brave. Always had been.

Heart swelling, Hunter reached for her, and as if sensing he was coming Britt's hand had already slipped across the table to meet him halfway, linking their fingers. One tight squeeze, two, and Hunter felt the zing of Britt's courage travel along his nerves, up his veins, and settle into his heart. She was beside him. She would always be beside him. If Britt could do this, so could he.

"Definitely." Eric straightened up a little more, his shoulders pulling back, chest puffing out. Hunter recognized it as the posture Eric used when he prepared for battle.

"Okay, but what's their end goal?" Ava sat up, brushing her hair back from her face. "Why all the theatrics? And the hostage taking? Why leave you alive? What's it all for?"

"They're fucking vampires, Ava, do they need a reason to mess with people's heads?" Kalla asked furiously from where she glared down at the coffee pot like that could make it fill faster.

Which meant she missed the way Eric's shoulders tensed at the questions and the comment. Missed how his brows pinched in the center before he smoothed them out. Maybe only Hunter and Ava had caught it.

Ava made eye contact with him, a whole conversation in a single look. Eric had never hidden the way he felt about how similar vampire and Venator were, at least not from them. He might have tried, but it was always transparently obvious to the two people closest to him that he felt a kinship toward the vampires that he couldn't explain. Felt that their abilities lined up too closely for him to shrug vampires off as just another boogeyman in the night. He was conflicted. Ava and Hunter may not understand it, but they could see it. Kalla, as always, missed it.

Hunter shook his head. "Whatever the reason, it doesn't matter. We're getting Tony back. We can worry about their motivations later."

Kalla grunted but didn't push the subject any further, and the room lapsed into a tense silence once more.

The clock ticked ever closer to the witching hour, and Hunter wondered if the vampires would show themselves at all that night, or if they'd wait. But Eric had a feeling they would, and Hunter had learned long ago to trust Eric's gut above all else. It was how he'd met Britt, after all. So he tapped the screen, refreshing the map once more, and—

And his fingers tightened around the phone in his palm. "We've got something."

Chairs scraped loud enough against the floor to wake the sleeping kids in the other room, then Hunter was surrounded by way too many people, all staring at the blinking dot on the east side of Ironport. A single dot. A single vortex of negative energy in all of Ironport. Definitely a trap.

"That's only a few streets down from where they ambushed us." Eric rubbed at his eyes, grabbing his chin so he could tilt his neck one direction and the other, cracking the vertebrae and stretching out the muscle. Then he dropped his hands, shaking them out.

"You couldn't have known," Hunter said, not needing to see Eric's face to feel the guilt radiating off him in waves. All he could hope was that Tony McMahon was alive when they got to him, or Eric would never *ever* forgive himself. This would hang above Eric until it eventually killed him, likely in the line of duty. And that wasn't something Hunter was willing to watch happen.

"I should have checked!" Eric snarled, baring blunt teeth

at Hunter like *he* was the enemy and not the vampires who'd taken Tony.

Hunter raised his brows in question. In challenge. In warning. A reminder that Eric didn't do *that* anymore, he didn't direct his anger at people who didn't deserve it. Not since the last time when it'd almost gotten him killed.

Eric relented, his hands carding through his oily hair, and nodded. "Sorry. I'm just—"

"I know. But we can't go into this thing waving our dicks around." Hunter took a screencap of the map, just in case the vamps decided to cloak themselves again. He didn't think it was an accident that they'd shown up when they had. He knew Eric was right. The whole nest would be ready and waiting for them. It was a good thing Eric wasn't alone. A good thing he had a team. It would give him an advantage. *Them* an advantage.

"He's right, Big Ricky," Ava said, patting his shoulder and offering him one of those sharp smiles that always came with her teasing. "You're too smart for that shit these days."

"And you've got us now," Bert chirped.

"He's right, you've got us," Kalla agreed.

Eric ducked his head in a nod, like he was trying to gather himself, like he was preparing himself for war. But Hunter clocked the glassy sheen of his eyes before they disappeared under that mass of brown hair. He bit back a snort and did not roll his eyes at the idea that Eric *ever* thought he was *alone* in this. Stupid boy.

When Eric raised his head a second later, his eyes were clear and his jaw was set into a determined clench that left no room for argument when he said, "We leave in ten."

Chapter 28

THE WORLD WAS all soft edges and floaty-ness. A warm hue layered over everything, settling against his skin, making it hard to focus on anything. But he didn't want to. Didn't want to come back down.

How Tony ever could have thought himself in love with anyone else was beyond him now. Unfathomable. How could he have been when this bright angel, his Dash, existed?

"You're mine," Dash mumbled against Tony's temple, dragging a fang over the thin skin not quite hard enough to draw blood to the surface, but enough to send a shiver of pain down Tony's spine, pooling liquid heat in his belly. "You were made for me."

"I was." It was the truth, Tony felt it down to his marrow. He had been born of the Goddess, crafted by the huntress Diana, all for this man. For the one holding him so tightly, he felt pinpricks of pain in his hips. But the weight of Dash's hands kept Tony rooted, kept him from floating away on a cloud of cotton.

But something niggled at the back of his mind. A voice. The words *I'm coming for you, Tony* said in such a sure, clear voice that they rang true as a bell, echoing through his head. Who had said that to him? He tried to latch on to the voice, to follow it like a string through a labyrinth and let it lead him to the man who'd said the words, but the way was blocked, distorted. This was the most lucid he'd felt in hours, days, *years* maybe. Because of that voice guiding him back to himself, even if Tony didn't know who it belonged to. Couldn't picture anything aside from a constellation of moles on skin.

"What if he comes for me?" Tony asked, leaning more heavily into Dash, seeking comfort and reassurance where he'd never needed it before. Maybe he had though. Maybe he'd always needed someone else to prop him up, there had just never been anyone else to do it till now. Because he was made for his Dash.

"He who?" Dash countered. He reached for Tony's wrist, blood still dribbling down his arm toward his elbow from the last bite, lazy and slow. Congealing in a cold wet pool at the crook of his arm that Tony didn't have enough energy to wipe away.

Tony made a sound of discontent, of confusion, as Dash lifted his wrist and bent to lick the lazy trail of cooled blood from his elbow up to his palm where he pressed a toothy kiss, soft and slow.

"He who, my darling?" Dash pressed, nuzzling into the skin he found there, nibbling at it with teeth too sharp.

"Eric." The name crawled up Tony's throat, unbidden. Not there one moment, and suddenly there the next. As if it hadn't existed before he formed the letters on his tongue. A face appeared behind his eyelids. Dark hair flopping into honey-brown eyes. Pink lips stretched into a wide smile. A single delicious beauty mark set off to the side of that smile, begging to be kissed, to be bitten. Pleading for tongue and teeth and lips alike. "He said he'd come for me. He said he'd rescue me. He *promised*."

"He needs another dose," Dash growled.

"Fucking Venator metabolism," someone said from across the room.

Tony leaned into Dash more heavily, making a soft, plaintive sound that he hoped would quell the irritation in Dash's voice.

Dash soothed him with a hush, nuzzling into his neck and brushing fingers down over Tony's hips.

"We should have run more tests."

"Yes, and how would you have liked me to do that, *Mayor Chadwick*?" Dash snapped. His nails dug more deeply into Tony's hips, drawing a whimper from him that went ignored. "You wouldn't bring me the Marcelino boy when I asked for him a *decade* ago."

"I told you, we need him. For the prophecy." Janet sounded like she was rolling her eyes, but Tony was too tired to open his own to find out. "It's the only reason I've kept the Huntsmen from fucking killing him."

"The prophecy. The prophecy. You Huntsmen and your fucking prophecies." Dash laughed, sharp and biting. The sound had teeth, and it raked across Tony's senses. "What of this one?" He grabbed Tony by the scruff of his neck and forced his face away from where he'd buried himself in Dash's shoulder, giving him a hard shake that made Tony's teeth rattle. "He's a part of the prophecy. Your precious Mac Mathghamhna blood. The last of his line, just like Marcelino. I smelled it on him from the very first."

"Which is why I told you, you can't kill him."

"*Told* me." Dash snarled, spittle dripping from his fangs as he bared them at Janet in a feral show of dominance. He was still clutching Tony by the scruff of his neck, the grip so tight Dash's sharp nails drew blood, bringing burning tears to Tony's eyes. "What gives you the right to order me around, Janet Chadwick? Have you forgotten who your maker is? Who dragged you from the fiery wreckage and made you *whole*? Who are *you* to order *me*?"

"No one, sir." Janet bent her blond head, her shoulders curving inward. Making herself smaller, even as she stood above where Dash and Tony leaned against the wall opposite.

The picture of graceful submission. "But if we want to end the reign of terror the Huntsmen bring down on our people—"

"I *know* what it's all for, *Madam Mayor*," Dash seethed. "Tell your witch we're almost ready. She can peel back the cloaking spell. Tony is almost there, and I want Marcelino to come to me now."

"What if he doesn't come alone?" Janet shifted on her feet, her hands fidgeting where they were clasped in front of her.

"Then there will be casualties." Dash licked his teeth, his tongue tracing the hints of red that remained from where he'd bitten Tony over and over again. Pumped him full of venom.

Casualties. What did that word mean again? Tony couldn't remember. He struggled to focus, to keep his eyes open as every blink seemed to last longer and longer.

"Maybe that little witch Marcelino is so fond of. The one who thinks he knows so much about our kind. Weren't you supposed to kill him *weeks* ago?"

Janet gritted her teeth, the sound of grinding loud in Tony's sensitive ears. "Unfortunately, Marcelino managed to save him."

"That's a funny way of saying that you failed, Madam Mayor."

Tony barked a laugh, then descended into a fit of giggles that made his belly ache. He wriggled out of Dash's hold on his neck and buried his laughter in Dash's warm shoulder again, curling languidly against his bright, fearsome angel.

"He's been listening this whole time?" Janet sounded like she was frowning, the words slightly accusatory.

"Of course he has, I *told* you he needed another dose." Dash's fingers stroked through Tony's hair, soft and soothing. "Don't you, my pet?"

"Mm-hmm," Tony agreed, but he wasn't really sure what he was agreeing too. All he knew was the world felt too sharp, too hard all of the sudden. He wanted the softness again, the blurry edges and the indistinct sounds. He wanted to go back to that place. Floating. "Please, Dash." He arched into the hold his Dash had on him, his throat open and waiting. "Please, can I have some more?"

"Soon, my darling. Soon." Dash shushed him again, giving his hair a soft tug as a warning. "It doesn't matter if he was listening. By the time Marcelino reaches us, he'll be too late. I'll have full control over this one. You won't tell a soul, will you, my pet?"

"Tell them what?" Tony slurred.

"Exactly." Dash chuckled softly, the sound like wind chimes in the air, brightly colored and vibrating with happiness. It tasted like popsicles in summertime. Brushed Tony's skin like silk and satin. He leaned into it, wanting to feel more. "Good pet," Dash cooed, then turned his attention back to Janet. "Go and do what you're *told*, Chadwick."

Janet dipped into a bow and exited the room, the locks clicking into place behind her, trapping Dash and Tony inside. Tony didn't quite understand why, but he didn't think he minded at all as Dash sank his fangs into Tony's neck again, and the world hazed over beautifully.

Chapter 29

KNOWING he wasn't alone was both a gift and curse wrapped into one, Eric found.

It was a gift. It bolstered him. It made him stand tall.

It was a curse. It terrified him. It made him paranoid.

It made him strong.

It made him weak.

Eric wavered on his feet in the cold and the dark. His pockets were heavy. Loaded down with stakes, and silver, and even a few wolfsbane-dipped daggers—they wouldn't kill a vamp, but they would sure as shit slow them down. Give Eric the time he needed to decapitate the fucker or stake them, whichever was more convenient. But now that he was here, he was waffling. He knew the plan. Knew it was the best chance they had at getting Tony back. It was just—

What happened if he lost someone else in the process? It would be all his fault for bringing them here. This wasn't their fight, it was his, and they shouldn't be forced to lose their lives to it.

"This is the Mystery Machine to the Scooby Gang. Are you sure you don't need a few extra sets of hands, Big Ricky? Over." Bert's voice crackled in his ear on the earbud, ripping Eric from his cold indecision. Lu was counting on him to get her brother back. The kids were counting on him to keep them safe. If he couldn't do that, what the fuck was he even here for?

"You know exactly what your orders are, Bert," Eric hissed back, his hands clenching and unclenching at his sides as he watched the front door to the house where the nest had moved. It was a far cry from the one where Eric and Tony found the last nest. Nicer, more well-kept. Freshly painted siding. Uncracked windows. And a door that looked to be locked tight. "Can you get the door from here, Ava?"

"What if it's not locked?" But already her sunshine magic rose to her fingertips, sprouting like buttercups in the spring, a spell on her lips as she held out a hand to send the glittering stream of magic across the several feet toward the door.

"I'm just saying," Bert pressed, "we have field training. Britt, Hunter, and Ava don't. We'd be the better option. Over."

"And I'm just saying that what you're proving to me right now, Humbert, is that you can't follow fucking orders out in the field. If I can't trust you to do as you're told on something like this, how can I trust you to have my back when we're in the middle of a horde of vampires?" Eric's eyes remained fixed on the door as Ava worked her magic slowly, and carefully. It would have been easier to burst through the door like a battering ram. To break the frame and slam it against the opposite wall. But that would defeat the purpose of them standing there out of sniffing range for the vamps.

"Sick burn," Nik muttered into his own mic. Someone must have smacked him because a moment later he said, "What?! It was!"

Humbert huffed but didn't argue further. Instead, he said, "All known exits are covered, sir."

"Good. No one gets out." Eric cracked his knuckles, then his neck, then dropped his hands to his sides to shake them loose. He wished he'd brought the sword Bert had tried to sneak into his bag. He knew Bert only wanted to bring it because it looked cool, but it hefted like a bat, and Eric would be far more comfortable with it than the small daggers strapped to his hips.

"Yes, sir," Kate answered.

Eric relaxed a little more into his stance, something in his shoulders going loose and liquid, more tiger on the prowl than frozen prey animal. "No survivors," he muttered to himself, hoping the kids didn't hear it. They didn't need to know exactly why he wanted the exits watched. They didn't need to know the horrible thing he planned to do once he was inside. But he was going to end this. For them. For Lu. For Tony.

"Keep the van running," he said after a heartbeat of silence when Ava's magic had finally worked the door open.

"Keep supplies on hand," Nik said, and Eric felt a surge of pride for his kids. They were ready. Maybe not to fight vampires, but to have his back. To do what they were doing right now. Maybe one day soon, they *would* be ready to fight vampires.

"Call for backup at your signal," Chase said softly.

Not that Eric actually thought backup would come. Even if they were trained, the Huntsmen would never send their non-Venator sons and daughters into the fray like this. No. There was too much money and power at stake for that. They would leave him and his to die. He didn't tell the kids that. Didn't want them to see the truth of their world yet. But he had a feeling they knew. Still, they agreed to do what he said.

"Ready?" Kalla asked. The safety on the pistol in her hand clicked off, and she braced the weapon at her side.

The answer was *not really*, but he took the talisman Ava had created to keep his air clean from his pocket and slid it over his neck anyway. He turned to look over his shoulder at Britt and Hunter—who lingered at the back of their group—

nodded once, then started up the walk with Ava and Kalla flanking him.

The front door opened onto a two-story foyer, open and echoing—hence the quiet entry—a smaller room on either side of it. With two quick nods, he, Ava, and Kalla broke off from each other. Ava took the room on the right, Eric the room on the left, and Kalla watched the stairs.

Three vampires waited for Eric in the first room, and although they all rose and kicked up a fuss—hissing at him—they were dust before the bottle one of them had knocked over spilled onto the floor.

Younglings then. Slow and sloppy.

Would that be all there was?

No. Couldn't be. Younglings didn't plan. They were too driven by hunger.

And unless one of them had been a biochemist—they didn't look like biochemists to Eric—there was no way they had created the drug used to knock him and Tony unconscious. Hunter hadn't had long to study it, but what he found told them that either it was created by a human with way too much time on their hands—and a degree in biochem coupled with a deep understanding of magical anatomy—or a witch. Probably a healer.

Eric was moving through the room, inspecting the table— the vamps had been playing cards—and making his way to the other door when the first shot rang out and all hell broke loose.

"Kalla," Eric hissed into the com at his ear, ducking his back to the wall so he couldn't be seen in the entrance to the room, "what the fuck are you doing? This was meant to be a quiet thing. Clear a path, extract, burn the place to the fucking ground."

"I've been spotted," Kalla growled, followed by another echoing shot.

"How many?"

"Just two. I can handle these; you go on ahead."

"Ava?" Eric closed his eyes, listening for the sounds of approaching footsteps, but he couldn't hear anything above the echoing shots of Kalla trying to bring down two vampires with silver bullets. Hopefully she succeeded before she ran out.

"I could use a hand," Ava grunted into her mic, and Eric took one last breath before he crossed the room back to the door he'd come in.

"Stay where you are."

"Not gonna be a problem. They got me pinned."

The sulfur of gunshots and the biting, blistering smell of desert sunshine burned at Eric's nose as he pushed through the foyer. The two vampires that Kalla could "handle" were rapidly getting within range, too close for the pistol in her hand to be effective anymore. One lunged for her and Eric moved quick, stake already in hand, meeting them halfway and using their momentum to bury the wood into their heart.

"Eric?" Hunter's voice came through, tense and clear over the comms. "Do you need us?"

The other vampire turned tail and ran up the stairs.

"No." Eric reached for one of the daggers at his side, grabbing the hilt in such a way so he could throw it, but Kalla beat him to it, her aim ringing true this time, burying the silver-and-wood bullet into the creature's heart. They had a moment to release a soft surprised noise right before they burst into dust, leaving behind only the fangs that clattered to the floor.

"Eric?" Hunter asked again, worry making the words tight.

"You and Britt stay put," Eric ordered, jerking his head toward the next room where he could hear a struggle and Ava cursing up a storm while her magic sent flashes of light through the open doorway. "We don't need our second wave yet."

And the longer he could keep his not-so-great fighters off the field of battle, the better.

"You comin' or *what*?" Ava snapped from where she was.

"Next time, you're bringing the crossbow," he said to Kalla and motioned for her to press to one side of the door while he took the other. Tilting his head, he got a good view of where Ava had backed herself against the wall, her Cross— a rag doll made of the blanket she'd used as a child—held out in front of her, creating a barrier while she hurled spells at the four vampires biting and snarling to get at her. The sunshine-sweet hiss of her magic bit into their flesh, but it did nothing to stop them coming, and Eric knew that if they didn't reach her soon, her faith would waver, her fear would take over, and the Cross would be useless.

"You go in this way. I'm going to circle around through the kitchen." He pulled two stakes from his pocket, holding one out to Kalla, who scowled at the piece of wood like she hadn't been trained to use one from the age of six.

"What if there are more of them? What if they see you?" Kalla hissed, her fingers wrapping tightly around the weapon.

"You let me worry about that. Just get in there and give Ava some room to breathe."

Without even pausing to nod, Kalla stepped inside, the fresh scent of blood drawing the vampires away, and Eric crept through the foyer toward the kitchen. Why all the vamps hadn't come running at the same time, he didn't know. Either they were told not to, or they expected him and his people to pass out from the drug in the air. But when he reached the kitchen, he found five more waiting for him.

Not younglings this time, but hungry enough for them all to lunge toward him at once.

On quick and sure feet, Eric danced out of their way, separating them as they spun to try to follow his movements, making it almost too easy to pick them off one by one. But by then, he'd drawn the attention of others. From the big open room off the kitchen—a living room maybe, he thought he saw the edge of a couch as they crowded through the door—came six more.

Because of the width of the doorway, they had to come through a couple at a time. The first two went down with thrown daggers, paralyzed by the wolfsbane coating. The next Eric met halfway to the door, kicking out to knock them back into the two behind them, sending them down like dominos. While they scrambled to get up, he thrust a stake into one's heart and retrieved his daggers from the first two, trading the buried knives for the stab of a stake as he moved. Slicing through the next three was like cutting through butter with his stake and dagger in hand, then the first floor was clear but for the vampires with Kalla and Ava.

"I need heat signatures, Mystery Machine," Eric said as he pulled a device from his pocket, sticking one end to one side of the hall and stretching the thin silver wire across to the other. "Where are they keeping our people?"

"Third floor," Bert replied, quick and efficient.

"There's two up there," Kate said.

"Human?" Eric cocked his head thoughtfully. Why would the vampires keep more than just Tony hostage? Why had he not heard about any recent disappearances?

"Based on the body temp, it's a Venator and a normie," Chase murmured, soft but confident. "Venator run a little warmer than normies."

"It's all the magic," Finn added. There was delight in her voice, like knowing this made her a good student.

"Gold stars all around. Remind me to pick up ice cream on the way home." Eric smiled to himself at the soft cheers that went up from the kids, quiet hope blossoming in his chest. "Any word on how many stand between me and our target?"

"Hard to say." Lu's voice was strained, but he was glad to hear from her, for perhaps the first time since he'd told her what happened to her brother. He knew she wanted to help, knew she'd rather be at his side fighting her way to Tony, but this was better. This was safer. And Tony would have Eric's head if Lu got hurt. "The heat signatures outside of those two are all over the fucking place."

"And what does that mean?" Eric pressed, willing to turn any moment into a teachable one. Besides, when would they get this kind of experience again? Not anytime soon, if he could help it.

Eric heard Bert make a noise like he wanted to answer, but someone must have smacked him because he grumbled and stayed silent.

"That the time since they fed last varies. A vampire's heat is based on the amount of blood in their system."

"Ding, ding, ding. You get extra fudge sauce, Miss McMahon." The wire set up and his kids momentarily mollified, Eric returned to the task at hand: getting Kalla and Ava the fuck out of that room.

"Hey, fuck face," Eric called, drawing the attention of the vampires in the room to him. Kalla and Ava had managed to dust one of them, but that still left three bearing down on them. They all whirled, their pupils narrowing to slits, their teeth dripping with saliva. Eric blew them a kiss and took off running. The wire he'd set up beheaded the first vamp to follow him, but the next two were smarter; they ducked it. But not smart enough as they'd turned their backs on Ava and Kalla, who shot one then staked the other through.

"Is that all of them?" Ava asked. She favored her right side, blood dribbling down from under one of her sleeves.

"Not by a long shot. How bad are you hurt?" Eric had already started toward the stairs. Two more floors full of vamps. Honestly, he wished they'd rushed him—that would have been better.

"I'll manage." Ava's magic flared back to life around her hands, burning hotter this time. "I just need a little kindling."

"That's my girl!" Eric whooped. "Kalla?"

In answer, she pulled bullets from her pockets, reloading her pistols, not making eye contact with him as they started up the steps.

Chapter 30

IT DIDN'T SIT RIGHT with Hunter. Not that he was some brave soul who wanted to go charging into the line of fire—he was a fucking coward, as a matter of fact. But it didn't sit right with him to wait outside, listening to the shouted commands and imagining the blood splattering the floor inside, making it slick and slippery. He knew that was all in his head. He knew his imagination was playing tricks on him. Kalla and Ava wouldn't let it get that bad before Eric called him in. But he couldn't seem to stop his mind from conjuring up such images.

The thought of losing them—any of them—made him antsy, jittery. He was pacing before he even knew that he'd started moving, circling Britt on the sidewalk. Her eyes followed him, her brow creased in concern.

And Goddess bless her—his wife, this beautiful, wonderful, perfect woman who knew him inside and out—she didn't reach for him. She didn't try to stop him from pacing and calm him. She didn't soothe him. She reached up, tapped her own earpiece, and said, "Eric, is the first floor clear?"

"Yeah. But I told you—"

"It'll be fine. We'll stay downstairs, out of the way," Britt said, her tone making it clear that she wasn't one of his soldiers and he didn't get to order her around. Hunter stopped in his tracks, a smile twitching at his lips. "It'll be better if I'm closer in case they're seriously injured."

Hunter wondered how much of that was true. How much of her choice to go in was driven by a desire to be closer to the injured? And how much was from her knowledge that he needed to be within shouting distance of his friends? He'd wager it was mostly the latter. She knew him. She knew what he was like. Knew that being in the house and seeing the walls not covered in Eric's and Ava's blood would settle something within him.

"Britt," Eric huffed a warning, and Hunter could imagine the exasperated expression on his face. Could close his eyes and see Eric standing there with his hands on his hips, looking like an overworked mother of three.

"Eric." Britt returned the warning in kind. There was a challenge in the word, daring him to go against her, and yeah okay, so Hunter found it intolerably sexy. Sue him. That was his wife, damn it! And she was standing up to a Venator. Talking him down like an errant child. "That wasn't me asking for permission. That was me telling you what I'm doing."

"I don't have time for this shit right now," Eric muttered to himself, probably running his hands through his ridiculously fluffy hair that was now matted down with sweat, and blood, and two days of not washing. "Fine. But be careful down there, all right? Neither of you play at being hero."

"Hero?" Britt snorted. "I'm just the medic."

Eric grunted. The lines fell silent as Britt grabbed her bag and started up the walk without once looking back to check if Hunter followed her. It took him a moment to do just that. For his body to catch up with his mind. Then he was loping along behind her like a gazelle, so he could keep pace with her.

There was blood inside the foyer, a couple droplets here and there on the floor. Not a lot. Not enough to make the floor slick. Hunter found himself fixated on it anyway, his eyes focused like he could tell whose it was if he looked hard enough. Like he could make out the DNA and the cellular makeup. Know if it were magical or mundane. Male or female. Venator or witch or Huntsman. Tell which of his friends had been hurt, and fix it somehow.

"Babe," Britt called, ripping Hunter's attention away from the splatter and taking his hand to squeeze it tight enough to ache, "you should probably collect the fangs if Eric means to burn it down."

Fangs. The magic word. Hunter's face lit up, and he nodded once, hard enough to almost bend him into a deep bow. He pulled a plastic bag from his pocket. "You, my love, woman of my heart, my life's sole purpose, are a genius."

Britt laughed, the sound high and bright. She said, "Tell me something I don't know" and blew him a kiss. He pretended to catch it, stumbling back under the force of her love and banging into a wall behind him, his smile so wide he could barely see.

He was just about to straighten back up, to set about his work, when two arms burst through the drywall and grabbed him around the neck. A choked-off breath left him. Britt screamed, horror draining the color from her face. But it was hard to focus on that, hard to even hear her over the thumping of his own heart in his ears. Over the voice pressed close to his cheek whispering, "Kill the witch. Kill the witch. Kill the witch. Master says he knows too much. He sees too much. Kill the witch" over and over again like a mantra.

Hunter scrambled against the tight grip, his nails dragging grooves into the creature's skin, but even as he tried to breathe, tried to regain focus enough to use his magic, he couldn't. It remained stubbornly out of reach. The tattoos on his arms slithered as if they wanted to help but stayed trapped on his skin without their witch to call them forth.

The creature stopped muttering long enough to lift their head from where their mouth hovered over Hunter's neck and sniff. One deep, long inhale, like smelling fresh air for the first time after being cooped up too long. Then they released Hunter and he dropped to the floor, gasping and choking.

He looked up, searching for Britt, and found her. His heart plummeted, lurched. He was going to throw up. He was going to die. Red. Blood. The shine of a scalpel in her hand. Her wrist dripping crimson onto the floor. It took him a second too long to register what she'd done, then he was screaming, struggling to his feet. "Britt, no!"

The vampire was faster.

They tore the artery open wide, sucking down Britt's blood in deep hiccuping gulps.

There was a stake in Hunter's hand. He didn't know where it had come from, and he'd found his feet, his boots sure beneath him. With the vampire distracted, it was almost too easy to jam the stake through their back, into their heart.

They wailed, thrashed, spilled precious blood from their mouth down the front of Britt's navy-blue shirt where it disappeared into the dark fabric, never to return where it came from. Then they *poof*ed into a cloud of dust, two pointed fangs clattering to the ground along with the stake as Hunter lunged for Britt.

He pulled her wrist to him first, grabbing gauze and bandages from the pack to wrap tight around the wound, but she was too pale already. It would take more than this to stanch the bleeding. More than this to keep her heart beating. He needed a healer. She *was* their healer.

"Hold on hold on hold on," Hunter chanted, the words blurring together as he dug through the bag she'd brought with her. There had to be fucking sutures in her kit. If he could just find them, he was sure—

"Remember what I told you?" Britt asked, her voice weak and thready. "Remember what we said when we got married? What I said?"

"You said you'd go before me." Hunter didn't look at her.

He kept digging for the suture kit, his other hand so tight around her wrist, he was sure he was cutting off circulation. But the blood was still flowing. It coated his palm, making it hot and sticky. His heart raced in his chest, threatening to lurch up his throat along with what little he'd eaten over the last few hours. "Because—"

"Because I'm human." Britt reached for him with her other hand and pulled his face around by the chin to look her in the eyes. Goddess, she was so pale. So very pale. How much blood could a vampire consume per minute again? He couldn't—he couldn't remember. He knew the numbers, the exact rate per second depending on body weight and point of entry, but his memory failed him. "Just another normie."

"You've never been a normie, Britt." Hunter sobbed, his face wet with something. Maybe tears? Maybe snot? Maybe blood? What the fuck did it matter.

"Your magic was always going to keep you alive longer than me. I made my peace with that a long time ago."

"But it's not supposed to happen *today*! Not today! We're supposed to have another fifty or sixty years before I have to say goodbye! I'm not ready, damn it. Britt, I'm not ready!" He would never have been ready, not really. Even if she lived to be a hundred, he'd still not be ready to let her go. She was everything he'd ever needed in his life. The grounding force that kept him from flying apart at the seams most days. And he'd always thought, stupidly, that he'd get to keep her. Even if witches did live a lot longer than humans.

She seemed to realize this because she shook her head, a soft sad smile on her face. "I know, baby, I know. But this is when it happens. It was always going to be when it happened."

"You don't know that! Like you said, you don't have any magic! You couldn't know!" There were other ways to know. Hunter was well versed in them—his gran had been a fortune teller. He'd watched her read the cards, cast the runes, commune with the spirits, and even look into a crystal ball sometimes. He'd sat outside her door and listened to her tell people how their lives would go. She'd told a youth they'd die young a time or two, said it was a kindness in its way—it reminded them to live while they were still living. A sentiment his mother had repeated to him over and over again growing up. Like she *knew*. Like she could see *this* coming. But she'd never said. Never warned him. A sob strangled him.

"Didn't I though?" She smiled in that mischievous way of hers, the way she'd smiled at him years ago when Eric brought her around to one of their friend gatherings, and it stole his breath now like it did then.

"If you knew, why the fuck did you come in here with me then? Why not stay behind? Why not stay in the van with the kids?"

"What's that thing your mama always said to you?" Britt asked instead of answering his question. "Life is for the living."

Her heart was slowing down now. He could feel it. He needed help. He needed someone. He tapped the comm in his ear. "Ava. Ava come quick. Britt's been hurt. There's—Just get here!"

"Ava's not a healer." Britt tsked lightly, a soft admonishment.

"She's a mender. It's close enough." It wasn't, not really. Ava fixed clothes and furniture. She patched shirts, and darned socks, and occasionally refinished a chair. She had never once set her arts to healing, said she didn't know enough about the body to do it. But it couldn't be that different, could it? And Hunter was desperate.

Britt shook her head like she did sometimes when she was shaking off a thought, then she scowled. "Dizzy."

"Save your energy, Ava's coming." He didn't know if she was or not. She hadn't answered him, or if she had, he hadn't heard her over the pounding in his ears. But she had to be. Because he couldn't lose Britt. She was his family. She was all he had aside from Chase, their parents long gone.

"Won't matter." Britt shrugged, focusing back on his face. "Like I was saying." Her speech was starting to slur, her lids growing heavier. "Life is for the living."

"I could—I could bring you back."

"No!" Her eyes flew open, fierce determination lending her one last bit of strength to clutch his chin so tight, it hurt. "You will not do that, do you understand me, Hunter Delacroix? You promised me when we got married. No necromancy. No bringing me back. One life."

"It's too short. I don't—I don't—There's not been enough time. How am I supposed to do this without you?" Hunter bent forward, pressing his forehead to hers, begging, pleading with his eyes for her to stay. For her to hang on until Ava came. For Ava's magic to do its work. But the blood had begun to squelch through his fingers a long time ago, and now that he gave himself time to look, it wasn't the only bite. There were others that Britt hadn't drawn his attention to, splattering the floor, soaking in through the legs of his pants. When had those happened? When had there been time? While he was swimming in his panic? His inability to act in a crisis was going to lose him the person who meant the most to him. Tears burned down his cheeks.

Britt hummed, her fingers stroking through his hair. "You just will," she said simply. "You'll live for me, like we always planned. Move on. Love again. That's what I always wanted for you when our time was up."

"Our time isn't up!" Hunter snarled, tugging her in closer.

"Oh Hunter, I think it is." Britt sighed, but she didn't close her eyes. She didn't look away. And her heart kept right on beating. Her breathing, however shallow, kept coming.

He could fix this.

He could make it better.

If he just knew the spell. If he just knew how to make his magic do what he wanted. If he was just strong enough. If he could just call on the land to help him. But he was covenless. Not tied to the land. And the land wouldn't give where it hadn't received. He was alone. Cast adrift.

Powerless.

"I've got her now," Ava said, sliding onto the floor on the other side of Britt, her bright magic already leaping from her fingers to start her work.

"You'll save her." Hunter looked at his best friend, his eyes wide and wild, and begged with every fiber of his being for her to say yes.

"I'll do what I can. But Eric needs—"

A shout from up the stairs ripped through Hunter like a blade, and fear sliced through him. Fresh panic made it hard to focus on the way his heartbeat ratcheted up another notch. He was going to give himself a fucking heart attack this way.

"Go to him," Britt said, her fingers brushing featherlight along Hunter's jaw. "And don't forget what I said."

"You're going to be here when I come back. This isn't goodbye." There was no other option. Hunter couldn't lose her.

"Of course." Britt nodded. Her smile didn't reach her eyes.

Another shout tore through the air, and Hunter was on his feet, running up the stairs.

CHAPTER 31

IT WAS like one of the kids' fucking video games in this house. And not in the fun, brightly colored, amusing-soundtrack way. More in the horror-game way. The ones Eric couldn't sit there and watch them play because jump scares drew up too many memories and made it impossible to sleep.

But every floor of the house seemed to be like going up a level in a video game. The first floor had been full of younglings, slower, more unwieldy, easy enough to dispatch. The second boasted older vampires. Not elders—Eric imagined the elders had gotten out before the raid, since they knew it was coming—but old enough to become a real problem for Kalla and Ava, who hadn't trained for this every day of their lives for the past twenty years like Eric had.

By the time he got to the third floor, Kalla was out of bullets.

"Wait here," Eric panted and lifted his shirt to rub sweat, grime, and blood away from his face with the hem of it.

Kalla opened her mouth to argue, but Eric stopped her with a shake of his head.

"I'll call you if I need you." He wouldn't though, he knew that. If it was too bad on the third floor, he would simply let whatever was meant to happen happen. He wouldn't draw the others in, let them go down with him. He'd drop the fire charm Ava created for him and send the whole place up in flames while he was still inside of it, and count on them to get out when they smelled the smoke. End all of this before it had really begun. He'd pray to the Goddess that it would be enough.

Eric stepped up onto the third floor, and the vampires there didn't give him time to finish climbing the stairs before they were on him. Nails sharpened to points ripping into his clothes. Fangs tearing into his skin.

He stumbled back, nearly falling down the stairs in a bid to get away, to get some breathing space, to reach for a weapon, or his Cross. A grip like a steel band wrapped around his wrist and yanked him forward. His chin hit the carpeted floor, leaving behind a burn, clacking his teeth together in a way he was sure had cracked at least one.

He must have shouted because he felt the rip of a scream at the back of his throat, even if he couldn't hear it over the pounding of his heart in his ears.

They dragged him across the floor, his shirt stretching and tearing from the force where it got caught on a bit of blood-tacky carpet. His shoulder screamed in agony, popping out of its socket where Britt had just put it back in, still tender and sore from the previous fight, and Eric had to bite down on another shout of pain.

But their distraction gave him enough time to reach into the back of his pants and grab the dagger stuffed into a holster there. His swing was wild, careless, but it landed just the same, slicing deep into the muscles and tendons, making the vampire's grip slacken enough for Eric to scramble away. To get to his feet.

Hunter was at his side then, before Eric could think to call for backup. Slamming a wall of ink-dark magic into the approaching horde of vampires, giving Eric enough time to pop his shoulder back into place and pull another dagger from his boot. When he rose to his feet, Eric got a better look at Hunter's face in the low light of the hall and his magic.

"Britt?" He had to ask, he had to know, even if somewhere deep in Eric's bones, he knew already. Knew that Hunter wouldn't be so pale, so drawn, if Britt was all right. Hunter met his searching gaze, and the feral heartbreak in his eyes told Eric all he needed to know.

Hunter shook his head. Which was worse than anything he could have said. Guilt gnawed at Eric's insides, making his joints ache in a way nothing else could. That was his fault. He'd done that. He'd brought her here. And now she was gone.

"Kill the witch. Bring the hunter," one of the vampires said, starting up a chant that rippled through the group of them held at bay by Hunter's power.

"Kill the witch?" Eric asked, his head tilted as he examined the vampires. They hadn't taken a step forward to retrieve him or Hunter, but he knew they wouldn't have long to wait. Hunter could hold up the shield for only a short time, even with his body on high alert as it was. He wasn't built for battle like Eric was.

Hunter didn't answer that question. Instead, he reached into Eric's pocket to retrieve a silver-tipped dagger, then smiled at him, all teeth. "Make 'em pay."

It was the only warning Eric got before Hunter lowered the shield and the vampires were on them once more. Eric spun, his back to Hunter, putting himself between the vampires and the man who had already lost too much tonight. But more came from behind, grabbing Hunter and ripping the two of them apart.

Eric slashed through the vamps with his dagger, cutting through bone and tissue, trying to clear a path back to Hunter, back the way he'd come. Hunter's dark eyes glittered in the dim light and the dankness of the upstairs, his magic flaring to life, sucking the light from the space around him. Beautiful and deadly. A riot of color.

Eric could see that it took Hunter a moment to realize

what he was doing. Eric was almost to him, within reach. When Hunter figured out what was happening, he snarled and threw a wall of power at Eric that sent him stumbling backward again.

"Don't worry about me," Hunter hissed through his teeth. Blood trailed from his nose, a sure sign that he was overexerting himself, but he didn't stop moving, dancing through the vampires, letting them rip and tear at him, using magic and blade to keep them at bay so fast and sure, it almost looked natural. But Eric knew better. Knew that Hunter was running on adrenaline and little else. He needed to stop this before Hunter collapsed. "Get to Tony. Get him out. Then we end this."

Eric nodded, spinning on his heel and slicing a path through the vampires that stood between him and the doors on the other side of the house. Their dust made it hard to see in the dim light of the hall, but he kept moving. Spinning and twisting. Jabbing and slashing. Taking down one. Three. Seven vampires. Now that he knew they didn't want to kill him, it was almost easy. He was less afraid. And in more of a hurry, knowing they *did* want to kill Hunter.

All the doors on this side of the house were flung open apart from one: the room at the very end of the hall. A giant vampire stood in front of it. Broad shoulders and rippling muscles. Like someone had turned a body builder or a bouncer. Eric took a moment, sniffed the air, sized them up.

The final boss.

Not a youngling, but not an elder, just like the others.

Was this their maker? The source of all the rest? He couldn't tell. The bloodline was the same, for sure, but that could mean they'd all been sired by the same vampire.

"Venator," the vampire said, their lips peeling back to expose fangs far longer than any Eric had seen before. Hunter would kill to have those fangs in the archives. Which was ironic, since Eric was going to have to kill to get past them.

"My reputation precedes me, I see." Eric laughed, biting and snarky, and gave a little bow. It was stupid. He'd been watching way too many movies with the kids lately. But there was no taking it back now.

"I didn't think you'd make it this far." They leaned casually against the doorframe, not a care in the world for the danger Eric posed. Which was just plain insulting, but it could play right into Eric's plans.

"Get used to disappointment." *Fuck.* That was a *Princess Bride* quote. He really *had* been watching too many movies with the kids lately. He planted his feet, the toe of one shoe squelching in the blood-soaked carpet, and firmed up his grip on his weapons.

The vampire snorted a laugh, eyes dancing with dark humor.

Eric didn't wait for them to continue the banter; there wasn't time for that, not with Hunter behind him fending off at least six vampires on his own, Britt bleeding out downstairs, and Tony—

Well, Tony behind that door, suffering.

His dagger sliced through the vampire's chest, burning and hissing along skin and muscle, but only doing enough damage to piss them off. They rammed their shoulder into Eric's torso, jarring his already injured body, snapping what felt like at least two ribs.

The next breath he took came out on a sob, a cough, a gasp.

A punctured lung, probably.

Still, the proximity had given him the space he needed to ram one silver dagger into the vampire's chest. He missed the heart. Fuck.

The vampire snarled. Snappy. Tore fangs into his shoulder, into his upper arm, ripping out chunks of flesh that would take weeks to heal properly, even with his accelerated Venator healing. They tried to rear back, tried to get away from the other dagger making thin, deep cuts along their side, their back. Burning and smoking.

Eric gripped them by the back of their neck, fingers so tight they could break bone, hand slick with sweat and blood as pain raced through his body. But it was almost done. He was almost there. He just needed to finish this.

The dagger slipped around in his hand, but he managed to keep a hold of it, even as something wet trailed down his arm to make the grip slicker. Blood, most likely. It was always blood with vampires. He tightened his fist around it, the muscles in his arm screaming, his joints aching, got a better angle on it, and rammed it up between the vampire's ribs at their side, under their arm, directly into their heart.

They stuttered, stopped, mouth falling open. Blood dripped down their chin onto Eric's shirt, coating him in it. Their eyes rolled back for a second, two, then the decay finally took hold and they crumpled to dust at his feet.

Someone made a sound behind him, a restrained cheer maybe? Eric looked over his shoulder to find Hunter and Kalla standing there. Both bloody. Both panting. But alive. Upright. The relief that washed through Eric was only half baked, still raw, like undercooked cookie dough. But he didn't have the energy to examine the feeling.

He turned to the door and pushed it open.

Huddled together in the dark and the stink were Dash Chadwick and Tony McMahon. Their breathing was even. Their heart rates were a little high, but that was normal in a panic situation.

"Help me get them up," Eric called back to Hunter and Kalla, then he bent before the two men, telegraphing his movements. "What are your injuries like?"

Tony blinked at him blearily, head lolling onto Dash's shoulder where he hid his face in Dash's neck, not even willing to look at Eric.

"Just bites," Dash replied for them both, the words a bit

choked, a bit strangled. "Blood loss. Venom. They—" He swallowed roughly, his Adam's apple bobbing. "It's been a bit since they fed on me. I think I can walk."

"Then you'll stick with Kalla. What about Tony?" Everything in Eric's body ached, itched, *longed* to reach for Tony. To pull him into his chest. To give comfort. But it didn't look like it would be well received, and honestly Eric was so injured himself that it was probably best he *not* try to bridal carry Tony out of there like he wanted to. Some hero he was.

"Couple-a hours maybe? It's—it's hard to tell in here." Dash shook his head, but his hand gripped Tony closer, as if he could shield him from the world, and Eric's heart sank toward his feet.

"Kids," Eric said, tapping the comm in his ear and putting some space between himself and the injured men on the floor, leaving Hunter and Kalla room to work.

"Yes, sir," Nik replied quickly.

"Call the Huntsmen-sanctioned EMS workers. Tell them we have three wounded and need emergency transport."

"Yes, sir."

CHAPTER 32

THE FUNERAL WAS HELD the following week, as was the custom of witches.

Even in the dead of winter. Even with the ground frozen over so hard, there would be no way to dig a hole for the body. The funeral was held.

Britt Delacroix hadn't wanted to be buried anyway.

And honestly, Hunter didn't think he could watch her be lowered into the ground. Not that cremation was better.

"She thought it was bad for the environment," Hunter said, his hand fisted around a tissue someone had handed him but he had yet to use.

He hadn't cried. It had been a week, and still he hadn't cried.

He couldn't explain why. Maybe somewhere deep inside, he thought she'd come back? Thought she'd pop out from behind a door somewhere and tell him it had all been some kind of prank.

It didn't feel real, he knew that much. He felt like he was living in an alternate timeline. Like the Matrix had fucking glitched and was buzzing, waiting to right itself. Then he'd walk around the corner of their apartment, and there would be Britt. Waiting. Beautiful. Smiling. Happy. Maybe that was why he hadn't cried yet. Because it wasn't real to him yet. Because she wasn't dead yet.

But she was. He'd held her cold body. He'd pressed bloody kisses to her face before the coroners took her away. She was dead. He knew that.

And yet he couldn't cry.

He couldn't cry. He couldn't go home. And every time Eric so much as looked at him, he felt like he wanted to throw up. Guilt crawled along every nerve ending in his body. Like he'd secretly wanted this. Like he'd been waiting for Britt to die so he could move in with Eric.

Objectively, he knew that wasn't right. He knew he hadn't been. But . . . but it was hard to turn the intrusive thoughts off sometimes. Hard to convince himself, inside his own head, that this wasn't all his fucking fault. That he didn't make this happen, somehow.

"Said she didn't want to clear living things just so we can plant dead ones." Goddess, Hunter had loved that about Britt. Loved the way she saw the world, and the way she wanted to change it. But she hadn't had the time to, had she? Because of him. Because she'd fallen in love with a witch and fallen in with monsters. Goddess, he was fucking disgusting. Toxic. A fucking biohazard just missing the steel drum. That's why his magic was black, wasn't it? Because he was *sludge*.

"That makes sense," Lu said, a note of approval in her voice that made Hunter's shoulders unhitch a notch. Eric's fucking kids. They were the only thing keeping him sane these days, Hunter was sure of it.

"We should take our seats," Dash murmured. He stood with the McMahon siblings, Hunter noted distantly. His hand pressed low and possessive into Tony's lower back. If Hunter weren't so fucked up, maybe he'd feel something about that. But . . . Well. He was fucked up.

And he still hadn't fucking cried.

———

The services started shortly after, and Tony tried to pay attention. He did. Knew that he should. Britt had died while helping to save him, to save his Dash. But it was hard to focus with the way Dash's fingers curled in the hairs at the back of his neck, and Tony wondered if that was intentional. If Dash was trying to take his mind off things. To alleviate some of the guilt they both felt.

When everything was said and done, Tony stood by his car, waiting for Dash and Lu to say their goodbyes, spinning his keyring round and round. He didn't know why they were bothering. Lu would see everyone on Monday when she went back to class. Dash didn't even know these people, not really. But Tony supposed that, as the mayor's brother, there was some face to be kept.

He heard Marcelino coming, his dress shoes squeaking in that way unbroken-in leather did, before he'd announced himself, but still Tony waited for Marcelino to say, "Tony" before he looked up.

"What is it, Marcelino?" Tony tilted his head back, lifting one arrogant brow. Marcelino looked like absolute shit. Dark circles sat under his eyes, bandages poked out from his dress shirt at the collar and at the wrists, and one of his arms was in a sling. But Tony didn't have it in him to feel bad about that. Not after Marcelino left him in that fucking place to be feasted upon by too many leeches to fucking count.

"We need to—" He swallowed, his throat bobbing, his hand fisting at his side. "We need to talk about what happened."

"There ain't nothin' to talk about." Tony shrugged. He stuffed his hands into his pockets, searching out the blunt he'd rolled that morning and secreted away before Lu could give him a lecture about getting high at a fucking funeral. It wasn't for the funeral. It was for after. But fuck off if he was going to explain that to her.

"There is." Marcelino straightened up, lifting his chin,

trying to make himself look taller, stronger. It just made him look small. One tin soldier fighting against the tide. *Pfft*. And Tony had thought him a hero, the best damn Venator in ages. He had everyone fooled, didn't he? Couldn't even clear one nest all by his lonesome. "I know you came with Dash, but we never officially—I need to know where we stand."

"Where we stand?" Tony scoffed, rolling his eyes. "We don't stand anywhere, Marcelino. We're done. Over."

"Over?" Marcelino frowned. He rocked back on his heels, looking like he'd been struck. "You're breaking up with me?"

"Breaking up requires us to have been a thing in the first place." Tony sneered, anger rising in his blood. He felt loose tongued, dangerous, out of control. Like he might take a swing at Marcelino right there in front of the funeral home where they'd held the service. Maybe he would. Maybe he'd make a scene. Marcelino would definitely get the message then, but it'd probably make the kicked-puppy look that had settled onto his features about a million times worse. And then there was Hunter to think about, and Britt. Was it worth it? Probably not.

"Sweetheart." Marcelino reached for him, his fingers crooked from where they'd been broken at one point or another and healed over wrong.

"Don't call me that!" Tony snapped, smacking Marcelino's hand away as it got too close to his cheek. "I'm not your sweetheart. I'm not your *anything*."

He didn't wait for Marcelino to say another word, just spun on his heel and shoved himself into the driver's seat, slamming the door behind him to cut off further conversation. Out of the corners of his eyes, he saw Marcelino still standing there, hand slightly outstretched, like he'd try again. Like he'd reach for the door and rip it open, make Tony face him. But he didn't.

Once he was gone, Tony let out a long, slow breath, deflating against the leather. He flicked down the visor to check that his eyeliner hadn't run in the mirror and frowned at what he found there.

He'd lost his tie and unbuttoned the top three buttons on his shirt a while ago. Now, slumped in his seat, the shirt splayed open further, he saw a bite mark on his collarbones. Red. Raw. Fresh.

But . . . that couldn't be right.

"You don't have to be such a prick to him just because you have a new boyfriend," Lu said, the passenger door flung open wide so she could fold the front seat down and climb in the back. Tony shifted in his seat, tugging his collar to hide the fresh bite mark, feeling oddly protective of it.

"Fuck off, Lu. If you're so worried about Marcelino's feelings, you can move in with him and his rug rats."

Lu huffed, muttered, "Maybe I will" under her breath, and crossed her arms over her chest to throw herself into a sulk when Dash rejoined them in the car.

———

A month had passed, and everything was different and yet the same. The night in the house full of vampires had changed so much about Eric Marcelino's life. He wasn't alone anymore, he knew that now. He knew he could trust his friends, his little family, to have his back when shit hit the fan. But he was even more committed to protecting them, to keeping them safe.

"The more things change, the more they stay the same," Eric muttered to himself, reaching for the kit he kept at the front door now instead of inside his car, just in case. A subtle change—the leaving of his gear out where anyone could touch it, could use it—but it was progress. Or he thought so, anyhow.

"Don't forget this." Hunter came around the corner, holding the Bluetooth earbud Chase set up for him. Another subtle difference in his routine. A way for him to call for help if he needed it. A way for his kids—his team—to check in on him, to guide him to where they thought the real danger was in Ironport so he didn't waste precious time and energy wandering around.

Eric took it, his gaze catching on the boxes still sitting in the living room over Hunter's shoulder. "I'll deal with those tomorrow."

"It's all good." Hunter shrugged, but there was a smile ticking at the corner of his lips. He hadn't smiled much at all since Britt's funeral, hadn't even met Eric's eyes much. He tried. Play acted at being happy. But Eric could see how ripped up inside he still was. That's why he'd told Hunter to stay—stay here with him, with the kids—the morning after everything had gone down when Hunter had still been in Eric's bed, his body curled so tight on itself, Eric couldn't tell his limbs apart.

"Nah. It's been long enough." It had been a month, and Eric knew it was partly because Hunter didn't want to think of this arrangement as permanent. He didn't want to think that he wasn't going to get back on his feet, live on his own. Eric hadn't pushed him. Knew this was a big change. But he didn't want Hunter to leave either. "Ava's right, you're not going anywhere anytime soon. Might as well be comfortable."

"I could. I've still got my lease."

A lease on an apartment with nothing in it apart from furniture. Hunter had scraped it clean of everything else, putting it all in boxes, and shown up at Eric's door with them during that first week after the funeral. Had told Eric it wasn't permanent, but he just couldn't be there right now.

"Still. Might as well be comfortable," Eric said again, deciding to skirt around the elephant in the room. If Hunter felt better knowing he had his own place still, could leave if he wanted, Eric wasn't going to take that from him. "But the boxes seriously have to go, dude. They're gonna draw roaches."

Hunter blanched. "Fine. I'll unpack the boxes."

"Good." Eric smiled gently and tugged Hunter into a hug, then turned for the door.

"Be safe out there tonight," Hunter said, a gentle order.

"Always am." Eric stepped out into the cold early April air and tapped on the device in his ear as he made his way to the car. "Who's my buddy tonight?"

"You've got Finn on the hammer," Finn replied right away, making Eric chuckle to himself and roll his eyes.

"It's the horn, Finn. That's what the truckers say: on the horn."

"Oh." He imagined her shrugging where she was tucked into the spare room in the attic of the dorm house, the one they'd remade into their command center. Packed with monitors and wheely chairs. Weapons, and charms Ava had put together for them. The perfect place for his team to keep an eye on him, where they were safe but still able to mobilize at a moment's notice. "I'm sending you coordinates to some activity going on downtown. It's near the hospital."

"Must be a blood delivery night."

Finn murmured her agreement, and Eric's car rumbled away from Moondale U, pointed toward Ironport.

ABOUT LOU WILHAM

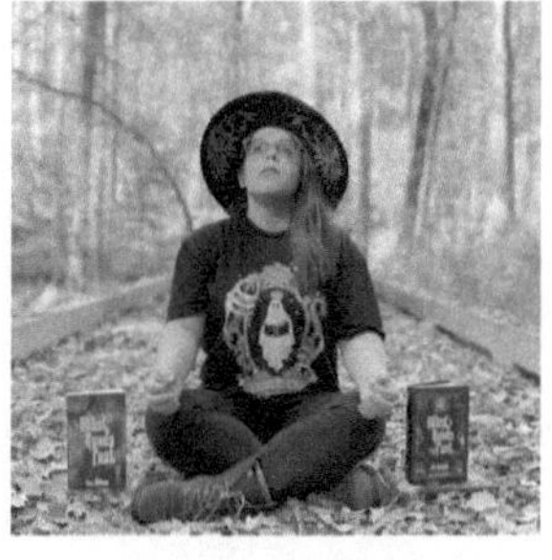 Born and raised in a small town near the Chesapeake Bay, Lou Wilham grew up on a steady diet of fiction, arts and crafts, and Old Bay. After years of absorbing everything, there was to absorb of fiction, fantasy, and sci-fi she's left with a serious writing/drawing habit that just won't quit. These days, she spends much of her time writing, drawing, and chasing a very short Basset Hound named Sherlock.

When not, daydreaming up new characters to write and draw she can be found crocheting, making cute bookmarks, and binge-watching whatever happens to catch her eye.

Learn more about Lou and her future projects on her website: http://louinprogress.com/ or join her mailing list at: http://subscribepage.com/mailermailer

 facebook.com/LouWilham
instagram.com/lou.wilham

ALSO BY LOU WILHAM

The Heir To Moondust
   The Prince of Starlight
   The Prince of Daybreak
   The Crown of Night

The Witches of Moondale
   The Hex Next Door
   The Ghost of Hexes Past

The Hunters of Ironport
   Overkill

Sanctuary of the Lost
   Of Loyalties and Wreckage
   Of Love and Ruin

Completed Series
   The Tales of the Sea Trilogy
   Villainous Heroics
   The Clockwork Chronicles
   The Curse Collection

Sneak Peek!

continue reading for a sneak peek of Hunters of Ironport
Book 2: Fresh Kill

Please note: This is an unedited sneak peek.

FRESH KILL

INACTION SAT a buzz along Tony's nerves, making his skin feel too tight. It manifested in the jittering of his right leg. The heel bouncing up and down just above the floor hard enough to make the water in their glasses vibrate on the table. If he bounced it just a little harder, they might spill over. The water. His nerves. All of it. Rise to a boiling point that would make him look like a complete dumbass.

Why had he even come to this fucking dinner? It wasn't like he had anything to offer to the conversation. And he certainly wasn't making Dash look good by acting like a child who couldn't sit still.

His collar was too tight, and the polished shoes Dash had picked out for him pinched his toes. Trapped in his own skin, that's what Tony was. He couldn't breathe.

Dash reached down beneath the table cloth to squeeze Tony's knee. His hand was dry, and cool, like he didn't have a care in the world. Like he did meetings like these every day.

Well. He was the mayor's brother, so he probably did. But that didn't make Tony any less stressed out. Because fuck he was the *mayor's* brother. And so far out of Tony's league he wasn't even sure how he'd gotten Dash to agree to that first date a couple months back.

Trauma bonding, probably. Shit like that happened to people who had been in life or death situations together. It didn't change the fact that Tony wasn't really worthy of Dash's notice.

He kind of missed the easiness of spending time with Marcelino. How they'd been able to just hang out, and shoot the shit—even if missing someone who'd left him to fucking die left a bitter taste in his mouth. Things weren't like that with Dash. Everything with Dash felt. . . loaded.

"You need to calm down," Dash murmured, his grip tightening on Tony's knee enough that Tony could feel his nails through his immaculately pressed slacks. They were Dash's slacks, actually. Tony didn't own slacks. He'd never had a need for them.

"It's dark out." It had been dark out for a solid hour at that point. It was early spring, the days were still short, and that meant Tony shouldn't be sitting at a table-clothed table wondering which fucking fork was the salad fork. He should be out in the cool night air, following his nose to the nearest undead thing. He had a fucking job to do.

Dash's gaze flicked over to the the couple on the other side of the table. Tony hadn't caught their names, but he had caught their professions. A doctor, and a lawyer. Fucking power couples. How did that even work? They both had to work really long hours, right? When did they see each other? Second thought. Maybe *that* was how it worked. They just never saw each other, except at dinners with the mayor's brother where they put their best face forward.

"Charlie, Jake, would you please excuse us?" Dash didn't wait for their agreement, he rose, and held his hand out to Tony, a silent command that Tony was helpless not to heed.

There was no ignoring Dashfield B.M. Chadwick when he looked at Tony like that, all glittering eyes, and mouth turned up in a slight smile. So, Tony went willingly. Let Dash lead him away from the table toward the bathrooms at the back of the restaurant, then into a little alcove tucked away where no one could see or hear them. Tony was hemmed in, his back to the corner, goosebumps rising along his skin. He wasn't sure if he liked it or not, the feeling of Dash looming over him like a predator. On one hand, it was kind of sexy. On the other, Tony was very much unused to being prey.

"What's this all about?" Dash pressed, straightening himself up further as if he needed to emphasize the few scant inches he was taller than Tony. The feeling of being smaller didn't actually make Tony feel safer in this circumstance, the way it had with Marcelino. Why was Tony still comparing the two? "Is this about Eric?"

That might be why he couldn't stop thinking about Marcelino. Because Dash kept fucking bringing him up, like some jealous asshole. Which was stupid, Tony had hardly spoken to Marcelino in the months since Britt's funeral, not even via text. They'd found a way to avoid each other while out on patrol, each sticking to their own particular side of Ironport. A feat only achieved through Lu and Finn's interference.

"No." *At least, not entirely,* Tony didn't add. Having a fight in the middle of a fancy restaurant that required collared shirts was probably not the best thing for his relationship, or Dash's image, so Tony decided to keep that last bit to himself. "I just feel like I should be doing something."

"Doing *what*, exactly?" Dash asked. He brushed a strand of Tony's long strawberry-blond hair back behind one pierced ear, his fingers lingering cool and shiver-inducing along Tony's skin.

"Hunting." It came out breathier than Tony intended it to, and he realized how close they were all of the sudden. Dash leaning in closer, bracing his weight on one hand behind Tony's head, and Tony leaning back, his neck craned to give

Dash the best possible view of his throat. Fuck. He was hard up for it, wasn't he? He needed to get fucking laid. "I should be out on patrol."

Dash tilted his head, more bird like than confused puppy, and not half as cute as it should be. His blue eyes narrowed, tongue poking out to lick his lips. Definitely not cute. Sexy, maybe. Interest zinged along Tony's nerves, heading south.

"You worry too much," Dash said, his voice soft, just this side of chiding. "Let Eric take care of things for a bit. You're allowed to have a night out."

It sounded true, when he said it that way. Tony found himself relaxing back against the wall, his muscles loosening as Dash's voice washed over him like a siren's call.

"Besides, there haven't been any attacks in months. Not since Eric took out that nest." Dash hummed, his fingers lifting to trace along the length of Tony's neck, nails scraping light enough to not leave marks, but hard enough for Tony to feel the pressure of them right down to his toes. "Eric doesn't need your help."

Tony flinched, the words stinging. But. . . Dash was right. Marcelino *didn't* need him. He'd been doing fine before Tony showed up to Ironport, and since Marcelino and his team had taken out that nest, things had been quiet. Tony couldn't really blame Marcelino for not wanting to go out on patrol with him, not after what happened. He was a liability. Likely to drag Marcelino down, and get someone hurt. Couple that with the fact that Tony couldn't fucking trust Marcelino to have his back anymore and it didn't make sense for them to work together as a team anymore. Not when the threat levels were low, and Marcelino was so clearly capable of dealing with the leeches on his own.

"Let's just go back to dinner," Tony said, trying to hide the way his eyes burned a little with unshed tears. Why was he crying? He didn't need *Eric Marcelino* or his friendship or anything else. He didn't need anyone. Least of all some stuck-up pretty boy Venator who had left him for the vampires to feast on for what felt like weeks.

Dash sighed, the air blowing too cold against Tony's neck where Dash's mouth had gotten impossibly close. When had he closed that distance? Tony's head was swimming a little with the darkness of the alcove, and the smell of Dash's expensive cologne. He wondered if Dash would be okay with making out in the bathrooms for a bit. Just to take the edge off. Probably not. He never seemed up for PDA, at least not to the degree that Tony was.

"You're allowed to have time for *you*," Dash murmured against the skin of Tony's neck, brushing first cool lips, then his tongue along the spot at the hinge of Tony's jaw. He shivered. Leaned into the contact. He needed more. He'd *been* needing more for months now. But every time they got close to that, Dash pulled back. Strung him along a little more.

"I know that." He did. Sort of. Tony knew that Dash kept saying it, giving him what felt like explicit permission to take time off, to focus on himself. But still in the back of his mind lingered a voice that said he wasn't good for anything other than slaying, it sounded oddly like his *father*. He gave himself a mental shake, hoping to clear it the way one might an Etch-a-Sketch.

"Well, even if you don't seem to believe me," Dash's lips twitched up into a smile which should have been kind but showed a little too much teeth, "I'll keep saying it until you do."

Tony grumbled, but let Dash reach down, take his hand, and lift it to his mouth where he pressed a lingering kiss to the inside of Tony's wrist. A gentle nip at the tender skin made Tony's toes curl, and his head go fuzzy. His body relaxed entirely, all thoughts of patrol, and Eric slipping away as Dash sucked a bruise into the spot. A strangled sound left Tony, his body all but slumping against the wall, and nearly sliding down it.

"There, that's better, isn't it?" Dash's voice floated through Tony's brain, warm and syrup sweet. "Good boy."

The soft words startled a moan out of Tony and he turned to putty in Dash's hands. Dash said something else, another instruction probably, then he was pulling Tony away from the wall and back into the main dining room.

***

"Are you high right now?" Lu asked, her green eyes narrowed on him where he was leaned against the frame of her bedroom door.

He'd only meant to check on her, and tell her to shut her fucking light off. It was past ten and she had school in the morning. But after a night with Dash he was left feeling slow, and languid. So he'd pressed his weight into the door to watch his little sister where she was on her bed, head bent over a textbook. She looked peaceful.

"No," he answered after perhaps a moment too long of just staring at her, trying to catch up with what she'd asked him.

Lu snorted.

"Why?"

Lu ducked her head back to her textbook as if by avoiding eye contact she could avoid the fight that was brewing between them. Fat chance. It had been brewing for weeks now. Not that Tony knew why. Maybe they were both on edge with the lack of activity? Or maybe it was the fact that he was pent up, needing to get laid? Maybe Tony's discontent and anxiety were rubbing off on Lu? There was no way to really tell.

"You always seem to come back high when you go out with *him*," she said to her textbook, not even making an attempt to hide how she felt about Dash. Not that he didn't already know. Lu was never the type to hide her feelings, and when she'd learned that Tony and Marcelino were officially over, she'd been nothing if not vocal about how absolutely stupid she thought Tony was being about this whole thing.

She'd also wanted answers he didn't have. It all played out oddly like a divorce might on TV. Which was just fucking weird. He'd only been sleeping with Marcelino for all of a couple of weeks, and they hadn't been anything more than that. At least not officially.

"Maybe I'm just happy." Was he though? He couldn't really tell . . .

"You were never like this with Eric."

"Maybe I wasn't happy with Marcelino." But that didn't feel right, and he couldn't explain why. His time with Marcelino was blurry, hazed over by the immediacy of the threat looming over them, and the trauma that came after it. Tony wasn't sure what had been real and what he was making up anymore. Maybe all of it.

"Bullshit." Lu cut him a hard look, her lips pursed. "I've never seen you—"

"Well it doesn't fucking matter now, does it Lu? It's over."

"Yeah but—"

"Go the fuck to bed. It's late." He turned on his heel and headed for his own room. The need to get out, to beat the shit out of something, taking hold of his muscles again. Dash said Marcelino didn't need him out on patrol. Dash told him to take a night off. And maybe Dash was right, but what Dash didn't know wasn't going to hurt him.

ACKNOWLEDGMENTS

I always start these things but thanking the reader, and this one is no different. I want to thank you—whether you're a returning reader or Lou is new to you—for picking up my little indie published book, supporting my dream, and following along with Tony, Eric, and Hunter on their journey. Without readers, I can't do what I do, so I greatly appreciate the support.

If you loved every moment of Eric, Tony, and Hunter's story (as I hope you did) please leave a review, follow me on social media, or give me a shout out. I love hearing from you guys, it's really the best part of writing.

Next I'd like to thank my family who supports me in this weird journey I'm on to become an established author. They show up to my signings, they listen to my rants about my characters, they look at my covers and tell me when they're complete shit (I design my covers FYI), and they're the best people to have in my corner, no joke.

Then there is the small hoard of beta readers I had look at this bugger to tell me if any of it actually made sense, and if I'm as funny as I think I am (turns out I am). You guys provided so much helpful feedback you don't even know.

And of course my editor, Brenna. Who loves these idiots as much as I do, and it shows!

And last but certainly not least, thank you to my small writing support group. Tiss, Elle, Whitney, and Nancy— without you there would be no Lou.

MORE BOOKS YOU'LL LOVE

If you enjoyed this story, please consider leaving a review.

———

Then check out more books from Midnight Tide Publishing!

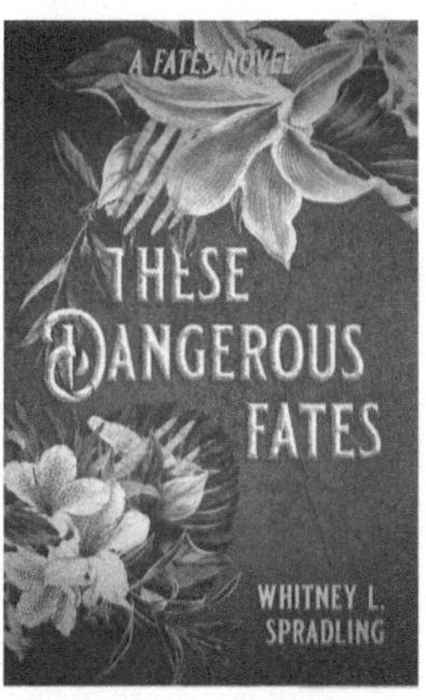

These Dangerous Fates by Whitney L. Spradling

I LIVE IN A MAGICAL WORLD. **A world filled with vampires, shifters, and mages.**

Mysteriously, I was born without powers.

After living the past two years in a personal hell, enduring abuse from a fiance I didn't choose, I finally snapped. An act of self-defense against my fiance angers my father, and in retaliation for my actions, he creates the ultimate contest. One that only the most powerful magicals can compete in to win my hand in marriage.

It sounds bleak, but anything has to be better than my current situation. At least, I thought so, until *they* appeared in the middle of the night to whisk me away.

A vampire prince.

A wolf without a pack.

A powerful mage.

My three captors do everything they can to win the contest, and as the attraction between the four of us grows, so does their desire to keep me safe.

When the mystery of my birth comes into play, we begin to question everything I thought I knew about my life. Am I just a human with no magical powers? Or am I something else entirely? One thing is certain, if my captors cannot keep me safe, more than my heart is at stake: my life is on the line.

Available Now

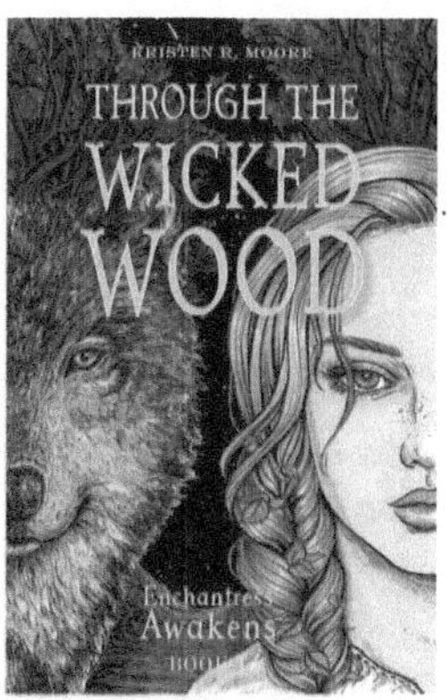

Through the Wicked Wood by Kristen M. Moore

ELORA LEIGH IS IN HIDING.

As an Enchantress, she has spent the last several years running not only from a King that hunts magick, but from her own grief and guilt from losing her mother.

Content in her solitude, Elora's life among the trees is disrupted when she crosses paths with the most unlikely of allies.

A thief determined to keep his village afloat, Sorin will do whatever it takes to provide for his people. Even if that means stealing from the King himself.

When they discover a common thirst for justice in the Kingdom of Valebridge, Sorin and Elora set out on a journey to fend for those who cannot fend for themselves.

But the deeper they go through the Wicked Woods, the more Elora realizes those she thought she could trust may not be who she thinks they are.

Family secrets, ancient magick, a kindling romance, and tangles of lies begin to reveal themselves. Elora must make a decision; trust this stranger to help defeat those harnessing magick in the Kingdom, or let the demons of her past push her back into hiding and away from who she was born to be.

• • •

Through the Wicked Wood is an adult fantasy romance and intended for readers over 18 years of age. Please check content warnings as some material may be sensitive for some readers.

Available Now